Yesterday's Secrets

Peggy P. Parsons

A Wings ePress, Inc.
Contemporary Romance Novel

Wings ePress, Inc.

Edited by: Joan Afman
Copy Edited by: Jeanne Smith
Senior Editor: Joan Afman
Executive Editor: Marilyn Kapp
Cover Artist: Peggy Parsons

All rights reserved

Wings ePress Books
www.wingsepress.com

Copyright © 2013 by
ISBN-13: 978-1-61309-854-7
ISBN-10: 1-61309-854-4

Published In the United States Of America

Wings ePress Inc.
3000 N. Rock Road
Newton, KS 67114

What They Are Saying About

Yesterday's Secrets

Yesterdays Secrets—A page turner...filled with surprising twists... sweet love's fight to survive is told at its finest. Peg Parsons has done it again.

Nancy Damato
Author

Dedication

To my sisters, Kathy and Lorraine.
Thanks for your love and support for so many years.

* * *

One

Sometimes when you're not looking
Love sneaks through a door
You didn't know you left open

Cold chills skittered down Saree's spine as Papa and Belle returned to the dining room after walking their six guests to the front door.

"You shouldn't have kicked Jerry under the table," Papa said, his green eyes narrowed to thin slits. "You disgraced me in front of my boss. After you do the dishes, go to your room. You're grounded for a week."

Saree knew better than to argue, but she dared one squeaky question. "Y'all will let me go to work won't you, Papa?"

"No." Hatred filled her stepmother's beady eyes. "I'll call the librarian and tell her you're sick."

Don't react, Saree ordered herself. *You can handle this.*

Hoping to escape to the kitchen, she picked up the gold-rimmed plates she had stacked on the table and took a cautious step sideways.

"Don't walk away from us," Belle growled, her voice slurred from the alcohol she had consumed before, during and after dinner. "Your father isn't finished talking to you."

Saree gripped the dessert plates so tightly her hands hurt. But if she set the plates down, Papa might extend his tirade. And if he didn't, Belle would likely goad him until he did.

"You deserve to be punished," he growled in a drunken slur.

"Let me handle her, Franklin," Belle snarled, an ugly gleam in her cruel eyes.

Saree's stomach balled into a twisted knot. If she complained, the punishment might be worse. Still, she couldn't resist defending herself tonight. "Jerry—Mr. Vickon put his hand on my leg, under my skirt and started to slide it up my leg, toward my—um—privates. I kicked him to dislodge his hand."

"You're lying." Shades of purple mixed with the red already coloring Papa's mottled face. "Jerry would never act with improper conduct."

"Why would I lie?" she blurted, hurt that he didn't believe her.

"Because you're trying to excuse your own bad behavior," Belle shrieked.

"A month," Papa roared before Saree could defend herself again. "You're grounded for a month."

"No," Belle shouted. "For the rest of your life." She raised her fist and waved it menacingly. "You'll not step foot out of this house ever again, you lazy good-for-nothing brat."

Saree blinked, unable to swallow the lump clogging her throat. Did Belle really think she could keep her grounded forever? If so, the Yankee lady had more than one screw loose.

When Belle sidled closer, Saree took a cautious step backwards. Her stepmother's breath reeked of alcohol and garlic from the shrimp and grits dinner Saree had cooked after she got home from work. "If I don't show up at the library, I'll lose my job," she said, forcing herself to speak with quiet reasoning.

"You're only volunteering," Belle wheezed with an ugly sneer.

Saree didn't react. She had worked part-time at the Spartanburg County Library Headquarters since her junior year in high school. After graduation last week, she had started working full-time. Although she had always been paid, Belle didn't know that. If she did, the greedy lady would have seized every cent, just as she always confiscated whatever money Saree earned babysitting.

"You owe your father for raising you," Belle said, with another unpleasant sneer. "And you'll work off your debt by cleaning and scrubbing this house every day until it shines." She shook her finger, missing Saree's nose by a mere inch. "You'll do exactly as I say, and there will be no talking back. Do you hear?"

Afraid to disagree, Saree meekly nodded.

Watching Papa, wishing he'd stick up for her just this once, she didn't realize Belle raised her arm higher. When she rammed her fist against Saree's face, excruciating pain slammed through her head.

Blood spurted from her nose. She raised her hands to stem the flow as shattering glass clattered around her bare ankles. A few chips bounced off the hardwood floor and lodged between her toes. When she jumped back to avoid another punch, sharp glass cut into feet. Unfortunately she had removed her sandals before she started to clear the table.

In a stupor, she stared down at the blood seeping out beneath her heels, then at the broken china scattered across the shiny floor. Holding her breath, she waited in fear of what might happen next.

To her surprise, Papa turned on Belle, yelling at her instead of his only daughter.

"You shouldn't have hit Saree," he said. "She was holding my wife's priceless china."

"Well, I'm your wife now, Franklin, and don't you forget it." Belle pointed her finger again, shaking it at him. "And your stupid daughter shouldn't have been holding so many plates. Why didn't you and your precious Minnie teach her to carry one at a time?"

Disgusted with Belle's drunken logic, but relieved to have her attention focused on Papa instead of on her, Saree decided to make herself scarce. In her haste, she bumped the table. The white linen tablecloth began to slide. She reached out, trying to stop it, but failed. The cattywampus cloth and everything on top, including crystal water glasses and wine goblets, crashed to the floor.

Belle's shrill scream rattled throughout the house, bouncing off the walls. "Now look at what you've done, you clumsy bitch."

More scared than she'd ever been, Saree dashed away. The glass trapped between her toes and embedded in her feet cut deeper, but she didn't dare stop. If Belle caught her, she might beat her, and in his drunken state, Papa probably wouldn't be able to stop her, even if he tried.

Pain of a different kind shot through her as she ran, cupping her sore nose, blood oozing between her fingers. Papa cared more about the broken china than he did about her. That truth hurt more than anything had since Mama died three years ago. But in a way, it also set her free, and cemented her decision to leave. For months she had been planning her escape. It was time to go.

Inside her bedroom, Saree slammed the door. Her breath came in short gasps as she heaved the dresser in front of the door, then shoved her single bed against it for reinforcement.

With her pulse hammering, she swiped her bloody hands on the flowery lavender comforter before she bent to remove the shards of glass from her feet. As she dug it out, sharp edges pricked her fingers, making them bleed as well.

Panic built inside while she wiped them on the bed again. She had to hurry.

Grabbing her pillow, she jerked off the flowered sham and stuffed it with clothes and shoes. Having planned this in total detail, she knew exactly what to pack, and what to ignore.

The shouting match in the dining room escalated.

Afraid her escape might be thwarted, she jammed her bloody feet into a pair of sandals while she twisted the sham together. Pushing the window open, she slammed the bulky contents at the screen. It bounced, but stayed in place.

She heard Papa and Belle raging at each other as they made their way through the house toward her bedroom. They'd be even more furious when they couldn't get in.

Adrenalin poured through her veins as she hurtled the stuffed sham against the screen again. Still, it remained rooted in its track.

Her parents pounded on the door. Belle shouted obscenities when they couldn't budge it open.

In desperation, Saree spun a chair over to the window and climbed up, kicking the screen, sending it clattering to the ground. Without wasting another precious second, she jumped.

The hard landing jarred her head, a painful reminder of Belle's vicious punch. Ignoring the sharp pain, she scampered to her feet, clasping the sham to her chest as she dashed across the recently mown lawn.

When she reached the sidewalk, dogs began to bark and lights turned on in two houses across the street. She groaned. It must be past midnight. Papa's friends had stayed late. Had the loud shouting match awakened the neighbors? If so, it wouldn't be the first time they called the police to report Belle and Franklin Naisbet were disturbing the peace.

Afraid someone might stop her, Saree ran as though her life depended on it. Clutching her possessions with one hand, she swiped at the blood still dribbling from her nose with the other. The metallic taste made her gag and she nearly retched. She forced the nausea back. But she couldn't ignore the cuts on her heels and between her toes. Or the painful throbbing at the bridge of her nose. Was it broken?

Fear added to her haste. She wouldn't be free until she got out of town. Even then, she doubted she'd feel safe. Never would she go home. Belle hated her. Saree didn't know why. She loathed Belle's drinking and despised her screaming rants. Most of the time she convinced Papa to drink with her, and if an argument occurred, which it usually did, he always sided with Belle against her.

A siren sounded in the distance.

Saree screeched her sore feet to a halt. Her gaze darted in every direction. Where could she hide?

Spying a lamppost ahead, she dashed behind it. By some miracle, the light at the top was out. Praying the post concealed her, she arched her neck and pinched her nose, trying to squelch the bloody flow while she held her breath.

Her heart pounded like a loud drum, and terror made her whole body shake as a black and white police car whizzed by, red lights flashing, siren blaring. When the driver turned left at the intersection, she heaved a ragged sigh of relief. *They weren't going to her house.*

Spurred into action, she ran again.

When her racing heart or the pain in her feet made running impossible, she slowed to a jog or fast walk, concentrating on her plans. First she had to get the money stashed in a locker at the bus station. The money was her ticket to the future—her way to disappear and put Belle out of her life.

She kept the locker key taped to her skin, inside the modest panties Belle insisted she wear. The only time she removed the key was when it came off in the shower. She always taped it to a new spot after she dried off.

Months ago, she had withdrawn all the money from her secret savings account and stashed it in her locker, along with a few other necessities, including the social security card and driver's license of her best friend's deceased cousin. For a while she had considered assuming the dead girl's name, but the driver's license photo didn't look anything like her, so she had decided to use a name that had lived in her head from her earliest memories—Janalou—the name from a rhyme she couldn't forget. *Janalou loves Jeri Sue. Jeri Sue loves Janalou. And Winnie the Pooh loves both of you.*

Although she didn't know anyone named Janalou or Jeri Sue, she dreamed about them often, and every time she thought about the rhyme, an odd warmth speared through her, reminding her of her dear dead mama's warm smile and kind, gentle nature. How could Papa marry someone like Belle after being married to an angel princess like Minnie?

~ * ~

Seated on the bus across the aisle from Reina, his middle-aged friend and his reason for flying to the east coast, Kree Winterton glanced at his watch. Not quite 1:00 a.m. When today's bus had been late, he had suggested checking into a hotel room and catching tomorrow's bus. Reina had persuaded him to take this one, instead, convinced it would be less crowded and they could sleep while they traveled.

She'd been right. And wrong. Most of the passengers had opted to wait, so only a dozen people occupied the big bus. But Kree couldn't sleep. Not only was his mind working overtime, it was alert and in full gear, as though waiting for something exciting to happen.

Through the dark window he spotted a mileage sign. Fifty miles to Spartanburg, South Carolina. A grin curved his lips. If his friends could see him now, riding a bus in the middle of the night, they'd burst out laughing. He'd done it for Reina. Years ago she had worked as a domestic for his parents, and he loved her almost as much as he loved his own mother. He'd do just about anything for her, including taking time off to fly east and ride the bus back home with her because after attending her niece's wedding, Reina didn't want to fly ever again.

Kree leaned back and crossed his ankles, hoping to catch some shut-eye. Sleeping might make the journey go faster. But his mind wouldn't slow down. Usually he could sleep anywhere. But tonight anticipation pumped adrenalin through his system, making him feel hyper, as though he were expecting some sort of life-altering change to occur.

Telling himself nothing unusual or monumental would happen on this uncrowded bus, he closed his eyes and let his thoughts wander back to a happier time. How different would his life be now if Bethany, Reina's daughter and the only girl he had ever loved, hadn't died three years ago?

Her death had been such a shock he still hadn't recovered. There were times when he half expected to see her again, blinking impishly, winking flirtatiously, or smiling because they were together, happily planning their next date. Or their future.

Two

Just when Saree thought her lungs might burst, she reached the bus station. Gasping for breath, she peeked through the door. No other travelers. Thank goodness.

Too pumped up to worry about her sore feet or the new pain throbbing in her side, she dashed inside and ran to the lockers. *Too bad she didn't have the money she earned for her last paycheck, but she didn't dare hang around to collect it.*

As she peeled off the tape holding the locker key against her skin below the waistband of her blue denim skirt, she grimaced. *Thank goodness her nose and fingers had finally stopped bleeding.*

Glad to be alone in the historic station, she opened the locker, dug out her new backpack and stuffed her blood-stained sham inside, leaving all but one envelope filled with money in the pack's zippered pockets. She had saved almost six thousand dollars. *Hopefully it would last until she found another job and got her first paycheck.*

Although the station was old, the technology was new, up-to-date state-of-the-art. As she'already practiced a thousand times in her mind, she fed the computerized ticket machine some bills. When her ticket gushed out with a noisy swish, her insides quivered with relief.

High on one wall a computerized screen displayed schedules. A delay worked in her favor. Instead of having to wait for tomorrow's 7:10 a.m. bus, tonight's 9:30 p.m. would arrive around 2:00 a.m. Having checked her destination on a library computer, she knew the journey would take three days of continuous travel, and entail six transfers along the way.

Too keyed up to relax, she went to the ladies' room and washed the blood off her hands and face. She glanced in the mirror. And frowned. *Belle's punch had given her a puffy red nose and the beginning of two black eyes.*

Grateful to be away from her cruel stepmother at last, she changed her blood-stained blouse. *If she threw it away, someone might find it and somehow track it to her.*

She stuffed the blouse in her backpack. After squeezing the zippered pouch closed, she dabbed at the dried blood between her toes, not surprised her feet felt as numb as her hands after clutching her possessions for the three miles she had run.

When she left the ladies' room, she stood by the station windows. *Where was the bus? Were Papa and Belle looking for her yet?*

Terrified they or the police might show up, she constantly looked up and down the street.

A few minutes before two 2:00 a.m., she ventured back outside. The late May night had turned chilly. She dug inside the backpack for her jacket, shaking so badly from nerves her teeth clattered. The only way she kept them still was by clenching her jaw, but that made the bridge of her injured nose hurt even more.

By the time the bus arrived, her raw nerves were in jeopardy of getting the best of her. As soon as the twin doors slid open, she climbed on board. After the bus driver accepted her ticket, she turned toward the aisle.

A short man dressed all in green, including an old baseball cap with the letter "L" embossed in white on the top, stood in front of her, a green duffle bag in hand. A merry twinkle lit his green eyes and he smiled before he hefted his bag up to the overhead bin and sat down.

Thinking he had been about to get off, and wondering why he had changed his mind, Saree tiptoed down the aisle, belatedly trying to protect the cuts on her sore heels. She took mental notes of the other passengers. There weren't many, only twelve, and two were children. All except the middle-aged man wearing green, and one considerably younger man, had their eyes closed and she assumed they were asleep. The young man's stare made her insides cringe. With a swollen nose and ugly facial bruises, she knew she looked frightful. Regretfully there was nothing she could do about it.

At the back of the bus, she plunked on the last seat opposite the onboard john, then slung her blue pack onto her lap and clutched it to her chest. Two of the passengers looked like grimy swamp rats, so she'd be wise to stay on guard.

Although the bus was warm, she couldn't squelch the shivers playing tag up and down her arms and legs. Never had she done anything this daring. In the space of a few hours, she had accidentally destroyed some of Mama's precious china and crystal, then packed a few meager belongings and run away.

Loosening her grip on her pack, she tried to relax, but couldn't. Her nose hurt. So did her feet as the numbness began to wear off. The metallic coppery taste of blood was still in her mouth, too, and the pain in her side gnawed with each breath she drew. But thankfully none of it was unbearable.

When the sound of sirens pierced the dark night air, her heart jumped half way up her throat. *Had Papa or Belle called the police? Were they looking for her?*

Renewed panic clamped around her chest like a vise, and she found it difficult to breathe when the bus driver pulled off the road and braked to a stop on the gravel shoulder before he turned on the inside lights.

Saree gulped. Fear had a smell. She inhaled it like bitter medicine. Suddenly sick to her stomach, she clamped a hand over her mouth, willing herself not to barf. *Were the sirens the police? Were they after her? She knew bus drivers always turned on the interior lights when they stopped at night, but why did he have to do it now? Couldn't she have just a little bit of luck?*

She scrunched her shoulders, trying to shrink inside her skin, wishing she had someplace to hide.

Bile rose in her throat, and her queasy stomach threatened to rebel as a police squad car sped by, red lights flashing. The blaring siren awakened all the adult passengers. Each one stared out the dark windows. Seconds later, a loud ambulance rushed beyond them, followed by a noisy fire engine.

After the emergency vehicles whizzed out of sight, the driver pulled back onto the road. Saree's heart settled back down. Almost.

When the young man turned his head and stared again, Saree's breath got trapped in her throat. *He's so good-looking.* And she had caught a whiff of his pleasant spicy masculine scent when she'd tiptoed past him. His jet black hair was as dark as hers and his curious blue eyes seemed to peer inside her quaking heart.

Calm down, she admonished herself, sucking in a quick breath. *And don't be impressed with the blue-eyed stranger. You don't have room in your life for guys right not. Not even one as handsome as he. Besides, with his looks he must already have a girlfriend. Maybe more than one.*

Her heart raced as he continued to stare. She forced herself to look away. Her gaze settled on the stocky middle-aged man in green.

He smiled and touched the brim of his green baseball cap. Saree blinked. *Was he flirting? He looked harmless enough.*

An icy chill froze her thumping heart. She was all alone with no one to protect her. Not that she'd had much protection at home. After Papa married Belle last year, he had ignored her, often drinking himself into a stupor when he was home and totally unaware of Belle's cruelty.

Misgivings twisted through Saree. Had she done the right thing by leaving? *Should she have stayed home and continued to put up with Belle's tantrums and abuse? Was the devil she knew better than the one she didn't?*

Riddled with fear and doubts, she drew in a batch of shallow breaths, relieved when both men turned their heads and the driver flipped off the lights. The other passengers leaned back in their seats. Saree assumed they fell back asleep.

Some of her apprehension retreated, and her heartbeat slowed. But she couldn't relax. Turmoil and fear held her in separate clutches. *If she slept, she might be taken unawares. Someone could steal her possessions, and her money.*

She clutched her backpack tighter. *From now on she must be careful. Very, very careful. Her pack contained everything she owned.*

~ * ~

Although Kree closed his eyes, sleep continued to elude him. Was the stranger the reason he couldn't settle down? Was she in some kind of trouble? If so, would he be able to help her?

He shook his head at the absurd thought. He couldn't be responsible for every person he encountered. Still, he couldn't help wondering why the girl had caught a bus in the middle of the night. Where did she live? Where did she intend to go? And why did she look like a frightened, injured rabbit who was much too young to be traveling alone?

~ * ~

When the sky began to lighten with the dawning of the first day of her new life, Saree squared her shoulders. Determination surged inside. *In spite of Belle's caustic criticisms, she wasn't a lazy good-for-nothing brat. She was a GRITS—a Girl Raised in the South, and dear, dead Mama would approve of her finally taking control of her life and putting mean-spirited Belle behind her.*

Riding high on those positive thoughts, Saree reveled in the marvelous sensations flooding her. Freedom. Independence. A sense of wonder. Maybe now she could live, not merely exist.

The logical part of her mind issued a few words of caution. *Don't look back. And never use your given name again. You don't like Saree anyway. Most people sound like they're saying Sorry instead of Saree.*

Her new name, Janalou, had a familiar ring, almost as though it were her real name. It was her alter ego, the name she had chosen for her new life, her new identity—Janalou Madsen, whose parents she had already decided, were both dead.

As the bus approached the outskirts of Atlanta, the driver announced, "Since we're off schedule, I'll stop for everyone to eat breakfast before we go to the station. There are no eating facilities at or near the Atlanta bus station. When we reach Knoxville later today, there will be a layover for those with transfers. On behalf of Greyhound, I apologize for the inconvenience our delay might have caused."

After quiet reigned again, Janalou made more plans. By the time the bus stopped, she had invented an entire history that didn't include Saree Nesbitt or Franklin and Belle.

~ * ~

Kree bit into the gooey center of his cinnamon roll. The sweet pastry satisfied his taste buds as he smiled at Reina, perched on a chair across from him in a small café on one side of the busy Atlanta street.

Reina smiled back, a gentle expression in her kind brown eyes. Years ago when he had fallen in love with her daughter and asked Bethany to marry him, she had replied with a joyful 'yes,' and thrown herself against his chest so fast they had both stumbled backwards and fallen onto the grassy lawn in front of her mother's home. Shortly after they announced their plans, his parents fired Reina, and told Bethany she wasn't good enough for him. Before he had a chance to convince her it didn't matter what his parents said, Bethany stepped out in front of a bus and got herself killed. She'd been unable to bear the pain and humiliation of their rejection. And part of him still blamed them for her death.

"Your smiles always be sad," Reina said, "like they contain loss of the whole universe."

Kree licked the icing off his lips before he replied. "Perhaps because Bethany was my universe."

"It's been three years, Kree. I love you like you my own *nino*, and I no like to see you unhappy for so long a time."

"I'm not unhappy."

Reina shook her head in vigorous disagreement. At forty-five, she didn't have a single gray hair. It was still as coal black as Bethany's had been. "You must bury the past," she said. "Bethany not come back from dead."

Kree hiked his brows, but kept his tone low. "Do you think I don't know that?"

Reina glanced down at her plate of scrambled eggs, sprinkled with Tabasco in lieu of salsa. "I thought a reminder might be helpful. You need find someone else to love."

"Easier said than done." Although he dated, Kree didn't intend to open his heart to love again, at least not for a long time. "Bethany was my soul mate," he said, doubting he'd ever find another. "Besides, I have a bunch of bachelor buddies, and I like being single." *And I don't intend to change my status just to please other people.*

"What about family? I see you with nieces and nephews. They adore you. And you love them, too, no?

"Yes, and someday I'll probably marry," he said. But not until he was ready. Maybe in ten or twenty years. But not yet. It was still too soon, and would feel like a betrayal to Bethany.

"Let's talk about something else," he said as Reina forked a bite of her fluffy eggs.

"You have idea?" she asked, her brown eyes locked with his.

Not sure what to suggest, Kree raised his glass and sipped orange juice.

"I want to ask something," Reina said.

"What?"

"Were your mama and papa upset because you flew across the country to accompany me home on bus?"

Kree forced himself not to frown. When he arranged for time off, he had been purposely vague. His two sisters understood his relationship with Reina. His parents didn't. Sometimes he thought they acted jealous of the time he spent with her. He made no secret of the fact that he talked to Reina every week, bought her chocolates on Valentine's Day, flowers on Easter and Mother's Day, as well as birthday and Christmas gifts. He took her out to dinner at least once a month, too. Reina was his only link to Bethany, and he kept her spirit alive by staying in touch.

"I work with Mom and Dad," he said, "but I don't tell them everything I do."

Reina stared him in the eye, her message clear before she spoke. "You should not blame them for Bethany dying. You must accept her death as I do. It be her time to go."

"I can't make myself believe that," he said, because part of him would always blame his parents and himself for their part in her death.

An emotion he interpreted as regret clouded Reina's dark eyes, but all she said was, "Your mama and papa—they only want the best for you, no?"

"Bethany was the best." He swallowed a slug of hot coffee before he said, "You're beginning to sound like them. They keep nagging me to find a wife, and start a family."

"Fault them not for that," she advised. "You be their only son, and it be up to you to carry on family name. Besides, you not getting younger. You be quarter of a century now."

Not used to having Reina poke into his personal life, he said, "Why don't we find something else to discuss?"

She shrugged her plump shoulders, but didn't hesitate this time. "The girl who got on bus in middle of night—she look like somebody beat her up."

Kree did his best to keep his expression neutral. Reina had caught him staring at the stranger, but she couldn't know his gut reaction. He had drawn in a deep breath, feeling as though somebody had socked him in the gut. Hard. The girl didn't look like Bethany exactly but she did resemble her with that long black hair and those dark soulful eyes. She had an attractive figure, but her face was a mess. Had she been beaten as Reina suggested? Or did her nose always look red and swollen, and too big for her delicate face?

He glanced around, expecting to see her, but didn't.

"She stay on bus," Reina said. "She look worried and very alone. We take her something to eat, no? She must be hungry."

Kree nodded and finished his coffee. How like Reina to suggest helping someone else. Yesterday she had reached out to a young mother traveling with two kids, and helped keep them entertained while they waited for the late bus.

As he chewed another bite of his sweet roll, his thoughts reverted to the newest traveler. Last night when the bus stopped in Spartanburg, he had gotten a good look at her before the driver turned off the lights. Her fear-filled eyes had dredged his protective instinct out of hibernation. What lay behind the hurt? And fear?

At first glance, she had reminded him of a scared, wounded rabbit. Even so, when she teetered past, she had stirred something deep inside him. And later, when sirens sounded and the bus driver pulled over for the emergency vehicles to pass, he turned to study her again. She had looked terrorized. Why?

At that moment, his protective instinct had almost gotten the best of him. The overwhelming urge to wrap his arms around her and promise to protect her had astounded him. How he'd remained in his seat still surprised him. She looked so young and frightened, he had wanted to race to the back of the bus and promise to help her, no matter what problem she faced, and despite the consequences he might encounter for sticking his nose in somebody else's business where it didn't belong.

He bet she had a story to tell, and figured Reina would draw it out. And if he didn't befriend her, Reina might nag. They had a long journey ahead of them, and he didn't want it filled with friction.

He had no real interest in the girl. At least that's what he told himself. Still, one part of his brain admitted he wanted to get to know her because of the electric jolts she had sent zipping through his system. Part of him felt as though he'd been asleep for a long time and seeing her had snapped him out of a deep slumber.

Was she the reason his senses had been on high alert last night? The reason he couldn't sleep? Had he somehow sensed she was about to board the bus? Was the sudden thrumming of his pulse due to the anticipation of seeing her again and talking to her?

Telling himself those ideas were insane, he ate the last of his sweet roll while Reina finished her toast. Somehow the attraction churning inside him had to be squelched. The girl was too young for him. Probably not even out of high school yet. And some days he felt years older than his actual age.

Three

The instant they climbed back on the bus, Kree felt the tension inside. A confrontation was going on between two dirty scumbags and the dark-haired girl in the back of the bus. Nudging Reina aside, he strode down the aisle. Anger pulsed through him. *Why did some guys think they had a right to harass defenseless women?*

"What's the problem?" he asked, stopping behind the two slimeballs, his hands balled in tight fists. He hadn't thought it possible for anyone to look more frightened, but the girl did. Instead of relief or gratitude, tears filled her exotic brown eyes and she clutched her blue backpack tighter against her chest.

"Butt out," one greasy, long-haired guy said.

"Yeah. This is none a' your business," the other added.

Ignoring him, the first hooligan badgered the girl. "We wanna know what you've got inside that backpack. You're hanging onto it like it's full a' gold."

"It's none of your business what's inside," Kree said, doing his best to convey with a glance that he meant her no harm. A slight nod was the only indication she understood.

"If you want to get off the bus, we can settle this with our fists," the second punk said, frowning at Kree.

"Be my guests." It would take some fancy footwork to fight them both, but he didn't hesitate. Thinking the lowlifes might attack from the back, he stepped in front of an empty seat and motioned for them to precede him. He was in excellent physical condition but two against one didn't stack in his favor. *Could he somehow outsmart them*?

While he was pondering that, another male passenger who had apparently witnessed the exchange, said, "I'll help even the odds, lad."

Dressed all in green except for his shiny brown shoes, the pudgy, white-haired man stepped in front of Kree and followed the two hooligans. Studying the back of the hefty guy who stood no more than five feet tall, if that, Kree wondered how much help he would be. Probably not much. His short stature and age were both against him. But maybe he could distract one guy while Kree dealt with the other.

He sucked in a breath of fresh air when they climbed off the bus. Both bullies stunk of body odor and their snarly hair looked like rat's nests. Kree wondered when they'd last had a shower or used a comb.

To his surprise, the bus driver climbed off right behind him, carrying two garbage bags that appeared to be half full. "You two get back on," he said, nodding at Kree and his squat volunteer helper. "I have a better way to handle this. Greyhound doesn't need passengers who bully others. We'll continue our journey without these dudes."

Kree nodded, but waited in case the driver needed help.

"Your tickets were for Atlanta," the bus driver said, "and we're there. Here's your luggage, such as it is." The instant he shoved a grungy garbage bag into each punk's dirty hands, they froze. Kree had a weird sensation they had been struck dumb. Rendered completely immobile. And speechless.

"They can find their own way to the station," the driver said, not even bothering to look at them again. "They're no longer welcome on my bus." He followed Kree and the hefty short man back onto the bus and shut the doors with a noisy, hissing clang.

The two guys outside came out of their stupor and started banging on the glass. Already seated behind the steering wheel, the driver merely shifted gears and drove away, ignoring the scumbags' obscene gestures and loud, threatening shouts.

Kree scratched his head. Had the two ruffians been struck dumb for a few seconds? While he was wondering if he had witnessed something extraordinary, or if his imagination had gotten the best of him, the girl cleared her throat.

"Thank y'all," she said.

No longer clutching her backpack, she stood in the aisle near the front of the bus, her blue pack strapped on her back. He swallowed, unable to ignore the sight of her white blouse stretched across her chest, her breasts thrust into prominence with the straps of her pack flattened near her shoulders.

The man in green grinned. "Allow me to assure you it was our pleasure, lass."

Instead of commenting, Kree took his time studying her. She had the longest hair he had ever seen, longer even than Bethany's had been. The silky black strands covered her slender shoulders and arms, all the way past her elbows. He knew from watching her last night that the lush locks fell below her waist in back.

Her dark almond-shaped eyes made her look a bit exotic. Another wave of awareness zinged through him. Stunned by the sensual jar, he drew air into his lungs like a swimmer who had stayed under water too long.

While he watched her, the girl blushed. She wasn't very tall, only an inch or two over five feet. Once again, her tiny size tugged at his protective instinct. No wonder he had stared last night, and kept staring now. Without a swollen nose, puffy cheeks, and bruises beneath her eyes, she might be beautiful. Even with them, she looked frail and delicate, and more appealing than he wanted to admit. In spite of not wanting to be attracted, desire streaked through him, along with fury that anyone might mistreat her in any way.

Not pleased with his sexual reaction, Kree stuck his hands in his pockets, trying to ignore the electric shock waves that continued to jolt through him like blinking neon lights.

The short man in green found his seat.

When the girl turned and made her way to the back of the bus, Kree watched her long hair caress her slender hips as they swayed enticingly against her full blue denim skirt. He gawked at her shapely behind until Reina leaned close and whispered, "Maybe she didn't have enough money to eat. You think she be offended if we offer food?"

Kree shrugged before he waved Reina in front of him. "Only one way to find out."

She trekked down the aisle, and he followed.

After the girl sat down, Reina said, "We notice you didn't get off to eat, so we brought you a cinnamon roll."

"And a bottle of milk," Kree added as Reina extended a white paper sack.

Although the girl looked startled, she accepted the bag, a half smile quivering on her pink heart-shaped lips. "Thank y'all."

"You're welcome," Kree said, charmed by her soft southern drawl in spite of silent admonitions to the contrary. "I thought you might enjoy coffee or hot chocolate, but Reina said milk goes better with sweet rolls."

The paper sack crackled as the stranger opened it and peered inside, then pulled out the cinnamon roll and plastic bottle of milk.

Reina sat down on the seat across the aisle from her, watching.

Kree stayed on his feet, his hand anchored on the back of Reina's seat. He didn't want to intimidate the girl or make her more uncomfortable than she already looked. Soon he would walk away. He had no intention of getting involved with her or any woman, but if he knew who had hurt her, he'd be willing to retaliate on her behalf.

"My name be Reina Ruiz," Reina introduced herself. "And this be my friend, Kree Winterton. We live in California and we on our way home." Reina paused to smile. "How far you be traveling?"

The young woman glanced away, then looked back at Reina, her gaze wary when she replied. "Across the country."

"To California?" Reina asked.

The girl lowered her head, staring at her lap, before she nodded.

Kree wondered if she might be hiding something. Or running away. Why those suspicions surfaced baffled him. He didn't make a habit of speculating or taking an interest in total strangers. But for some odd reason this one intrigued him. Suddenly he wanted to know as much as possible. And that annoyed him.

He clenched his jaw, intending to keep his mouth shut.

"I be glad." Reina's friendly expression radiated warmth. "That will give us a few days to get better acquainted, no?" She crossed her arms over her ample bosom and when the girl didn't reply, she asked, "What be your name?"

Once again, the girl hesitated, licked her lips, and stared out the window. Finally she looked at Reina again, and said, "Janalou. Janalou Madsen."

"I happy to meet you, Janalou." Reina's brown eyes twinkled as she stuck her hand across the aisle.

Janalou shook it, but the sadness in her eyes tore at Kree's gut.

Her long black lashes were spiked from the tears that had filled her eyes when the two lowlife punks had threatened her.

Seized by a sudden urge to say something to make her smile, he unclenched his jaw, and raised his hand in mock salute. "Here's looking at you, kid."

He hadn't seen the old Humphrey Bogart classic *Casablanca* since Bethany had died. The old movie had been one of her favorites. So why was he glomming onto a line from it now? He stifled a grimace, feeling guilty for showing interest in another female, as though he were betraying Bethany.

Janalou's reaction startled him as much as his own had. She didn't smile. She simply raised her hand, waved, and said, "Goodbye, Rick."

More pleased than he wanted to be, Kree grinned. She had picked up on his message and followed his lead, mimicking Ingrid Bergman, but in her own slow Southern drawl.

When she closed her eyes and inhaled slowly as though it hurt to breathe, he took a step closer. "Are you all right?"

Her eyelids flickered open, her expression at odds with her reply. "Yes. Of course."

"You don't look all right." Reina stood and moved closer too.

Janalou's dark slanted eyes opened wider. "How do I look?"

"Like you've been in a fight and lost your best friend," Kree said.

The sadness in her eyes deepened. "Actually, leaving my friends feels like I have lost them. I suppose we can stay in touch, but it's never the same when someone moves away, is it?"

Aware that she had avoided his mention of a fight, Kree wondered what had caused the swelling on her face and the purple bruises beneath her eyes.

"So, you be moving," Reina continued the conversation as though it hadn't been interrupted. "I didn't think you be from West coast. Your Southern accent be pleasant to hear." She smiled. "You have relatives in California, no?"

Janalou shook her head.

"Then why you going there?"

"Because that's where I want to live."

"How do your mama and papa feel about your move?"

"I—a..." She cleared her throat, her cheeks turning pink before she tried again. "I don't have any parents. I'm an orphan."

She must have sensed all Reina's questions begging for answers because she raised her hands, palms out, as though to ward them off. "I didn't grow up in an orphanage. I lost my parents recently, and I don't want to talk about them. It's too painful."

Reina nodded, and Kree had an urge to take her by the arm and lead her away so Janalou could compose herself and eat the cinnamon roll.

He didn't though, and Reina plowed on. "If you want work when you reach California, Kree might help you find job."

His shocked expression must have revealed he didn't have a clue why Reina had said that because Janalou looked as though he'd struck her. Filled with remorse from all the emotions swimming in her dark, soulful eyes, he found himself forcing a smile he hoped looked genuine. "Yes, I might." He let go of the seatback and braced his hip against it to maintain his balance as the bus turned a corner.

"What—a—part of California to do you live in?" Janalou asked.

"Lodi."

She licked her lips. The sight of her pink tongue awakened a hunger he had believed dead. "I'm going to Los Angeles," she said quietly.

Reina spoke again before Kree could collect his thoughts. "Maybe we help change your mind."

"Are y'all related?" Janalou asked, doubt evident in her exotic eyes.

"No. Years ago I work for Kree's family, and we still be friends."

Janalou eyed the sharp creases on his tan pants, his eighty-dollar shirt and three hundred dollar cashmere sweater. From her expression, Kree guessed what she was going to ask.

"Why are you taking the bus instead of flying?"

Kree let Reina answer.

"Weeks ago, Kree convince me to fly across country for niece's wedding. But when we talk on phone afterwards, I tell him I no like crowded airplane or take-off, landing, or windy, turbulent sky. I decide to ride bus back home. I never want to fly again." Reina paused to smile at Kree. "Feeling responsible for convincing me to go, he didn't want me to travel on bus alone. So he flew east and met me." Reina hiked her black brows in question. "Why you be on bus instead of airplane?"

"Because it's cheaper."

"Well, if money be a problem, you might change your mind about L.A. I think it cost more to live there, and Kree did offer to help you find work."

Kree still didn't understand why he had agreed, but he knew why Reina felt Janalou should go to Lodi. She looked like she needed friends, also like she might cry, and Reina had a weakness for lonely people and their tears. Truth be told, under his macho façade, so did he.

"Could you really help me find a job?" Janalou asked, her drawl a notch above a trembling whisper.

"Sure," he said, thinking she might fit in at the office, and help Martina, their receptionist.

Janalou cleared her throat, and her voice sounded stronger when she asked, "What kind of work would it be?"

"What experience do you have?" he countered.

"I worked in a library for two years, and I took computer and office classes in school, so I'm good with people and qualified to work in an office."

"Have you graduated from high school?" he asked, trying to determine her age.

Her nod surprised him.

"When?"

"A little over a week ago."

Relieved, although not sure why, he said, "My family owns a real estate company. Mom, Dad and I work full-time, and my two sisters work part-time. We keep our receptionist busy. I'm sure she could use help."

"Thank y'all. I appreciate your offer, and I'll—a—think about it."

He nodded. "Why don't you eat now? We'll talk again when you're through."

Janalou unscrewed the bottle of milk. Gratitude filled her dark eyes when she glanced up. "Thank y'all once more. You're very kind."

"You're welcome." Before Kree walked away, he thought he caught a glimpse of a smile, and a sparkle in her exotic eyes.

As Reina preceded him down the aisle, using the seat backs for support as the bus swayed around another sharp corner, his steps felt lighter, and the weight near his heart less heavy. He told himself it wasn't because he had any interest in Janalou Madsen. He just wanted to help. That's all.

Why then did he want to turn back around and try to convince her to settle in Lodi? Convince her she didn't belong anywhere else? Not because she was beautiful. She might not be sporting two black eyes. Those dark smudges could be a permanent skin discoloration.

And her swollen nose might look like that all the time, rather than the result of an injury.

In spite of those possibilities, a strange new attraction kindled inside him. Bothered by the emotion, he frowned. He was used to dating gorgeous women. *Why couldn't he be attracted to one of them instead of a young chick who reminded him of a stray, wounded cat who feared he might step on her tail? Or whack it off?*

Four

Janalou nibbled on the cinnamon roll, staring at the back of Kree's head, a durn attractive head, she decided as he sat across the aisle from Reina near the front of the bus.

A silent reminder poked through her thoughts. For months she had practiced talking like a Yankee, but today she had completely forgotten her plan not to use words or phrases that might give away her background.

Kree turned his head and smiled at Reina. His handsome profile made Janalou's pulse flutter. Although he had a military type haircut, the top of his black hair laid in short cropped curls, and looked as though he'd had it styled by an expert barber or beautician.

She released an inward sigh, telling herself not to be too impressed. But the way he had stood up to those two swamp rat bullies made him a hero in every sense of the word. Her heart still hadn't settled down from the confrontation with the lowlifes, or her encounter with Reina and Kree, either. With alert blue eyes and an athletic build, he was one of the most striking men she'd ever met.

She gave herself a mental shake. At this stage in her life, she had no interest in men. Still, she couldn't repress a shiver of regret. What would it be like to get close to a man who cared so much about the welfare of others that he flew clear across the country to ride the bus back with a woman of Mexican descent who had once worked for his parents?

The sweet scent of sugar and cinnamon wafted up from the cinnamon roll. She took her first real bite. While she chewed the delicious pastry, she decided Kree must come from a wealthy family, like Tony, the only boy she'd ever had a crush on, the only boy she had dated steadily.

Tony had been two years ahead of her in school, and after Mama died, he had taken her to school dances, ball games, movies and parties. The junior prom and senior hop were two of the most romantic, magical nights of her life.

Unfortunately they had grown apart after Tony graduated because his family moved to Virginia. He had promised to stay in touch when he went away to college. During her junior year, they had communicated regularly by email, phone calls and text messages, but after Papa married Belle, Tony's texts and calls stopped. She hadn't received any letters either, not even a card or phone call on her birthday or at Christmas.

As it had for the last year, suspicion threaded through her. *Did Belle have anything to do with Tony's neglect? Had she intercepted his phone calls and texts, and destroyed his emails?*

She had confiscated her computer, cell phone and car keys. Belle had also convinced Papa to keep her from dating. She had done her best to thwart activities with girlfriends, too, but she hadn't entirely succeeded. Her best friend, Margie, knew about Belle's cruelty and had encouraged her to leave home, giving her the driver's license and social security card of her dead cousin so she wouldn't have to use own and risk being found. Margie was in Europe for the summer, traveling with her grandparents and two cousins. When she returned, Janalou would call and tell her she had finally escaped.

Her thoughts returned to the present and she found herself smiling for the first time since her adventure began as another passenger, a little boy, toddled down the aisle, sucking his thumb.

When he reached her, he sat on the floor, pulled his thumb out of his mouth, poked at her toes, and muttered, "Oow-ee."

She glanced down and saw dried blood. Although she had tried to clean her injured feet in the ladies' room at the bus station, she'd been too nervous to do a very good job. Fumbling in her backpack, she found a pair of socks and put them on inside her sandals, satisfied that the cuts on her feet were healing.

The short white-haired man who had offered to help Kree with the two swamprat bullies, wandered to the back of the bus next. Dressed in a green shirt and trousers with a battered baseball cap of the same grass-green shade, he spoke in a cheerful melodic voice. "Hello, lass."

Stunned when he sat on the seat right beside her, she gasped, "Who are you?"

"My name's Guggles. Duke Guggles. Rhymes with struggles, and that's why I'm here. To help you with yours."

Janalou looked around, wondering how many people had heard him. But other than the little boy, toying with the velcro straps on her sandals, no one seemed to be paying them any attention. "Y'all— want to help me with my struggles?" she asked.

Duke nodded, a cheerful grin spreading across his cherubic face. "Ye do want help, don't ye, Janalou?"

Startled that he knew her new name, she merely stared.

"I overheard ye introduce yerself to the young man and his Mexican lady friend." Duke smiled and dimples winked on both cheeks. "Janalou Madsen be a foine name, lass."

"Thank you," she said. "I like it."

He nodded, his gaze friendly. "Is that the name ye were born with, lass?"

Suspicion snaked through her, although she sensed no fear. "Why do you want to know?"

"Curiosity," he said. "Ye see, 'bout a week ago I attended the Spartanburg High School graduation, and a lass who looks a lot like ye received a four-year scholarship to the University of South

Carolina. But her name wasna Janalou. It was Saree. Saree Naisbit. That be ye, lass? And if so, why did ye change yer name?"

"If that was me," Janalou lowered her voice to a desperate whisper, "maybe I don't want anyone else to know."

Duke waved an arm at the passengers several rows in front of them. "Dinna ye worry, lass. The others, they canna hear me jest now."

She folded her hands on her lap, certain he must be jesting. "Whatever does that mean?"

His eyes twinkled when he winked, and the strangest sensation she had ever experienced descended. She had no idea where her next thought came from, but suddenly she knew, just as surely as she knew the sun would rise again tomorrow, that he must be an extraordinary being—someone special, someone not of this world, someone above mere mortals.

"You're not from this world, are you?" she blurted. "You're a... you must be..."

"A leprechaun?" he suggested with a kindly smile.

"Well, y'all are wearing green," she said as though that made sense, which it didn't.

"If I look like a leprechaun, then 'tis a leprechaun I shall be. And, just so you know, I'm using a bit of magic to keep this conversation private atwixt the two of us."

Janalou clapped her hand over her heart. The rapid thudding shouldn't have surprised her, but it did. "Using magic?" she echoed, wondering if she had fallen asleep and might be dreaming.

"Yep. And proud to admit it to ye, lass." He removed his green ball cap, and reached inside. "Here's me credentials, if ye want to see them."

Nervous laughter escaped as she read the words on two small plastic cards. One resembled a driver's license issued by Triple A, the other a business card. "Duke Guggles, Irish Leprechaun, Services rendered for free." She glanced up, saw his grin, and decided to go along, at least for the time being. "A leprechaun with credentials. I can hardly believe it."

"Well, lass, if it's all the same to ye, I'd be pleased to keep that bit 'a news atwixt the two of us."

"Okay." Smiling, she returned the cards.

Duke tucked them back inside his baseball cap and stuck it on top of his mop of unruly white hair again. Then to her surprise, he moved his hand to her face, and touched the bridge of her nose ever so gently before he ran his fingers below each of her eyes. His soothing touch felt as soft as butterfly wings fluttering against her skin. He lowered his hands and touched the cuts on her fingers.

"I wish I could heal yer injuries properly, lass. I canna for I possess not that kind 'o power, but I promise no complications shall arise from the attack ye had last even'."

"How did you know?" she gasped. Although Mama had always said she could read her mind through her eyes, she hadn't thought about Belle's attack for some time. A spooky sensation stole over her. "Are you a mind reader?"

Duke shook his head. "Nay, lass. Some leprechauns be capable of a bit a' magic now and then, but I havena the power to poke around in yer head. 'Tis plain to see ye musta been attacked from the swelling on yer lovely face and the cuts on yer hands. Ye dinna look like this last week at graduation."

Not knowing what to say, Janalou didn't reply. *Was he real? Or was she hallucinating? And if he was a Leprechaun and capable of magic, what kind? Good or bad?*

She stared ahead at the other passengers. None of them seemed aware of her and Duke.

Had he really spun some kind of spell to keep them from hearing their conversation?

Her silence didn't seem to bother him. "Had I known ye were in a situation that might cause ye harm, I woulda come to help ye before now, lass."

"Why?" she asked, still wondering if she might be imagining this conversation.

"Why not, lass? I sense ye've had a difficult time. Tell me about yer life."

To her amazement she did, feeling as though he had injected some kind of truth serum into her veins without even touching her. She revealed things she hadn't told another soul, not even Margie, her best friend, and she ended by saying, "Belle is an awful human, and a terrible stepmother."

Duke nodded, a grim expression in his brilliant green eyes. "Then ye should understand why I want to help ye, lass. Surely ye deserve something good after what ye've been through since yer papa married that hag. She be the one who struck ye in the face, right?"

Mesmerized by his keen gaze, and still unable to avoid the truth, Janalou nodded. But she regretted it immediately and panic whizzed through her. "Y'all—you won't tell anyone else anything I've said, will you?"

"Nay." He shook his white head, his tattered ball cap teetering to one side. "We'll keep yer secret atwixt the two of us."

"Thanks. I'd appreciate that."

"Welcome ye be, lass." He patted her hand. "The hag's out of yer life now, so ye can relax."

How she hoped that was true.

Duke then spoke in a voice so quiet she had to strain to hear. "I truly want to help ye, lass, and I'd be pleased to advise ye regarding some of the other passengers, if ye care to hear what I have to say."

"Please do," she said, still wondering if she might be talking to a figment of her imagination.

"*Senora* Reina Ruiz and Mr. Kree Winterton be good folks. Ye can rely on them. Believe what they say. And the mother of this youngster, she's in need of friends. I'm looking out fer her as well as ye, and if ye befriend her, 'twould make me job a might easier."

Janalou pondered his words a few seconds before she said, "Why are you on the bus now? You looked like you were about to get off when I first got on."

"I was," he admitted. "I was returning to Spartanburg to see ye, and ye surprised me when ye boarded at the station. Now that we're together, I'll go where ye go."

"Why?"

"I told ye, lass. To help ye with yer struggles. They'all be easier if'n ye don't try to conquer them all on yer own."

"That's very kind," she said. "But I don't understand why you or anyone would want to help me."

"In due time, ye'll know why, lass. In due time." Tipping the brim of his cap, he stood and winked. "Top 'o the mornin' to ye, lass. I hope ye'll enjoy yer food now that I've had me say."

He whistled as he walked back up the aisle. Other passengers turned their heads to stare. Kree's gaze met Janalou's, and her heart did a crazy flip.

She lowered her eyes, and pretended interest in the cinnamon roll, although her side hurt and her stomach felt too queasy to eat very much.

When she glanced back at Kree, he was still watching her.

Excitement warred with trepidation. Both emotions gurgled inside like a fountain about to burst. She told herself she couldn't be attracted or get involved with him—or any man. She had too much to do first—establish a new life, get a job, find a place to live, learn how to talk like a Yankee, and most important—conceal her past so Papa and Belle couldn't find her.

A pang of regret tumbled through her. Kree probably wouldn't want anything to do with her anyway, not looking the way she did. Besides, she had lied about being an orphan, and if he ever found out, he might hate her. That thought made her feel guilty, and unworthy of his help or friendship.

Sensing Reina also watching her, Janalou forced a calm she was far from feeling, and once again bit into the sweet cinnamon roll the friendly woman had provided. There were nice people in the world. They weren't all like her wretched stepmother.

A shiver of fear raced up her spine. By now Papa and Belle must know she had bolted. Had they called the police? Filed a missing person's report? Let the head librarian know she wouldn't be at work?

Unwilling to dwell on unwelcome questions or the knowledge that she would probably never see Papa again, she turned her mind back to Duke Guggles. Was he truly a leprechaun? He reminded her more of a guardian angel with the kindest eyes she'd ever seen.

She raised her fingers and touched her face, more than a bit startled to discover the painful swelling and soreness had lessened, along with the cuts on her fingers that had stung all night. *Was Duke's touch responsible? Did he have the power to heal even though he said he didn't?*

Doubt shot through her. If he weren't a leprechaun or an extraordinary being, she didn't really want to know. Believing he was added to the mystique of her new life.

Breathing a little easier, she relaxed her tensed fists.

For months she had made plans to seek her destiny, and challenge the future. Now she had finally taken the plunge. Already she felt like a different person, much stronger and more confident than she had been during the last difficult year.

The sudden urge to laugh surfaced. She tamped down the happy bubble, just barely, but couldn't suppress a smile. The future lay before her, bright, cheerful, and full of promise.

Five

Janalou only nibbled half of the gooey cinnamon roll, but the milk felt good going down, so she drank all of it, wishing she had tea. As she wiped her fingers on a paper napkin, the little boy's mother wandered down the aisle, holding her daughter's hand. The girl looked about five, a year or two older than her brother. Tall and willowy, the blonde mother had friendly blue eyes, long dark eyelashes, and a gorgeous face.

"Hi," she said. "I came to check on Toby. I hope he's not being a nuisance."

"No, not at all." Janalou decided to take Duke's suggestion and befriend her. "Toby's darling. So is your little girl. What's her name?"

Pride radiated in the mother's pretty eyes. "Misti. I named her after my mom." Her smile faded as she sat across the aisle in the seat Reina had briefly occupied. "I'm Cherilyn Byrd. What's your name?"

"Janalou Madsen, and I'm happy to meet you." She offered her hand as Reina had done. "How far are you traveling?"

"I haven't made up my mind. I bought tickets to Denver, but I don't know anyone there so I might go on to Utah or California."

"Where's your family?" Janalou asked.

Sadness crept over Cherilyn's pretty face. "My daughter and son are all the family I have now."

Janalou raised her brows, wondering about the children's papa. "Are you a widow?"

Cherilyn shook her head. "I never got married. Unfortunately I fell in love with the wrong man."

Sensing Cherilyn wanted to talk, Janalou said, "I'm a good listener, if you'd like to unburden yourself, and I can keep secrets, too."

Relief flooded Cherilyn's expressive eyes. She shoved her long blonde hair behind her shoulders and glanced at her children. Both sat on the floor, playing with the velcro straps on Janalou's sandals.

"His name is Ryan," she explained. "His parents think he's too good for me and he doesn't have enough backbone to stand up for himself or to defy them."

"I'm sorry." Janalou didn't know what else to say.

"Me too." Cherilyn blinked back tears. "When I got pregnant with Misti, I was sure Ryan would force them to accept me or elope with me. He did neither, although he helped support us financially. Not long after Misti was born, he got engaged to a high-society, social-climber. It broke my heart. I ended our relationship and didn't see him for a whole year.

"Then he came back, begging to spend time with Misti and me, claiming he wasn't happy in his marriage, vowing he loved us, and intended to get a divorce. Like a fool, I believed him. But saying he would get divorced was a bald-faced lie." A frown marred her forehead, and sadness crept into her eyes again.

"We were careful, but not careful enough, and I got pregnant with Toby. When I told Ryan, he admitted he had to stay married to please his family, but he wanted me on the side."

She swallowed a couple of times before she continued. "I worked up my nerve to go see his parents. I thought they'd want access to their grandchildren. But they don't. They gave me money to leave Philadelphia and I promised to stay out of Ryan's life. We moved to North Carolina where my parents live. I worked for a couple of years but I hated leaving Toby and Misti with a sitter who cared more about the money I paid her than she did about them. Besides, my parents are ashamed of me for having two children without getting married. So now, we're off on an adventure." She licked her lips and crossed her arms, a fierce look of determination now in her eyes. "That's my story. What's yours?"

"I had an abusive stepmother," Janalou admitted, more to commiserate than a desire for pity. Sticking close to the truth, she didn't say her parents were dead, but stuck to the facts. "I'm starting a new life too. I thought I'd go to California. I've always wondered what it would be like to live there."

"Not in Los Angeles, I hope."

"Why not?"

"Statistics, that's why. The last I heard, Philadelphia had six thousand policemen. Los Angeles had nine thousand and that isn't enough to handle all the crimes committed there."

Janalou shivered. She had no special reason for choosing Los Angeles except that it was clear across the country, and she wanted as much distance as possible between her and Belle. "How do you know those facts?"

Cherilyn grinned. "My cousin's a policeman in Philadelphia, and he told me when I lived there."

Janalou nodded. "The Mexican lady sitting up front suggested that I settle in Lodi, California. Maybe you should consider settling there, too."

Interest sparkled in Cherilyn's pretty blue eyes. "Where is Lodi?"

"Near Sacramento, I think."

"Is it by the ocean?"

Janalou shook her head. "I don't think so, but a freeway would probably make it easy to get to the beach in an hour or two, if that's what you're curious about."

"I am." Cherilyn winked. "I brought a road atlas. I'll go get it. Is it all right if I leave Toby and Misti here?"

"Sure."

A few seconds later, she returned with toys and the atlas. After she bent and gave the toys to Toby and Misti, Janlou patted the seat beside her. "Sit here so we can look at the map together."

"Good idea." Cherilyn plopped beside her, and flipped the atlas open to California. "Here's Lodi." She pointed with a bright red polished fingernail.

"It's closer to Stockton than Sacramento," Janalou said.

"Might be a good place to raise my children."

"Might be," Janalou agreed, and guided by instinct, she smiled and shed the reticent shell she had hidden behind during the last year. "I need friends. I think you do, too. Maybe we should settle in the same place. It would be nice not to feel so alone, and to know someone else who's new in town."

"Another grand idea." Turning sideways, Cherilyn smiled. "So, my friend, what do you think of that handsome curly-haired guy who brought you food and stood up to those two scoundrels?"

"I—I don't know," Janalou stammered.

"Well, don't read me wrong. I'm not interested in him, but he looked interested in you."

"I doubt it." Janalou shook her head, wishing her heart would stop spinning so crazily. "He offered to help me find a job if I go to Lodi instead of Los Angeles. Well, he didn't really offer. His friend, Reina, sort of coerced him into it."

Cherilyn winked. "I think you've made more than one friend on this bus."

"I hope so." Turning her gaze from Cherilyn, she looked ahead. Duke Guggles had started up an animated conversation with Reina and Kree.

"We could move up front," Cherilyn said, "if you'd like to get better acquainted with them."

"No," Janalou said. "I don't want to butt in."

"I'll go get my things then, and sit back here with you."

"I'd like that."

After Cherilyn returned, Janalou said, "I expected more passengers."

"There probably will be after our next stop." Cherilyn looked lovingly down at her children who were playing contentedly with their toys. Glancing back up she asked, "How did you get those black eyes?"

Janalou tucked her upper teeth over her bottom lip. When she didn't reply, Cherilyn said, "I'm not the only one who might ask. If you don't want to admit the truth, maybe you should invent an answer." She paused and winked again before she added, "You could claim you bumped into a door."

"Sounds good," Janalou said, hoping no one asked so she didn't have to lie again. Since talking to Duke Guggles, she regretted not being a hundred percent honest with everyone.

As the miles zoomed beyond them, she and Cherilyn discovered they had several things in common, including growing up in the South and sharing the same birthday in June, a few weeks away.

"I'll be eighteen," she said. "How old will you be?"

"Twenty-four."

"You look younger."

"Thanks. Some days I feel much older. Being a single parent isn't easy, but my kids are the best thing that's ever happened to me. I know I sound like a bragging mother, but they both listen to reason and they're easy to live with."

"I can tell," Janalou said, recalling some of the high-strung, spoiled youngsters she had tended.

She glanced down the aisle and saw Kree approaching. Her pulse picked up speed, and her conversation with Cherilyn ended.

"We change buses in Knoxville," Kree reminded them, his blue eyes warm, his expression friendly. "If you're going to Lodi instead of Los Angeles, you'll probably need to change your tickets, and since we'll have spare time because we're ahead of the next regular schedule, Reina wonders if the four of you would like to eat with us and Duke Guggles before we re-board."

"Yes," Cherilyn answered. "We'd love to join you for lunch, wouldn't we, Janalou?"

She nodded. "Thanks for inviting us."

Kree grinned. "You're welcome." Then he surprised her by hunkering down and talking to Toby and Misti. "Are you two getting hungry?"

Toby rubbed his tummy. "Me hungry like Winnie, the Pooh."

Chills skidded up Janalou's spine. She always reacted to any mention of Winnie the Pooh. Why? Because of the rhyme that lived inside her head? *Janalou loves Jeri Sue. Jeri Sue loves Janalou. And Winnie the Pooh loves both of you.*

All her life she had dreamed about a girl named Jeri Sue, but the dreams were usually too vague to recall. In those she did remember, Jeri Sue was a little girl, playing with another little girl named Janalou, and in the background there was a boy a few years older named Paul. She'd never been able to make sense out of the dreams, but she couldn't forget them either. She had vague memories of a man and woman in the dreams, too, and always wondered why she dreamed about a family she didn't know.

When Kree glanced up and flashed another grin, she found herself wishing again that she wasn't already living a lie, pretending to be someone with a fictitious name. But she couldn't tell him or anyone else the truth. If she did, Papa and Belle might find her and force her to go back home. She wouldn't take that chance. Not for any reason. Not for any person. Not even one who made her heart beat faster. She had already confided too much to Duke Guggles, although that hadn't been intentional. With him the truth had gushed out as though it had a voice of its own.

~ * ~

After Janalou and Cherilyn changed their bus tickets in Knoxville, they all went to lunch. Everyone ate with gusto. Everyone except Janalou. She didn't have much appetite.

The nagging pain in her side had gotten worse. Wondering if she should be worried, she listened but didn't add much to the conversation.

Finished eating, they boarded a bus already half full of passengers. Their small group found seats together near the back.

A little bit later, Janalou helped Cherilyn settle Toby and Misti down for naps, with Misti's head on her mother's lap and Toby's on Janalou's.

Although she enjoyed listening to her new friends, the long bus ride began to wear on her, especially after the children woke up, and afternoon gave way to dusk.

The adrenaline high she had been on waned. She was tired from not sleeping last night, but too tense to relax or doze.

When the pain in her side intensified, she drew in a batch of slow breaths. They didn't help. A bitter taste gurgled up from her stomach and the small amount of lunch she had eaten threatened to come back up.

Shifting on the bus seat, she swallowed the bitter taste and tried to get comfortable. But the pain increased until it was almost unbearable. Her head started to hurt, too, rivaling the terrible pain in her side. Suddenly her head and stomach felt like they both might explode.

When she wiggled again, Duke Guggles, seated across the aisle, eyed her with his keen gaze, and said, "You don't look like you feel well, lass."

"I don't," she managed through gritted teeth.

He rose and called out, "Is there a doctor on the bus?"

No one answered, but his question claimed Kree, Reina and Cherilyn's attention. All three looked concerned. "You be ill," Reina said.

"Yes," Duke agreed before Janalou made a beeline for the on-board john.

Inside she lifted the lid. A sweet chemical smell assaulted her senses as she bent over and retched.

Instead of feeling better, she felt worse. Sicker. Weak. Dizzy.

Self-pity slithered through her as she leaned her forehead against the cool wall. For months she had survived Belle's verbal abuse and last night she had survived a physical attack. Now something else was going to kill her. On second thought, Belle had punched her in the stomach last week after she graduated and dared to complain about Papa not attending the ceremony. Had Belle injured a vital organ then and was it just now manifesting itself?

Staggering out of the john, her brain muggy, her strength drained, Janalou felt awful. Sick enough to die.

"Where do you hurt?" Reina asked.

"Here," she gasped, holding her stomach. "I wonder if it might be my appendix."

"We should find a way to get you to the hospital," Cherilyn said.

Kree nodded. "I'll go tell the bus driver to find the nearest one."

Instead of thanking him, Janalou crumpled in a dead faint.

~ * ~

Kree reached out and caught Janalou before she hit the floor. "Hold her," he instructed Duke, transferring her to the short man's lap before he strode to the front of the bus to speak to the driver.

"We need to get a passenger to the hospital," Kree announced, already punching 911 on his cell phone.

As soon as the call ended, he asked the driver to take the next exit, then hurried back down the aisle. Propped on Duke's lap, Janalou was still unconscious, her face pale, her skin moist with perspiration. "Has she come to?"

Everyone shook their heads, worry evident in their somber expressions.

"I've arranged for an ambulance to meet us at the next exit."

"I want to go to the hospital with her," Cherilyn said.

"So do I." Reina folded her arms across her chest, a stubborn tilt to her head.

Kree bent to take Janalou's pulse. Faster than he'd hoped. And her clammy skin had taken on an ashen sheen. He made a quick decision.

"I'll stay with her. The rest of you should continue your journey. I'll call Reina and she can let everyone know how Janalou is the instant I know what's wrong."

It took some fast talking, but Duke finally helped him convince both women to stay on the bus.

"I'll watch over them," he promised as Kree lifted Janalou off his lap.

He might have harbored doubts about how much help Duke could be in a fist fight with those two scumbag hoodlums early this morning, but tonight he didn't have a single doubt that the sturdy little man would see Reina, Cherilyn and her two children safely to their journey's end.

A few minutes later, Janalou opened her eyes. Kree was sitting on the front seat with her cradled on his lap. As the bus left the freeway, she moved her lips but no words came out.

"Don't try to talk," he said. "I know you're in a world of pain, and you're probably afraid, but I've called nine-one-one." He hoped his words would soothe her. "An ambulance will meet us in a few minutes. Try to relax, and don't worry. We'll get you to a hospital as soon as possible."

Janalou's eyelids fluttered closed, and he wondered if she had passed out again.

The bus driver found a wide spot and parked.

At the sound of the ambulance's siren, Janalou opened her eyes and mumbled, "Sor—ry to be so much trou—ble."

"You're no trouble." Kree didn't know what else to say to comfort her. He didn't even know if she heard him because her eyes closed again and her body went limp.

When an ambulance pulled up next to the bus, he breathed a little easier.

"Here's the lass's backpack." Duke handed the blue pack to Kree while the EMTs transferred her to the ambulance.

"Thanks."

Worried and concerned, Kree climbed in the back of the ambulance with Janalou seconds later. As they sped away, the siren blaring, a lump formed in his throat, and a tight band wound around his chest. *Janalou looked deathly ill. Would she be okay? Or had he met her only to watch her die?*

<h1 style="text-align:center">Six</h1>

At the hospital, a team of skilled emergency workers lifted Janalou from the ambulance and wheeled her away on the gurney. Watching her lying so pale and still, it took all Kree's effort not to get in the way, to back off and let the medical team do their stuff.

Inside the ER, a nurse took her vital signs. Another summoned a doctor.

Janalou hadn't opened her eyes again, and Kree worried she might have gotten here too late.

"Elevated vitals," the doctor announced seconds later. "Possible appendix rupture. Could be too late to save her."

Kree stood in shock, afraid she might never open her eyes again.

"We need her next of kin to sign a release so we can operate," the doctor said.

"I'll sign. I'm the closest thing she has to family." Kree reached for the electronic tablet.

While he waited for Janalou to come out of surgery, he paced the waiting room floor. He'd feel awful if she died.

In spite of the talks he had given himself, he had already formed an attachment to her. He told himself it was friendship, nothing more. But part of his brain disagreed. She was special, although he didn't know why.

With nothing except worry to occupy his thoughts, he went through her backpack, feeling guilty for snooping, but needing to know more about her. Maybe he'd find her address, or at least a list of her friends.

The flowered pillow sham splotched with something that looked like dried blood took him by surprise. Finding a blouse in a separate zippered pocket caked with what must also be blood surprised him even more. Tempted to throw the blouse and sham away, he stuffed both back inside the pack. She must have had a reason for keeping them.

In a different pocket, he found a Baltimore driver's license and social security card. Both belonged to someone named Emily Watson. He scratched his head. There were two famous women with that name, both British movie stars. The older one had starred in *War Horse* and *Anna Karenina*. The younger actress had played Hermoinie in the Harry Potter movies. The photo on the Baltimore driver's license didn't look like either movie star or the girl who called herself Janalou Madsen.

Wondering why she toted someone else's identification and not her own, he stashed everything back inside the pack, including several envelopes stuffed with money. Then he sat down and braced his elbows on his knees.

Janalou was more of a mystery than she had been before. *Was it possible her real name was Emily Watson in spite of the photo that didn't look anything like her? Had she run away and decided to change her name? And why was she carrying a soiled, probably bloody, sham and blouse with her?*

~ * ~

Cloaked in a deep, dark blackness, Janalou slept without pain.

When she finally awakened, groggy and disoriented, a man dressed in green surgical garb was holding her hand, his warm fingers pressed against the inside of her wrist.

"Who are you?" she asked through dry, parched lips.

"A nurse."

She blinked. "Where am I?"

"In the hospital. In Recovery. You've had surgery. But you're going to be fine," he assured her. "Your vitals are almost back to normal." He slanted a nod at a medical screen. In her muggy state, she couldn't decipher what she saw.

"The lines and numbers indicate your heart rate, temperature and blood pressure," he explained, releasing her hand before he added, "You'll be taken to a room in about ten minutes, if you can stay awake."

With some difficulty she managed to keep her eyes open and focused on what was going on around her. There were two other patients in the recovery room. Unlike her, both were still conked out.

After what seemed like hours instead of minutes, the nurse summoned two orderlies to wheel her to her own room.

Not long afterwards, Kree stood at the side of her bed.

"Where—are—we?" So glad he was there and she wasn't alone, she choked up.

He furrowed his brow, alarm and concern in his gaze. "We're in a hospital."

"I know," she gasped. "I mean what city? What state?"

Relief covered his handsome features. "Evansville, Indiana."

"And the others? Are they here, too?"

He shook his head. "No, I convinced them to go on. But don't worry. We'll meet them in California."

"Are you sure?"

"Yes." Kree smiled. A dimple dented his right cheek. "Cherilyn said to tell you you'd better show up, healthy and well, or she'd find a way to haunt you."

"Thanks." Janalou glanced away, suddenly feeling awkward and shy. "I don't know how I can ever repay you for staying with me."

"It isn't necessary."

Too grateful to disagree, she asked, "Do you have any idea how long I might have to stay here?"

"The surgeon said you can leave tomorrow, provided there are no complications. He also said you're lucky to be alive." Kree reached across the rail and gave her hand a gentle squeeze. "You need time to recuperate. I'll go check into a motel tonight. We'll stay there tomorrow night, too. That will give you time to rest up before we hit the road again."

Janalou forced a smile. She did need to convalesce and his suggestion to stay overnight in a motel held a lot of appeal. "How long have I been here?"

"Just a few hours, and I've been told you're going to be fine. What you need now is a good night's sleep."

"Thanks again." When he took both of her hands in his, calm settled over her, and she almost forgot the pain in her stomach. Before she fainted, it had been so severe she really had expected to die. Vaguely she recalled being aware of Kree's strong arms holding her, and his calm voice soothing her. But she'd been so sick she didn't remember leaving the bus or arriving at the hospital.

Now she felt much better, although she was too drugged to think clearly. All she knew for certain was that she wasn't alone. A kind handsome man had stayed behind to be with her. More gratitude washed through her. The smile on his face slid inside her heart, heating her all the way down to her toes.

Kree stroked her hands in a gentle caress. Strangely comforted by his presence, and the warmth of his touch, she fell back asleep.

~ * ~

In the morning she awakened from a dream that seemed so real, she felt crying. All her life she had dreamed about the girl named Jeri Sue. But this time she remembered what she said and what she looked like—exactly like her.

The dream spooked her. It was like staring in the mirror and seeing herself, talking to herself. And the girl kept saying, *'Where are you, Janalou? Why did you leave? Please come home. We miss you. We want you here. This is where you belong.'*

As she laid there, memories of other dreams, old dreams crowded in. A younger Jeri Sue was playing with another little girl named

Janalou. The boy named Paul was in the dreams too, teasing them until the man and woman, their parents, chided him and threatened to take his computer away if he didn't stop tormenting them.

Baffled by the recurring dreams, she realized they had haunted her sleep for years, on a regular basis, as though somehow connected to the cycles of the moon.

Emotion clogged her throat, and she found it difficult to swallow. *Why did she dream about people she didn't know? Was her subconscious doing a number on her mind because she had changed her name?*

Blaming last night's anesthesia for her unruly emotions, she touched her stomach. Still tender and sore, but nothing like the pain before she passed out on the bus.

She inhaled antiseptic hospital scents and closed her eyes, feeling tired and drowsy. But she had to stay awake. Be alert so the doctor would let her leave today.

"Hello." A cheerful female voice said. "How are you this morning?"

Janalou glanced at the doorway as a cute young nurse walked inside, carrying a breakfast tray. "I'm fine, thank you."

The nurse smiled. "Are you hungry?"

"Not very, but I am thirsty."

Setting her breakfast on a tray table, the nurse wheeled it across the bed with the efficiency of much practice. "Maybe you'll get your appetite back once you start to eat."

"Maybe." Lemon Jell-o cubes and cranberry juice didn't look particularly appetizing but she hadn't eaten much for twenty four hours and knew she needed to eat to regain her strength and recover. Picking up the small plastic cup, she peeled off the lid, and took a long slow swallow.

"That tasted good." She licked her lips, savoring the sweet flavor still on her tongue.

The nurse eyed the empty plastic cup. "You should drink lots of liquids. Would you like more juice?"

"Yes, please, if it's not too much trouble."

"No trouble at all."

"Could I have some hot water too?"

"Would you prefer tea?"

"Oh, yes. That would be even better. And lemon, if you have it."

"I'm sure we do. I'll be back in a jiff."

As soon as she left, Janalou looked for her royal blue backpack. Panic set in when she didn't see it. *Had it been left on the bus? Had she lost all the money she had saved for so long?*

Deciding to search for it, she shoved the tray table aside with a weakness that surprised her. Slowly, she eased to the side of the bed. She jiggled the rail, but couldn't figure out how to lower it. Could she climb over it without hurting herself?

Another big problem confronted her—the I.V. tube attached to her left arm. If she moved too much, she might pull it out. She was trapped. Unless she could crawl over the end of the bed and take the I.V. with her. Would her legs reach the floor? Could she move the I.V. stand?

It was worth a try, she decided. If she had lost her pack and all her money, she'd be in deep trouble. Desperate to know, she rolled to her knees and inched to the end of the bed, careful not to dislodge the I.V.

The nurse returned, startling her when she asked, "What are you doing?" She set juice and a small stainless steel teapot on the tray table, then stuck her hands on her hips, frowning.

"I need to look for my backpack. Do you know where it is?"

The nurse relaxed her disapproving posture and waved at a small closet. "Sure. It's in there, along with your clothes and shoes."

Relief whooshed through Janalou when the nurse opened the small door near the TV. Her clothes and backpack hung on separate hooks.

She crawled slowly back to the middle of the bed, and leaned against the pillow, feeling as though she had performed a full day's worth of physical activity. *At least she wasn't penniless. Unless someone had gone through her pack and stolen her money.*

"I need something from my backpack," she said, unable to control the alarm warbling in her voice. "Would you mind handing it to me?"

"Not at all." The nurse lifted the blue pack off the closet hook and set it on Janalou's lap before she left again.

Janalou went through every pocket, not relaxing until she found all her envelopes and counted her money. Like Southern women who didn't trust anyone to clean their skillets except themselves, she didn't trust anyone with her backpack. Strangers should not have been trusted with her valuables. But she hadn't had any choice. She'd passed out, and according to Kree, the doctor had said she was lucky to be alive.

Forcing herself to calm down, she sucked in some slow breaths before she picked up her spoon and ate the Jell-o, somewhat surprised it tasted so good.

After the nurse took the breakfast tray away, Janalou raised the lid of her roll-around tray table, and used the mirror to study her face. Belle's vicious punch had not only made the bridge of her nose hurt, it had given her a terrific headache. Thankfully the headache was gone, along with some of the facial swelling, but her two black and purple shiners looked like she'd been in a fist fight and lost.

While she was hoping no one would mention her black eyes, a doctor dressed in green surgical garb, entered the room. "I'm Dr. Menton," he said. "I performed surgery on you last night. How are you feeling?"

"Pretty good," she said.

"We need to discuss your black eyes. How did you get them?"

"I bumped into a door." She crossed her fingers under the white blanket, thinking the fib wouldn't count if she did.

"Are you sure someone didn't hit you?"

She nodded, hoping he couldn't read the lie in her eyes.

To her dismay, he didn't give up. "If someone beat you or abused you, we should report it to the authorities."

"No one beat me. I was in a hurry and bumped into a door."

"If that's the story you intend to stick with, we can't help you."

"I don't need help, but thanks for your concern. I'm not from around here. I'm traveling across the country."

"Alone?"

"No. With a friend."

"Male or female?"

"Male."

"Did he give you those black eyes?"

"No." She shook her head. "He, my friend, is very kind. I don't think he would mistreat a flea. I ran into the door before he–a– picked me up."

Although the doctor didn't look convinced, he made notes on her tablet chart and hung it on the end of the bed.

"I'll check your incision now." Lowering the guard rail, he pulled the blanket and sheet down. He stared at her fingers as she uncrossed them, but said nothing, merely slid her hospital gown out of the way.

"Your incision looks fine, but it will take six weeks for your body to heal. When you leave the hospital, don't overdo. No heavy lifting, pushing, or pulling. Don't vacuum, don't over-exercise and don't have sexual intercourse for at least six weeks."

Her face went red. She'd never been intimate with a man. "I won't."

He eyed her with a grave stare. "You might have complications if you fail to follow my instructions. All of them."

"I'll follow them, I promise."

"See that you do," he said sternly.

The nurse waited until the doctor left before she said, "I'll tape plastic over your incision and help you get out of bed so you can shower."

"Thanks. I'd really appreciate having a shower."

The sunny-natured nurse confided, "I love patients who are grateful for help. Some of the ones we get are grumpy and not just bad-tempered but ill-manned as well. They make it difficult for me to do my job."

Janalou smiled. "I can't imagine anyone being ornery with you. You're a terrific nurse."

"Thanks." With careful deft practice, she removed the I.V. from Janalou's arm and pushed the covers away. Then she taped clear plastic over her bandaged stomach, and helped her get out of bed.

As the nurse pulled her clothes from the locker, Janalous said, "I'd like my backpack too."

After the shower, she dressed in a clean blouse and underwear, brushed her long hair, and applied make-up, doing her best to camouflage her black eyes. Not wanting anyone else to ask about them, she applied a second coat, deciding the make-up masked them pretty well.

Back in her room, she sat in a chair and turned on the TV to watch the news, curious to discover if her disappearance might have made the national news. Commercials were on every channel she flipped to.

Kree walked in, claiming her attention before he asked, "How do you feel?"

"Like I might live. Last night I wasn't sure."

"That bad, huh?"

She nodded, noting his clean clothes, and thinking again how attractive he was.

"Have they given you anything to eat?"

"Yes." She punched the remote to turn off the TV. "Jell-o, juice and tea."

He grinned, and her heart fluttered. "Doesn't sound like a very substantial breakfast."

"Maybe not, but it tasted good nonetheless."

His smile faded to concern. "Are you sure you feel okay?"

She nodded, her heart racing from his nearness. "We're a long way from California."

"Yes," he agreed, lounging against the side of her bed. "I saw your doctor in the hall. He said your vital signs are all back to normal, you had a restful night, and he left instructions for you to leave whenever you're ready."

"Great. I don't have insurance, and the longer I stay, the more I'll be charged."

"You're probably right. I'll go take care of the paperwork and get you checked out."

"I have money in my backpack. And thanks for making sure it came here with us. I may not have enough to cover all my expenses, but maybe the hospital will allow me to pay part of my bill off over time."

"We'll discuss the charges later. For now I'll put them on my credit card."

"Thank you." Although relieved, she wondered how she would ever pay him back. Maybe they could set up some kind of monthly repayment schedule. Hope blossomed near the vicinity of her heart. If they did, that would ensure they kept in touch whether she worked for him or not.

Seven

Kree fished a credit card from his wallet and signed the papers to get Janalou released. He had always appreciated his family's wealth. Right now he appreciated it more than ever.

Minutes ago, the doctor had put him through the third degree, all but accusing him of giving Janalou those two shiners. They didn't look as bad today, probably because she had covered them with make-up. Without them to detract from her appearance, she looked so stunning he had almost been bowled over when he walked into her room.

He stuck his credit card back inside his wallet, folded the documents and slid them into his hip pocket. The doctor's interrogation made him wonder again if Janalou had an abusive boyfriend. If so, had he beaten her? Is that why she had run away? Caught a bus in the middle of the night? Would she tell the truth if he asked? Not sure, he decided to wait. What she needed right now was a friend, not an interrogator.

As he drove the rental car away from the hospital, Kree watched Janalou out of the corner of one eye. She looked nervous. What could he say to put her at ease?

Unable to think of anything clever, he said, "In case you don't remember what I said last night, we're going to a motel so you can rest today. I'll stop at a pharmacy to fill your prescriptions first. The doctor prescribed one to prevent infection, and one for pain. He wants to see you in his office in the morning. If you pass muster, we'll head for California afterwards."

"Will we take the bus?"

Kree shook his head. "I cashed in our bus tickets. We can either drive or fly. Which would you prefer?"

"Driving," she said, sounding excited by the prospect, and sounding less nervous. "I've never driven clear across the country, and I'd like to see as much as possible while I have the chance."

"Me too, and if we drive," he added with a grin, "we can stop and rest whenever you feel tired. If you need to see a doctor along the way, that won't be a problem."

An angelic smile covered her lovely face. "I don't know how I'll ever repay you for everything you'd done to help me."

"I'm sure we can find an agreeable solution once you're recovered and back up to full steam."

"Do you have something in mind? If so, I'll willingly cooperate."

A sensual shiver traced down his spine. Trying not to read too much into her comment, he stopped at a red light and turned his full gaze on her. "I'll do my best not to expect too much."

Still smiling that innocent smile, she winked and another shiver shot through him. "Thanks. You're a true hero."

The impact of her softly spoken words created a glow inside his chest. "Thanks," he said, hoping he didn't sound too pleased.

How had she slipped under the protective layer guarding his heart? She hadn't, he told himself, trying to believe it. *I can't allow that to happen. All I feel for her is concern, nothing more.*

Why then did he want her to become a permanent part of his life? He didn't, did he? All he wanted was to help her until she got on her feet and could take care of herself. Although his brain tried to believe that, his heart couldn't quite agree and his mind ignored the guilty feeling that he was betraying Bethany's memory by taking Janalou to a motel, something he had never done with his beloved Bethany.

~ * ~

Janalou cautioned herself not to read too much into what Kree's staying with her meant. Still, a tendril of hope crept through her. *The future has real potential. It might be better than good. It could be fantastic. Her life was already better because it no longer included Belle.*

Thoughts of Papa crowded in. *She missed him, but didn't expect to see him ever again.*

To keep her bottom lip from quivering, she tucked it beneath her upper teeth. Under other circumstances, she would have called to let Papa know she'd been in the hospital and that she was okay. But during the last year, they had grown apart. And now that she'd left, he was no longer part of her life.

Although saddened by that fact, excitement crawled through her, slowly at first, then more rapidly, filling her with eager anticipation as Kree drove. She attributed the sensation to the opportunity to travel across the U.S. in a car, and then realized that being near Kree in such close confines added to her happy state. When she had dated Tony, they had been alone sometimes but that was more than two years ago, and being with Kree felt like a brand new adventure, one to be treasured.

When Kree pulled into a parking lot in front of a CVS Pharmacy, she covered her mouth to stifle a yawn. He rolled the windows down, then said, "I'll go get your prescriptions filled."

"Thanks." Having already dug inside her pack for money, she extended two fifty dollar bills.

"I'll use my credit card."

"I prefer to pay for my medicine myself."

With a shrug, he accepted her money, and climbed out.

Worried about medical expenses gobbling all her cash, Janalou had to force herself not to dwell on negativity. But she didn't want to be any more indebted to Kree. He could have stayed on the bus and she'd be here alone. She could have been stranded without her backpack, too. *What would have become of her if that had happened?*

She released a quiet sigh, forcing worry aside, and feeling a bit loopy, probably from last night's drugs. Her mind cleared enough to realize that driving to California would give her black eyes more time to heal, and she didn't want to meet people she might work with while she still had them. *Two shiners and facial bruises would be difficult to explain, and she wasn't about to tell anyone the truth. What had happened was in the past and there it must remain.*

Fatigue rumbled through her, and she closed her eyes, wishing they were at the motel so she could lie down.

By the time Kree returned, she felt exhausted.

Unfortunately, traffic was heavy, and even though the morning rush hour was over, the ride to the motel seemed to take forever.

Finally they arrived.

Kree ushered her into what was, without a doubt, his room. Some of his possessions sat on the dresser and masculine clothes hung in the doorless closet.

"Are we going to share the same room?" she asked, not having thought about room arrangements until now.

He cleared his throat, looking a bit uncomfortable when he nodded. "The doctor said you shouldn't be alone. You might need something. And you will need to be reminded to take your medication at the right times."

Janalou swallowed with difficulty. *She'd never slept in the same room with anyone except during sleepovers with girlfriends. But she really didn't want to be alone tonight.*

At least there were two beds.

She sat on one, and decided she must look worn out when Kree said, "Why don't you lie down and rest? In a little while, I'll go buy some lunch. The nurse said you can eat anything you want now. What sounds appealing?"

"Chicken soup," she said, longing for the chicken soup Mama used to make. "Do you think there's a restaurant or cafe around here?"

Kree grinned. "Yeah. There's one right across the parking lot."

"Good." She hadn't noticed. Unfastening her sandals, she said, "I don't understand why you stayed with me, Kree. I'm a stranger. You don't know anything about me. I could be a very unscrupulous person."

"I doubt that. My first impressions are usually on target. Besides, I believe in helping others."

Her eyes rounded in surprise. She couldn't help it. "I've never met a man who admitted that."

"You might when we reach Lodi. A lot of terrific people live there."

"I'm impressed. Tell me more."

"I will later, maybe while we travel. First you should rest. You look like you can hardly hold your head up. Close your eyes and take a nap."

Janalou took his advice. And slept.

~ * ~

Kree alternated between trying to concentrate on reading a book on his Kindle, and watching her. He couldn't stop thinking about the soiled blouse and pillow sham he'd found in her backpack. The sticky stuff had to be blood. *Had someone hit her and bloodied her nose? Is that why her face looked swollen, bruised and puffy? Why she had black eyes? Or had she just had a bloody nose?*

When he stared at her again, he realized her face no longer looked swollen. *Even with black eyes she looked beautiful. Or, was he wrong when he first saw her? Had he looked for something then to make her less appealing to fight his instant attraction?*

After that disturbing thought, he leaned back, set his Kindle on the table, and thought about the new clothes he had bought for her after he'd discovered she had so few in her backpack. *When should he give them to her?*

He decided not to rush. She needed rest, not any kind of confrontation, and he was fairly certain she'd want to pay for the clothes even though he didn't intend to let her.

As they often did when he sat still, his thoughts turned to Bethany. For a long time he stared at the blank TV screen, and while he did, he realized two things—*his memories of Bethany were growing dimmer and he no longer felt guilty for being with Janalou. Somehow she had managed to crawl through his protective shield and made him want to feel alive again.*

He shook his head with that thought. Janalou was young and innocent, which made her dangerous. Young, innocent chicks formed attachments easily. She might fall in love and he couldn't return the sentiment. He wanted to be near her. Yes. But love her? No. He didn't. Couldn't. His heart wouldn't allow him to love again. Even if it did, his heart no longer ruled his life. His sensible brain did. When the time came for him to marry in five or ten years, he would choose a wife with rational thought, not emotions he couldn't control.

~ * ~

Janalou awakened from a dream she couldn't quite remember, but she knew it had included the young girl Jeri Sue and the boy named Paul. Why she kept dreaming about them was a mystery, one she decided might never be solved.

This time she wasn't disoriented, and didn't have to wonder where she was. She knew. With Kree. In a motel room.

She looked around. And discovered she was alone. Panic erupted inside her.

Where was Kree? Had he left her to fend for herself?

Another quick glance around the room calmed her a little bit. Her backpack sat on the dresser. Believing she could trust Kree, she hopped off the bed anyway, and regretted the fast move when her incision rebelled.

Holding her stomach with both hands, she hobbled over to the window, parted the drapes, and looked out. Relief soothed the panic thumping through her when she saw the rental car parked by the door. Only then did she notice Kree's clothes were still hanging in the closet.

The clock on the night stand between the beds read 7:00 p.m. Apparently she had slept all day, and Kree must have turned the corner lamp on before he left. Once again relief and gratitude flowed through her. Both emotions tripled when Kree returned a few minutes later.

He shut the door, then hiked his brow. "Feel better?"

When she nodded, he grinned. "You slept through lunch. Are you hungry?

"Yes."

"Me, too." He set two bags on the table by the window, and turned on another light before he unwrapped a straw and stuck it through the slot in one of the plastic cups before he handed it to her.

"What is it?"

"Sprite."

"Thanks."

"You're welcome." Kree consulted his watch. "Time for your medicine." He opened her prescription bottles and extended two capsules.

Janalou swallowed both pills, unable to ignore the awareness of being alone with him behind closed doors. "Whatever is in those bags smells scrumptious," she said, feeling awkward and somewhat shy.

"I brought chicken soup for you, and a hamburger and fries for me." He handed her a bag, unwrapped his burger and took a bite before he turned the TV on. "Do you mind if I watch the basketball playoffs?"

"No, not at all. Who's playing?"

"The Lakers and the Salt Lake Jazz." He clicked to ESPN.

"Who's ahead?"

"The Lakers," he answered with a satisfied grin.

"Is that who you're cheering for?"

"Yeah. They're my team."

~ * ~

During halftime, Kree tossed empty containers in the trash, pleased to see Janalou had eaten all her soup. He muted the TV, pulled out his cell phone and called Reina.

"Janalou's fine," he assured her. "I sprung her from the hospital this morning." He winked at Janalou. "We just ate, and she rested all day. We'll hit the road tomorrow, if the doctor gives the go, and if she feels up to traveling."

Kree looked at Janalou again. "Would you like to talk to Reina?"

When she nodded, he offered his phone. Their hands touched before he released it. His pulse gave an odd jerk.

They talked for several minutes, and he heard her say, "Yes, please. I'd love to talk to Cherilyn."

When the conversation ended, Janalou returned his phone and explained. "Cherilyn and her children are staying with Reina until they find a place of their own. Reina's a very thoughtful person, isn't she?"

Kree nodded. "Yes, she is."

He picked up the TV remote, and unmuted the volume.

Janalou stayed by the small table for a few minutes, then migrated to her bed, where she stacked her fluffy pillows against the headboard before she reclined against them. One of the pills had been for pain, and he thought she looked drowsy again.

The rest of the evening passed quickly. Kree was surprised how much of it Janalou spent dozing, and how little he saw of the game because he kept looking at her. Each time he did, his stomach clenched. Emotions he hadn't felt for a long time surfaced. *Where had they come from? Why was he so concerned about her? Why did he want to touch her? Spend more time with her?*

Around 11:00 p.m. she stirred.

"You should take another pill," he said.

"Why? I feel fine."

"You need one to fight infection." He reached for her prescriptions. "You might want one for pain to get you through the night."

She shook her head. "I don't think I need one yet."

A few minutes later, he turned off the TV and lights, and climbed in the other bed.

Lying in the dark, he couldn't relax. He worried about Janalou, not just because she'd had surgery but also because he thought she might be in some kind of trouble.

No one had ever affected him as she did, and he didn't much like how that made him feel—a trifle shaky. Also like a traitor to Bethany.

Being alone in a motel with Janalou made him think about the things couples did in bed, and his imagination almost got the best of him.

Eventually he fell asleep and dreamed he and Janalou were in each other's arms. Without clothes. Kissing and exploring each other's bodies. Hot and eager, he kept trying to get closer. And she kept trying to slow him down.

He woke up and kicked the covers off. Embarrassed by his aggressive behavior in the dream, he blew out a slow breath. It felt good when his breath fanned his hot face. Forcing himself to think about Bethany, he finally cooled off. After a long time, he pulled the covers back on, and fell back asleep.

Once again he dreamed about Janalou. This time she was in danger. Someone was chasing her. He found out too late, and couldn't catch them. Somehow he knew she was approaching a cliff. He yelled, trying to warn her of the danger ahead, but she stumbled on. And tumbled over the edge.

"No," he yelled, awakened by his own loud voice.

Shaken by the dream, it took a few seconds to realize she hadn't fallen over a cliff. She was okay. Right here in the same room. He climbed out of bed and stepped close to hers. Relief tumbled through him when he touched her soft cheek and heard her gentle breathing. *It was a dream*, he told himself. *She's okay.*

Still, he worried. *Did the dream have a special meaning? Was she in danger? Had she been in danger before they met? If so, would it return? Or haunt her even if it didn't?*

The questions couldn't be ignored. *How could he protect her when he didn't even know if she needed protecting?*

While he stood in the dark, barely able to see her, he sensed she might need help even if she hadn't fled from danger.

And he wanted to be there to fill that slot. He hadn't saved Bethany from harm, but if Janalou needed help, he had already committed himself to do whatever he could.

Not only did she look small and defenseless, she made him feel like a hero.

Would she agree to do him a favor? One that might change both of their lives?

Eight

Wide awake the next morning, Kree saw Janalou open her eyes and stare up at the ceiling. He waited for her to look at him. She didn't.

Did she feel awkward after sleeping in the same room? If so, what could he say to make her more comfortable?

Unable to think of anything suitable, he finally said, "I'll shower first, if that's okay with you."

"It is." She kept her gaze straight up and continued to avoid looking at him.

For some reason, he had expected her to take a peek to see how he'd slept. In his clothes, as she had, but she didn't look. He decided that was fine. If she had, it might make things seem more intimate, and he already felt guilty for insisting they spend the night together. But he hadn't dared leave her alone, and didn't know when or even if he would. *How could he protect her if they weren't together?*

After his shower, Janalou kept her gaze averted until he said, "It's your turn to use the bathroom."

She looked at him then, and smiled. "Thanks."

He smiled too, and his heart began to pound. She had a beautiful smile, but then she was beautiful, and he was glad he had stayed with her. Just as glad he had agreed to help her find a job.

Ideas were blossoming inside his brain. The bruises on her face made him nervous about introducing her to his family and friends. *If we slow our journey down, the extra time will give them time to heal before she meets them. It will also give us time to get to know each other better.*

While he waited for her, he flipped the TV on to hear the morning news. Finding only commercials on most channels, he flipped to ESPN and got caught up on the sports. Seattle had lost to the San Antonio Spurs. The Lakers had beat Utah, and only needed to win one more game to finish the series and wind up in the finals.

During a commercial break on ESPN, he flipped to CNN and caught the tail end of a news bulletin.

"Once again," the newscaster said, "if anyone has seen this girl or knows anything about her whereabouts, please contact the police near you as soon as possible. Her name is Saree Naisbet, and her parents said she disappeared from her home two nights ago. Kidnapping is feared. Her bedroom window was open and furniture had been pushed against the inside door."

Shock reverberated through Kree as a commercial took over. *Could the missing girl be Janalou? The time fit.*

It took a few seconds to remember she was an orphan. *Her parents are both dead. So it can't be her.*

Relief whipped through him as he flipped back to ESPN. Still he wondered if the missing girl had run away or been kidnapped. He assumed her picture had been plastered on the TV screen. If so, he had missed seeing it.

He waited until Janalou was ready to go eat before he said, "While you were in the bathroom, there was a news bulletin on the TV about a missing girl."

She looked up with an expression he could only interpret as interest, not guilt, in her dark exotic eyes. "Did they say where she came from?"

He shook his head. "I just saw the tail end. If there was a photo of her, I didn't see it, but the newscaster said she disappeared the night you got on the bus."

"I hope she's not in danger," was all she said.

"Me, too."

Not a trace of guilt crossed her face, and he relaxed again. In his head she was already part of his future plans and he'd hate to have to give them up.

~ * ~

After breakfast, Kree drove toward the doctor's office.

Still upset about the missing girl Kree had mentioned hearing about on the TV, Janalou stewed in silence. She must have masked her emotions pretty well because he hadn't grilled her or asked if she could be that person. Having learned the wisdom of keeping quiet while living with Belle, she hadn't asked the girl's name and he hadn't mentioned it.

Trying to take her mind off Belle and the news bulletin, Janalou removed the rubber band holding her damp hair behind her head, and finger-combed the long strands—until she saw Kree watching her with an odd expression. Self-conscious and more aware of him than she wanted to be, she drew in a shaky breath.

"Are you nervous about seeing the doctor?" he asked.

She nodded.

"Why?"

"Yesterday he asked how I got the bruises on my face. I told him I ran into a door, but he didn't act like he believed me."

"Is that how you got those shiners?"

She nodded again, and turned her head, hating the lie, and hoping he wouldn't know she had fibbed. It was easier without Duke Guggles nearby, but the reminder brought a huge flush of guilt. She didn't want to be an accomplished liar. She wanted to be open and honest. *But how could she stay free if she told the truth?* Her birthday was still a few weeks away, so she wasn't yet considered an adult.

"Do you want me to go in with you to see the doctor?" Kree asked when a nurse called her name some time later.

She weighed her choices before she answered. "Yes, if y'all don't mind."

"I don't."

In a patient room, the nurse handed Janalou a blue paper gown and disposable white sheet. "Put this on and sit on the examining table. You can use the sheet to cover yourself."

Flooded by embarrassment, heat covered Janalou's face. She hadn't thought about having to undress.

Kree's face also turned red and she knew he was embarrassed, too, as he backed toward the door. "I'll wait in the hall while you change."

All she managed to say was, "Thanks."

When he returned, she was sitting on the examining table with the sheet covering her from the waist down and she had put the short paper gown on backwards to cover her breasts. He walked to her side, and reached for her hand.

"You're cold. Are you all right?"

"Yes, just nervous," she said before the doctor came in. Kree's touch felt wonderful, and she was experiencing emotions she didn't quite know how to deal with.

"Lie down," the doctor instructed.

She did, and Kree let go of her to adjust the pillow under her head.

The doctor didn't mention her facial bruises again. Much to her relief, he didn't lower the sheet very far so he didn't expose much of her stomach either and Kree didn't see a lot of bare flesh. Even so, she felt embarrassed, and her face stayed uncomfortably warm.

After the surgeon checked her incision, he said, "You're healing nicely. If you don't overdo, you should have nothing more than a small scar."

"Will you need to see her again?" Kree asked.

"No. She's fit to travel as long as she doesn't overdo." He turned his attention back to her. "Take all the medicine I prescribed for infection. I cannot emphasize that strongly enough. You could have died, Janalou. If you hadn't arrived at the hospital when you did, you wouldn't be alive. Take care of your body. It needs time and ample rest to recover. Make sure you see your own doctor when you get home."

"I will," she promised. Although she disliked the idea of spending more money on medical expenses, she saw no way around it. From what she had learned about Kree so far, she suspected he would set up a doctor appointment for her and make sure she kept it.

~ * ~

The first day of travel wore Janalou out. Even though they left late, stopped to eat lunch an hour later, and only drove a few hours more, she dozed off and on, and fell asleep shortly after they checked into a motel, once again without changing to pajamas, and before they had a chance to eat.

Wondering if they should have waited another day before beginning their journey, Kree pulled his phone off his belt, opened the phone book, and called to order a pizza. His idea to turn the trip into a vacation had grown, so he called his oldest sister, too.

When Jocelyn answered, he said, "Hi Joce. I won't be back in town for a week or so. Will you pass the information on to the others in the office?"

"Sure. Where are you?"

"In the Midwest. I don't have any sales pending, so I don't feel guilty for taking extra time off."

Jocelyn laughed. "You shouldn't ever feel guilty about taking vacation time, Kree. You usually go fishing a couple of times in the summer, or skiing in the winter, but you rarely go for more than a day or two, and those are often over a weekend. You're way overdue. Have a great time."

"I plan to."

"Are you traveling alone, or are you still with Reina?"

Kree chuckled. "Not going to answer that, sis."

"Why not?"

"Because it's none of your business."

"Kree," she gasped, "you've met a girl, haven't you?"

"Don't you wish you knew?" He chuckled again. "I'll talk to you later, Joce. Goodbye." He hung up before she could ask more questions, half expecting her to call back or send a text. When she did neither, he appreciated her willingness to leave him alone.

While growing up, they had been a close-knit family. He still felt close to his sisters, but after Bethany's death, he had pulled away from his parents. Part of him knew he shouldn't blame them for her accident. But another part couldn't help feeling that if they hadn't interfered, he'd be married now. Maybe even have a child or one on the way.

Knowing it was senseless to dwell on what might have been, he turned the TV on to watch the Lakers, keeping the volume low so Janalou wouldn't be disturbed.

His gaze, as it had last night, kept straying to her. With her eyes closed and her long black hair spread over the white pillow, she looked innocent and fragile.

It occurred to him that if he had married Bethany, he wouldn't be here, and if he hadn't been on the bus, those two scumbags might have hurt Janalou and stolen her money. She might have been alone at the hospital. Alone right now. Or she might not have made it to the hospital in time to save her life.

For the first time in three years, he realized Reina could be right—maybe Bethany died because she was meant to—because they weren't meant to be together.

The realization didn't make her loss easier, but it made things different, although if asked how, he couldn't have explained.

Janalou was a comfortable person to be near, and even if he might not be as happy as he would have been if Bethany hadn't died, for the most part he was content. One thing made complete contentment impossible. Desire. But he wasn't going to use her. Lust had no place in their relationship, even though he didn't intend to let anyone except her know that. His brain had hatched a plan, one with a lot of appeal, and she might be willing to help him pull it off.

~ * ~

Janalou awakened in the middle of the night. Disoriented and frightened, she froze solid until she remembered where she was. With Kree. Not home where Belle could yell and threaten or hurt her.

Kree's quiet presence had a calming effect, just as his holding her hand had in the doctor's office earlier today.

She rolled onto her side, facing his bed. Awareness flitted through her, creating tiny tremors of excitement. Not only was Kree handsome, he seemed too good to be true. *Would he be different when they reached California? Or would he continue to befriend her?*

Her thoughts drifted to Duke, the self-proclaimed leprechaun. *Had he been teasing her?* If so, how had he been able to draw out her life history so easily when she hadn't intended to share any part of it with anyone?

With her limited knowledge of leprechauns, she remembered they had a reputation for brewing mischief, and they lived in Ireland. So what was he doing in the U.S.? And whether he was a leprechaun or not, did he really want to help her?

When she had talked to Cherilyn and Reina on Kree's phone last night, they both said Duke would be in California when she arrived, and he had promised to stay there and help her, although she didn't have a clue what that meant or why he had even mentioned it.

She recalled how the sting had left her face after he touched the bruises while they were on the bus. She had momentarily wondered if he might be an angel. If he were some kind of magical being, and capable of healing, could he have helped her avoid surgery? He hadn't, but the doctor did say she had almost died, and would have if she hadn't made it to the hospital when she did. *Had Duke's magic somehow kept her alive?*

Deciding only time would tell, she closed her eyes and listened to Kree's steady, even breathing. She had always slept alone, but now realized she liked having someone else nearby, in the same room.

After she closed her eyes, a vague memory wiggled through her, one of sharing a bed with another little girl when they were both very young. But she hadn't participated in sleep-overs until after she started school. *Had the memory come from one of those dreams about Jeri Sue?*

Whether it had or not, Janalou always felt as though she had lost something or someone precious whenever she had one of those recurring dreams about the family she didn't know and had never met.

In the dark motel with Kree, a few dreamy fantasies played through her head. The one she liked best was his asking for a date after they reached California.

Regret crept in. If he did ask her, she'd have to turn him down because she was putting on airs, pretending to be someone she wasn't, and that was dishonest.

Remembering Mama's wise counsel as she'd grown up, she drew in a deep breath, determined to take each day as it came, without wishing any part of it away, and to enjoy every moment.

Eventually she fell back asleep. And this time she didn't dream.

~ * ~

In the morning, Kree's presence seemed to steal all of the air in the room, and Janalou found it difficult to breathe. She sat up, and waited for him to break the silence.

"If you feel up to it today," he said, his voice husky from sleep, "we could stop along the way and do something touristy."

Thrilled by his suggestion, she turned an enthusiastic smile to him. "That would be wonderful. I'm afraid I didn't pay much attention yesterday. Are we near a big city?"

"Yes. Almost in St. Louis. We could tour the famous arch, referred to as the Gateway to the West. I've always wanted to see it up close."

"Me too," Janalou said, delighted he was willing to slow their journey and visit a tourist attraction.

"Are you sure you feel up to it?"

"Yes. Absolutely, and I'll try not to sleep while we drive."

"It won't bother me if you do, so don't worry. Okay?"

She shook her head. "If I sleep during the day, I might not sleep tonight."

"Maybe you will if we get some exercise."

Janalou grinned. "Y'all are probably right."

"I like the way you talk," he said. "Your drawl sounds kind of musical."

She laughed, pleased she hadn't lied about being from the South, and proud of her heritage. "Southern girls are taught that a drawl should be beautiful to hear, and we pronounce it as 'drol,' not drawl. We deliberately speak slower than Yankees, prolonging our vowels. And please don't confuse that with the slurring of a drunken cowboy."

Kree laughed. "I won't, and your drawl is beautiful."

"Thank you." A blush heated her cheeks and something else warmed her heart. She looked away, hoping he wouldn't notice how much his compliment meant to her. He was one terrific man, and the more time they spent together, the more she admired him.

Nine

They reached the Jefferson National Expansion Memorial Park before noon. As they strolled toward the arch, Kree reached for her hand and clasped it in his. "Are you sure you're up for this?"

"Yes. Walking isn't strenuous, and I need exercise."

He squeezed her hand gently. "Me, too."

Her insides were quivering, and her heart had picked up speed. She shouldn't like the way his touch affected her. Not with her life so unsettled. Besides, she was living a lie and if Kree ever found out, he might wind up hating her.

She squared her shoulders, strengthening her resolve. She would not fall in love with him. Her heart sagged a little with that thought. *What if it was too late? What if the damage had already been done?*

Below the arch inside the visitors' center, Kree said, "Why don't you go look around while I stand in line to buy tickets?"

"Thanks, I'd love to." She wandered into the Levee Mercantile, an 1870's-style river-front general store, and felt as though she had stepped back in time. Closing her eyes, she inhaled unique scents from the past—an earthy smell of freshly cut wood, rich flavors of vegetables and fruit—and sweets in the form of all kinds of candy, licorice and pickles.

When she opened her eyes, she had a purpose—to pick out inexpensive souvenirs for Reina, Jerilyn, Misti, Toby, Duke and Kree. Although she felt guilty about spending money when she hadn't given Kree a single dollar for their shared expenses or her medical bills, she bought things anyway, telling herself she could afford the expense because she already had a job lined up.

Buying things gave her a sense of freedom she hadn't had for more than a year, and she enjoyed selecting each gift. Tonight she would offer Kree as much of her money as he would take. Maybe that would eliminate some of her guilt.

When Kree found her, she had two plastic bags in each hand filled with her special purchases. "Let me carry those," he said.

"They're not heavy. Just a few trinkets I bought for my new friends."

"I'll carry them anyway." He took the bags, his fingers brushing hers, and her unreliable heart started to pound while he collected them all in one hand.

As though he hadn't even noticed the contact, let alone been affected by it, he said, "I bought tickets for the ride up to the top of the arch, and to the Odyssey Theatre to see the documentary film, *Monument to the Dream.* It's on an IMAX, a four story high screen."

Excited by their stop here as well as his generosity, she said, "We're not on a date, and I feel guilty for letting you pay for everything."

"Don't feel guilty. Guys like to pay for things, and I can afford it." He grinned again and reached for her hand with his free one. "Let's go see the show."

Once more her heart trembled. She cautioned herself not to get used to his touch or his attention. They were friends. That's all they could be. Never would she tell him the truth about her past or her real identity. She was too ashamed to admit she had put up with Belle's abuse instead of doing something about it, like calling Child Protection Services. Why that thought had never occurred baffled her. Why had she been so afraid of the Yankee?

She wasn't a dumb ninny who didn't have enough brains to take care of herself. She possessed above-average intelligence which had earned her a four year scholarship to the University of Columbia. So why had she lived through such a miserable year without doing anything about it?

Then she knew why. Because of Papa. She loved him and wished he could still share her life. Part of her wanted to call and tell him where she was, where she planned to go. A stronger part feared he might tell Belle, and that part worried about what they might do if they came after her. Hurt her? Beat her? Threaten her? Lock her in a room? Tie her up? Refuse to let her go out?

She gave her head a mental shake. Belle's latest threat—grounding her forever—didn't make a lick of sense. Most parents wanted their children to grow up and move out. Why didn't Belle? And why hadn't Papa disagreed or taken any stance to protect her?

Janalou scraped her free hand over her face. No way would she be trapped inside a brick box called home for the rest of her life. She licked her dry lips. Would the fear of being found ever go away? *I'm almost eighteen, so they can't force me to go back, can they?*

The reminder didn't ease the fear that they might show up and tell Kree the truth.

Inhaling a calming breath, she issued herself a warning to be careful, and not to say or do anything that might help Papa or Belle find her. Maybe they wouldn't look. Maybe they were as happy to have her gone as she was. She didn't really believe that. But she could hope.

They entered the IMAX. The big theater made her feel as if she were in a new world. And with Kree still holding her hand after they sat down, she felt like a different person. She shoved her long hair behind her shoulders, and leaned back, craning her neck to see the entire screen.

"We just made it," Kree whispered as the lights dimmed and the huge screen came to life.

As the documentary began, Janalou marveled at the story unraveling before them. The builders had started on separate sides of the arch and met at the top, over six hundred feet in the air, weaving the middle together in the exact center high above the ground. How anyone could accomplish such a feat was a mystery to her.

When Kree stroked her fingers, her heart raced. She lost track of time. And the story. All her awareness focused on the man at her side. And the way his gentle strokes made her insides quiver.

After the film ended, he released her hand. She couldn't help being a little disappointed.

Outside the theater, they strolled around the museum, reading signs about the construction and also studying displays, saving the ride up to the top of the arch for last.

Janalou thought her petite height in the round cage-like elevator must be more comfortable in the confined space than Kree's tall six feet. He didn't complain though, just smiled as other tourists filled each small round seat, their eyes eager with the same kind of anticipation she felt. Although somewhat claustrophobic, she was still excited to be doing something unusual.

After the doors closed, a recording began. "The Park was established on December 21, 1935, to commemorate the westward growth of the United States between 1803 and 1890. Construction of the nation's tallest memorial began in 1961, topped out in 1965, and was dedicated in 1966. Cost for the thirty million dollar national monument was shared by the federal government and the City of St. Louis..."

As the elevator ascended, the recording repeated information they had heard in the film. "Made of stainless steel, the arch is six hundred and thirty feet high from its sixty-foot foundation and spans six hundred and thirty feet at ground level. The classic weighted curve at the top sways one-half to one inch in a twenty mile per hour wind."

Thinking about swaying so far above ground turned Janalou's stomach. Maybe going up to the top was a mistake.

When the elevator stopped, she felt okay standing at the side of the arch. They had a lot of steel beneath them to support everyone's weight. But as she and Kree walked toward the center of the arch, her heart moved up to her throat, and she almost forgot to breathe.

There was nothing under them except the floor and six hundred and thirty feet of empty air.

Fear clutched her stomach into a tight knot.

Part way across the arch, Kree stepped up on a ledge on one side to look out a window. Janalou told herself to stop being a ninny, gathered her courage, and stepped up beside him. Her uneasiness escalated and her insides began to tremble, and that was before she looked outside. All she saw were a few puffy clouds and blue sky. Her nervous stomach filled with butterflies. Then she looked down. And saw nothing but air between her and the ground, so far below.

"Amazing, isn't it?" Kree asked.

"Yes." Almost afraid to breathe, she barely moved her lips. Having nothing below except open space freaked her out. She didn't dare look down again, not even at the Mississippi River which she knew must be there.

Kree reached for her hand. "Don't be scared. We're safe."

"Are you sure?" Intellectually she knew they were, but emotionally she felt unsafe. Insecure. Nauseated. Sick enough to heave.

In spite of her resolve not to look straight down again, she finally did. Her stomach fell about a mile.

For a few seconds, she closed her eyes, trying to calm her jittery nerves. Then more focused, she said, "It's spooky to see nothing beneath us except land, and it looks so far away."

"Yeah," Kree agreed. "The arch is a testament to man's ingenuity." He shifted her bags of trinkets, stepped behind her, and wrapped both arms around her. "Does this make you feel safer?"

Not trusting her voice, she nodded, but barely. *Safe from what?* she wanted to ask. Certainly not from him. Her hormones or something inside had gone berserk, orbiting away from the arch, up toward the sun high in the sky. She didn't know what disturbed her most—being so far above ground or having his arms around her.

Hardly daring to move for fear of weakening the crowded structure, she swallowed and stared at other tourists after she stepped down from the ledge. *Did anyone else feel as unsafe as she did?* A half smile blossomed when she saw two children stretching their parents' arms practically out of their sockets by planting their feet on the floor and stubbornly refusing to get near the windows.

When she saw a short stocky man who resembled Duke Guggles standing a few feet away, a strange sensation whooshed through her. Relief followed, magically removing her fear, as though he had touched her, even if only with his gaze, and taken away all her misgivings. *Was Duke responsible?*

Her heart skipped a beat. Instead of green clothes, he wore a dark charcoal suit, white shirt, and colorful green and white tie.

"Duke. There's Duke," she gasped.

"Where?" Kree released her arm and glanced around. "I don't see him."

Janalou blinked. She couldn't see him either. Was her imagination playing tricks on her? Or had the pill she'd taken for pain earlier made her hallucinate?

Telling herself she must have imagined Duke, she reached for Kree's hand and clung, as though that would keep her anchored in reality, but she didn't understand what had happened to her fear. *Why had it suddenly evaporated?*

Kree walked across the short walkway and stepped up on the opposite ledge. Without any fear, Janalou stepped up beside him. Once again he moved behind her and wrapped his arms around her. Shivers raced down her arms, not from fear this time, but from his nearness, as she inhaled his wonderful spicy scent and reveled in the strength of his arms holding her close.

Still wondering if she had seen Duke, she studied the other tourists again, hoping for another glimpse of Duke. But if he had been there, he was nowhere in sight.

They finished their stroll across the tunnel-like arch. While they waited for the elevator, she breathed easier.

Maybe she hadn't hallucinated. Maybe she had seen Duke and he had removed her fear. Or maybe her brain had figured out that the sides of the steel arch and the rounded structure could support tons of weight, and her fear was unwarranted.

"Do you regret stopping here?" Kree asked as they headed out to the parking lot a short time later.

"No. I'm glad we did. I don't know why I got so spooked up there."

Kree smiled. "I thought you were very brave."

She laughed, trying to mask her nervousness. "You don't have to fib. I know I acted like a scared ninny. I felt like one—for a few minutes anyway."

"We won't do anything else that feels risky."

"Don't limit what you'd like to do, please. This is your trip, too."

He slid his arm around her shoulders and gave her an affectionate hug. "I'll enjoy whatever else we plan, so don't worry your pretty little head."

Janalou didn't know whether to be thrilled by his hug, complimented by his use of the word *pretty*, or upset by the words *little head*.

He smiled after he unlocked the car door. Deciding he hadn't meant anything uncomplimentary, she smiled too. This journey truly was an experience to remember and savor. She rated it right up there with the magical prom and senior hop she had shared with Tony more than two years ago.

She heard Kree whistle a snappy tune as he walked around the rented Ford Taurus. Although they weren't on a date, he made her feel special, and treated her with respect and kindness. Too bad she didn't possess a sparkling wit so she could charm him, entertain him, and somehow pay him back for all the time and attention he was devoting to her.

"We don't have to follow the bus route," he said as he maneuvered the rental car through St. Louis's crowded downtown streets instead of getting back on the freeway. "We could deviate, if you'd like, and stop and see things along our way, turn the trip into a mini-vacation."

"I'd love to do that," she said, unable to contain her excitement. "This is the first time I've ever been west of the Great Smokey Mountains."

"Fine. Decision's made. I'll pull over when I get a chance and find the nearest Triple A so we can pick up some maps and brochures." A few minutes later, he said, "Wish I'd brought my iPad. Didn't think I'd need it. Maybe I'll stop and buy one."

"You paid my medical expenses," Janalou reminded. "Can you afford a new iPad? Don't they cost as much as a computer?"

He grinned. "Probably, but I'm due for an update. When I get home, I'll donate my old one to a worthy cause. I can write it off as a business expense."

"Are you sure your credit card isn't maxed out?"

"I'm sure," he said. "Besides, I have more than one credit card."

"You must be a fortunate man."

He grinned. "I like to think I am."

Kree wove through more traffic to the outskirts of St. Louis, and drove around until he found a mall he had located on his smartphone.

After he paid for the iPad, he handed his phone to Janalou and they both searched for a Triple A office. She found one first, and by his expression she knew she had impressed him.

He drove there and they both loaded up on tourist information.

Back outside, Janalou raised her arm to shield her eyes from the bright sun. "Are we staying here tonight, Kree?"

"Sure. I think we've done enough today, don't you?"

She nodded, so happy he had suggested prolonging the journey that she wanted to hug him. Of course she didn't, but she did smile. *Slowing down their trip would give her incision and her black eyes time to heal before she met his family and started to work.*

~ * ~

After checking into the Marriot, a uniformed bellman delivered more luggage than they'd had when they left the bus. "He must have left someone else's bag," Janalou said, eyeing the pink suitcase with wheels.

"No. That's yours," Kree said. "I bought it while you were in the hospital. Thought it might make checking in and out of hotels easier." He cleared his throat. "I also took the liberty of buying you some clothes."

Janalou's tired, exotic eyes popped wide open. "Why?"

He shrugged, unwilling to admit he had gone through all her possessions. "Because I doubt you have room in your backpack for very many."

"I can't let you pay for my clothes. You're practically a stranger. Mama would turn over in her grave." Janalou flipped her long black hair behind her shoulders. "How much did the rollaround and clothes cost? I'll pay you for them."

Kree hoisted the new case onto a stand and opened it, revealing several plastic bags. "You make it tough for a guy to do something nice for you. Most girls would be thrilled, wouldn't they?"

"I don't know. I'm not most girls. You paid my medical expenses. And for our motel rooms. Even today's adventure. I say that's nicer than I deserve. I intend to repay you for that and these." She raised the bags of new clothes from the suitcase, dangling them in front of his face, and he resisted an urge to grin. "I'll give you four thousand dollars now and set up a monthly payment schedule for the rest of what I owe you as soon I start to work."

"Let's talk about that later, after we reach California," he said, wondering if she would consider repaying him with a favor instead of money. "I bought some things you might not think you need. Just give me fifty bucks."

She looked inside one bag, then another and another. "Well, I declare," she muttered a phrase Kree hadn't heard her use before, which made her sound exactly like a Southern belle. "Looks like you've been as busy as a one-armed paperhanger."

"Is that good or bad?" he asked, doubtful. Had he been complimented or insulted?

"I'm not sure," she said, without smiling. "It means y'all have been durn busy, and this stuff cost a bucket more than fifty dollars. That won't even pay for the luggage." She pulled an envelope from one of her backpack's zippered pockets, withdrew some greenbacks and extended five one hundred dollar bills. "Will this cover it?"

He took one bill. "I went to a discount store. This will more than pay for my purchases."

"You wouldn't lie to me, would you?"

He laughed at her skeptical expression, and patted her gently on the cheek, thoroughly enjoying himself. "I might, but only if I think it's for your own good."

She raised her chin a notch, dislodging his fingers before she took an audible swallow.

"Please take this." She held up the four one hundred dollar bills he had refused. "I'd like to help pay for the car rental and some of the gas and room charges, too." She dug more money from an envelope and extended a wad of bills.

He shook his head, refusing her offer. "I cashed in your bus ticket. That will pay for your share of our travel expenses, and to put your mind at ease, neither one of us has to worry about your medical expenses until I see my next credit card statement at the end of June."

She smiled then, and his heart reacted with cheerful elation, as though he had won a hard-fought battle.

"Y'all are just too good to be true," she said, her voice soft and quiet, the expression in her exotic eyes full of respect and admiration.

Kree gave in to the urge to caress her cheek. "Keep thinking that and we'll get along great, Janalou."

"We do get along well," she agreed. The warmth in her eyes indicated she liked his touch as much as he enjoyed touching her. But when she backed away, the warmth disappeared. All he saw was wariness.

She sat down on one of the beds.

He moved close and touched her shoulder to get her attention. She looked up. The warmth was back.

His pulse picked up speed. "You never complain, so I don't know how you feel. How's the incision?"

"As the surgeon said, it's healing nicely."

"It hasn't even been three full days since your surgery," he reminded.

"Well, it looks okay," she said, staring at his feet, and making him wonder what she was thinking.

"I'll feel better after we reach California and my doctor checks you."

She glanced up, gratitude in her eyes. "I've never known anyone like you."

He gave her shoulder a gentle squeeze, and spoke in a quiet tone. "I've never met anyone like you, either."

For long moments they stared. She looked away first.

"I bought a cooler and some drinks and snacks as well," he said, pulling her attention back to him.

"Terrific. You thought of everything. Thanks again," she said. "Next time we stop, I'd like to buy a notebook."

"You want a computer?" he asked. "If you're willing to wait until we get home, I'll give you my old iPad."

She laughed, shaking her head. "That's very generous, but I meant a paper notebook. I like to doodle, and I want to write things down as we travel. Keep a journal of the places we stop and all the things we see and do."

He grinned his approval. "My sisters usually kept journals every time we went on a family vacations. Sometimes I played tricks on them just to see if they'd write them down."

"Did they?"

"Yeah."

She reached up, touched his hand on her shoulder. "This is a trip I'll always treasure."

"We'll make it one to remember," he promised, resisting the desire to lean over and kiss her. He convinced himself it was a natural urge. Any guy would want to kiss a pretty girl who treated him like a hero.

Ten

Sound asleep, Janalou lay flat on her back, the covers pulled all the way up to her chin, as though she used them to hide behind.

Kree wondered if the bruises near her eyes hurt. Although they looked better each day, they were still a long way from being completely healed. A knot formed in his gut as he wondered again if she had she run away from an abusive coward who had punched her in the face.

He recalled the news bulletin on CNN two nights before and his first reaction when he wondered if Janalou might be the missing girl. They hadn't watched much TV, but when they did, he hadn't seen the bulletin again, so maybe she had been found.

Janalou didn't act like a runaway, at least not anymore. No, now she acted like a lovely young Southern lady who possessed charm and wit. Tonight at dinner she had opened up enough to tell him about her parents. She had loved them, but admitted her father had drunk too much, so she never touched alcohol, and she was uncomfortable being around people who did.

He had his own reason for not drinking. He'd been drinking beer with his buddies the night Bethany died, and he'd been too hung over to drive to the hospital. His friend, Jason, who never drank, had driven him there. By the time they arrived, Kree had been cold sober, and he'd stayed that way ever since.

Janalou stirred and rolled over onto her side, facing him. Tenderness washed through him, easing some of the tension kinked inside. He'd never watched a girl sleep. Her long black eyelashes looked like miniature fans shielding her closed eyes, and her face, relaxed in sleep, seemed innocent and vulnerable. She'd said she would be eighteen in a few weeks, which confirmed his earlier thought that she was too young for him. Even if he had a romantic interest, which he didn't, and the seven year age difference didn't bother him, which it did—*she had been eleven and still in grade school when he was eighteen and starting college*—their backgrounds were too far apart, and created a gap impossible to bridge.

He sat back, crossed his ankles, and steepled his fingers beneath his chin. In spite of their differences and his reason for not wanting to be romantically entangled, she might be a perfect candidate for an idea that had hatched and wouldn't go away. If he had a make-believe fiancée, his parents and sisters would stop trying to line him up with potential brides. Even Reina would approve of his being engaged.

Would Janalou go along with his twisted inspiration? She wasn't like any girl he had ever known. Shy one minute. Friendly the next. Proper always. And refined. But never forward. She didn't flirt. And hardly even looked at him when they were alone in a motel room.

Still, she had backbone. She didn't want him to buy things for her. Didn't even want him to pay for her meals. Didn't complain, either. Half the time she acted embarrassed. Why didn't she know how to accept compliments without blushing? That endeared her for reasons he didn't understand.

He plowed his fingers through his hair. Those kinds of thoughts were dangerous. They lured men to do serious things, like consider marriage.

To avoid thinking about the M word, he compared Janalou with Bethany, who had been much worldlier. And spoiled. He didn't like that reminder. He loved Bethany, and spoiling her had been a pleasure. Even so, he kept wondering how Janalou would react if he kissed her. Why did he want to? She was young, far too young for him. Also naive. And unspoiled.

He checked his thoughts again, feeling like a traitor for remembering Bethany always wanted more than she had. Someone always got it for her too, including him. He shoved those thoughts aside as well. His heart belonged to Bethany. And he didn't want it any other way. He knew how much losing someone you loved hurt and he wasn't about to go through that possibility ever again.

When Janalou kicked the covers off, he found himself wishing her long-legged yellow pajamas revealed more. With a mental shake, he twisted a bottle of Gatorade open and took a long swig.

Janalou had examined the clothes he'd bought for her with an expression of awe, but she hadn't badgered him about the cost again. She had merely folded the slacks and blouses into neat piles, and placed everything except one outfit back inside the new pink suitcase. He wanted to see her in clothes he had selected, although he couldn't explain why. And in slacks, instead of the long denim skirt she had worn four days running.

He uncrossed his ankles, and swallowed another slug of Gatorade. Earlier, he had called his sister again, admitted he was traveling across the country with a female, and that he had offered her a job in their office. Joycelyn had jumped to the conclusion that he was romantically involved, which had given credence to the plan of a fake engagement. It was a brilliant idea. And it would work, for a while at least. Not only did he and Janalou get along well, she was easy to look at, even with those black eyes she camouflaged with make-up. And he was attracted to her. Any normal guy who wasn't blind would appreciate her looks—a terrific figure with lovely curves, dark exotic eyes, a pretty face, and all that long, silky black hair.

If he asked her to pretend to be engaged, the worst she could do was say no. Nothing ventured, nothing gained. He convinced himself it wouldn't be dishonest. It would be a game. An odd sense of anticipation swept through him. Pretending to have a fiancée would outwit everyone. And it would keep his sisters and parents from trying to line him up with chicks he didn't want to meet.

It would also protect Janalou from other men. And she needed protecting, at least until she got settled. After a reasonable time, they could break the fake engagement, and go their separate ways, although that might be difficult if she worked with him. But he would cross that bridge when they came to it. In the meantime, a pretend engagement seemed like a perfect solution for him. Hopefully for her, too.

~ * ~

The next morning, Kree said, "I can't find much to stop and see in Kansas."

Janalou stood behind him, watching while he searched for tourist attractions on his iPad.

"There are just small towns along the freeway, but going any other way will add miles to our trip. If we drive across Missouri today, we could stop in Independence tomorrow and tour the Harry Truman Library before we tackle Kansas. The White House in Miniature is on display until July ninth."

"Sounds cool," Janalou said, so delighted about his suggestion to turn their journey into a vacation she wanted to hug him. Just thinking that was way out of line. But she couldn't control her thoughts. Like her heart, they yearned for more than friendship with Kree Winterton.

During the long drive across I-70, Kree said, "Tell me about your family."

Janalou felt her throat choking up. "Perhaps I can discuss it later," she said, "but not right now."

He'd probably mistake the warble in her voice, think it was due to grief. But she couldn't correct him. She was too ashamed to admit she had lived like a scared ninny for the past year—ashamed she had let Belle intimidate her and allowed her to dictate what clothes she wore, where she went, almost everything she did.

She forced her thoughts off Belle, and watched the scenery, so glad to be with Kree and traveling across the country in a car she wanted to shout with joy. Instead she inhaled slowly, savoring the fantastic scent of his spicy aftershave each time one of them leaned closer to ask a question or make a comment.

After lunch, she had an almost overpowering urge to ask Kree to pull off the freeway and stop the car so she could slide closer, lean against his solid chest and melt in his arms.

Her reaction to him was getting out of control. Why? Tony hadn't affected her like this. Sure she had enjoyed his kisses, but he had never tried to do much more. He had been sensitive to her mourning after Mama's death, and hadn't taken advantage of her weakened emotions. He had been an ideal boyfriend, not too pushy or forward. And he'd never tried to make her jealous by flirting with other girls. All her memories of Tony were sweet, and she would always remember him with enormous fondness.

If she knew where he was now, she might call him. But the last time she'd heard from him, he'd decided to change universities, and she didn't know which one he had moved to. She didn't even know what state he might be in.

Maybe she could look him or his parents up online, and contact them when she had access to a computer again. She wasn't about to ask Kree if she could use his gadgets to find her old boyfriend.

That's when she realized she shouldn't try to find Tony. He was part of her old life. A life already far behind her. And it would be foolish to contact anyone who might help Papa and Belle find her. Anyone except her best friend, Margie. She had promised to let Margie know she was okay if she left, but she didn't have to take care of that until the end of the summer, after Margie returned from her three month tour of Europe—her high school graduation gift from her grandparents.

She glanced at Kree again, wondering what he was thinking about. "Are you tired of driving?"

"No." He flashed a grin. "I like to drive. How about you? Are you tired of being cooped up in the car?"

"Not at all. I'm enjoying seeing this vast country we live in."

"Me too, and I like sharing the experience with you."

Nothing he might have said could have pleased her more. Joy pumped through her, making her heart pound hard, as though she had just run a bunch of miles nonstop, like those she had run to the bus station. *Had that only been four nights ago?*

In some ways, it seemed like a lifetime.

~ * ~

As they began their tour inside the Truman Museum, Janalou read some displays out loud.

Watching and listening, Kree resisted the temptation to raise his hand and caress her cheek. He didn't know why he kept wanting to touch her.

A sudden sensation of being watched descended. He looked around, but didn't see anyone paying attention to them.

"Let's go see the permanent exhibition that explains Truman's story," he said.

Janalou grinned. "Lead the way."

"Here's something you might enjoy first." Kree stopped by the Benefactors' Special Exhibition Gallery.

"Caroline Kennedy's dolls!" she exclaimed. "How marvelous." She read the display out loud. '*Enchanted by a young family in the White House, the world responded with gifts to the Kennedy children. The Truman Presidential Museum & Library is proud to host an exhibition of dolls given to Caroline between 1961 and 1963, before the President's tragic assassination ended their brief residency in the White House. On loan from the Kennedy Library, the collection showcases more than a hundred dolls and puppets from thirty different countries. Many were gifts from foreign dignitaries and first ladies, including India's Indira Gandhi, Monaco's Princess Grace, and France's Madame de Gaulle. Others were given by ordinary citizens.*"

While Janalou studied the dolls, Kree had the sensation of being watched again. He glanced behind his shoulder. And did a double take. Then he blinked, as he noticed Duke Guggles staring at him. The short stocky man, dressed in a dark suit, with a white shirt and striped green tie, motioned for Kree to follow him.

"Excuse me," he said to Janalou, compelled by an invisible force to answer the summons. "I'll be back in a few minutes."

Duke Guggles waited around the corner, his gaze somber.

"What are you doing here?" Kree asked, his heart pounding like a drum. "I thought you were in California."

Duke didn't reply. He simply waved one arm.

Kree sucked in a sharp breath. Then wished he hadn't. A cloud of fog surrounded them, sealing them away from other museum visitors, making him feel as though he had entered a different dimension, one located in a cloud or cyber-space or the nether world where he had never ventured, and a place he didn't really believe existed.

Was he hallucinating?

Duke reclaimed his attention when he said, "I'm checking on the lass. How is she?"

Kree scratched his head. *Was he listening to a figment of his own imagination?*

Duke's green eyes demanded an answer, compelling Kree to speak. He licked his lips, still confused. "She seems fine. Why don't you ask her yourself?"

"No need when ye can tell me, is there, lad?"

"I guess not," Kree said. "Do you want something?"

"Just to tell ye that ye'll be fine with the lass, as long as ye don't take advantage of her."

"I have no intention of taking advantage." Kree squared his shoulders, feeling out of sorts. "Taking advantage of women isn't my style." The mere idea went against his grain.

"Ye shared a motel room last even," Duke said, "and I be thinking it weren't the only night ye've slept in same room."

Stung by the implied accusations, Kree demanded, "How do you know? Have you been spying on us?"

"No need, lad. Ye made no secret of the fact. She be a foine lass, and she has the possibility of a foine future. Don't ye be messing it up, ye hear?"

Before Kree could form a reply, Duke added, "She may think she's no good enough for ye, lad, but that be not true. Might well be 'tother way 'round." With barely a pause, he added, "One word of caution. Ye'll both weather the storm that's about to erupt outside, although ye might have trouble if ye try to drive in it. What's more, ye be wrong about the deceased lass, Bethany. She weren't the lass fer ye, lad."

"Am I supposed to make sense out of this jumbled conversation?" Kree demanded. *How did Duke know about Bethany? Had Reina told him?*

The short man flashed an indulgent grin. "Twould be good if you could, lad, but yer no supposed to understand me musings, although I'd wager ye'd know what I mean if'n ye put yer mind to figuring it out."

Kree tried to look away, but he couldn't. Duke's magnetic stare held his as though captured, trapped. He wanted to say something too, but his tongue suddenly felt numb and he couldn't force a word through his lips.

"About tonight's storm," Duke continued, "attempt not to drive in the rain. I can save the lass if ye do, but I canna promise to save ye, too. Do ye ken what I say, lad?"

"Are you telling me I might die if I drive in the rain tonight?"

"No, lad, ye'll not die. Yer time on earth be far from over, but I'm thinking ye'll no like the circumstances under which ye may have to live if'n ye heed not my words of caution. Tell me ye ken, lad. Do ye?"

He nodded, still wondering if he was imagining this bizarre conversation. *Was it a hallucination? A product of too little sleep last night?*

He sucked in a deep breath, wondering if the fog around them would pollute his lungs as it had apparently befuddled his brain.

"There be a bed and breakfast inn within walking distance from the museum," Duke said, claiming his attention once more. "They will have one room open before the night ends. I'm thinking that be where ye and the lass should spend the night to avoid being out in the storm."

"We planned to put a couple of hundred more miles behind us before we stop for the night."

"There's dark clouds in the sky, lad, and yer chances to spend long hours alone with the lass may be limited. I suggest ye enjoy what time fate has allowed ye now. Also, ye may want to re-think that plan of yers to wait until yer forty or fifty to find yerself a wife."

Kree shook his head, unable to believe the white haired man was real. No one knew his plan. *No one.* He'd never told a single soul. Not even his closest friend, Jason. "Am I hallucinating?"

Instead of answering, Duke said, "I've had me say now, lad, so I shall take me leave."

He didn't walk away. Instead he floated backwards out of the mist. Still facing Kree, he disappeared around the corner, leaving Kree with an eerie sensation that he had just been visited by an other-worldly being.

Kree rubbed his chin and felt the sandpapery bristle of more than a full day's growth, only then realizing he hadn't shaved that morning. *And he never forgot to shave. Never.* Unless he was fishing with his buddies. Then it was deliberate. *Why had he forgotten today? Because he'd been distracted by Janalou? Worried that she might miss taking her medicine?*

Baffled, he shook his head, trying to make sense out of what had just happened.

Had he really just seen the short man who had worn green on the bus now dressed in a business suit? Or had his imagination gotten the best of him because Janalou thought she'd seen him yesterday in the arch?

Eleven

Delighted by every doll she saw, Janalou moved through Caroline Kennedy's collection slowly. A wisp of nostalgia spiraled through her. She had left her own cherished dolls behind, stored in boxes on the highest shelf in her bedroom closet to hide them from Belle. The dolls were one of the few things Belle hadn't seized and destroyed or given away. Chances were, though, that she would get rid of them and Janalou would never see them again. Just as she would never see Papa.

Trying to ignore her regret, she focused on the future. It was easy now with Belle out of her life. All her tomorrows looked bright and promising. Only the thought of missing Papa marred her happy anticipation.

As she reached the last doll display, Kree rejoined her. Startled by his pale complexion, she said, "You look spooked, as though you've seen a ghost."

His grin looked forced. "A ghost? In here? Have you seen one?"

She shook her head.

"Good. Are you ready to look at something else?"

"Yes."

He took her hand and led her away, caressing her fingers in an absentminded way. Every time she stopped to read a description, he stopped too, and he didn't rush her. Instead he encouraged her to wander slowly, and take her time. It really was like being on vacation.

When they finished looking at everything, Janalou smiled. "I'm glad we stopped here, Kree. I loved the White House in miniature, including Caroline Kennedy's doll collection. And I'm impressed by all the difficult decisions Harry Truman had to make during his first year in office."

"Me, too." Kree seemed a bit more at ease now, and Janalou relaxed.

"Truman assumed the presidency at a difficult time, less than three months after being sworn in as vice president. He oversaw the ending of World War Two, and later he recognized the new state of Israel, desegregated the armed forces and implemented a loyalty oath for federal employees."

"Yes, and I've always loved his phrase, 'the buck stops here,'" Kree said.

She gazed up, her pulse racing because he had curled his fingers around her arm and was caressing her flesh again, even though he didn't seem to realize what he was doing.

"Did you ever consider going into politics as a career?" she asked, unable to ignore the butterfly emotions whirling around inside her.

Kree shook his head. "I admire those who are willing to get involved, but a politician's life isn't his or her own. There's too much limelight, not to mention all the ridicule they're subjected to if they make an unwise decision, or even say one wrong word. Sometimes even when they think they're confiding something in private, it gets blabbed, picked up by the media and blown out of proportion, often out of context."

Janalou nodded. "I agree, but being around anyone in politics isn't something I'll ever have to worry about."

Kree released her arm. "Me either, and I'm glad you're not related to any politicians or people who are involved in serving the public. You're not, are you?"

"No." She shook her head, pleased he knew one true thing.

His touch had ignited a burning sensation way down deep inside. Each physical contact seemed to affect her more strongly than the last. She told herself that would end when they reached California, but couldn't make herself believe it.

Kree had snuck inside her heart and, although she hadn't expected that to happen, she couldn't squelch the excitement he created, nor could she stop hoping something would come of it if she ever found the nerve the tell him she had lied about being an orphan.

As they headed for the exit, thunder rumbled outside, so loud it sounded as though it had shaken the building. Kree's forehead creased into a troubled frown.

"Sounds like it's going to storm." He opened the door. They walked outside. Not a drop of rain hit the ground but the smell of moisture filled in the air.

Lightning flashed a few feet away.

Janalou gasped, unable to believe how close it hit the ground. "How that missed us and the building, I'll never know."

"Me either." Kree reached for her arm and they hurried toward the parking lot.

A started squeal escaped Janalou a few seconds later when lightning flashed again, this time barely above their heads.

Thunder roared, sounding very near. She jumped half a foot in the air and came down inside the circle of Kree's arms as another streak of lightning struck the paved parking lot, leaving a sizzling hiss behind, mere inches from their feet.

"Easy," he soothed. "You're going to be okay."

With her heart pounding, she glanced up, caught the worry in Kree's eyes and wondered if he believed what he'd just said.

It started to rain, big droplets pelting against them with the sudden ferocity of a full gale wind.

"Looks like we're in for a bad storm. Maybe we should we go back inside the museum," he said.

"The car's closer," she disagreed. "If the storm lasts beyond the museum's closing time, we might get wetter if we wait inside. Let's make a dash for it." She grabbed his hand and they raced through the parking lot.

She didn't understand what happened next. One second they were getting struck by rain from one direction. The next instant water splashed down in a solid sheet, as though someone had parted the clouds and aimed a huge vat of water directly at them. It wasn't merely a deluge, it was as though a lake had flooded them from heaven. They were both soaked.

Drenched to the skin, they plunged through inches of rain. Water squished inside her soaked shoes. Clinging to Kree's hand, she used her other to shove her wet hair out of her eyes. The storm blew it right back. She found herself sputtering, gasping for air, as though she were trying to swim through an angry ocean and barely able to stay above the surface.

Before they reached the rented Taurus, more thunder sounded and lightning cracked in the dark gray sky. Never had Janalou experienced anything like it. *Now that it was raining, shouldn't the thunder and lightning be gone? Or have moved farther away?*

By the time they reached the car, the flooded parking lot looked like a pond, the water more than ankle deep.

Wild wind flapped their wet clothes, and rain plastered their hair to their scalps as Kree unlocked the driver's side of the car, jerked the door open and barked, "Get in."

She jumped inside and wiggled beneath the steering wheel, her wet clothes soaking the seat as she scooted over to make room for Kree. He jumped in behind her, and slammed the door shut.

"Holy moly. What a downpour!"

"You can say that again." She liked his choice of words. A lot of men might have cursed or used crude language, but he didn't, and that pleased her. Truth be told, she couldn't think of a single thing about him that didn't impress her.

"I've never seen anything like this. Have you?" he asked.

She shook her wet head, flicking drops of water onto the seat, and onto Kree as well before she realized it and stopped. "I don't have an inch anywhere on my body that's still dry."

"Me either." Kree stuck a key in the ignition. As soon as the engine started, he switched the air-conditioner off and turned the heater on.

Glad he didn't shift gears, Janalou said, "I don't want to travel anywhere in this storm."

"Neither do I." He sounded even grimmer than he looked.

The inside windows fogged, making it impossible to see out. While rain continued to pour, the wind blasted against the car so hard it wiggled.

"I wonder how long this will last," Kree said, after a few minutes of stark silence.

"Me, too. I remember the news about floods in Missouri a few years ago. The storm went on for days."

Kree flipped on the car radio. A newscaster was issuing traveler's warnings. "Stay home unless you have a medical emergency. Do not go out. I repeat, do not go outside or drive anywhere unless you absolutely must. This is a severe storm, one of the worst that has hit Independence in five decades. More flooding is expected. Some roads are already closed."

"Do you think we should have stayed inside the museum?" Janalou asked.

Kree's lips thinned into a grim line. "We're as safe in a car as we would be in a building. At least we're grounded, if lightning strikes again."

Janalou wasn't so sure, but she wanted to believe him. "You're not going to try to drive in this, are you?"

"No. I don't think we should move. The tires might not stay on the ground, and the car could hydroplane. We'll stay put, and hope the storm blows over."

"Sounds like a good plan." Shivering in spite of the warm air blowing from the heater, Janalou gathered her long wet hair behind her shoulders, wishing she had a rubber band to hold it together, also wishing she had her dry jacket. But those things were in the trunk, packed in her new suitcase.

Minutes ticked by. The storm didn't show any signs of slowing down, and the radio newscaster didn't give any hope that it would. To make matters worse, the water in the parking lot deepened, turning from a shallow pond into a lake.

They sat so close, Kree felt Janalou shiver. "Do y'all think we'll have to spend the night here in the car, in wet clothes?"

"Maybe." He tried to decide what to do. After the warning from Duke, he didn't plan to drive anywhere until the storm ended. "Let's go back inside the museum," he finally said. "We're already wet, and it might be a better place to wait out the storm. We aren't the only ones who might be here all night."

"Yes, and we can't get much wetter."

He opened his door, and slid out. Janalou followed. Instead of heading for the museum, however, he turned toward the parking lot exit, and slogged through the lake-like pool. Janalou plodded along behind him.

A car had stalled in the middle of the road, blocking the parking lot exit and traffic in both directions. Cars were backed up, and drivers impatiently honked horns.

"What's wrong?" Kree asked, when he reached the stalled driver.

"I think a manhole cover came off and one of my tires is stuck in the hole," the driver yelled to be heard above the howling wet wind.

Other drivers continued to honk. Kree raised his arm and waved, just once. As though by magic, all honking stopped.

"Why don't we go into the museum, and get out of the storm?" he suggested to the driver of the stalled car.

"Good idea." The man opened his car door and motioned at the woman inside.

As they hopped out, Kree forged through the rain to the car behind to explain. "We think a car tire is stuck in a manhole in that stalled car. Not much we can do to get it out until the storm slows down. We're going to seek shelter in the museum. You might want to join us."

He didn't have to talk to every driver. As soon as a few people headed for the museum, others followed, trekking through calf-deep water.

Kree locked hands with Janalou, wanting the contact, but trying to convince himself he did it out of concern for her. Rain continued to pour, and the wild wind whipped at their clothes, blowing debris in front of them, making it difficult to see. Kree forged on, Duke's dire warning fresh in his mind. *"Attempt not to drive in the rain. I can save the lass if ye do, but I canna promise to save ye, too. Do ye ken what I say, lad?"*

Not about to ignore what he knew had not been a hallucination, Kree plowed on, wrapping one arm around Janalou, trying to shield her with his body.

Inside the museum, staff members were offering paper towels and serving complimentary coffee, tea and hot chocolate. In addition to towels, they had miraculously come up with a variety of donuts, too—glazed, frosted, chocolate, maple and cherry pink icing.

"I'll go get our suitcases so we can change to dry clothes," Kree said to Janalou. 'Wish I'd thought about that earlier."

"I'll go with you."

He shook his head. "Stay here. No sense both of us getting wetter." When he released her hand, her bleak expression made him feel like he was abandoning her. Without conscious thought, he bent and brushed a quick kiss on her cheek. "Don't worry, sweetheart. I'll be back. I promise."

She didn't say a word, but her eyes spoke volumes. He saw surprise. Relief. And gratitude. Plus something more, something he couldn't quite define, something he didn't think he should acknowledge. *Why had he called her 'sweetheart'?* It wasn't like him to use terms of endearment with anyone.

He raced outside, back to the car, fighting wind and rain, soaking the inside of the trunk when he lifted the lid.

Back in the museum, he gave Janalou her suitcase, and they headed for separate restrooms. After he changed to dry clothes, he shared most of what he had in his suitcase with other men whose clothes were soaked.

He found Janalou in the hall. She looked terrific in one of the new outfits he had bought—red capris and a white blouse with short, red-trimmed sleeves and a red collar.

"I offered my other dry clothes to women until I emptied the suitcase," she said. "One lady is wearing my pajamas. She didn't care what she wore as long as they were dry."

"I did the same thing with men." Kree smiled before he glanced around at the crowd. "Let's go get a donut while there are still some left. That might be all we get to eat tonight."

They hurried to the table set up for refreshments.

"Hot chocolate never tasted so good," Kree said a few minutes later.

"Neither did a donut." Janalou bit into the pink-frosted one she had chosen.

"I'll share a bite of my chocolate donut if you'll give me a bite of yours," Kree said, winking.

"All right."

She licked her lips, and he wondered what it would be like to lick them himself. *Why had he kissed her cheek earlier when he'd wanted to kiss her tantalizing mouth? Would he get another chance?*

To get his mind off how tempting she looked, he said, "Let's go see if we can find a room to stay in tonight."

"Sounds good to me." When she shivered, he gave in to the urge to wrap his arm around her shoulders.

The museum worker who was trying to help people find lodgings said, "Sorry, everything's already filled up."

"If there are any cancellations, please let us know," Kree said. "My girlfriend had surgery a few nights ago, and she needs a bed to rest in."

The worker wrote their names down, and promised, "I'll let you know if anything comes up."

What little daylight had been outside disappeared and dark descended. The storm raged on. Parents and museum workers kept busy entertaining children, and trying to reassure everyone the museum was sturdily built and would withstand nature's abuse.

A few minutes before 9:00 p.m., the power went off.

Plunged into darkness, Janalou groped for Kree's hand. He pulled her close, and hugged her tightly against his side.

Museum workers found some flashlights, and staff members walked around, encouraging people to find a place to sit, and try to relax. Kree was sure part of their strategy included making sure no one ruined an exhibit or destroyed museum property.

He and Janalou found a vacant spot on the floor, sat down and leaned against the wall. He continued to hold her close, thinking he could spend all night, and longer, right there, holding her in his arms.

The rain finally slowed. But the wind gave no sign of blowing away.

A worker walked through the museum announcing, "Some roads are closed, and travel advisories are still in effect. If you're not from around here, you may want to settle down for the night. Those of you who asked for help finding a room, please come talk to me. A few more accommodations are now available."

Kree urged Janalou to her feet, and guided her back to the staff worker's desk.

"Other people are parting," Janalou whispered, "letting us pass, allowing us to be first in line. Do you think it's because we shared our dry clothes?"

Kree nodded and whispered back, "Probably."

The museum worker, an elderly woman, looked tired, and probably should have gone to bed long before. She covered the phone's mouthpiece with one hand before she said, "The Serendipity Bed & Breakfast has one room left, and it's walking distance from here."

"Terrific. Tell them we'll take it." Kree gave her his name again so the owner would hold the room for them. Seconds later, the museum worker handed him the address and phone number of the B and B.

"Should we change back to our wet shoes, and pack our dry ones in your suitcase?" he asked Janalou.

"Good idea, and if we roll our pant legs up and put our jackets on, that might help."

"Right."

A museum worker extended a flashlight. "You might need this to find your way."

"Thanks," Kree said.

"Thank you both for sharing your dry clothes with other people."

"Happy to do it," Kree said.

"Yes," Janalou agreed.

Kree was grateful for the room reservation, but not anxious to go back outside. Janalou was already shivering.

He opened the door and waited for her to exit.

They sloshed through water almost reaching their knees. With one hand, Kree carried his shared suitcase, having left Janalou's new pink one with the museum worker. With his other hand, he gripped her arm to steady her if she stumbled.

She grasped the flashlight with both hands. "I'm trying to keep the aim steady," she said, "but it's not easy with the parking lot turned into a river and the current going against us."

"Walk slowly," Kree advised. "We don't want to trip over something we can't see under the water."

"Right, "Janalou agreed, shivering again. "I've never slogged through water at night. Have you?"

"No." Kree tightened his grip on her elbow. "Keep your chin up, little one. We shouldn't have much farther to go."

Little one. Even spoken in a near shout, his words sounded like an endearment. He heard Janalou gasp, felt her tremble, and hoped she hadn't taken his comment seriously. Earlier he had called her 'sweetheart,' and hoped she hadn't taken that to heart, either. *He hadn't meant anything special when he'd used those words. But he'd never used them with another woman..*

He exhaled a deep breath, a bit surprised by the strange warmth heating his insides while the cold weather cooled his face.

Twelve

After what seemed like miles instead of blocks, they reached the B and B. Relief flooded Kree when he saw the welcoming light by the front door.

"I'm glad the power outage didn't extend this far," Janalou said.

"Me, too."

They climbed four steps to the top of the porch. "It feels good to step out of the water."

"Right," Kree said, ringing the doorbell.

A tall middle-aged woman opened the door. "Sorry. We only have one room left, and it's been promised to a man who's coming here from the Truman Library."

"That would be me," Kree said.

"Come in then." She opened the door wider, holding her flowered housecoat together when the wind tried to whip it open. Her long salt and pepper braid bounced over her shoulder as she slammed the door shut behind them and yanked a sturdy deadbolt home. "Never seen anything like this storm, have you?"

Kree and Janalou both shook their wet heads.

"Take off your shoes and leave them down here. Hang your coats on that." She pointed at an old-fashioned clothes tree. The woman reminded Kree of a drill sergeant he'd seen in a movie.

A few seconds later, she led them up the staircase. The stairs creaked a little, as though protesting their weight. Kree wondered how old the house was, worried if would weather the storm if it started to rain again, and wondered if they should have stayed at the museum until he remembered what Duke Guggles had said. Even though he had half-chastised him for spending nights in the same room with Janalou, the stocky man had suggested they spend the night in a B and B.

Kree's attention shifted to Janalou. He couldn't take his eyes off her shapely behind. The thought of being alone with her again in a cozy room wreaked havoc with his hormones.

In spite of wet feet and cold skin, desire rumbled through him. He wanted Janalou Madsen with a fierceness that startled him. He'd never felt this way. Never. Sexual hunger had often been a problem for some of his friends, but not him. He was too attuned to a faithful marriage like his parents and sisters had, and commitment to one woman to allow lusty thoughts to get the best of him.

At the door to their room, he thanked the proprietor, and followed Janalou inside.

Only one bed. Not twins as he had hoped. Not even a queen. A double. And it would be crowded unless he never got in it. But if he didn't get some sleep, he might not be fit to drive.

With Duke's bizarre warning still fresh in his mind, Kree knew he needed to be well-rested and alert before he drove anywhere again. The dire warning conjured up images he couldn't ignore. *If he had tried to drive in the rain, would he have been injured and maimed for life as Duke had insinuated?*

Feeling as though he might have escaped a terrible fate, he swallowed with difficulty. He didn't believe in other-worldly beings. So what was Duke? A guardian angel in the flesh? Someone assigned or destined to take care of Janalou?

The night had already been long. Kree feared it might be even longer. *It couldn't be filled with more tension than what they'd lived through during the last few hours, could it?*

He glanced at Janalou, wondering if he should let her set the tone for their sleeping arrangements or take charge himself.

Her gaze fixed on the inviting bed. She looked cold and the quiet in the room was so intense he heard her teeth chatter. "I wish I could soak in a hot bathtub before I climb under the covers," she said. "But the other guests are probably already in bed, and a bath or shower might disturb them."

"I wish you could get warm, too," he said.

A few seconds passed. Each one seemed like an eternity. Finally he said, "Come here."

She didn't hesitate. She walked right between his spread arms. "You're cold, too."

"But I'm not shaking like you are."

"I'm getting warmer, thanks to you."

"Looks like we might have to share a bed." Expecting her to argue, he was startled when she nodded, even though her head was resting against his chest.

"Maybe we could put pillows down the middle," she said. "I saw an old movie once where the hero and heroine did that. They called it the Wall of Jericho."

"That'll be like having two beds." *Two very narrow beds.*

"Twins," she agreed, but she didn't sound very enthusiastic.

He wasn't eager to be separated by a wall of pillows. The bed was barely big enough for two, and pillows would be like having a third body in bed with them. Besides, after holding her in the dark museum as well as now, he wanted to keep her close.

"Guess we should try to get some rest," she mumbled.

"You're right." He let go of her.

Someone knocked on the door. Janalou opened it.

"Feel free to take a shower, if you'd like," the tall woman who had let them in said. "You might need one to warm up after trekking through all that rain on the ground."

"Thanks."

"I put towels on the rack warmer in the bathroom," she said.

"We appreciate that." Kree's opinion of the drill sergeant owner edged upward, filled with gratitude as she walked away.

"Go take a shower," he said to Janalou. "I'll see if I can warm up the room." He walked to the window and bent to adjust the controls on the wall heater beneath it.

While Janalou was gone, he rolled his pant legs down, put on dry shoes and socks, then turned on the TV, keeping the volume low as he listened to the local news, all about the storm, blocked roads and empty cars.

Janalou returned with a big fluffy towel wound around her head.

"Wish I had my iPad."

"Where is it?"

"In the car."

"Don't you have your phone?"

"Yeah." He pulled it off his belt.

"Does it work in this storm?"

He punched buttons. "Yeah. Guess I should turn it off, though, to keep it charged," he said, then added, "Guess I'll go shower."

~ * ~

While he was gone, Janalou found an extra pillow in the small closet, and lined it, along with hers, down the middle of the bed. She felt silly but decided it might be good to stake out her space and leave Kree his.

When he returned, he looked so good she thought she might drool. Like her, he was still completely dressed. Unable to ignore her racing heart, she wondered if he might be nervous, too, when he paced the small room like a caged lion.

She couldn't help wondering what he looked like wearing nothing more than his pants. So far she had only seen him completely dressed.

Rubbing her wet hair with the towel, and concentrating on the news on TV, she perched on the only chair in the room and kept her eyes off Kree by sheer force of will.

Had Kree been blessed with calm insides? He sure looked calm right then.

She felt so nervous she wanted to hide in the closet, except there wasn't much room in it, and she'd likely feel claustrophobic.

The room was small and Kree so close she could smell his clean, soapy scent. Not only that, the reporter on TV was getting under her skin.

"Except for fire," the newscaster said, "floods are the most common and widespread natural disasters. And they're the number one killer related to weather in the U.S."

Goose bumps formed on Janalou's arms.

On TV, the outside reporter's coverage ended, and the screen changed to the weather man at the studio. While he was discussing the storm, the TV went blank and the lights blinked off.

"So much for being glad the power outage didn't affect this area," Kree grumbled.

Plunged into darkness for the second time that night, Janalou inhaled a startled gasp.

"Are you all right?" he asked.

"Yes," she said, her voice a mere whisper in the sudden blackness.

While her eyes adjusted to the dark, she fashioned the damp towel on her head into a turban, then moved to the edge of the bed. When she eased down, onto her back, she wondered if Kree would get in bed with her or sleep in the chair.

As she lay in the dark huddled under the covers, he stood by the window. His posture indicated he was brooding. Funny how she knew that, yet somehow she did.

Outside the wind howled and the rain started again, pelting the roof and hitting the windows.

Janalou yearned to be closer to Kree. She wanted him to hold her again. *But could he when she'd built a wall of pillows to keep them separated?*

~ * ~

Finally convinced he could control himself, especially if he kept remembering Janalou's recent surgery, Kree climbed in bed. The mattress dipped beneath his weight. He didn't disturb the covers, though. Instead he stayed on top, and lay very still. His side of the bed felt small, especially with pillows lined up between them.

Lightning flashed outside the window. A scream tore from Janalou's lips. Thunder sounded. More lightning followed. With the next crack of thunder, she jumped.

Surprised she hadn't fallen off her narrow side of the bed, Kree tossed the pillows aside and pulled her close.

"Good riddance to the Wall of Jericho," she said, laughing so hard her whole body shook.

Kree laughed too. Some of the emotions clamoring in his gut relaxed. "Shouldn't have been built in the first place."

"I'm glad we agree." She let out a soft sigh. "Thanks for holding me, Kree. Your touch makes me feel safe."

"You're welcome," he said, his voice a hoarse whisper.

She smelled good. Way too good. And having her in his arms felt great. Her warm breath fanned his cheeks, and he inhaled the clean scent of her skin. Her perfume was gone, washed away by her shower. He hadn't realized before how much he liked that perfume. He liked how she smelled now, too, though, a feminine scent unique to her, mixed with the same pleasant soap he had used in the shower.

He inhaled deeply before he said, "I'll have to remember nothing dull happens around you."

She laughed. "I could say the same thing about you. We really haven't had time to get bored."

His laughter joined hers, and more of his tension eased, although having her flesh next to his with only the bed covers separating them, made him hot. Very, very hot.

Still, he tried to relax. If he hoped to spend the rest of the night with her locked in his embrace, he had to force his lusty thoughts under control.

"Don't you want to get under the covers?" she asked.

He wanted that very much, but didn't think it would be wise. Before he could think of a reasonable excuse, she pulled away and invited him to get closer, warmer.

How he made it through the first hour in the same bed amazed him. He'd never been more tempted by a woman. Nor more determined not to pursue erotic desire. He would have felt that way even if he hadn't been warned off by Duke Guggles. Even if Janalou weren't still recovering from surgery.

Besides, she was too young for him, although his body didn't seem to know or care.

More than once his hormones threatened to get the best of him. Janilou was so tempting, the age difference didn't make a bit of sense.

An image of Duke flashed. *Was the man who favored green somehow responsible for the storm? Had he created it to delay their trip? If so, why?*

Telling himself that idea was impossible, Kree drew in a slow breath. It was also impossible that Duke had created some kind of fog to enclose them at the museum, but it had happened. *Was the short man trying to prove Bethany wasn't his soul mate?* If so, it wouldn't work. Kree firmed his hold around Janalou just the same. Tonight she needed him. It would be cruel to release her, and let her feel unsafe. At least that's what he tried to convince himself. It didn't totally work. She had gotten under his skin. And he didn't want that to change. At least not for a while.

~ * ~

Janalou awakened from a dream about a heavy rain storm and Duke Guggles. Unable to recall much more than that, she enjoyed the feeling of Kree still holding her close. Her thoughts turned to the past, and her experience with guys. In high school, her good grades had earned her the reputation of being nerdy, and although she liked boys, most of them had labeled her a geek and steered clear of her. A few who got good grades like her had asked for dates. Some had even kissed her after she went out with them. But she hadn't felt a strong connection with any of them and rarely accepted a second date.

Tony had been her only real boyfriend. Like Kree, he didn't seem to choose his friends to impress his peers.

Grateful for all the good times she'd had with Tony, she wondered where he was, what he was doing, if he had another girlfriend, if he might be married, if he still intended to graduate from law school.

As she lay in the dark, Kree's deep even breathing had a soothing effect. She couldn't help wondering if he had a girlfriend or two at home waiting for him. Her heart quailed at the image of him with another woman. Or women. But the pleasant sound of his breathing lulled her back to sleep.

Pounding rain awakened Janalou the second time. She stared up at the ceiling and saw a skylight she hadn't noticed before. The room lay in shadows. Still snuggled in Kree's arms, a sense of contentment stole through her. Being held was the safest and most comfortable she'd felt since before Belle entered her life.

Kree shifted. Every inch of Janalou's flesh reacted. She could happily spend a week or two right here in this room, alone with him. Knowing that was impossible, she stirred. He withdrew his arms. She felt strangely alone when he slid off the bed, and went to the window.

When he parted the curtains, she caught a glimpse of the dark overcast sky and steady downpour. He turned, and Janalou's breath caught in her throat. With his curly black hair tousled, and his eyes still sleepy, he looked like he belonged back in bed.

He flipped the light switch. "Looks like the power's still off."

"Maybe they have a portable radio downstairs," she said. "If so, we can listen to the news down there."

"Good idea." He grabbed his dry shoes, put them on, then left, giving her privacy to prepare for the day.

She put on her shoes, applied make-up to cover her bruises, and joined him downstairs. Other guests were clustered in the breakfast room, all anxious to hear news about the storm.

"Sorry we can't cook breakfast," the female owner said. "We have cold cereal, bananas and juice. Take whatever you want." She motioned at the sideboard.

Her husband, also tall with thick graying hair, cleared his throat. "I'll turn up the volume on the portable radio so everyone can hear the news."

"Today's news is good and bad," the radio announcer said. "The good news is major roads no longer resemble rivers, therefore, driving shouldn't be as hazardous as it was last night. The bad news is the area near the Truman Museum suffered severe damage, and the storm in that part of the city doesn't show any signs of letting up any time soon. Travel advisories are still in effect. People are cautioned not to go out unless it's an absolute necessity—a medical emergency. Manhole covers came off on a number of streets, and traffic jams are expected. Near the Truman Museum, abandoned cars have already created problems."

"Looks like you might have your house full for another night," one guest said.

Both owners nodded, their expressions somber. "We have books, magazines, games and crossword puzzles to help keep you occupied today. They're in the living room. Sorry we don't have a generator, but we can make sandwiches for lunch, and we'll find something for supper, too, even if the power isn't restored."

All of the guests mumbled their thanks. Some returned their attention to the small radio while others began to fill cereal bowls, and juice glasses and started to eat.

Throughout the dreary storm-filled day, Kree and Janalou took advantage of the books and magazines in the downstairs living room. They also helped half a dozen other guests put a thousand-piece jigsaw puzzle together on a card table set up in the spacious room.

Around noon when the electricity was restored, everyone kept close to the big screen TV, watching and listening to the local news.

~ * ~

"It's been a lazy day," Kree said that night when they were alone in the small guest room they shared.

Janalou smiled. "Yes, I'm more relaxed than I expected to be after a day cooped up with a bunch of strangers."

"Resting all day was probably good for you."

"It was. I feel stronger tonight than I have since before my surgery."

"Good." She looked better as well. The bruises beneath her eyes were still purple but she had camouflaged them with make-up, and the swelling on her nose and face had disappeared. *When?* Kree couldn't remember because after the first day he had looked beyond her injuries. She had a perfect nose, he decided. Her figure was kind of perfect, too, and her body fit perfectly with his. He knew from holding all through last night.

"Do you think we'll be able to travel tomorrow?" she asked.

"Yeah." But he was in no hurry to get home. He wanted her black eyes completely gone before she met his family and friends

He walked over to the small window, but couldn't see anything outside except the dark because the back yard had no lights, and the moon and stars were hidden behind clouds.

With his back to Janalou, he saw her reflection in the dark glass panes, watching him. Behind those exotic brown eyes and that mane of glorious black hair, he sensed an aura of mystery. *What secrets did she hide? How could he discover them? Why did he want to try?*

With somewhat of a jolt, he realized it would be easy to fall for her. He checked his thoughts right there, unwilling to let them wander any farther. Relaxing his guard would make it more difficult to get through another night in the same bed.

He broke eye contact in the window, relieved when she said, "I'd like to finish this book, in case we leave in the morning." Sitting on the chair by the door, she opened the one she had borrowed from downstairs and started to read.

"I think I'll go take a shower," he said.

She nodded without looking up.

After his shower, Kree turned his phone back on and called his other sister, Sirena. He answered her questions about the storm, relieved she didn't ask about his traveling companion. Maybe Jocelyn hadn't said anything.

"Looks like my trip will be delayed longer than I anticipated when I talked to Jocelyn."

Sirena laughed. "I'll pass your news along, and don't worry about being out of the office, Kree. We miss you, but the business won't fall down around our feet without you. The only thing we care about is your safety."

"Thanks." He hung up, grinning, and wondering how much longer it would take for Janalou's facial bruises to heal. A few more days might work wonders.

In the meantime, he'd find a way to broach the subject of a pretend engagement. If she didn't agree, he didn't know what he'd do. He'd already indicated to Jocelyn that they were more than casual friends.

Thirteen

The B & B owners cooked a big breakfast of bacon, sausage, toast, eggs and fruit.

"Coffee never tasted better," Kree said.

"Neither has tea," Janalou replied, smiling before she took another sip.

After they ate, Kree and Janalou headed toward the stairs, but paused when a loud knock sounded on the front door.

As the proprietor opened it, Janalou spied people from the museum, the ones she and Kree had given their dry clothes to. A few stood on the small porch, but most crowded the sidewalk. Every person had something clutched in his or her hands. One person carried her new pink suitcase.

"We have some things for two of your guests," one lady said. "Their names are Janalou and Kree."

Kree took her hand, and they walked closer to the door.

"Hi," the woman who had apparently agreed to act as spokesperson said. "We're returning your clothes. Ours dried yesterday, and we brought gifts for you as well."

"It wasn't necessary to bring us anything," Janalou said. "We were happy to share what we had with you."

"We appreciate that, and now we're happy to repay your kindness."

"Yes," a man chimed in, followed by a chorus of others.

"Come in," the owner invited, "and let's see what you brought."

Soon the expansive living room was filled with people. Janalou felt like she was at a birthday party or opening presents on Christmas morning. A variety of gifts were stashed inside plastic bags that bore the museum's logo. Most were items she suspected had been bought from the museum's gift shop. But there were envelopes with money in them, too... ten, twenty, and fifty dollar bills.

Surprised by the strangers' generosity, Janalou fought to control her emotions. There really were some wonderful people in the world.

"Thank you," she said, again and again.

"You're more than welcome," people took turns repeating.

When the well-wishers finally decided to leave, she and Kree stepped outside with them and waved goodbye.

"The water level has gone down considerably," she said, relieved.

"Yeah," Kree agreed. "I'll go get the car. I think it's safe to resume our journey."

She flashed a smile. "I'll go upstairs and collect our things."

"Great. I'll take some of the gifts and your case with me now."

"Fine. See you in a few." Mere days ago, she would have feared he might not return, but now she didn't have a single doubt that he would.

~ * ~

With not much traffic on the roads, a hush filled the air, as though humans were loath to come outside and see the damage.

As he drove, Kree turned up the volume on the car radio. The newscaster announced the storm had wreaked havoc all over the city. Light poles were down, as were street signs.

He and Janalou saw the devastation first hand. "Wow," she said. "Not only were tree limbs and branches broken off and scattered across lawns and roads, entire trees were blown over." She pointed at exposed roots.

Kree glanced out the side window. Oversized gnarly roots, washed clean by the rain, poked out of the ground, many aimed up at the still-gray sky. Parts of roofs had blown off, and windows were broken in homes and office buildings alike.

"The National Guard has been called in to control looting," the newscaster announced, "And builders are already in demand to the repair damages. It will take construction crews months to repair and rebuild."

"Doesn't surprise me," Janalou said. "Look at all the debris. The storm scattered it everywhere."

"Right," Kree agreed, recalling Duke's warning not to drive in the storm.

They reached the I-70 freeway entrance, and left Independence at a slow crawl, eventually gaining speed.

"Are you feeling okay?" Kree asked, after they'd been on the road about an hour.

"Yes. Actually I feel good. It's hard to believe I had surgery a few nights ago."

"Yeah," Kree said, remembering how difficult it had been to keep his hands from wandering during both nights in the same bed. "You'll tell me if you don't feel up to traveling, or if you need to stop, won't you?"

"Yes. Of course." She smiled. "This trip is turning into a real adventure. Educational, too."

"More than that. It's like some force in the universe is trying to delay our trip, and keep us together."

Janalou laughed. "You can't believe the storm had anything to do with us."

Kree grinned. "Right now I might be convinced of almost anything." His thoughts veered off in a different direction because he didn't want to dwell on the possibility that his time with her might be limited as Duke had insinuated.

"The other day you asked about my family. Should I tell you about them now? "

"Yes. Please do."

"My parent's names are Helen and Max. My two sisters are Jocelyn and Sirena. They're both older than I, and each has two kids, a boy and a girl."

"Two nieces and two nephews. How nice." She turned her smile to him. "Where does Reina fit in your life?"

"She worked for my parents for a number of years. She had a daughter named Bethany, and I ignored her until I turned sixteen. Then one day I realized she had grown up, and she was gorgeous. We dated, fell in love, and during my first year of college, I asked her to marry me."

"What happened?"

"We decided to wait until I graduated, but my parents said she wasn't good enough for me. Before I found out and had a chance to convince her their opinion didn't matter, she stepped out in front of a bus and was killed."

"That's terrible," Janalou sympathized, and he heard the concern and empathy in her voice. One more thing to admire.

"Yeah," he agreed. "It is."

"How long ago—did it happen?"

"Three years."

"I lost Mama—my mother, three years ago," she said, "so I know how difficult it is to lose someone you love."

He thought she might not continue the conversation, but then she said, "Do you still love Bethany?"

He nodded. "I always will."

"Do you ever date?"

"Yeah. But I'm not serious about anyone. I don't know if I ever will be. Losing Bethany took a lot out of me."

"I can imagine," Janalou said. "I marvel at your devotion. You're an amazing man."

"No, I'm not," he disagreed, uncomfortable with her praise. "There are a lot of guys like me."

"I haven't met very many."

~ * ~

They rode in silence until Kree said, "Tell me more about your life. Do you have a boyfriend?"

"Not anymore. I did, but he moved away." Janalou told him about Tony. But not about Papa and Belle.

She was ashamed to admit they both had drinking problems, and she had endured abuse from Belle for a whole year. His parents might not have thought Bethany was good enough for him, but she knew she wasn't, and didn't have to be told.

Hopefully she could work with him and meet his family. If she used Margie's deceased cousin's social security number, Papa and Belle couldn't find her or force her to return to Spartanburg. Although she'd soon be eighteen, she still feared Belle might find a way to make her life miserable.

In spite of being glad she had finally left, a wave of homesickness washed through her when she thought about not seeing Margie again. Even though she was gone for the summer, Janalou missed her and probably always would.

She straightened her shoulders, reminding herself she had new friends—Reina, Cherilyn and her two children, plus Duke, who had promised to help with her struggles. How strange, she thought, that he claimed he wanted to help her, but he'd let Kree stay behind instead of staying himself.

More thoughts intruded. *Was Duke in California? Or had he somehow managed to locate them in St. Louis? Had she seen him up in the arch? If so, was he following them for a sinister reason? Or to watch over and protect her as he had indicated?*

Deep down she wanted to believe the latter, and chastised herself for even thinking the jolly-looking man, who really did resemble a plump leprechaun, might be a threat in any way. But after her experiences with Belle, she didn't find it easy to trust strangers.

Why then did she feel so safe with Kree? A few days ago, she hadn't even known he existed. Now he stood at the center of her world.

~ * ~

After lunch she said, "We could take turns driving."

"Works for me." Kree jingled the car keys at her. "Do you feel up to it?"

Excited, she smiled. "I do."

"Sorry." He pulled the keys back. "I didn't put you on the rental agreement. I didn't even think about it."

She tried to hide her disappointment as he unlocked the car.

And then he drove. For miles and miles, across eastern Kansas, the Sunflower State, through Topeka, toward Salina.

Because Belle had hijacked the keys to their second car and squashed her driving privileges, Janalou hadn't driven for a whole year, and she longed to be behind the steering wheel again. If she made enough money, maybe she could buy her own car.

Pleased with that idea, her new life stretched ahead, inviting and welcome. She'd have to take the California driving test, but she needed a license with her new name anyway, especially since she'd left her other one behind. Her stomach clenched with that thought. Thankfully Kree hadn't asked if she had a driver's license. If he did, she'd have to tell the truth. She didn't intend to compound her guilt with more lies.

Without a lot to claim her attention along the freeway, she and Kree talked almost non-stop.

Enjoying their easy camaraderie, she learned more about him, his family, his friends and his work.

After a while he said, "You know what sounds good?"

"No. What?"

"Ice cream. If we pull off the freeway in Salina we can stretch our legs, and find a place to buy a treat. Are you up for ice cream?"

"Yes." She flashed a grin. "Absolutely."

She fiddled with his phone and found a Dairy Queen.

When they arrived, he ordered a Blizzard and she ordered a peanut buster parfait.

"Would you like to sit inside or out?" he asked, hiking a dark brow.

"Outside. I don't think it's too hot, do you?"

"No. We've been cooped up all day. Fresh air sounds good." With his free hand, he opened the door and waited for her to exit.

"This is so good, it's decadent," she said, licking thick chocolate off her plastic spoon a few minutes later.

"Probably has about a gazillion calories."

She laughed. "I refuse to worry about calories while we're on vacation."

"Me, too." A grin covered his handsome face "Or high cholesterol," he added, still grinning.

As they enjoyed their treats, he said, "Remember when you thought you saw Duke Guggles in the arch?"

She nodded. "I must have been hallucinating."

"I'm not so sure."

"Why?"

"I saw him at the Truman Library. He told me about the storm and warned me not to drive in it. Said if I did, we might be in an accident and he could save you but wasn't sure he could save me, too."

"Did he say you might get killed?"

"No." Kree shook his head for emphasis. "He said it wasn't my time to die, but he implied I might be crippled for the rest of my life if I didn't heed his advice."

"He's a strange man."

"Yes," Kree agreed. "While we were talking in the museum, some kind of fog or mist surrounded us. I think he created it."

Goose bumps raised on Janalou's arms and the back of her neck. "When we were on the bus, he said no one else could hear our conversation, and he showed me a card that said 'leprechaun service rendered free.'"

Kree wrinkled his forehead. "Do you think he is a leprechaun?"

"I haven't decided. I don't know anything about them, but I did wonder if he's some kind of magical being. Maybe an angel—a guardian angel, perhaps."

"An angel?"

She nodded. "He said he was on the bus to help me. But if that's true, why didn't he stay behind with me?"

"Probably because I volunteered, and asked him to make sure Reina and Cherilyn and her children made it safely to Lodi."

"I see." Still confused, she wondered if Duke were some kind of extraordinary being or if she and Kree had both hallucinated.

But she was glad they had discussed him.

Back on the freeway, they passed a billboard. Janalou read it out loud, "Friends are angels who lift us to our feet when our wings have trouble remembering how to fly."

"Wouldn't surprise me if Duke put that up there," Kree said.

"Me either," she mumbled, beginning to think anything might be possible, even some kind of supernatural being who called himself a leprechaun.

"I'd like to stop early tonight, if that's okay with you," Kree said.

"Of course it is." She'd half expected him to suggest driving late to get as close to home as possible, but she didn't want their journey to end until it was absolutely necessary.

She glanced at the spiral-bound notebook she'd bought to keep track of their expenses, along with the plans they'd made, hoping he wouldn't suggest ditching any of them.

They had started to learn the nicknames of the states they were seeing, and he said, "Colorado's our next state. What's it called?"

"Centennial State," she said, having already looked up the ones they had and would drive through.

"I know what Utah is, do you?"

"Yes. The Beehive State. And Nevada is called the Silver State."

"California is the Golden State."

"I know because the Gold Rush helped establish it as a state. I read that in a history book. Otherwise the growth would likely have been much slower."

Kree flashed another grin. "Right."

~ * ~

The next few days passed almost in a blur.

They did and saw so many things in Colorado and kept so busy, Janalou was exhausted by nightfall. Kree said he was, too.

On their fourth night there, they stopped at a cafe near the freeway in Grand Junction. It was called 'Starvin Marvin's.'

Janalou ordered soup and salad. Kree ordered the special: chicken, mashed potatoes, gravy and corn.

"This cross-country journey is the most fun I've ever had," she said while they waited for their food. "You said your first year in college was the best year of your life. Well, this summer is my best one. Thanks for making it happen, Kree."

Looking uncomfortable with her praise, he asked, "Did you ever go on vacation with your parents?"

"Yes. Every year before Mama died." Then realizing she might be admitting too much, she clammed up, not wanting to lie, or explain any more.

She had enjoyed trips with her parents, but this one was very different. The first time she had traveled so far. And her first adventure with a man. She rated it higher than anything she'd ever done, although she wished she hadn't admitted that to Kree.

While they ate he said, "We've traveled a lot of miles."

She frowned. "Are you taking too much time off work?"

He shook his curly-haired head. "I can take as much time as I want." His wink made her heart do a strange flutter thing. "That's one of the benefits of working in real estate, and being self-employed."

"I'm sure it must be. I'm looking forward to meeting the people you work with, and hopefully working with them."

"You'll meet my family." He pulled his wallet from his back pocket and flipped it open. "I have photos, if you'd like to see them."

"I do." Janalou studied each one before she said, "You've made me feel as though I already know your family. I hope they'all like me."

He grinned. "I do, and I'm sure they will, too."

Her heart did another funny flip. She told it to behave. Unfortunately it didn't obey. And that's when she realized she had fallen in love.

The admission knocked the breath from her chest.

She glanced away, hoping he wouldn't see what she might not be able to conceal. *When had it happened?*

To her relief, Kree set money on the table for a tip, picked up the check, and stood. At the cash register, the cashier looked at their slip, and said, "It's already been paid." She handed the bill back to Kree.

"Who paid it?"

The buxom cashier shrugged. "I don't know."

"I'm sure a mistake has been made," Kree said. "Please charge our food to my credit card. I don't want to cheat you or another customer."

Once again the cashier shrugged, but she took his credit card and processed the transaction.

Janalou couldn't help being impressed. In addition to all the other qualities she admired, Kree had integrity.

Back in the car, they drove to Green River, Utah. After Kree filled the gas tank, they found a motel.

"We had another full day," she said, flopping on one of the double beds before she kicked off her shoes.

"Have I worn you out?" Kress asked, concern in his gorgeous blue eyes as he sat beside her.

She shook her head, shoving her long hair behind her shoulders after it fell across her face. "I love everything we've seen and done, and it was okay to drive today. It's difficult to believe how many miles we've covered since we left Indiana."

They sat so close his leg touched her from hip to ankle, making her body tingle with awareness. He reached out and lifted a strand of her long hair.

"I've wondered how this feels," he said, his voice low and husky.

Enjoying his closeness, she reached up and fingered a lock of his curly hair. "I've had the same thought about yours." Did she look as flustered as she felt?

Suddenly, to her surprise, he drew her into his arms and kissed her.

Janalou melted against him. For days she had wondered what it would be like. Now she knew. Wonderful. Exciting. Thrilling.

She wrapped her arms around his neck and kissed him back, amazed at her boldness, stunned because the kiss felt so good. So right. So perfect.

As far as she was concerned, he ended it way too soon.

"I don't know how I've resisted doing that," he murmured, his gaze warm, his voice husky as he stared into her eyes.

Her mind went fuzzy, and she saw him through a haze. "Would you—a...?"

"What?"

"Mind doing it again?"

"Only a fool would say no." He tightened his arms around her, and claimed her mouth again.

Lips locked, they fell back on the bed, turning to face each other in a motion so smooth it seemed as though they had done it a dozen times.

Her heart was soaring, lifting her up, taking her away from the ordinary world into the sublime.

Without conscious thought, she molded her curves against the contours of his strong, lean body.

And still the kiss went on. Janalou had never experienced anything like it. His mouth tasted marvelous. Wonderful. Joy pounded through her entire body, making her want more. Guilt descended with that realization. If they got any more carried away, she might not be able to stop.

Sanity returned like a demon. She pulled away. "I think we'd better stop while we can," she choked out.

"You're right." Kree agreed, his eyes heavy lidded with passion. "And I think I need a cold shower."

He rolled off the bed, and headed for the bathroom.

Fourteen

The next day, as they drove across southern Utah on I-70, Janalou said, "The scenery's fantastic."

"Right."

Every mile was filled with spectacular landscapes, fascinating deserts, deep canyons with sheer cliffs and unique red rock formations.

Eventually Kree turned south, leaving the freeway to visit Capital Reef National Park, some sixty miles away.

"Look at that mountain," he said when they neared the park. "Gorgeous, isn't it?"

"Sure is," she agreed, consulting a brochure. "The ridge is a hundred miles long, and was thrust up millions of years ago. The strata folded back on themselves, trapping water in the process. It's called a waterpocket fold."

"The color's fantastic. Vermillion, I think."

"Or cinnamon," she added, staring at the dark red sandstone.

After they visited the visitor center, they drove around, stopping whenever the mood struck, strolling along easy trails, listening to tour guides, learning about storms that had changed rivers, trails and roads, and making more memories Janalou knew she would never forget.

The lack of crowds added to the experience. Most places they visited had teemed with tourists, so it was a nice change of pace.

The next day they headed north, along highway 89, a scenic byway.

Janalou glanced through the notes in her paper notebook, then consulted maps and brochures they had collected from visitor centers. Kree's new iPad had proven invaluable, and they had used it to map out their entire journey, which included two more major stops—Salt Lake and Lake Tahoe.

In a few days they would arrive in Lodi.

She felt anxious and nervous. But Kree had assured her she already had a job, so that was one thing she didn't have to worry about.

They had been together more than a week. Each day, Janalou had fallen more deeply in love. *Would Kree ever kiss her again?*

She was beginning to fear he wouldn't. He hadn't said a word about their first kiss. Neither had she. Every time she thought about their passionate kisses in Grand Junction, her heart picked up speed.

If he kissed her again, would she be able to stop before they went too far?

Tony had never pushed her for intimacy. She'd always been glad. Dear Mama had warned her about getting sexually involved before she was ready, encouraged her not to rush, and assured her there would be plenty of years to enjoy sexual activities when she was ready. *Was she now?*

Most of her girlfriends had slept with more than one guy, but Janalou hadn't been tempted until Belle came into her life. For a short time she had considered getting pregnant just to upset the miserable hag. Good sense had prevailed though. Sex wasn't a weapon to be used for selfish purposes. Besides, she hadn't really had a candidate in mind, and Belle had kept such close tabs on her she'd rarely had a chance to be alone with a guy. If she had found one, she would have had to sneak out, probably through her window late at night, and that went against her grain. So instead she had planned to disappear. And she had. Pleased that she didn't think about Papa and Belle nearly as often, she looked out the window, marveling again at the changing scenery. The red rock formations along I-70 yesterday had been spectacular, but the tall green mountains were equally as beautiful in an entirely different way.

~ * ~

In Salt Lake, they checked into a room at Little America before they drove to Temple Square. As they walked along a wide sidewalk, admiring well-tended flowers and shrubs, Janalou said, "The grounds are so beautiful they feel kind of sacred."

Kree nodded. "Sometimes I'm surprised our thoughts are so in tune."

"I read that the Mormons are a cult," she said.

"I have to disagree. Some of my best friends are Mormons, and I've been to a lot of their church meetings and parties, even on some scout trips with the guys. They're Christians and they believe in the Bible, just as other Christians do. In addition, they're very focused on the family."

"Sounds like a durn good church, although I understand their religion is strict."

"It is a good church. Do you have a religious preference?

"I was raised as a Baptist."

"I've heard Baptists are even stricter than Mormons."

"Will I get to meet your Mormon friends?"

"Sure, if you'd like to."

"I would. What are they like?"

"Like us, you and me. Jason, my best friend, is a great guy. He doesn't smoke or drink or cuss or swear. He spent two years on a mission in Canada, teaching or preaching the gospel to complete strangers."

"Has he ever preached his religion to you?

Kree shook his head. "He offered to tell me more about it, but I haven't taken advantage of his offer. I admit though, that when

Bethany died, his church helped Reina arrange the funeral and they couldn't have been more wonderful."

A short time later, Kree said, "I'm ready for dinner. There's a restaurant across the street, at the top of what used to be the Hotel Utah and is now headquarters of the Mormon Church."

"Is it indoors?"

He nodded, "Outside, too. Would you like to eat under an umbrella?"

"Yes. Definitely."

~ * ~

After they ate, Kree lifted his hand and touched the fading bruises beneath Janalou's dark exotic eyes. "How did you get these?"

Although she flinched, she answered with what he thought was the truth. "Someone hit me."

He didn't think she had really bumped into a door. "A guy?"

"No."

"Not a man?" he rephrased his question. Wanting to know more he probed with his eyes, forcing her to maintain eye contact by reaching for her chin.

"No," she said again. "Not a guy or a man."

"If one had, I'd be willing to go beat the living daylights out of him."

As he had hoped, she smiled. "It was a woman. A very mean woman."

"Is she related to you?"

"No. Not by blood."

He had heard about abuse given by people who worked at orphanages and senior care centers but he didn't understand that kind of behavior. *Did hurting others make some people feel big and strong?*

"Are they—my bruises—black eyes the reason you decided to take our time driving to California?" she asked.

"Part of the reason, yes."

She licked her lips and squinted against the setting sun. "What are your others?"

"Let see," he held up his pointer finger. "First, I wanted you to have time to recover from your surgery before you start work." He raised his index finger. "Second, I wanted to get to know you better. Third, I wanted to see parts of the country I hadn't seen. I thought you might enjoy that, too."

He lowered his fingers and reached for her hand. "Are those enough reasons, or should I go on?"

She smiled. "They're enough. You're a very thoughtful man. And thanks for offering to retaliate on my behalf. I haven't had anyone offer to stick up for me for a long time."

He squeezed her fingers gently. "You have someone now."

"Thanks. I appreciate that."

Kree smiled. He liked her drawl, the musical lilt of her Southern voice, the twang he could listen to for a long time without becoming bored.

He was relieved she had said a woman had hit her, glad she hadn't run away from an abusive boyfriend or a husband. Apparently she had left an orphanage that had hired an abusive employee.

~ * ~

At breakfast early the next morning, Kree said, "I think we should spend another day here."

"Why? Is there something special you'd like to do?"

He nodded his curly-haired head. "I have a few suggestions."

Janalou's heart filled with gratitude and love. "What are they?"

"We could go to Hogel Zoo, or visit the planetarium, or go to Lagoon—that's an amusement park. Let's see, what else?"

He plowed his hand through his hair, as though concentrating. "Capitol's are always a popular tourist attraction. So is the "This is the Place" monument up by the zoo. There are historical museums to see like Brigham Young's home. Utah also has three Olympic places to visit." He paused again. "Should I continue?"

"No. Everything you've mentioned sounds fantastic."

"You're easy to please."

She winked. "I'm glad you think so."

"How about going to Lagoon? An amusement park is different from anything we've done so far."

"Great. Sounds like fun."

"If you didn't have that recent incision, I'd suggest buying swimsuits."

"Why?"

He grinned. "In addition to amusement park rides, there's a beach water park and a small pioneer museum village."

She hiked her brows. "An actual village?"

He nodded. "Complete with log cabins and some small shops."

"I'd love to see them."

"Then we will." He licked his lips.

She licked hers too, tasted maple syrup from her French toast and wondered if he did, too.

"Lagoon doesn't open until about eleven," he said. "We could check out the Pioneer Memorial Museum first, if you'd like to see it."

"I would."

"Are you sure you feel up having such a full day?"

"Absolutely."

"We should get started. The museum opens at nine."

"Maybe we have time to go look at swimsuits first. Do you think a discount store might be open this early?"

"Probably."

She grinned. "Even if I don't get in the water, you can. I can wade, or lie on the sand or a lounge."

"Works for me." He stood up and smiled. "Let's go."

~ * ~

At the pioneer museum, Janalou said, "This place is fantastic. It's like we've just walked back into history."

"I'm glad you're impressed."

"It's huge. Did you know there were six floors?"

He nodded. "We don't have to see all of them."

"Yes, we do. I don't want to miss anything."

Kree winked, and she asked, "Have you been here before?"

"No."

As they studied artifacts from the pioneers who had migrated two thousand miles across the plains from Nauvoo, Illinois, to seek religious freedom, Janalou identified with them and their desire to find a new place to live where they could be free from persecution.

Some items were a surprise. In addition to things needed for everyday life, she saw remarkably ornate decorative objects. A few were as small and delicate as crystal salt and pepper shakers, others as large and cumbersome as heavy pianos.

"It's hard to believe some of these things were carted all the way across the continent by oxcart."

Kree nodded, studying a furniture display. "Pioneer craftsmen were astonishingly adaptable. This display says they used material available in Utah to make pine furniture and painted it to look like expensive wood."

"That dresser looks like mahogany."

"And that table looks like walnut."

About an hour later, Janalou said, "Thanks for suggesting we come here, Kree. I enjoyed every minute."

"You don't have to keep thanking me. I'm enjoying myself, too." He raised his hand, and touched her cheek. "Are you hungry?"

"No. Are you?"

He shook his head. "I thought we might wait and eat at Lagoon."

"Sounds good to me."

As he drove north on I-15 toward Farmington, she asked, "Have you ever seen where the railroads were joined at Promontory Point in eighteen sixty-nine?"

"No. Not yet, but I hope to someday."

"Me, too." Would she ever return to Utah? She hoped so, but felt certain she'd never enjoy herself as much as she was enjoying this trip with Kree.

~ * ~

Seeing Janalou in a swimsuit shook Kree to his core. She had a fantastic body. He thought he had prepared himself for the onslaught, but his imagination hadn't come close to the realty of actually seeing her bare arms, shoulders, and legs all at the same time. Although the one piece suit was modest, it exposed enough cleavage to make him swallow. Twice. Then again.

"Do you swim?" he asked when he could speak.

"Yes. I had lessons years ago. Started when I was about five. Mama didn't want me to be afraid of the water, so she took me swimming often."

"You're not going to swim today, are you?"

"No. I don't think I should, but I'd like to wade."

She eased into the cool water slowly, up to her knees, then turned to walk sideways.

Kree flattened his body and swam behind her, glad to have the exercise and admiring her backside when he paused.

"You're a good swimmer," she said, after turning back to watch him. "Like a trained athlete, you barely make a ripple. Have you ever won any swimming contests?"

"No, I never competed in swimming." He stood up, enjoying the heat of the warm sun. "I competed in race and track."

"You're a runner?"

"I was, in high school and college."

She flicked her gaze down to his chest, then lower to his legs. "No wonder you have such an athletic build. You must have run a lot of miles."

"I did, and I won enough races to get a full scholarship to Stanford.

"Did you enjoy all your years at college?"

He raised his hand to shield his eyes from the sun. "Yes. In some ways they were the best years of my life." He studied her a few moments, then asked, "What were your best years."

She lowered her gaze to the water. "I don't think I've had them yet."

He lowered his hand, and used his fingers to lift her chin. "Maybe you'll have them now."

"I hope I do." Her tremulous smile made him want to pull her close, hold her for a long, long time, and promise that her future would be good. He resisted the temptation, but only because children splashing water nearby helped remind him they were in public.

Sometime later, they dressed, went on rides, snacked on popcorn and ice cream in lieu of lunch, toured the small pioneer village, ate dinner and ended up staying until Lagoon closed at 11:00 pm.

"Are you tired?"Kree asked as he drove back toward the hotel.

She turned her head to him. "Pleasantly so. How about you?"

"I feel the same way." He kept his eyes straight ahead, focused on the freeway.

"Bed will feel good tonight."

"Yeah," he agreed, and then wanting more time with her, he said, "If you'd like, we could stay another day."

"I'd love to, but can you take more time off?"

"Sure. I'm self-employed, remember?"

"If we stay, what will we do?"

"We could drive up to Park City and see the Olympic Park where athletes trained for the two thousand two bobsled, luge and ski jumping. I understand visitors are treated to a seventy mile-per-hour bobsled ride, zipline rides, Quicksilver alpine slide rides and there's also an Olympic museum."

"How far is Park City from Salt Lake?"

"About an hour."

"Will it take all day?"

"I doubt it."

"Maybe we could spend some time in the afternoon at the pool at the hotel," she said.

"Or we could go see the Olympic Oval in West Valley. It's still an athletic training center with public skating, speed and figure instruction, soccer, curling and hockey games. There's also the, "This is the Place State Park, a monument dedicated to the arrival of the pioneers in eighteen forty-seven."

"We could probably spend a week here and still not see everything," she said.

"That's true of lots of places."

She nodded, and he conjured memories of all the things they had seen so far, and the things he had most enjoyed. Holding her close in the St. Louis arch, and kissing her in Green River topped the list.

~ * ~

"What's your favorite experience so far?" he asked the next night, after a seafood dinner. They were walking back to the rented car, and she looked up at the sky, still light due to daylight saving time.

All the things they had shared flashed through her mind—the physical ones more vibrant than what they'd seen and done. She would always love the precious memories, just as she would always love him in secret. "I can't say," she finally answered. "It's too difficult to pick only one. I've loved every activity."

"Except your surgery," he reminded her.

"No, I didn't love that, but I did appreciate getting rid of the pain."

"Do you still have any?"

"Just occasional twinges if I move too fast."

"Maybe we tried to do too much too soon."

She heard the concern in his voice and smiled at him. "I'm not overdoing, Kree. I'll tell you when, if I think I am. Please don't worry about me."

"It's impossible not to worry. You looked so ill that night before we got to the hospital, I thought you might die."

"I thought so too, but I didn't. I'm very much alive, and I intend to stay that way for years and years."

"I sure hope you do."

~ * ~

They slept late the next day and drove to Wendover, Nevada, just over the Utah border in the afternoon.

"I'm afraid there isn't much to see here except casinos," Kree said. "It's still a long drive to Lake Tahoe, but we can make it there tomorrow."

"We've done more than I could have hoped for."

"If this were a real vacation, we'd have done much more."

The old adage, *'Beggars can't be choosers,'* came to mind, but Janalou kept quiet. So far he hadn't let her pay for anything, and she was feeling more indebted all the time. Someday, somehow, she would find a way to reimburse him for her share of their trip as well as her medical expenses. In the back of her notebook she was keeping track so she'd know how much she owed him.

They checked into a room at the Peppermill, ate at the buffet in the casino's restaurant on the main floor, and went to bed early.

Janalou's sleep was disturbed by a jumbled dream about Papa and Belle. Someone had reported her missing and the police went to their home, found blood on the floor and in her bedroom, and arrested them on suspicion of murder. The sluggish dream wouldn't end, and she struggled in her sleep, fighting images that wouldn't let go.

When she finally managed to shake the dream away and wake up, she was perspiring, and shaking so badly the bed shook. She had to find out if there was any validity to the nightmare or if her own anxiety had caused it.

Relieved to see daylight through the slit in the drapes, she got out of bed. After she showered and dressed, she said, "I'm going for a walk. I'll meet you downstairs by the restaurant where we ate last night." She left without waiting for Kree's reaction.

In the lobby, she counted her change, knew she had enough, and found a rare pay phone to call home. Belle answered. "Hello."

Startled to hear her voice because she hadn't expected her to be home, Janalou sucked in her breath, almost afraid to breathe.

"Hello," Belle repeated. "Who is this? What do you want?"

Janalou hung up, glad to know Belle wasn't in jail, but not surprised to discover the cantankerous woman still sounded as ornery as ever.

To clear her conscience, she called Papa at work.

He answered during the second ring. "Hello."

Once again she didn't speak. She didn't want him to know it was she. He might have the call traced. Relieved to know he was at work and not in jail either, she hung up and turned around.

Kree stood a few feet away. "Who were you calling?"

She shrugged. "Someone back home."

"You could have used my cell phone."

She shook her head. "You've already done too much for me. I don't want to take more advantage than I already have." In truth, she didn't want Belle or Papa to be able to trace the calls she'd made to Kree's phone. If they had access to his number, they could conceivably find her, if they tried.

Convinced she had done the right thing by calling to make sure they weren't in jail, she smiled up at Kree. "I'm ready for breakfast. How about you?"

He nodded, took her arm, and guided her to the restaurant's breakfast buffet.

~ * ~

They were quiet while they ate.

Kree couldn't stop wondering who she had tried to call, or why she'd hung up without leaving any messages.

He had learned more about her each day, and liked each new trait he discovered. As far as he knew, she didn't have any bad habits that might turn a guy off, but she did have some that could turn one on.

Soon they would be home, in California, and she would meet his family. The black and blue bruises under her eyes were almost healed. He could only detect them early in the morning, before she applied make-up. Soon they wouldn't be visible at all, with or without makeup.

Chewing a slice of bacon, he thought about the kisses they had shared a few nights ago. That's what he would remember about southern Utah—those passionate kisses, and her ardent responses when they rolled on the bed. It felt as though they couldn't get enough of each other, and he'd only stopped when she said they should. He had forgotten her surgery, forgotten everything except her. That couldn't happen again. To some girls, sex meant commitment, sometimes marriage was expected, and he wasn't going to get married, not for a long time anyway.

He drew in a breath to calm the heat pulsing through him. They had made memories in each state, and although he didn't expect them or her to be important in the years to come, he saw no reason not to continue to enjoy her.

A short time later, they checked out of their hotel room, and hit the road again.

When they reached Tahoe, Kree drove to the visitor center instead of the hotel where he had booked rooms online.

Outside of the car, he asked, "Ready to do something touristy again?"

Janalou nodded, grinning. "Always."

Appreciating her enthusiasm, he took her hand in his, and led her the from the parking lot, following the interpretive trail from the visitor center to a profile chamber below ground, next to the creek. With floor-to-ceiling windows, they watched fish and other marine life in their natural habitat.

"It's great to see what's below the water's surface," Janalou said, studying a small school of fish. "Do you know what kind of fish those are?"

Kree nodded. "Trout."

"Do you ever go fishing?"

"Yeah. Every summer.It's one of my hobbies."

"Do you go alone?"

"No. With fishing buddies."

She glanced back at the underground display. "The only time I've ever seen anything like this was on TV."

"There's a cool aquarium in Monterrey," Kree said. "Maybe someday you can go there."

"I'd like that."

After exploring the inside of the visitor center, they strolled back to the car, his hand holding her elbow.

"I'd suggest going to Vikingsholm Castle," he said, "but it doesn't open until June fifteenth. We're about a week early."

"That's all right. We've seen much more than I ever dared dream I'd see."

He smiled. "You're easy to please."

"And you're easy to be with. Thanks again for staying behind. I don't know what I would have done without you."

"You might have been alone, but I'm sure you would have managed quite well."

She blushed. "If that's a compliment, thank you."

"It was, and you're welcome." He reached out to cup her cheek. "You're pretty and brave, and I'm glad we met."

"I feel the same way about you, well not the pretty part, but you are handsome."

Kree laughed. "Thanks."

~ * ~

At the motel, Kree checked in, then extended a key card. "I booked separate rooms. Thought you might appreciate some space tonight."

"That was thoughtful," she said, not sure whether to be happy or sad. Had he grown tired of her constant company?

"I thought we should end our trip with something memorable so I made reservations for dinner on a boat, a three deck paddle-wheeler."

Janalou's mood perked up. "Sounds marvelous, but I don't have anything dressy to wear."

"Would you like to go shopping?" he suggested.

Although she didn't want to spend money on clothes until she had a job for certain, she nodded.

"I'll drive you to a mall." He jangled the keys inside his pocket, his eyes gleaming with amusement. "I don't want you to feel rushed while you shop, so I'll use my iPad to catch up on some work."

Janalou's heart skipped a couple of beats. They hadn't even reached their destination and already he was pulling away. "Should we unload our luggage first?"

He nodded. "Shouldn't take long. Our rooms are next to each other."

She still didn't know whether to be delighted or disappointed to have a room by herself.

A few minutes later, they headed toward the shopping center they had passed earlier.

"Would you mind if we turned the air off and rolled the windows down?" Janalou asked.

"Not at all. Go ahead."

She did, loving the sensation of the wind blowing her long unbound hair behind her.

At the mall, Kree found a table inside Starbucks, plopped his iPad on top, then said, "Our dinner reservation is at seven."

"I won't be long," she promised, grinning before she skipped off, her half-empty backpack bouncing against the straps anchored over her shoulders.

In spite of her misgivings about Kree's reason for booking separate rooms, her heart was singing a happy tune. They were going out on what she thought of as a date. She couldn't think of anything that would please her more.

Selecting something new to wear made her feel giddy. She didn't want to overdress. Neither did she want to embarrass Kree.

She found what she hoped was the perfect outfit on sale. A long black skirt with slits up both sides, and a sleeveless sequined top with a high neckline. She'd never owned anything more elegant. Her prom and senior hop dresses had been pretty, but she'd been used to nice things then, and too young to appreciate the fashionable clothes her parents allowed her buy. Only after Belle had denied those things did she realize how fortunate she had been.

Back at the motel, Kree said, "Can you be ready by six-thirty?"

"Yes."

She showered and washed her hair, using the blow dryer hanging on the wall to dry her long black hair before she twisted it in back and held it there with clips she had stowed in her backpack weeks before. Then she donned her new clothes, and was ready before 6:30.

"You look terrific," Kree said, appraising her with his warm gaze when she opened the door to his knock.

"You look nice too," she complimented, admiring his white shirt, dark blue suit and striped tie she hadn't seen before. He must have left those clothes in the trunk when they were in Independence and he'd shared his clothes with strangers during that terrible storm.

The sun was still up when they boarded the dinner boat, but it was beginning to lower and she expected the sky to be dark before they finished eating.

All during the trip, Kree had turned down cocktails and wine, which only endeared him more. He did it so smoothly, Janlou envied his charm.

"Do you ever drink alcohol?" she asked.

"No. Why?"

"I just wondered."

"You said you were uncomfortable around people who drink," he reminded.

"I am," she said, wondering if he would drink when they reached California. Would he do other things he hadn't done while they were together?

She gave herself a mental shake. That was none of her business. She had no claim on him, and shouldn't be interested in his life. But she was.

"Should I tell you why I don't drink?"

"Yes, unless you'd rather not."

He raised his glass, swallowed some water. "I was drinking the night Bethany died. I've always regretted not being with her. I knew she was upset about Mom and Dad's reaction to our engagement and I feel kind of responsible for her death."

Instead of commiserating again, she asked, "What was she like?"

His eyes took on a far-away expression, as though seeing back into the past. "She was the most beautiful girl I've ever known. Like you, she had dark eyes and long black hair. But you don't look anything like her. Your eyes are almond-shaped, kind of exotic. Hers were round and...'

"And?" she encouraged when he paused.

"I never saw any fear in them."

"Like you've seen in mine?"

He nodded. "Were you afraid of the woman who struck you? The one who gave you those black eyes?"

"Yes. I still am, but I don't expect to see her ever again, so I'm not as afraid now as I was when you first saw me on the bus."

"Good." He glanced away as a waiter arrived to take their order.

Live music played softly in the background and while they waited, he said, "Would you like to dance?"

"I'd love to," she said, "but I might be a little out of practice."

"Me, too."

The instant he took her in his arms, she knew he must have been kidding. He was an excellent dancer, and he guided her so expertly around the small floor, she felt like she was in a dream. *Was there anything he didn't do well?*

She hated to have their journey end. Kree was considerate, and they got along like two peas in a pod. If her wish came true, their camaraderie would continue when they reached Lodi, and they would work together in harmony. He wouldn't turn into Jekyll and Hyde as Papa had after he married Belle. Trust, she realized, wasn't easy, not after the torment she had endured from her stepmother.

Forcing Belle and Papa from her mind, Janalou focused on Kree, hanging on every word he said, enjoying every smile they shared while they ate at a leisurely pace.

When they finished, the sun had set, and they danced again.

"I understand this vessel has a glass bottom for viewing the mysteries of the deep," he said. "At night nothing much can be seen. Do you wish we'd taken the cruise during the day?"

"No. I love what we're doing now." She stopped short of saying it was romantic. "It's a perfect ending to a perfect trip. I don't know how I'll ever begin to repay you."

Kree looked as though he was about to say something, but he remained quiet.

Curious, she asked, "Were you going to suggest something?"

He nodded, tightening his arms ever so slightly as the next dance, another slow one, began. "I've thought of a way you can repay me."

Anxious to know what, she said, "I'll do anything. Well, almost anything. I really do appreciate all you've done to help me."

He cleared his throat. "My parents keep nagging me to get married. I'm not ready for that yet, but if they think I'm engaged, that would get them off my back for a while. You can repay me by pretending to be my fiancée."

Shock reverberated through Janalou. *Pretend to be his fiancée?*

She couldn't say no, could she? Not after all the things he'd done for her. Could she live with one more lie?

Disappointment that he didn't want to get married dribbled through her. She didn't want to consider marriage, either, at least not until she had proven she could take care of herself, and not until she met the right man. She refused to dwell on the fact that she might be in his arms right now.

While she considered his suggestion, she drew in a long, slow breath, half expecting him to say more to convince her.

He didn't.

Finally she said, "All I'd have to do is pretend? We wouldn't really be engaged, and you wouldn't expect anything more from me?"

"That's right. Well, I'll expect you to accompany me to family get-togethers. And you'll have to pretend we're in love. Do you think you can?"

"I don't know. People say my expression usually gives me away."

"I doubt your face will be a problem."

"But our lives are very different," she reminded. "Our backgrounds are so far apart. You're a Californian and I'm from the South."

"You make our differences sound like a crime."

"Sorry. I didn't mean that as an insult." She swallowed before she asked, "Do you think we can pretend to be engaged and pull it off?"

He nodded. "I'm a man. You're a woman. Nothing else matters. Nothing." He said that with such authority, she almost smiled.

The look in his eyes turned gentle. "You don't have to give me an answer right now. Think about it, Janalou. You'd be doing me a huge favor. And I'm not talking about forever. It only needs to last a few months. By the time the pretense ends, you'll be settled in Lodi. In the meantime, it'll give me some breathing room. People will stop trying to line me up with potential brides."

"They do that?"

"All the time."

"Okay. I'll think about it."

And she did. Couldn't get it out of her mind.

As they drove back to the motel, Kree said, "We don't have to get up early in the morning. If you'd like, we can sleep in."

"Why don't you call when you wake up?" she suggested. "It won't take me long to get ready to leave."

"I've noticed that. And I'm impressed. When I was growing up, my sisters spent hours in the bathroom primping. I can't believe how much time they wasted."

Janalou laughed. "I should probably take more time than I do. Mama always said if anyone could be ready to leave in less than thirty minutes they probably shouldn't leave the house at all. Most of my friends think the same thing. If it doesn't take an hour to get ready to go somewhere, they believe they haven't succeeded in looking halfway decent."

"I'm not complaining," Kree said. "I like your speedy showers and quick packing in the mornings. I like a lot of things about you."

"I like you too, Kree, and the fact that you don't drink is a real plus. Liquor drove a wedge between me and Papa after Mama died."

She hadn't meant to admit that. Most of the time she avoided discussing her parents, even when he asked about them. Thankfully, he didn't comment. Relief waved through her, mixing with gratitude.

~ * ~

Kree frowned as he drove. Although Janalou had mentioned her father had a problem with alcohol, she had led him to believe her parents died together, recently. Now she had contradicted that notion with something entirely different.

"I'm anxious to meet your family and the people you work with," she said, sounding a little breathless.

"You will, shortly after we get to Lodi."

So far she had avoided talking much about her life. He still thought she had a story to tell. But he wouldn't probe. If she wanted to keep her past a secret, that was her business, not his.

Why then had he spent so much time checking out the driver's license and social security number he'd seen in her backpack?

His discovery had surprised him. The girl, Emily Watson from Raleigh, North Carolina was dead. And had been for more than two years.

He had convinced himself snooping in Janalou's backpack and checking out the identification cards weren't underhanded. He just wanted to satisfy his curiosity. Instead it had increased.

What was she doing with a deceased girl's driver's license and social security card? Where were her own? Or was she Emily, and had somehow faked her own death? Or had her own cards been stolen? If so, why hadn't she obtained new ones?

He had a sneaky suspicion she intended to use the deceased girl's social security number. Although he didn't want to believe she would, he had stored the driver's license and social security card numbers in his iPad. When she filled out the required application form to work with him, he would know if she was trying to hide her identity.

Fifteen

Unable to fall asleep Janalou stared at a shadow on the ceiling, continuing to mull Kree's idea of a fake engagement.

Although she hadn't wanted to associate their trip with romance, she would always remember tonight as one of the most romantic of her life. It had even ended like a fantasy, almost. He'd asked her to be his pretend fiancée.

Would it work?

They had some things in common. Three years ago they had both lost someone they loved. And neither one of them wanted to get married yet.

She smiled in the dark. Pretending to be engaged might be exactly what she wanted. It would ensure they stayed connected. It might also make her feel less obligated for the money he had spent on her behalf— medical expenses, the trip, new clothes. No way had he paid the small amount he accepted for those.

Her smile grew, and happiness bubbled inside as she considered all the positives. Kree had given her a way to continue sharing his life. At least for a while. They wouldn't be serious, but they would be friends.

Was it possible to love him more than she did right now?

In all honesty, she didn't know.

~ * ~

As soon as they were on the road that would take them to Lodi the next morning, Kree cleared his throat, anxious to hear Janalou's decision. "Have you thought about the suggestion I made last night?"

"I've thought of little else," she admitted.

"Have you decided?"

"I guess if you can pretend, I can, too."

Relief poured through him. "Don't worry about me. My family will think I'm crazy about you."

They had spent enough time together for him to sense her frown while she stared at his profile. "Do you really think we can fool them?"

"Sure." He made his voice sound light, almost teasing. "From our phone conversations, my sisters already think I've got a thing for you. That's what gave me the idea."

"I see."

He flicked his gaze at her, then focused back on the road. "You won't regret our agreement."

"I hope not, but you might have to coach me. Tell me what you expect me to do."

"That'll be easy. And having you work with us will make our engagement believable."

"Giving me a job will be a huge favor."

"Good. It's settled then."

"Yeah, I guess it is."

Kree told himself a pretend engagement wasn't dishonest. It was just temporary. He couldn't be serious about another girl. Bethany had claimed his heart, all of it. No one could take her place. Ever. He doubted anyone could come close. Even if he married someday, it would be more for companionship than love.

His long ago conclusions had become such a habit he couldn't believe otherwise. Still, a niggling doubt crept in, forcing him to wonder what would happen when he and Janalou ended the pretense. He didn't want her to get hurt.

"There is one thing I'd like to discuss," she said, jostling him from his thoughts.

"What?"

"The money you spent on my behalf. I'd like to set up a repayment schedule."

"Repayment won't be necessary. Your agreement is enough."

She shook her head defiantly. Long strands of hair flew in wild disarray around her shoulders and face and he realized she looked younger than she had last night. With her hair fashioned in a thick twist behind head, she had looked elegant and older than a girl still in her teens.

"I agreed because y'all are my friend," she said. "I might be a GRITS, but I'm not a fragile faint-hearted southern belle who can't pay her debts."

"I thought grits were something people eat," he deadpanned.

"They are." Janalou laughed. "But the initials also stand for Girls Raised in the South, and we all consider ourselves to be very strong females. I'll accept your willingness to put off repayment for a while, but someday I intend to make it up to you."

"Why?" he asked, curious.

"Pride, I guess. And gratitude. Besides, just because y'all might be wealthy doesn't mean I should take advantage of your generosity."

Pleased with her reply, Kree increased the car's speed, and reset the cruise control. Introducing her to his family would cause a stir, especially if he told them ahead of time they were engaged.

~ * ~

In Lodi, Kree drove straight to a modest house and pulled into the driveway.

"Is this where you live?" Janalou asked when he shifted into park and turned the engine off.

"No. My house is a little bigger. This is Reina's place. I promised we'd come here so she could see for herself that you're okay."

"I'm better than okay," Janalou smiled. "I'm great."

Reina opened her front door almost as soon as Kree rang the bell.

When Janalou saw Cherilyn, Toby, Misti, and Duke, who was dressed in green again, tears clouded her vision. "What a wonderful surprise!" she exclaimed. "It's so good to see y'all again."

"How ye feeling, lass?" Duke asked.

"Marvelous. We saw so many things traveling across the country, and Kree has agreed to arrange for me to work with him."

"That isn't all we've agreed to do," Kree said, smiling, as he reached for Janalou's hand. "We're engaged."

"How romantic," Cherilyn gasped. "A whirlwind romance. I'm so happy for you, I think I might cry." Tears puddled in her eyes.

"Don't cry or I will, too," Janalou said, feeling as though she had known Kree much longer than twelve days. Their time together had made her feel very close.

"Kree make you happy. He good man," Reina said. "He love my daughter but she die. Now he love you. I be glad. You lucky girl. He take good care of you."

While Janalou was digesting Reina's comments, Duke said, "You work fast, lad." He studied Kree with his keen gaze before he turned his attention back to Janalou. "Have you ever been in love, lass?"

She thought about Tony, and shook her head. "I had a crush on a boy once, but I don't think I loved him." Tony had been her boyfriend and confidant, and they'd had fun together. But he hadn't made her heart sing the way Kree did.

"I wonder if you know how fortunate you are," Duke said to Kree.

"I think I do," he said, sounding as though he meant it. "I'll buy a ring and give it to her soon."

Janalou gulped. *A ring?*

Not a real diamond, she hoped. That would increase her guilt. Make her feel more obligated.

She forced a smile. "I'm the fortunate one," she said.

He squeezed her hand. When she looked up, his gaze seemed to say, *don't worry. Everything's going to be all right.*

She dragged in a fortifying breath. Simply being in the same room, breathing the same air as Kree affected her as she'd never been affected.

What would she do if he kissed her again? The mere thought made her heart race and her knees wobble.

"I found an apartment," Cherilyn said, interrupting her chaotic thoughts. "You can stay with me until you find one of your own. The manager said there are some available in the same complex, if you're interested. I'm sure you'll want privacy, especially now that you're engaged."

Janalou did want her privacy, but not for her engagement's sake. For a whole year, she had yearned to have her own place. Looked forward to having no one else around to expect anything from her. No one to boss her. She had enjoyed keeping the house clean and tidy before Belle came into her life, and issued orders like a cruel drill sergeant.

She stifled a sigh. Her own space was almost within her grasp, and according to Kree, she also had a job. She exhaled, and forced herself to relax.

The reunion with Reina, Duke, Cherilyn and her children was wonderful. Not as good as her adventures with Kree, but nothing could compare with their time together.

As the evening progressed, Janalou felt as though she were living in some kind of fairy-tale world. Everything seemed too good to be true, too much in harmony, too perfect.

Would it end? Would her euphoria come crashing down on her?

She forced worry from her thoughts. Her new life was good, and she intended to enjoy every single minute.

After the early dinner, they continued to laugh and talk until Reina said, "We take up collection. This money help pay your medical expenses." She thrust an envelope at Janalou.

"I'll give it to Kree." Janalou opened the envelope and stared at ten one thousand dollar bills.

"I don't want it," Kree said, winking at her. "If Janalou is going to be obligated to anyone, I want it to be me." He accepted the money she had extended and gave it back to Reina. "Return this to whomever it belongs to, will you?"

Reina nodded, and the conversation turned to questions about their journey.

After a while, Kree said, "I need to return the car to the rental agency. Do you want me to drop you off at Cherilyn's apartment, Janalou?"

"No," Duke said, before she could reply. "I got meself a job driving a taxi, so I'll see the young lasses and children home."

"All right." Kree glanced at Janalou. "We have a lot to discuss. I'll call my doctor and arrange an appointment for you as soon as possible, and I'll take you out to dinner tomorrow night. Here's my phone. It's charged, so keep it turned on. I'll call tomorrow and we can decide what time I should pick you up."

Then he surprised her by planting a kiss on her cheek.

Gripping his phone with one hand, she touched her cheek with the other and held her fingers there after he'd gone.

"You're in love," Cherilyn said, her eyes warm and dreamy.

Janalou dropped her hand to her side. "Would I be engaged if I weren't?"

Cherilyn shook her head.

But Duke studied her, making guilt pound through her.

Did he know the engagement was a farce? Could he sense such things? Was he truly a leprechaun? Or some kind of magical being? Or had he been teasing her?

"I have good news," Cherilyn said, interrupting her thoughts once more. "I have a job."

"Where?"

"At a nursery school. I start working on Monday. I'm delighted because I can take Misti and Toby with me. I'll get to teach them songs and rhymes, and play games with them throughout the day. We'll get to share lunch, too."

"That's marvelous," Janalou said, smiling, when Kree returned with her suitcase and the small plastic bags of gifts she had bought at the old-fashioned mercantile in St. Louis.

"Wait a minute," she said as he turned to leave again. "I have something for everyone, including you."

"Presents? You brought us presents?" little Misti's eyes glowed with excitement.

Janalou nodded, reached inside one plastic bag and gave Misti a small box.

"A baby doll with her very own bottle," Misti said, a huge grin spreading across her pixie face after she opened the gift.

"Me want toy." Toby took his thumb out of his mouth and wiped it on his yellow T-shirt, looking expectantly at Janalou.

She gave him a box, and Cherilyn helped him open it.

"Truck, he said, holding a miniature white truck up in the air, and spinning the tiny wheels with his little fingers.

"An old-fashioned milk truck," Janalou explained.

"Me like milk," Toby said, kneeling down to run the truck across Reina's clean linoleum floor.

Janalou distributed her remaining gifts. A necklace for Reina. Earrings for Cherilyn. A new green baseball cap to replace the battered one on Duke's head. And a book of cowboy poetry for Kree.

"You know me better than I thought," he said in a quiet aside. "I don't recall telling you I like cowboy poems."

Janalou smiled. "You didn't, but I saw you looking through that book after I bought it. I hope you like it."

"I do. Thanks." He gave her another affectionate peck on the cheek.

Once more, she fingered the spot he had kissed after he left. But when she saw Cherilyn grinning, Janalou dropped her hand again. She was acting like a love-sick teenager.

Duke stuck his new green cap on his head. "Are you lasses ready to call it a day?"

They both nodded, and thanked Reina for cooking dinner.

"It was delicious," Janalou said again.

Reina smiled. "It a pleasure to cook for people we love."

"The pleasure was ours," Janalou said.

"Yes," Cherilyn agreed.

Outside, Duke ushered them to a white cab decorated with green shamrocks on the hood, trunk and both sides. Janalou grinned. Trust him to find work connected with something Irish.

During the drive to Cherilyn's apartment, she said, "I saw a man who resembled you in St. Louis, Duke. Do you have a twin brother?"

He laughed. "Nay, lass, but certain I am that more than one man might resemble me." Without giving her a chance to pursue that topic, he said, "Are you sure you're healing, lass?"

"Yes. Thank you for asking."

~ * ~

Later that night, she lay on the couch in Cherilyn's two bedroom apartment, haunted by guilt. *Could she begin work at an office using a fake name?*

She didn't dare use her own. She wasn't eighteen yet and feared Papa and Belle might find her and force her to go back to Spartanburg.

Masquerading as Kree's fiancée compounded her problems. *If she heaped any more guilt on top of the pile, would life be bearable?*

Her thoughts turned to the past, and to Belle in particular. Janalou had read that abused people were consumed with the fear of being found and punished, if they ever worked up the courage to run away from their tormentors. Now she knew firsthand how true that was.

She closed her eyes, determined to be strong, and even if she failed, to exude Southern charm. She must do her real mama proud. In the process, maybe she could feel good about herself. There was no room in her new life for guilt. She should enjoy her pretend engagement and Kree for as long as possible.

<h1 style="text-align:center">Sixteen</h1>

Kree flicked his gaze over Janalou's pale blue skirt and layered blouses after they were in his car, a dark blue Cadillac. The top blouse, made of gauzy see-through pink fabric, had a V-neck and flared sleeves. Her under-blouse resembled a blue tank top. White lace trimmed the neckline, reminding him of underwear. Her modest outfit shouldn't tempt him, but on her it looked sexy and made him want to explore the curves beneath. Instead, he swallowed to moisten his dry throat

"You look nice. Are those new clothes?" he asked, knowing they must be.

"Yes. I went shopping with Cherilyn this morning. We both needed clothes for work. I left most of mine behind."

"Speaking about work, you can start on Monday if you feel ready. Martina, our receptionist, is on vacation so we need you, and my family's eager to meet you."

"I'm ready."

Although she said it with conviction, her eyes told another story. "You're ready to begin working," he guessed, "but not entirely ready to pretend to be my fiancée in front of my family."

She scrunched her brows in a frown. "What if I make a muddle of it, Kree?"

"You won't. Unless you come right out and tell them it isn't true."

"I won't. I'll do my best to pretend it is."

"And you'll do a terrific job. You have a lot of backbone, and I have confidence in you."

She fidgeted under her seatbelt. "I hope your confidence isn't misplaced."

"It isn't." He grinned. "Don't be nervous. You have nothing to worry about. Just pretend our engagement is real, and be yourself."

"I'll try."

"Good." Moving on, Kree said, "Mom invited us and my sisters and their families to an early Sunday dinner tomorrow, so you'll meet the whole crew."

Janalou twisted her hands on her lap. "Have you told them we're engaged?

"Yes." He flashed a grin, and reverted back to her earlier comment. "Why did you leave most of your clothes behind?"

Instead of answering, she stared out the side window.

"You don't have to explain, if you'd rather not," he said. "It's just that my life's an open book, and your past is a blank. All I know is that your parents are dead, you once had a boyfriend named Tony, and your dad drank too much after your mother died. I don't know your parents' names or your best friend's either."

"I'm sorry. I can't talk about them."

He saw her swallow, and felt her discomfort.

"Talking might help."

"It won't."

Kree decided not to push. "I thought we'd eat at Applebee's tonight," he said. "You mentioned you like their food but we never found one while we were traveling."

She smiled. "I do like Applebee's."

~ * ~

A short time later, Kree parked in the restaurant's crowded lot, and switched off the ignition. After he unfastened his seatbelt, he turned to face her. "I made an appointment for you to see our family doctor on Wednesday."

"Thank you."

"You're welcome." His gaze turned solemn. "I have something for you." He reached inside the breast pocket of his suit coat, and pulled out a small box.

Her heart leapt. *The engagement ring?*

Sure enough, when he flipped the lid open, a dazzling solitaire glittered on a bed of black velvet. Her heart began to pound. Again.

"It's gorgeous."

He smiled. "I hoped you would approve."

She laughed to hide her nervousness. "How could I not?"

Instead of replying, he winked before he slid the ring onto her finger.

She swallowed a lump of emotion. His touch clouded her brain, and made her heart zing. *Was the solitaire real? Or a fake?*

She wasn't about to ask. Part of her hoped it was as artificial as their engagement. Another part wished it were a real diamond, also that the engagement weren't a sham.

She had yearned to start a new life. Now she had. But it was based on lies and deceit. A false name. A made-up past. And a fake engagement.

Despite last night's pep talk to herself, uneasiness escalated as they walked into the busy restaurant and waited to be seated. Although she loved being with Kree, she felt like a fraud. *Did it show? Could she mask her emotions in front of his family?*

Kree held her hand as the hostess led them to a table. More awareness sizzled through her, and it took a lot of effort to shove her discomfort behind her. But once she did, she had a marvelous time.

As he had been while they traveled, Kree was fun to be with. He charmed the hostess, waitresses, people seated around them, even Janalou, telling anyone who acted the least bit interested that they were celebrating their engagement. Each time he held up her hand for others to see the beautiful new ring.

It was a night she would always remember with mixed emotions. Pride to be associated with Kree. Shame for lying to the world. Regret because they had no future. Envy for an unknown woman who would someday marry him. Yet delight, too, because he kept her so thoroughly entertained.

While he drove her back to Cherilyn's, she studied his profile, wondering if he would ever kiss her again on the lips. Cheek kisses like yesterdays didn't count. They were as fake as their trumped up engagement—perfunctory with no emotion.

Lip kisses were real, though. They were focused. Full of emotion. And spark.

Just thinking about lip kisses sent sensations pulsating through her like a bright rocket shooting through the night time sky.

At Cherilyn's apartment, Kree walked her to the door. "I know you're not thrilled with our agreement, but it's a perfect solution for me right now. Don't think of it as being dishonest or anything else that might make you uncomfortable. Think of it as our secret. Ours alone. No one else needs to know. Right?"

She nodded in the near dark, glad the outside lights were small and sparse.

"Good." Then, to her utter surprise, he wrapped his arms around her and drew her close. "I think we need practice."

"What—kind?" she asked, too befuddled by being held close to think straight.

"This kind." He lowered his head and kissed her. Lip kissed her.

Skyrockets went off inside her head, catapulting her into a different world, a world where only they existed, a world where nothing mattered except the two of them.

She couldn't seem to get close enough, and pressed against him. Her eager arms wound around his neck. With a will of their own, her fingers explored the texture of his hair, the skin at the base of his neck while her brain attempted to memorize every sensation whizzing through her.

The stimulating kiss devoured, consumed.

In way it filled her, too, satisfying the yearning she should have been reluctant to acknowledge.

Although she was sure Kree didn't know it, she gave him part of herself during the exciting kiss. She gave him her heart. And that was her secret. Her secret alone.

When the kiss ended, they stared at each other, although she couldn't see his expression clearly. All her senses focused on the wondrous sensations still buzzing inside. At that moment, she wanted to tell him the truth about herself. She could trust him. She knew that.

But he released her, and the moment fled, along with her desire to admit she had lied about her identity.

Grateful for the dark so he couldn't see all the emotions swimming in her eyes, she said, "Thanks for dinner, Kree."

"You're more than welcome, Janalou."

She turned and inserted the key Cherilyn had given her into the lock. "Good night."

"Yeah. It has been," he murmured, his warm breath caressing the back of her neck. *When had he stepped so close? If she turned, would he kiss her again?*

Afraid he wouldn't and she would be disappointed, she turned the key and reached for the knob.

But before she opened the door, he said, "I'm sorry if you think kissing was out of line. I'll stop," he paused, cleared his throat, and once more she felt his breath on the back of her neck. "I mean I won't do it often. I promise."

Tears sprang to her eyes. *He was sorry? And what had he just promised to do? Deprive her of the most exciting kisses she'd ever had?*

Glad he couldn't see her eyes, she didn't comment. If she did, he would surely hear the tears she couldn't choke back.

She walked inside and shut the door behind her. Grateful Cherilyn had already gone to bed, she leaned against the door. At least she didn't have to face her friend right now and pretend everything was all right.

What was wrong with her? Why couldn't she be content with the agreement she had forged with Kree? Why did she suddenly want him to offer more? Why did she want to back out unless he did?

Telling herself she was an ungrateful wretch, she got ready for bed.

She slept fitfully, and awakened full of pessimism.

In the shower the next morning, she gave herself a rigorous self-pep talk. It was too late for regrets. She had made a decision, and she would stand by it, regardless how much it hurt, regardless how much it bothered her.

Determined to make a good impression on his family, she primped more than usual. The new modest yellow dress helped her sagging confidence as she stared in the mirror. Not knowing what to do with her long hair, she fixed it up, then down, and finally gathered it behind her nape, securing it with a new clasp.

"Do I look too young or girlish?" she asked as Cherilyn studied her.

Her friend shook her head. "You look cool, and elegantly casual."

Janalou laughed and some of the tension inside her eased. "You're good for my ego."

Cherilyn's laughter filled the living room. "You've been good for mine, too. I'm so glad we met."

"The feeling's mutual. I don't know why we connected so quickly, but I feel as though I've known you for years."

"Me, too." Cherilyn agreed, all traces of laughter gone. "If you believe in reincarnation, maybe we were sisters in another life."

"I believe in the hereafter. I'm not sure about reincarnation, although sometimes I have strange dreams, as though I'm someone else with a family I can't quite remember."

"Maybe you have those dreams because they were your family in another life."

"I suppose anything's possible," she said.

But her mind couldn't accept that idea. It sounded too logical. Or too farfetched. And it had more to do with mystical religions than the Christian beliefs she had been taught all her life.

~ * ~

Janalou prepared to meet Kree's family by dressing carefully and making sure make-up covered the last tale-tale signs of her black eyes.

As Kree made the introductions to all ten members of his family—six adults and four children—she smiled, shook hands, and endured their quiet inspection.

Everyone except his dark-haired mother, Helen, smiled. Her expression bordered on frosty.

"We've heard a lot about you," she said, her voice crisp and cool, "and we're happy to meet you, Janalou."

"She's right," Jocelyn said, the warmth in her eyes almost making up for her mother's aloof attitude. "I'm Kree's older sister, and don't believe any of the childhood stories he tells you about me or Sirena. Being the youngest prejudiced him years ago."

"Yes," Sirena, said, twin dimples denting her cheeks as she grinned. "We used to drive him crazy teasing him about being the baby. He got even by teasing us about our boyfriends when we started to date." She placed her hands on her children's shoulders. "These two are mine, Ben and Tami. We're all looking forward to getting better acquainted as time goes by."

Kree's father, tall and black-haired Max, spoke next. "I'm delighted you've agreed to marry our son, Janalou, and happy you'll be working with us. You couldn't begin at a better time. Kree said he mentioned our receptionist is on vacation so you'll be solo your first week. Sometimes we're all out of the office at the same time. You'll need to take messages, and hold down the fort. Think you can handle that?"

Janalou nodded. She had assumed full responsibility for running the library when the head librarian and her assistants took time off or ran errands, so thankfully she did have some experience to fall back on.

The Wintertons chatted, good-naturedly, as families do, and Kree paid attention to his nieces and nephews. His family tried to include Janalou in their conversations, but she didn't have much to say.

Her thoughts wandered back to the library in Spartanburg. A lot of her work had included shushing people. She smiled at the memories. Working at the library had been a highlight in her life, and she would always cherish the hours spent there. The quiet solitude had been a safe haven, a place where she could pretend her life was normal, not filled with tension or out of control. She wished she'd had a chance to tell her co-workers goodbye. One more thing to regret. To feel guilty about.

"It's time to eat," Sirena's husband, Mark, interrupted her silent reverie. "I'll shepherd the kids to the table."

In the dining room, Janalou admired the big table, set for twelve. When they were all seated, she studied Kree's family again. He favored his slender, dark-haired mother. Their facial features were similar and they had the same dark brown hair and blue eyes.

Joycelyn favored their father, tall and lean with black hair.

His middle sister, Sirena didn't favor either parent. Small, petite, thin and short, she had curly sandy-blonde hair, and Janalou had a difficult time believing she had given birth twice.

"You don't look big enough or old enough to have two children," she said when Sirena glanced at her.

Sirena laughed. "Thanks. I haven't had a compliment like that for a long time."

Janalou's face turned warm when everyone focused on her. Suddenly she felt tongue-tied again.

"You look kind of young yourself," Sirena's husband said. "How old are you?"

"Almost eighteen."

"So young," Helen said, sweeping her gaze over Janalou. "People might accuse Kree of robbing the cradle."

Kree chuckled, but when he spoke, his voice sounded almost harsh. "If they do, they'all say it with envy, Mother."

Helen flinched, and looked away.

Sensing the tension between them, Janalou smiled at Jocelyn. She liked Kree's sisters. They shared one common trait: both were friendly, as were their husbands and children. So was Kree's father, Max.

But she could tell his mother didn't approve of the engagement. Not that Janalou could blame her. In her shoes, she doubted she would approve either. The engagement had happened too fast. His family didn't know her. Neither did Kree, at least not very well.

With an inward sigh, Janalou vowed not ever to do anything that might hurt or upset him or them.

Part of her envied Kree for having sisters and nieces and nephews. *What would it be like to have siblings?*

The closest thing she'd ever had to a sister was her best friend, Margie. But friends weren't the same as family. Family always came first.

While Janalou filled her plate, a strange question rippled through her. *Did she want more people in her family? Is that why she had dreamed about playing with another girl and a boy so often? Had she invented them to be her imaginary brother and sister when she was very young so she wouldn't feel alone?*

Her attention was drawn to Mark, Sirena's husband, when he said, "You look like someone I've seen before, but Kree said this is your first time in California. You have a pleasant accent. Where did you grow up?"

Janalou couldn't lie. She had already told too many. After wiping the corners of her mouth with her white linen napkin, she answered. "South Carolina."

"It's difficult for her to discuss the past," Kree explained, saving her from more questions.

"Everything is delicious," she said, giving Helen a shy smile. "You're a good cook."

"Thank you," Helen said, her gaze cool.

Trying not to be bothered, Janalou listened to the Wintertons' conversation, remembering to use her best table manners so she wouldn't embarrass Kree.

After dinner, she helped Jocelyn and Sirena do the dishes while Helen put the leftovers away.

Kree and Janalou spent all afternoon with his family, getting better acquainted. Janalou found herself wishing she really was going to be Kree's wife. But that was wishful thinking. She couldn't marry him anyway, not without telling him the truth, and she didn't want to think about that. Explaining her past and trying to justify her lies wasn't something she thought she could ever do.

~ * ~

When they left, Kree reached for Janalou's hand.

She glanced up, a question in her lovely eyes.

He winked, and raised their clasped hands between them. "This is for my family's benefit. In case they're watching us," he explained.

She nodded.

He looked away. His hormones were surging to the surface. Acting with Janalou was both pleasure and torture. "I'll pick you up for work in the morning, around eight-thirty, if that's all right," he said.

"It is, and thanks."

He smiled. "You made a good impression on everyone."

"Except your mother."

"Don't worry about her. I doubt she'll ever approve of any woman I take home." Pleased with the arrangements he'd made with Janalou, he said, "Tomorrow we'll get to the office by nine. That'll give me time to show you around before anyone else arrives. They usually get there around nine-thirty or ten."

When they arrived at Cherilyn's apartment, Kree walked Janalou to the door, but he didn't kiss her. Didn't even touch her. Didn't dare. Last night's kiss had made him want more. Much, much more. Not only was the doctor's warning to wait at least six weeks burned into his brain, his belief that he would hurt her if he allowed intimacy and then broke up with her kept nagging his conscience.

Even if those reasons weren't an issue, he couldn't get too personally involved. Janalou wasn't the type of girl a guy could love and leave. Neither was she the kind who could be intimate without some kind of commitment. He wasn't sure how he knew that, but he did. Maybe because it was there, in her sad, exotic eyes.

As he drove home alone, a barrage of emotions attacked.

Why did Janalou's touch excite him?

He had dated lots of beautiful women. Not one had ever affected him like she did, not even Bethany. With her he had always felt protective, and when he kissed her, their kisses were enjoyable, not passionate. Passion would have made him want more and they had both agreed that passion and sex belonged to marriage

He wished he hadn't kissed Janalou last night, and discovered how much he wanted her. And want her he did. But he didn't intend to do anything about it. So he wouldn't kiss her again, except maybe for an occasional peck on the cheek. That wouldn't be personal, and it would be expected when they were with other people.

Seventeen

Kree arrived at Cherilyn's apartment early. As anticipated, Janalou answered the door. She invited him inside, twisting her hands, a gesture he interpreted as nervousness.

"Do I look all right?"

"Sure. You look terrific."

She blushed. "Thanks. You said to dress casual. I wasn't exactly sure what that meant."

"You made a good choice." Pleased with her outfit—tan slacks and a red blouse—clothes he had purchased for her, he smiled. "Are you ready?"

"Yes." She slung the straps of her backpack over one shoulder and preceded him out the door.

The drive to the office took the full half hour he had predicted during the rush hour.

While he unlocked the office, he sensed her studying his dark trousers and blue dress shirt, and wondered what she was thinking. Her nearness was getting to him again, speeding up his heart rate, ramping up his hormones.

He flipped on the overhead lights, his breath uneven, as though he'd just finished a lengthy jog. Unable to ignore the awareness throbbing through him, he took Janalou's arm, and guided her through the lobby, down the hall.

"Mom and Dad share this office," he said, pausing at the first door. The spacious room contained two desks, with matching credenzas.

Kree tightened his hold and urged her away. "Sirena and Jocelyn share this room. As I mentioned, some days they're both in, some days neither one is."

He allowed time for Janalou to inspect his sisters' name plaques on their respective desks, along with photographs of their children before he guided her to his office.

"This is where I work," he said.

"It's nice. Like the others."

"I'm glad you approve." He took her to the conference room next.

"We do closings in here. We also use this room for meetings, and to discuss problems or new ideas."

When she glanced at the TV in one corner, he suspected she wondered what they used it for, but she didn't ask. He motioned to the wall lined with filing cabinets. "That's where we keep contracts. We'd like you to get familiar with them because you'll be doing the filing. Sometimes we can't find folders. I suspect they've been misfiled."

Janalou blinked, but remained quiet as he showed her the break room that housed a microwave, photocopy and postage machines, as well as a round maple kitchen table, six chairs and a full size refrigerator.

"My sisters usually bring snacks, and store them in here. Mom makes sure we have soft drinks for ourselves and clients." He opened the fridge, revealing a variety of canned and bottled drinks. "We usually have cookies and popcorn around, too."

"Sounds more like fun than work."

"Sometimes it is," he said, grinning. "We keep things kind of casual. I guess that's why I enjoy working."

They strolled back to the lobby-reception area. "You'll hang out in here. We'll have to get you a desk. You can use Martina's this week. I didn't mention this before, but she doesn't work on weekends, and we'd like someone in the office on Saturdays. Would you mind taking a different day off?"

"Not at all."

"After this week, if you take Mondays off, you'll have two days in a row."

"Sounds good to me."

"Great. I'll tell the family." He smiled, his heart full of approval, his hand still on her elbow.

He let go of her arm, wondering why he'd hung on so long. Trying to ignore his inner turmoil, he extended a file folder he'd picked up from his office during the brief tour. "Here's an employment form and application, along with government withholding forms. Fill them out when you get time."

Janalou nodded and set the folder on Martina's desk.

"We'll have to make arrangements for you to get to work," he said. "Maybe when I can't pick you up, you could take the bus."

"I appreciate your offer, but you don't have to take care of me anymore. Duke volunteered to drive me to and from work. He said it's on his way."

Kree grinned. "That's great." He tried to sound enthusiastic, and hoped he succeeded. He didn't want to be burdened with the responsibility of getting her to and from work every day, did he? No, of course not. Then why did the thought of her making her own arrangements and exercising her independence bother him?

Janalou walked behind the receptionist's desk, sat down, pulled a pen out of a drawer and started to fill out the application. His pulse drummed while he waited for her to finish the government withholding form. *Would she use the fake social security number he had seen stashed in her backpack?*

He could hardly believe his eyes when she wrote the number he had memorized. *Why was she using a deceased girl's identity?*

The answer came in a flash. *Because she had run away.* He didn't doubt that, not anymore. *But what did she have to fear by leaving an orphanage?* She had graduated from high school and was old enough to be on her own.

After her surgery, he had offered his phone so she could call her friends back home. She had thanked him politely, but refused. Not even a single soul had she contacted—until they'd reached Wendover on the Utah-Nevada border. Even then she hadn't talked to anyone. She had hung up shortly after punching two different numbers. *Who had she called? And why hadn't she said anything after going to the trouble of finding a pay phone?*

He walked to his office, scratching his head. *Would she confide in him if he asked? Or would she get upset and run away from him, too?* If she did, he might never find her again. Not willing to chance that yet, he banked his curiosity. Maybe when he was ready for the temporary engagement to end, he'd get nosy. If she didn't like his snoopy questions, she might leave. Why that thought disturbed him didn't make sense. They weren't in love or anything. They weren't even very close. He knew next to nothing about her or her past.

Behind his desk, he picked up the phone. The time off had been welcome, but he liked his work and was ready to get back to business.

~ * ~

While Janalou waited for Kree's family to arrive, a variety of emotions churned through her—pride, fear, worry, anxiety. She liked the prestige of sitting behind a beautiful teakwood desk in a sleek office, but was she qualified to work as the Wintertons' receptionist?

Plagued by another problem, she sucked her bottom lip beneath her upper teeth. *Could she keep the agreement she had made with Kree? Would staying in Lodi be a mistake? Should she push on to L.A., where she would be all on her own?*

For some reason, that thought terrified her. She didn't want to leave her new friends. She adored Reina, Duke and Cherilyn. And she loved Kree, and didn't want to leave him.

A shudder galloped through her when she glanced at her employment forms. *What would happen if anyone discovered she was using a dead person's social security number?*

The telephone rang. Taking a deep breath, she lifted the receiver. "Winterton Real Estate. How may I help you?"

"It's me," Duke's cheerful voice said. "Just checking on ye, lass. Everything all right?"

"Yes. As right as rain," she said, shivering as she recalled the Missouri storm.

"Will ye be needing a ride home?"

"Yes. Please. I'd appreciate one."

"Fine. I'll be there around five o'clock."

"Thanks, Duke."

"Yer welcome, lass."

Helen, Max, Jocelyn and Sirena arrived within minutes of each other, shortly after she hung up.

All morning they were kind, helpful, friendly, and acted glad to have Janalou there. Even Helen, although Janalou sensed she had misgivings about her relationship with her son.

Every time the phone rang, she answered without sounding like a ninny, and she greeted clients who came in with a smile, which they all returned.

The first day passed with relative ease.

So did Tuesday.

And Wednesday. During a late lunch hour, Kree drove her to see his doctor.

"Your incision is healing nicely," Dr. Bracken said. "But don't overdo. You shouldn't lift anything heavy, or vacuum or have sexual intercourse until I see you again. Make an appointment with my receptionist for a month from now."

The sexual intercourse remark made her cheeks feel hot, and she said meekly, "I will."

When she tried to pay for the office call, Kree shook his head. "You're on the payroll now, so it's taken care of."

She didn't know if that were true, but decided not to argue. Probably wouldn't win even if she did.

During her lunch hour on Thursday, she took a cab to a nearby bank and opened two accounts, checking and savings, and deposited the bulk of her money in the savings account. That night she wrote a check for a deposit on a one bedroom furnished apartment in the same complex where Cherilyn lived.

After work on Friday, she moved in.

To her bemusement, Duke moved in across the courtyard at the same time.

"I hope ye don't mind me being close, lass. But if ye have problems, and need help, I won't be more than a few steps away."

Having him nearby made her feel safe, and she smiled. "Thank you, Duke. I really appreciate everything you're doing to help me, especially driving me to work and home again."

His cheeks dimpled when he smiled. "The pleasure be mine, lass."

~ * ~

At the end of her first week in Lodi, Kree took her to a barbecue at a friend's home. In the back yard she met his friends.

"Jason is my best friend," Kree confided when the three of them stood a little away from the others on the patio in the back yard.

"We went to high school and college together," Jason said. "If you ever want to know anything about the guy you intend to marry, just ask me."

Surprised whipped through Janalou. *Hadn't Kree told Jason the engagement was fake?* He had said it would be their secret, but she hadn't expected him to keep the truth from his best friend. That meant she couldn't tell anyone either, not that she planned to, but it cemented her decision in place.

~ * ~

The regular receptionist returned to work on Monday. Janalou had that day off, and spent it at home, enjoying time by the pool, reading, catching up on the news.

On Tuesday she went to work early, and was seated behind the receptionist's desk when a girl of Mexican descent arrived.

"That's my desk and chair," she said, her brown eyes dark with accusation.

Startled by her hostility, Janalou stood up and backed away.

"I'm Martina," she added. "Who are you?"

"My name is Janalou." She spoke quietly, trying to placate. "The owners hired me to help lessen your work load."

"My load isn't heavy." Martina frowned. "Kree said I'm a good worker. Why did they hire you?"

"Because I needed a job, and they think you have too much to do."

Martina's frown deepened. "That's a huge rock on your hand." She eyed the solitaire with envy in her brown eyes.

Janalou didn't know what to say, so she didn't comment.

"Who gave it to you?"

"Kree."

Anger covered Martina's face, but all she said was, "I hope you know you'll be marrying into a *muy bueno* family."

Janalou forced a smile. "I do." How she wished she didn't have to pretend that the engagement was real.

A question swirled through her when Martina jerked a drawer open. *Did she love Kree too?*

The instant he walked into the office, Martina blurted, "I don't like sharing my desk or the lobby with a stranger."

Kree flashed one of his killer smiles. "That won't be necessary, Martina. We'll buy a desk for Janalou, and she can share my office."

Martina frowned again, and Janalou felt as though invisible battle lines had been drawn. No way did Martina intend to get along. Janalou tamped down a smile. The idea of sharing Kree's office held a lot of appeal.

In spite of Martina's negative vibes, Janalou loved her new life. The fear that she might be found receded more each day. If not for feeling guilty about the pretend engagement, and worrying about her fake identity, she didn't think life could be much better.

Janalou loved going to work. Each day she learned more about real estate as well as Kree and his family, except for his mother. Helen held herself aloof, rarely asking Janalou to do anything, and only speaking to her when it couldn't be avoided.

She didn't see Kree much outside the office, but her relationship with Cherilyn, Duke and Reina grew by leaps and bounds.

Unfortunately working with Martina deteriorated daily, and Kree's mother ignored her. Janalou wondered if some of Martina's hostility was due to Helen's attitude. They both wanted her gone, out of their lives.

"Have you set a wedding date?" Martina asked one morning before anyone else arrived at the office.

"No. Not yet," Janalou said with caution.

"You'd better not, or I'll make trouble. I'll tell Kree you're not good for him."

Hackles raised, Janalou lost her cool and snapped, "Our engagement isn't any of your business, Martina."

"Everything about Kree is my business," she snarled, anger turning her dark face red. "I will not let you marry him."

Although exasperated, Janalou kept quiet. She didn't want to make waves, but she was tired of Martina's antagonism. Thankfully, Kree walked in the front door, interrupting the conversation.

But Martina's threat put Janalou on high alert. From then on, she would have to be very careful what she said to Martina.

She spent most of her working hours at her new desk in Kree's office. In some ways, avoiding Martina was like trying to stay out of Belle's way. Both were mean-spirited with cruel streaks a mile long.

One afternoon Kree extended a file folder. "I need some photocopies. Would you mind making them?"

"Not at all."

He smiled. "I put paper clips on the sheets I need copied."

When Janalou walked into the break room, Martina was already there. She eyed the file. "I heard Kree say he needed copies."

Instead of replying, Janalou brushed past her, on toward the copy machine.

Martina grabbed her shoulder, spun her around and snatched at the folder.

Instinctively, Janalou jerked back. But Martina's grab dislodged the folder and she dropped it. The contents spilled, sheets scattering helter-skelter.

"What's going on?" Kree asked, standing in the doorway, surveying the mess on the floor.

Wondering how much he had overheard, if anything, Janalou said, "I think Martina resents me, and doesn't want me to make copies. She tried to grab the folder, and it fell."

He turned his attention to Martina. "Why?"

"Because I don't like her and I don't want her here."

Janalou lowered her head in defeat. "Maybe I should find another job, Kree."

"No. I want you to stay." He glared at Martina. "You're not in charge of who works here and who doesn't," he said, his tone ominous. "Go to your desk and stay there, and don't harass Janalou again. Understood?"

Martina nodded before she stomped out, but Janalou saw her mutinous expression.

Kree patted her shoulder. "How long has she been treating you like this?"

"Since I started."

He bent and helped her collect the papers. "Make the copies. I'll take care of Martina."

~ * ~

He marched to his parents' office and shut the door behind him. Alone in her office, his mother looked up from behind her desk, eyed the closed door, then smiled. "Is something wrong, Kree?"

"Yeah. Martina's attitude toward Janalou sucks."

"What do you expect me to do about it?"

"You hired Martina, so as far as I'm concerned she's your responsibility. Tell her to lay off Janalou or you'll fire her."

His mother cleared her throat. "What if I don't…"

"Then I'll walk."

Helen's brows arched. "What does that mean?"

"I'll leave the firm."

"You wouldn't. Real estate is the only business you know."

"Yeah, but this isn't the only company in town. Besides, I have a college degree. I could switch my occupation, and try something different. Maybe even start my own company."

Helen wrung her hands, her expression worried, concerned. "Are you sure Janalou is right for you, Kree? Is she even a Christian?"

Fury bolted through him. "Don't interfere with my engagement, Mom. If you do, I'll be out of here before you can blink."

He turned and stomped out, his angry strides more mutinous than Martina's had been moments before. No one was going to dictate his future, especially not his mother. She had already run Bethany out of his life. If he wanted to marry Janalou, he would. Without realizing that his mind was actually considering the idea, he entered his office and shut the door.

Janalou looked up. "I'm sorry I've caused a disturbance."

"Don't be. It's not your fault." He walked closer, stopped when he reached her side. "Are you busy tonight?"

"No. Why?"

"I'd like to spend some time with you. Any objections?"

"No. None. I'd enjoy seeing you outside of the office."

"Good. I'll take you home tonight. We'll stop by my place first. I want you to see where I live."

"Thank you, Kree."

"You're more than welcome."

Her warm smile filled his heart and he realized he'd missed spending time with her. Maybe it was time to change that. After all, in the eyes of his family and all their acquaintances, they were engaged.

Eighteen

"Your home is fantastic." Janalou looked around the huge living room, seeming to take in details, including the wall of windows and the huge deck beyond them that was shaded by tall trees and surrounded by grass.

"It suits me," he said. "Come, I'll give you a tour."

When they reached his bedroom, his heart pumped. Having her close was like a gift, a dream come true.

"This room, like most of the others, looks very masculine," she said.

"Yeah. My interior decorator did a good job."

Janalou nodded, staring at the big king-sized bed, which made him ache to share it with her.

He cleared his throat instead, bringing her full attention back to him. "I didn't bring you here for this, but I'm going to kiss you anyway."

He lowered his head and kissed her. Thoroughly. They were both breathless when it ended.

"I know I said I wouldn't do that again, but I enjoy kissing you," he said, his voice gravelly. He was testing her. Testing himself.

Wondering if he should consider turning the fake engagement into a real one. That might be the only way he could truly help Janalou—the only way he could gain her complete trust. In the back of his head he acknowledged that his mother's unfriendly attitude might be partially responsible for his thoughts, and that was the wrong reason to consider marriage. But he liked Janalou more than any girl he had dated since Bethany's death, and he didn't like the idea of breaking up with her.

"I have a suggestion," he said, acting on an idea that had popped into his head more than once.

"What is it?"

"Maybe you should study and take the California drivers' test so you can drive if you get a chance."

Her puzzled expression relaxed into a smile. "I think that's a terrific suggestion," she said. "I'll check into it as soon as I can."

"Let me know if I can help in any way."

"You already have," she said, smiling.

~ * ~

The next evening, while Janalou and Cherilyn sat outside reclining on lounges while they watched Toby and Misti play in the sand nearby, Cherilyn said, "I don't know how you put up with Martina. It sounds like all she does is cause trouble. Maybe you should ask Kree to get rid of her."

Popping open a can of soda, Janalou shook her head. "He knows how she treats me, and I don't want to make waves at work. Martina was there first, so if they decide to let anyone go, it might be me."

"You sound so calm about the whole thing. If I were in your shoes, I wouldn't be."

She smiled, thinking about her dead mama's advice. "I try to take each day as it comes, without wishing any part of it away. I want to enjoy every moment. Mama taught me to live with an attitude of gratitude, in other words to enjoy what I have and not wish for something beyond my means or my reach."

Cherilyn picked up her can of soda. "That's good advice. Sounds like something my own mother might say." She leaned back, sipped her drink. "How are things between you and Kree?"

"They're good."

"Does he kiss you every night before you leave work?"

Janalou laughed. "No, not every night."

"I envy you," Cherilyn said then. "Kree's a terrific man. I'm sure you're going to be very happy."

"I already am." Then to change the subject, she winked and repeated something she had read in a magazine that afternoon. "A kiss is such a strange thing. It's never understood. You eat it not, you drink it not, and yet it tastes so good."

Behind her she heard Kree say, "Would you mind repeating that?"

Janalou swung her head around, her cheeks burning as she stared up at him. All she managed to say was, "I don't think you need to hear it again."

He grinned, and her heart spun out of control. "Yeah, you're right, and your kisses do taste good."

He was flirting. She could hardly believe it. For Cherilyn's benenfit? Or because he enjoyed it? She couldn't be sure. And didn't dare ask.

"I wasn't expecting to see you tonight. Is everything okay?" she asked.

"Everything's fine. I hoped you might have time to go for a drive. Do you?"

"Sure."

"I'll buy you an ice cream sundae," he said, sweetening his offer.

"Maybe this time you could let me buy one for you."

"Deal," he said, reaching to help her off the lounge.

In her apartment a few minutes later, he said, "Before we part tonight, I might issue a challenge."

"Issue it now, if you'd like."

"Tell me about your past."

She lowered her head. "I can't, Kree."

"Why not?"

"I just can't."

"What if we decided to get married? Would you tell me then?"

"That's a moot question since we aren't going to marry each other."

Instead of arguing, he changed the subject. "I know a great place to buy ice cream sundaes."

"What's it called?"

"Baskin Robbins."

She laughed. "How many are there here?"

He grinned. "At least three."

~ * ~

On her birthday a few days later, Kree brought a dozen long-stemmed red roses to the office. After setting the full milk-white vase on her desk with a flourish, he smiled. "Happy birthday, Jana."

"Thank you." She blushed, pleased with the shortened version of her name. "They're beautiful."

"So are you." He leaned over and kissed her cheek, making her heart race, and her head spin.

Since that spectacular kiss the night he showed her his home, he hadn't shown much affection. Now, as then, the kiss made her quiver all over. But she had the presence of mind not to cup her cheek, or swoon, although she was sure her face turned as red as the roses. Seeing Martina frown from the hall didn't help. It added to her emotional tailspin.

"I wanted to give you flowers when you were in the hospital," Kree said, "but I thought they might get in the way while we traveled."

"They probably would have," she said, remembering all the time she'd spent sleeping and dozing during those first few days after surgery. "I'm sure I'll enjoy them more now than I might have then, but thanks for the thought."

"You're welcome."

Everyone who came into Kree's office commented on the flowers—his father, his sisters, and their clients.

"Who sent you roses?" they all asked.

Each time Janalou smiled, and said, "Kree." No one had ever given her flowers. Tony had brought corsages for two formal dances, but a whole bouquet of flowers was new.

She resisted the urge to sigh. Kree was so thoughtful, and she was grateful. She was also falling more deeply in love. Sadly she suspected Martina loved him, too. How and where it would all end was anybody's guess. And she couldn't help regretting her reply when he'd asked if she'd tell him about her past if they had decided to get married.

~ * ~

That night she, Cherilyn, Sirena, Jocelyn and their combined six children gathered at the park to watch Jason, Kree, and his two brothers-in-law, Mark and Brad, play softball on a community team.

At the top of the last inning the score was tied. Kree's team would be last to bat. The other team scored two runs before they made three outs.

When it was Kree's team's turn, Jason hit a double, and both Mark and Brad got walked. With the bases loaded, Kree picked up a bat. When he hit a home run on his second swing, his team and all those cheering for them went wild, jumping, shouting, cheering, clapping each other on the back.

As soon as Kree crossed home plate, the umpire ended the game. Since it was Janalou's first experience at a community ball game, she watched in fascination as men on both teams gathered in separate circles and chanted, "Bricka bracka, soda cracker, ziss, boom, bah, team work, team work, rah, rah, rah."

Afterwards all the men from both teams shook hands.

Janalou marveled at their camaraderie. They had played a friendly game without cursing, taunting or muttering foul language. She'd never seen anything like it. And it left her with a warm feeling that spread as Kree joined her in the bleachers.

"Did you enjoy the game?" he asked.

She nodded. "You played very well. Like a true hero."

"We all played well," he said. "We're a team, and it takes every guy to play."

"And win," Jason said, grinning.

"Let's go eat," Kree said. "I'm hungry."

Janalou and Kree piled into Jason's SUV and rode to Reina's for a pot luck party to celebrate both her and Cherilyn's birthdays.

All of Kree's family was there, including his parents, although Max and Helen hadn't been at the ball game. His nieces and nephews, who had played with Misti and Toby at the park, continued their fun in Reina's fenced backyard, along with Jamie, a little boy they knew from the daycare center. Cherilyn had invited him and his father, Brad, and Janalou was happy she had met a man she liked and wanted to date. Reina had invited Duke too, but Janalou was relieved not to have Martina there.

The adults joked and laughed as they ate. Then Reina lit the candles on a homemade birthday cake, and everyone sang "Happy Birthday" to her and Cherilyn.

"Make your wishes before you blow out the candles," Reina said.

Janalou closed her eyes and wished she would always have these marvelous people as friends. She wondered what Cherilyn wished for, and suspected they would tell each other before the night ended.

"Let's clear the table and save the cake until they open their presents," Jocelyn suggested.

"Good idea," Sirena said.

When all the dishes had been cleared away, Reina said, "You should open your gifts at the same time."

"Why?" Cherilyn asked. "Are they all the same?"

"Probably," Reina said, her even white teeth gleaming when she smiled.

The gifts she extended were practical. Small reading lamps to put by their beds. At different times they had both said they wanted one.

Kree's parents gave Janalou and Cherilyn each a huge box of chocolates. They also gave Janalou a cell phone.

"You don't have a home phone," Helen said in a no-nonsense tone, "and you said you see no reason to get one, so we thought this would come in handy."

"I'm sure it will. Thank you."

"Our gift includes the monthly fee," Max said.

"I can't let you pay for my phone," Janalou objected.

"Of course you can." Max grinned, a single dimple denting his cheek, similar to the one that often dented Kree's. "It's a business expense. Consider it as part of your salary."

Awed by their generosity, and feeling guilty because she had decided to tell Kree she would look for another job so things wouldn't be awkward after they broke up, she said, "I feel so indebted."

"Don't," Jocelyn said. "That phone will benefit us as much as it will you. I've wanted to call you a number of times, and found it inconvenient when I couldn't." She smiled. "Here. Open our gifts next."

"Perfume," Janalou and Cherilyn said in unison a few seconds later.

"Smells terrific," Cherilyn said after she sprayed her wrist.

"Here are our gifts." Sirena extended one to each of them.

"Books." Janalou smiled. "Mine is written by Judith McNaught, my favorite author."

Sirena winked. "You mentioned that a few days ago."

"Guess I'm next." Duke gave them each a wrist watch.

Amazed by his generosity, too, Janalou said, "My watch stopped working last week."

"I know," Duke said. "Ye told me, lass."

Tears glistened in Cherilyn's blue eyes. "I haven't had this nice a birthday for years."

"Neither have I." Janalou's heart reacted raucously when Kree extended his gifts. She opened hers slowly, savoring the suspense.

"Necklaces," she said, delighted when she unwrapped hers. "They look like alexandrite, our birth stones."

"They are," Kree said. His blue eyes twinkled as he winked at her, and she felt a rush of warmth heat her cheeks.

Jason extended his gifts next.

"More books," Cherilyn said, studying hers. "I love to read, especially when there's nothing good on TV after I put the kids to bed."

"Not just books," Janalou said. "Mine's a trilogy written by Nora Roberts."

"Mine are, too, but a different set," Cherilyn said, smiling up at Jason.

"I heard you were working at a daycare center," he said.

"I am."

"Do you like your work?"

She nodded. "I love it."

"You must be good with kids."

"I can vouch for that," Brad, Jamie's father, said.

"Time for cake and ice cream," Reina announced minutes later.

While everyone ate dessert, Duke drew Janalou aside to speak in private. "Now that ye have yer own phone, feel free to call if ye ever need me, lass. Remember always that I be only a phone call away."

She had the oddest sensation that he knew something she didn't, but she couldn't imagine what it might be, so she forced a smile. "Thanks, Duke. I won't forget."

There had been times at work, and that night, too, when she sensed tension between Kree and his parents. She wondered if anyone else felt it, but kept her thoughts to herself. To talk about that with anyone, even her new friend Cherilyn, would feel like a betrayal to Kree, and he had done so much for her she didn't want to say or do anything that might reflect poorly on him.

When the party broke up, Kree drove her home. She thought he only did it because it was expected. A few miles from her apartment, he said, "I have something else for you."

"What is it?" she asked, curious.

He pulled over to the side of the road before he extended a small gift-wrapped package. When she opened it, she found a pink cell phone holder, decorated with rhinestones. "It's for your new phone, and includes a slot for your driver's license," he explained.

A few days before, he had driven her to the courthouse and let her use his car for the driving test, after she passed the written one.

"Thank you." Without thinking, she flung his arms around his neck and kissed him on the mouth.

"You're welcome," he said, smiling down at her in the dim dashboard light. "I'll have to remember to give you things more often."

"No. Please don't," she pleaded. "You've already given me way too much.

He waited until they reached her apartment before he said, "I have a feeling you've been wanting to tell me something, but you're holding back."

Perplexed that he read her so well, she admitted, "I think I should look for another job, so when we break up, it won't be awkward for either one of us."

He shook his head. "Push that idea out of your head. We've only been engaged a short time, and I'm enjoying not having other women shoved at me."

Relief tumbled through Janalou. She really didn't want to make any more changes in her life yet, but she wished Martina didn't resent her so much. "There's another reason I've been thinking about working somewhere else," she said.

"Martina?"

Janalou nodded. "She doesn't want me around, and she makes sure I know that when the rest of you are out of the office."

"I'll have a talk with her."

"No, please don't. That might make her resent me even more. I think she's in love with you, Kree. That's why she doesn't like me."

"In love with me?" he said, as though the idea had never occurred to him.

Again Janalou nodded. "Haven't you noticed how she looks at you?"

"No." He sounded stunned, maybe even shocked. "I can't believe Martina has any designs on me."

"She said if we set a wedding date, she'll find a way to make me sorry."

"Then we won't set one. If people ask when we intend to tie the knot, let's tell them some time next summer."

Relief poured through Janalou. Next summer sounded so far away. *Could she really hang onto to their pretend engagement and continue to see Kree for a whole year?* Part of her hoped so. Another part worried about Martina, and problems at the office. Not in any way did she want to make Kree's family uncomfortable. So, if things got worse, she would look for another job.

~ * ~

About a week later, Kree sat down in front of Janalou's desk. Everyone else was at lunch or out showing houses to prospective clients. He leaned forward, propping an elbow on her desk. She wished they were closer, wished he would touch her, kiss her, tell her he wanted her again.

"If you were serious when you mentioned looking for work elsewhere, I have a suggestion."

"I did think about it, but that's about all," Janalou prevaricated.

"I have a suggestion that might help."

"What is it?"

"You could study for the real estate exam. If you had a license, you could work with our firm, if you like, or any other firm. I'm sure you'd make more money selling houses than you'll ever make working as a receptionist."

"That's a terrific idea," she said, delighted by his suggestion, and relieved he hadn't suggested that she pursue looking for work elsewhere.

But she was also disappointed that he didn't touch her. The fake engagement didn't even feel fake anymore. It didn't feel like anything. If not for the ring on her finger, she might have believed it had never happened at all. *Why had she been so quick to ignore his comment about the possibility of getting married?*

~ * ~

A few days later, Kree stopped by her apartment on Monday, her day off. Cherilyn had the day off too, and Janalou had volunteered to watch Toby and Misti and Jamie so their parents could go out together. The children were outside, playing on the grass with toys, and she was sitting on a blanket watching them when Kree arrived.

"Hi," he said.

"Hi yourself."

Kree hunkered down beside her, making her pulse throb and her heart race. Because she was so happy to see him, and ached to reach out and touch him, she kept her gaze averted until she got herself under control.

He waited until she looked at him. "On your days off, Martina repeatedly tells us she doesn't need help. None of us agrees because we don't have problems finding contracts or files with you doing the filing. Even so, my suggestion for you to take the real estate exam might ease the situation between you and Martina."

Janalou nodded. "I think it's a cool idea, but I don't know where to take classes. Can you tell me where I might find information?"

Kree nodded, and the action, along with a slight breeze blew his dark curls off his forehead. "I brought a manual for you. It's in my car. I'll go get it in a few minutes. The real estate classes last from three to six weeks, and I have both an address and a phone number. You might be able to attend class on your days off, or at night."

"I will, and thanks, Kree. I'd love to move into sales."

He reached for her hand. "You must know that people like you, and everyone in my family thinks you'd be a natural at selling. We'd be proud to have you continue to work with us after you pass the exam, and we'd all be above happy if you'd continue to do the filing so we can find contracts."

"I will. Thanks again. For everything."

"You're welcome."

~ * ~

Kree followed his impulse and wrapped his arms around her. He liked having her in his arms, and had decided to use any excuse to get her there. That she came of her own volition gave him hope that she felt more than friendship for him. And it gave him more ideas about something that had blossomed in his mind, and wouldn't go away. Just because their engagement wasn't real, that didn't mean they couldn't enjoy each other.

"I've been thinking about something," he said, inhaling her sweet feminine essence that threatened to drive him mad.

"What is it?" she asked, easing back to look up into his eyes.

He glanced around to make sure the children weren't within earshot. "I'm attracted to you, and you're attracted to me, right?"

She nodded.

"Then I see no reason not to consider getting closer."

Her mouth fell open, and he knew he'd startled her when all she did was stare.

"Don't be shocked," he said. "You must know I want you, Janalou. I've been lying to myself, and trying to pretend I don't. But I do. I've wanted you from the beginning. I can't give you my heart, but I can promise I won't hurt you, and I'll be faithful to you. I'll be good to you. I promise."

"I–a–need time to think," she said, sounding as surprised as she looked.

"I'm sure you do. And you have time. It's only been four weeks since your surgery. We have plenty of time to get closer."

He stopped then. He'd already said more than he'd intended, more than he should have said. *Closer? Is that all he really wanted?*

His conscience was getting the best of him. He'd made her think he wanted intimacy, and he did, but that hadn't been his intention.

"Why?" she finally asked.

"Why?" he repeated, trying to think of a reply that wouldn't irritate or insult her. "Because you're a beautiful woman, and I find you very desirable. Because I haven't met any other woman I'm attracted to. You've made me feel alive again, Janalou."

"I can't believe you're suggesting intimacy," she said, pulling free and scooting away. "You said if I agreed to pretend we were engaged, you wouldn't expect anything more."

"I don't." He raised his hand and stroked her cheek. "And I'm not suggesting intimacy, even though I realize that's what it sounded like. I'm suggesting we spend more time together, and get to know each other better."

"That's—all—you want? To spend some more time together?"

He nodded. "You feel the same way. I know you do. It's there in your eyes when you look at me. And we both sense it when I touch you. Some kind of chemistry shimmers between us even when I don't. So, you might as well get used to the idea of spending more time together. I have. It's going to happen. It isn't a matter of if. It's just a matter of when."

"Y'all sound pretty sure. Even cocky."

"That's because I believe in thinking positive." He bent his head, but she turned hers and his lips met her cheek instead of her tempting lips.

"If you need patience, I'll try to give you that, but I can't promise I won't be tempted to try to persuade you to see me outside the office."

Her cheeks were red and she sucked her bottom lip beneath her upper teeth. He'd seen her do that a few times early on, and taken it as a sign of worry.

Disliking himself for creating distress, he said, "If my suggestion doesn't appeal to you, tell me now."

"I don't know whether it appeals or not. How can I? I haven't thought about seeing ya'll much away from the office. I thought you'd made it durn clear you didn't want that."

"If I did, it wasn't intentional. And I apologize if my suggestion upsets you. Most women would consider it to be a compliment."

"I'm not most girls."

"I know that. Are you offended?"

"No. I might not be sure what I feel, but I'm not offended. I feel complimented, but, but I didn't expect this. Now, can we talk about something else? Please?"

"Sure. How about dinner? Will you eat with me tonight? We could go to a movie, too, if you'd like."

"Why?"

He laughed. "Don't look so suspicious. I won't try to seduce you. You know that goes against my grain, but I would like to spend more time with you. And we are supposed to be engaged. We should go out sometimes."

"You haven't asked me to go out for days—weeks. Why now?"

"Because I've missed you, Janalou. I liked traveling with you, and I like seeing you at the office. But that isn't enough. I want to share more of your life."

~ * ~

Janalou decided the subject needed to change, and blurted what had been on her mind since her birthday. "Don't you think pretending to be engaged is deceitful? Dishonest? Doesn't it ever make you feel unworthy of your family and friends' trust?

His expression looked as though she'd struck him, but he kept his voice quiet when he spoke, although he pulled back, stiffening his spine. "We're not hurting anyone, so don't let it bother you." He straightened his legs and rolled down to lie on his side on the blanket beside her. "How about tonight? Are you going out with me?"

"Yes. In spite of your cocky attitude I'll go, but tonight I pay for dinner and the movie."

"You're on." He came up in one smooth fluid motion, and planted a kiss on her surprised lips. "That'll have to hold us until later."

He looked and sounded so confident, she laughed. "Has anyone ever told you that you can't always have everything your way?"

"Yeah. But I don't believe them unless it comes true." He climbed up to his feet. "When do you expect Cherilyn to get home?"

Janalou glanced at her new watch, still grateful to Duke for giving it to her. "In about an hour."

"I'll be back in forty-five minutes. I have a short errand to run."

"What is it? Or shouldn't I ask?"

He grinned. "I need to go buy some flowers for the terrific lady in my life."

The warmth in his voice turned her insides to mush. He could be a very persuasive man. No wonder he was in real estate. He could probably sell snow to an Eskimo.

"By the way," he said, smiling down at her, "my family always spends the Fourth of July together. They'all expect you to be with me. Any objections?"

"No. None. I'd love to spend the holiday with you."

"Fine."

Half an hour later, he returned with a patriotic floral flower arrangement made of pretty red, white and blue carnations. Together they sat outside watching the children until Cherilyn arrived home.

After Brad lifted his son, Jamie, up on his shoulders and left, Janalou said, "How was the date?"

"Great." Cherilyn's blue eyes sparkled. "We had a terrific time."

"I'm glad."

"Me too," Kree said. "Now it's our turn. My fiancée is taking me out."

Before Janalou had a chance to explain, he took her hand and guided her around to the parking lot. "Want to drive?"

She looked up, surprised. "Your Cadillac?"

"Sure. Why not? You've got a license now."

With a shrug, she took the keys he dangled in front of her, then felt guilty. She was still taking advantage of him and his generosity, but at least she wasn't breaking the law.

In spite of her guilt, she drove to dinner and paid the bill afterwards—a first for them because she hadn't had enough cash to pay for the ice cream sundaes they'd ordered when they'd gone for a drive. But tonight she was in charge, and she paid for the movie after dinner, too.

"I like your style," Kree said, making her heart spin when he placed a quick kiss on the side of her throat after he drove back to her apartment.

"I like yours, too," she said, her voice a breathless whisper.

~ * ~

During the next week, she studied for the real estate exam, attended class, and tried to take Kree's advice not to worry.

But her conscience wouldn't let her rest. A demon seemed to live in her head, and wouldn't allow her to forget the dual lies she'd told. She hated the guilt. Hated that her new life was based on a shaky foundation. What should she do?

And she had something else to consider. Spending more time with Kree. Was she ready for that? She didn't know. Didn't even know whether to be insulted or complimented. He'd said he wanted her. And she wanted him too. But not just for a little while. She wanted commitment. And a future with him. But she couldn't have either one because of the lies she'd spun.

In spite of her misgivings, and the discord between her and Martina, Janalou kept so busy she rarely had time to think about her old life. If only she dared tell Kree her secret.

But the longer she put it off, the more difficult the truth became.

To keep her mind off her guilt, she studied harder, and swam laps every day after work so she fell into bed exhausted.

Nineteen

On the Fourth of July, Janalou and Kree joined his family at Lodi Lake. Adults and children alike wore red, white and blue, a Lodi tradition, Janalou had been told, which she heartily approved and followed. The red, white and blue carnations Kree had given her a few days earlier were still fresh and she smiled every time she looked at them.

"The city of Lodi knows how to celebrate." Kree's mother smiled as Janalou plunked her bowl of potato salad on the picnic table that Helen had covered with a colorful patriotic cloth. Since her birthday, Helen had acted friendlier, and Janalou was so grateful she wanted to hug her, but she didn't dare.

"I grew up in Elko, Nevada," Helen confided. "It was fun, but nothing like Lodi."

Placing a pot of fried chicken in the middle of the table, Sirena, said, "Living here is terrific. Every month Lodi has some kind of community-based celebration."

"Yes," Joclyn agreed, while she unpacked red, white and blue paper plates, napkins, and red plastic knives and forks from her picnic basket. "In the summer we have outdoor music performances on the second Saturday of every month, and evening concerts in the park."

"They like to brag." Kree reached for a slice of watermelon.

Sirena slapped at his hand, dislodging the melon. "You should take Janalou to a concert."

"I plan to." Kree grinned, nabbing another piece of watermelon.

Jocelyn smacked the table in front of him. "Not yet. That's for dessert."

He laughed. "I say life's short. Eat dessert first. 'Sides, I thought Mom's chocolate cake was for dessert."

"Grandma made apple pie, too," little Ben, Jocelyn's five year old son, said.

"But we want ice cream, too," his sister said. "Daddy promised we can have ice cream today."

"And you will," Kree agreed. "After we eat the fried chicken and potato salad our women made for us."

He winked at Janalou and her heart nearly stopped. *Our women?* Did he really think of her as his? Enjoying the banter, she smiled, duly noting that Sirena and Jocelyn's reprimands hadn't stopped Kree from eating and enjoying the watermelon.

"Spending the Fourth here is an event I wouldn't want to miss," she said.

"Me neither." Ben's eyes were bright with a big grin. "The fireworks go off over the water when it's dark. I love fireworks. Do you, Janalou?"

She nodded, looking around at other merry-makers. She had heard Lodi families celebrated the nation's birthday with a variety of activities—rides, crafts, beach projects and boating, all around the lake. To be sharing it with Kree's family thrilled her. To be accepted by his mother at last humbled her.

Last year she had celebrated the Fourth with Margie, her best friend, and Margie's family, including her grandparents, who had taken her to Europe this year. Those happy times were gone, but would never be forgotten. Sometimes she dreamed about the memories she'd made with Margie, and if she woke up during the night, she relived them when she had trouble falling back asleep, which didn't occur nearly as often as it used to.

Once again she thanked her lucky stars for boarding the same bus as Kree, and for being guided here to Lodi where she thought she could live happily for the rest of her life.

After lunch, the men and children tossed paper plates and plastic knives in a nearby trash container while the women cleared the table, stacking leftovers in the center and covering them with a clean cloth. As they finished, Janalou saw Martina walking toward them with a couple she decided must be her parents. Before Kree's family noticed her, Martina shot Janalou a venomous glare.

When Kree spotted them, he motioned them closer and shook her parents' hands. "Hope you're having a nice holiday, Jorge."

"We are," the Mexican man said, looking from him to Janalou. "This your *novia*?"

Kree nodded, and introduced them.

"Last year we celebrated with you," Martina said, her peevish expression sullen. "Why didn't you invite us this year?"

"It was an oversight." Helen smiled and filled the awkward silence. "I thought you might be spending the day with other friends." She patted the bench beside her, and Janalou wondered if the oversight might have been Helen's way to let Martina know the way she treated Janalou was unacceptable. Pleased with that thought, she smiled.

"Would you like to join us now?" Helen asked. "We can offer dessert. We have plenty left over."

"Thank you," Martina's mother, Katalina, said. "We eat already. Not hungry now." But her expression also seemed to blame Janalou for not being included in the Wintertons' plans.

Vowing not to let Martina or her parents upset her, Janalou turned away to entertain the children while the adults talked.

~ * ~

Kree watched Janalou play a quiet game with his nieces and nephews, shushing them with a finger at her lips so they didn't disturb their parents or grandparents. She was a natural with kids, and they adored her. So did he, but he still hadn't decided what to do about it. Neither of them had mentioned his proposal to spend more time together since last week, but he would continue the discussion before the night ended.

When Martina and her parents finally departed, he heaved a sigh of relief. Early on, he had suspected Martina had a thing for him, but he'd never returned the sentiment, and thought he had made that clear long ago. The mere fact that she worked for him and his family must have given her ideas. He thought announcing he was engaged to Janalou would have killed whatever hopes she might have pinned on him. Apparently it hadn't. He'd have to find a way to let her know that nothing was possible between them. He also wanted to make things easier for Janalou at the office. She shouldn't have to put up with Martina's petulance.

When she turned her head and smiled at him, he felt as though he'd been sucker-punched. Yes, they would talk about spending more time together, and about their fake engagement, too. Maybe it was time to convince her to make it real. He even considered suggesting a wedding date because he wanted her. *Would she agree? Or would she tell him he was crazy for even having such a thought?*

The afternoon passed pleasantly. In the evening, Kree and Janlou joined his friends, waiting for the fireworks to begin.

"Have you enjoyed today, Jana?" he asked, sitting so close their bodies touched from hip to ankle.

"Yes. Immensely. Thanks for inviting me to spend the Fourth with you."

"You're welcome." With a grin, he tucked her in the curve of his arm as they stared up at the first fireworks to appear in the dark starry sky. "This event is touted as one of the country's better fireworks shows."

She smiled. "I heard that, and I'm beginning to feel more obligated. Now that I have a job, I'd like to set up a repayment schedule. I feel as though I've taken advantage of you, and I don't much like the feeling." She spoke quietly so Jason and Kree's other friends couldn't overhear.

"You're repaying me by being with me on days like this," Kree whispered in her ear, turning her flesh into tiny goose bumps.

"This isn't repayment," she whispered back.

"I agree. It's fun."

"I want to pay you back."

"Let's not talk about it now. I don't need the money, and you're still getting settled. If I ever do need it, I'll let you know. Then maybe we can discuss some sort of payback arrangement."

Janalou smiled. "Sometimes I think you're too good to be true."

"Sometimes I think the same thing about this arrangement of ours. It has a lot of benefits."

"Such as?"

"This." He dipped his head and kissed her. The third time in less than a week, the last time being two nights ago after work, when everyone had left the office except them. The kiss had startled him as much as her. He hadn't intended to kiss her again. But when he did, he wondered why he ever resisted. Desire like he'd never known had punched through him when she'd leaned closer and boldly wrapped her arms around his waist, hugging him closer, something she hadn't done before. When he had tightened his arms around her, she had laid her head against his chest and said, "Thank you, Kree. For everything. I know I keep repeating myself, but I'm very grateful for everything you've done for me. "

"You're welcome."

"I don't want it to end."

"Neither do I." And that's when he had made his suggestion again. "Have you thought about my suggestion to spend more time together?"

"Am I a woman?"

When he'd stared, without understanding, she had shrugged. "How could I not think about it, but we agreed not to get too emotionally involved. Besides, I have classes now and I need to study."

"I know that." He deepened the kiss, ignoring everything except the desirable woman who trembled in his arms and kissed him back with as much passion as he offered her.

Then he was kissing her again, no longer willing to fight the attraction.

~ * ~

Janalou didn't need fireworks in the sky. They were lighting up inside her body, inside her head. She responded, kissing Kree eagerly, trying to tell him what she felt in her heart.

She had to force herself not to gasp for breath when the passionate kisses finally ended. "Those were pretty intense," she murmured, almost afraid to look him in the eye. But she did.

He was smiling. "Our kisses are supposed to be intense." He winked, sending her heart into another tailspin. "We're engaged."

"Hey, you two... knock it off," Jason said. "You're making me envious."

"Then maybe you should find yourself a girl," Kree said, without taking his gaze from Janalou.

Jason cleared his throat. "I'm looking. I'd like one like you've got. Do you have a twin sister, Janalou?"

"No. I wish I did, but I don't have any sisters or brothers." Her smile faded as she recalled the repetitive dreams about Jeri Sue and Paul. *Were they her make-believe family? Had she invented them because she wanted a brother and sister?*

"What do you think of Kree's palatial digs?"

She had seen where he lived and wondered if she ever would again. "They're terrific," she said. During Kree's brief tour, she'd been too aware of him to pay much attention to their surroundings.

"Are you going to live there when you get married?"

"We haven't discussed that," Kree said, thankfully saving her from having to reply. "We haven't set a wedding date yet, either. Janalou is mourning the loss of her parents, and she needs time to adjust to living here first."

Her face heated, and she was glad it was dark. Unable to think of a single thing to say, she trembled when Kree tightened his hold again. She had a feeling he wanted more than kisses and that's why he had suggested spending more time together.

As they drove home after the fireworks, Janalou said, "Today was very special. Filled with patriotic music, friendship, and good will... it was truly a day when people celebrate America, and being an American. Everyone's enthusiasm made me proud."

"Me too," Kree said. "There's always an outpouring of patriotism here, and I'm glad you settled in Lodi instead of Los Angeles."

"I'm glad, too."

When they reached the outskirts of town, and he turned east instead of west, she said, "Where are we going?"

~ * ~

"To my digs. I rushed you through the last time we were there." He didn't add that he had because if he hadn't, he wouldn't have wanted to let her leave. Now he wanted to convince her to spend more time there. With him.

"Your home is palatial," she said, making him grin as she looked around the living room again.

"Not really. Jason likes to exaggerate."

"You said someone decorated for you. Was she or he a professional?"

"Yeah. In addition to selling real estate, Sirena likes to decorate, so I gave her free rein. She wanted to do something here she couldn't do with her own home, and I was willing to let her experiment."

"She did a gorgeous job."

"I'll tell her you approve." He took her hand, and tingles of awareness shot up her arm as he showed her through the house again, this time at a more leisurely pace.

She had no difficulty imagining herself living there with him. Eating together in the roomy kitchen or more formal dining room. Watching the sixty-five inch TV in the family room, sitting side by side on the cushiony sofa. Welcoming company into the living room, and entertaining guests outside on the beautiful wooded deck.

When they reached the master bedroom, she could even see herself sharing the bed with Kree. Whether they were married or not. And then she knew what her answer would be if the subject of intimacy ever came up. She would agree. Because she wanted whatever they could share before they split up. And split up they would. She knew that in her heart, just as she knew she would never forget him or stop loving him.

~ * ~

As the warm summer days passed, Janalou grew closer to Kree and his family, and to Cherilyn. She had told her about her past, including Belle's cruelty, but she didn't reveal her real name.. Although she withheld that information, she decided to find an attorney who could help her arrange to change her name legally.

One night after work, she agreed to watch Toby and Misti so Cherilyn could go out on another date with Brad. She also agreed to tend his son, Jamie, again.

Brad was an attorney, and when he brought Cherilyn home, Janalou said, "I changed my name and I'd like to make it legal. Can you help me?"

"Sure."

"Do you know what it costs? If it's expensive?"

He shook his blond head. "Most attorneys charge by the hour, but I'll prepare the legal documents without charging you because you're Cherilyn's friend, and you watch all the kids sometimes so we can go out."

"Thanks. When..."

"I'll take care of it first thing tomorrow. Do you want to stop by the office and sign the documents on your lunch hour?"

"Yes. Of course."

The next day, as soon as that was accomplished, she breathed easier.

The day after that, she applied for a new social security number, although she didn't dare tell the Wintertons her employee records needed to be changed.

At the office, she was in charge of filing, so she found a new form, filled it out and destroyed the first one. She hadn't worked there long enough for a quarterly report to be filed with the IRS. For the first time since she had begun to work for the Wintertons, she relaxed, comfortable with the knowledge that she was no longer breaking the law by using a deceased person's social security number.

~ * ~

Occasionally Kree took Reina out to eat, and he invited Janalou to go along. When they spent time with his family or Reina, Janalou almost felt as though they were really engaged.

Although he kissed her often now, he didn't press her to sleep with him. Sometimes she wished he would. At other times she was grateful he didn't.

Duke continued to drive her to and from work every day.

"I don't know why I'm so lucky to have your help," she said one day.

"Perhaps this be yer lucky year, lass," he replied, smiling. "I'm thinking ye be overdue fer some good luck."

"Yes," she thought out loud, deciding this truly must be the luckiest year of her life. "I feel as though I belong in Lodi, and I love having my own apartment."

"Do ye love the lad, Kree?" Duke asked.

"Yes. Meeting him is one of the best things that's ever happened to me."

"Happy I be fer ye, lass."

"Thanks, Duke. That means a lot. So does your friendship. I feel safe with you living across the grass from me."

Duke winked. "That pleases me, lass.

~ * ~

More than halfway through her real estate classes, Janalou decided she had to tell Kree her secret. She wanted to explain away from the office. With that in mind, she invited him to eat at her apartment one Sunday afternoon.

Although she had cooked for Cherilyn and her children several times, it was the first time she had asked Kree over, and she was nervous for days beforehand. In the past, she had helped Mama entertain dozens of times, then she had cooked dinner for her papa's guests before and after he married Belle, but she had never entertained anyone alone.

Deciding to fix something that couldn't possibly fail, she put a pot roast with onions, potatoes, and carrots in her small oven.

After Kree arrived, she checked the oven and smiled. "Dinner or lunch is almost ready. I cooked pot roast, and I hope you're hungry."

"I am. I haven't eaten since last night."

"Me either. I skipped breakfast this morning."

"I did, too."

Kree eyed the chocolate cake she'd baked for dessert. "That looks delicious." Then he startled her by picking up a dishtowel and tucking it around his waist like an apron. "What can I do to help? Set the table? Or make gravy?"

"The table's already set."

He looked around and grinned. "Yeah, and it looks great."

She laughed. "Not really," and then a bit wistfully, she added, "I wish I had real china. Those dishes came with the apartment, and they'all have to do." She blinked then, realizing what he had offered to do. "You know how to make gravy?"

"Sure. All I have to do is make a smooth paste of flour or cornstarch and water, stir it into the juice from the pot roast, add salt and pepper, and bring it to a boil."

"Who taught you how to cook?"

"Nobody. I had to learn when I went to college. Either that, live on junk food, or eat what my roommate fixed, and most of that tasted awful." He stepped closer, and her heart gave a sudden leap. She was so glad Martina wasn't around to interfere like she usually managed to do at the office.

"With your wealth, I would have expected that you'd eat out often," she said, wishing he would touch her.

"We did, but going out often requires time and I did have to study."

"Have you ever tired of eating out?" she asked.

"Yes, since I do that more now than I eat in."

"I haven't had a chance to get tired of eating out," she said.

He winked, staring down at her. "A steady diet of the same thing day after day can get boring." He glanced behind her, at the table. "I could fill the water glasses, if you'd like."

She shook her head. "I'd rather watch you make gravy."

His grin deepened. "Do you have flour or cornstarch?"

"Both."

"Fine. Where's your salt and pepper?"

She showed him, and he got to work while she put ice cubes, lemon slices and water in two glasses, and set them on the table. He never ceased to amaze her.

The table was small, big enough for four people but no extra room for food, so better suited for two. And Janalou was so happy to have her own place, it seemed like heaven.

"I need to tell you something," she said after they sat down and filled their plates.

In the act of cutting his roast beef, he paused and looked up. "I have something I'd like to discuss with you, too."

Surprised and curious, she swallowed. Afraid his reaction to her news might be negative and he'd end the fake engagement right then and there, and fire her on the spot as well, she said, "Let's talk about what's on your mind, then we'll talk about what's on mine."

He set his knife and fork down, picked up his glass, and took a drink of water. If she hadn't known better, she would have thought he was nervous, but she'd never known him to be nervous before, not about anything. Embarrassed once or twice, but never nervous.

Kree set his glass down with deliberate slowness, and reached for her hand. Her heart started to sing. Would he say he wanted their fake engagement to be real, and no longer a farce?

He cleared his throat.

Again she wondered if he was nervous. Her singing heart started to pound like a loud drum. Would he say what she so desperately wanted to hear? She sure hoped so. "What?" she asked, warmed by the intensity in his gaze.

"I'm taking a few days off work to go fishing with my friends. I know you're not comfortable around Martina, and if you don't want to be in the office when I'm not there, you can take some time off too, if you'd like."

Janalou's throat went dry. If her life had depended on it, she couldn't have spoken. She had expected him to talk about them and he'd only been interested in telling her about his fishing trip.

She blinked. Disappointment warred with hurt, and she was too shocked to know which emotion was strongest.

"It shouldn't come as a surprise," he said. "I've mentioned my fishing trips before."

"Yes." She nodded, but the idea of not seeing him every day at work had shaken her. She'd become so used to being near him, her paralyzed mind couldn't think about much else.

"You could stay at my place and get used to being there," he said. "I'll give you to the keys to my car, so you can drive it too, if you'd like."

When she still didn't speak, his generous mouth curved into a grin. "We're attracted to each other, Janalou. Maybe we owe it to ourselves to explore our relationship and take it to a different level when I get back."

Her heart did a crazy flip. Was he suggesting making their engagement real? Or just exploring intimacy?

She didn't know what to say. Part of her wanted to shout 'yes' because he might then discover he loved her. But that was wishful thinking. He couldn't love her. Even if he did, he'd probably end up hating her when he discovered she had lied about being an orphan, lied about her name, her true identity.

While she stared, speechless, he picked up his fork and started to eat.

Trying to act as nonchalant as he, she cut a small piece of pot roast and raised it to her mouth. It tasted good, and she was surprised she noticed, because her mind was at war. After she swallowed, she finally found her voice. "I'd like some time to think about taking time off work."

He smiled. "I expected you to say that. If you don't mind working, I'm sure my family will appreciate having you at the office."

He chewed another bite, swallowed, and looked up again. "I failed to say something important. I think you should consider moving in with me when I return."

Once again her heart did a crazy flip. *Move in with him?*

"Are you serious?"

"Yes. What did you want to talk about?"

Too strung out over the agitation gyrating inside her, she couldn't even imagine discussing what she had intended to say, so she shrugged. "It isn't important."

The truth would have to wait until he returned, and until she worked up more courage. Right then, all she could think about was what he had suggested. Stay at his house. Get used to being there. Spend more time together. Consider living with him.

What a dilemma. If she said 'no,' she'd feel like a prude. But if she said 'yes,' she might wind up feeling like a tart.

One thought hammered through her. If Mama were still alive, she wouldn't approve of her jumping into a situation she didn't feel ready for. That was one of the reasons she hadn't been tempted to sleep with a man yet.

After they finished eating, Kree helped clear the table, and they did the dishes together, by hand, since the small apartment didn't have a dishwasher.

They sat on the couch, and talked some more. To her relief, he didn't mention their living arrangements again. Nor did he do anything suggestive. He didn't even touch her. She wasn't sure she liked that.

After a while, they took a long, leisurely walk around the apartment complex, stopping to watch swimmers playing volleyball in the pool, and again a little later to watch a badminton match. Kree didn't mention his fishing trip again, or talk about their attraction. And she didn't know whether to be relieved or upset.

He stayed all afternoon. They ate leftovers for supper.

"Guess I'd better go home," he said around 8:00 p.m. "I've been here all day."

"I've enjoyed your company, Kree."

"I've enjoyed yours, too. You will think about my suggestions, won't you?"

She nodded. And suddenly there it was. The excitement. The tension. She wished he would draw her close and hold her. But he didn't. He was giving her time to make her decision.

He stuck his hands inside his pockets, looking so handsome her mouth watered. Would he kiss her again? Just the thought had sensations pulsating through her like a rocket zooming through outer space.

"Thanks for lunch and dinner."

"You're welcome," she said as she walked him to the door.

Then, when she least expected it, he drew her close, and stared down into her eyes. "This is what it could be like, Janalou, if you agreed to live with me."

When he kissed her, surprise exploded in her brain while joy bubbled up inside. She had wondered when or if he would ever kiss her again, and this confirmed what it was like. Heaven. Better than anything she had ever experienced. And it made her wish she meant something special to him so she could say 'yes' to his suggestions, and see him more often without regretting her decision.

Breathless when the kiss ended, she couldn't speak.

He didn't either. He looked as surprised as she felt. Giving her a long look, he opened the door and left.

She watched him walk to his car, longing to be more important to him, yearning to have him look at her with love in his gaze.

In love. Yes, she fell more deeply each day.

Was he falling in love, too? How she wished he would. Maybe not right away, but some day.

Would he if they lived together? Slept together? Or would he tire of her and want to end their fake engagement before she was ready? Would she ever be ready?

Haunted by his comment about a steady diet of the same thing day after day getting boring made her want to plop on the sofa and cry.

~ * ~

Kree sat in his car without starting the engine. He was touched by Janalou's invitation to share the day together. Her quiet manner drew him like a magnet, and he was awed by her inner strength, certain she had lived through something unpleasant, and survived something ugly. He had a feeling something bad might happen to her and the only way he could protect her was to have her live with him. He worried about her, and wished he had insisted on living together from the beginning.

What had she wanted to discuss? He had a feeling it had been important, but his proposal to spend more time together had caught her off guard. After that, she hadn't been willing to confide. In hindsight, he should have let her speak first. Then he'd know what she'd had on her mind. His suggestion had probably ruined what she had planned to say.

He picked up his right foot and kicked himself on the ankle. What a knucklehead. For weeks he'd waited for her to confide, and just when she'd been ready, he'd opened his big mouth and stuck his foot in it.

Although he hadn't intended to push her, he had. Her willingness to confide without being asked ranked her pretty high in his estimation.

He pulled onto the street, his mind full of questions. *Why had he kissed her? He hadn't intended to, not after he'd said his piece and seen the shock in her eyes.*

He didn't want to push her into something she wasn't ready for.

That was a bald-faced lie. If she'd given him any encouragement, he'd still be with her, and he might even have suggested spending the night together.

Truth be told, he was surprised he hadn't kissed her more often. She tempted him as he had never expected to be tempted. And if they kept up the pretense of being engaged, he might wind up asking her to marry him.

How odd. That thought no longer bothered him. They had only known each other a couple of months, but after traveling across the country together, he felt he knew her well. He'd seen her in all kinds of situations, watched her play with Toby, Misti and his nieces and nephews, and marveled at her ability to adjust to cranky people in the office, and handle difficult phone calls as well as Martina's attempts to belittle her every chance she got.

He could certainly do worse. And he doubted he could do better.

Marriage began to have great appeal. *How would she react if he suggested making the engagement real?*

Feeling no need to rush things, he decided to give the idea more time, and not say anything until he had more time to think about it.

His thoughts returned to his proposal. *What would she decide? And how could he be patient until she did?*

He wanted her close so he wouldn't worry about her getting in trouble and him not being there to help her. He also wanted to see her again. Right now. And every night, as well. No one else had ever made him feel this way. And no one else would do.

~ * ~

Janalou sat alone in the dark. She hadn't turned the lights on even though it had grown late. She needed time to think. If she didn't want Kree to go out with other women, she should agree to his suggestion. Part of her felt guilty for thinking that way. According to Mama, if they became intimate, he would have all the benefits of marriage without committing himself in any way.

First he had asked her to pretend to be engaged. Now he wanted her to live with him. What would he ask next? A more personal favor? One that might require her to do something she'd never done?

Guilt descended with that mean-spirited thought. He hadn't asked her to do anything she didn't want to do. He knew she was attracted to him. He also knew about her Baptist background.

The sudden feeling that she wasn't alone descended. The feeling of having a guardian angel on her shoulder didn't happen often. When it did, she experienced a calm and an awe she couldn't begin to explain. Was Mama's spirit nearby?

She drew her knees up to her chest and mumbled out loud. "I wish I knew what to do."

And then she knew. The words seemed to come from thin air, and she felt them rather than heard them. *Follow your heart.*

Whether Mama was her guardian angel or not, Janalou knew she wouldn't approve of intimacy without marriage. If a man wanted a woman, he should have the old-fashioned decency to marry her.

But how could she tell Kree that, and make him understand, when she wasn't sure that was his intent? She couldn't, and that worried her. A lot. But she did owe it to him to tell him the truth about her past. And she would. Just as soon as she worked up her courage again.

~ * ~

As though he sensed her thoughts the next day, Kree shut the door after she entered their shared office. "Have you made a decision, Jana?"

He didn't have to say anything more. They both knew exactly what he meant.

She nodded, then shook her head. "I want to spend more time with you, but I'm afraid, Kree."

"Why?"

"There are still so many things I don't know about you, things you don't know about me, and I have to be honest about this. If we're together more, our relationship will change. I'm not sure I'm ready for that yet."

"Do you have any idea when you might be?"

"Sadly, no."

"Maybe we've both done too much thinking. Maybe we should just try it and see what happens."

"I wish it could be that simple."

He drew her close and kissed her, not passionately or persuasively as she expected, but slowly, tenderly. "I told you I wouldn't push or press, and I won't, although I think you know I'd like to do both."

She came close to telling him the truth then. But he kissed her again, and every single thought fled. She'd almost lost her ability to breathe. She did lose her balance, and might have fallen if he hadn't been holding her so close.

~ * ~

Two days later, Kree left on his fishing trip.

One night after watching baseball on TV with his buddies, Gary asked, "Is Janalou as good in bed as she looks, Kree?"

"We haven't slept together," he said, disgusted by Gary's tone. "She's not that kind of girl. Can't you tell?"

"You didn't sleep with her? Not even when you were traveling across the country? I thought you said you stayed in the same room."

"We did, but she was recovering from surgery."

"Come on Kree, you can level with us. What's she like in bed?"

"Lay off," Jason said.

"Yeah, give him a break," Marty added.

"When are you getting married?" Chaunce asked.

"We haven't set a date yet. She lost her parents recently," he repeated for the benefit of those he hadn't told, "and she's still mourning them."

The razzing from his friends had shaken him. Did people put Janalou through the same kind of questions?

Her delicate beauty couldn't help but catch a man's attention. It had caught his friends' and they envied him, he knew.

To save them both some hassle, he had considered suggesting they elope. But that would hurt his family, all of them, so he'd tossed the idea aside.

Jason surprised him by saying, "Maybe Kree got engaged to protect Janalou from guys like you, Gary."

Kree laughed. He wasn't suffering a mega-guilt complex over their fake engagement like Janalou apparently was, but he was hot and bothered day and night. He dreamed about her far too often and woke up turned on, wishing she were there beside him, in his bed.

June and July were already behind them. In a few weeks, his friends would expect him to come fishing again over the Labor Day weekend. He'd much rather use that time for a honeymoon with Janalou. He still had a nagging feeling that she needed to be protected. If only he knew from what.

When he returned to work, he intended to have it out with her. They both had a habit of arriving at the office early, so they'd have time to talk without anyone around to disturb them. He'd give Janalou an ultimatum. Either she move in with him or he'd move in with her, even if he had to sleep on that paltry thing she called a couch in her small living room.

~ * ~

The summer days had sped by, and Janalou had been working more than two months. Thankfully, Kree had returned from his fishing trip and called to remind her he'd be at work that day.

She loved being the first person to arrive at the office and unlock the door. She no longer checked messages on the recording machine, though, except on Saturdays, because Martina insisted that was her job.

While Kree had been gone, Janalou wanted to stay at his house and use his car, but she did neither because she felt that might obligate her more.

The phone rang. Since no one else had arrived, the office hadn't officially opened, but Janalou answered anyway. "Good morning. Winterton Real Estate. How may I help you?"

"It's me, Cherilyn. Are you all right?"

"Sure. I'm fine, but you sound upset. What's wrong? Where are you?"

"I'm at work, at the nursery school."

Janalou jumped to the first possible conclusion. "Are Misti and Toby okay?"

"Yes, they're fine, but I'm watching the news. I think it might have something to do with you, but I'm not sure."

Concerned by her agitation, Janalou said, "Spit it out."

"I came into the owner's office to get something. The TV's on and a photo of a girl with your face and long black hair is splashed across the screen. She looks so much like you she could be you. It's eerie. Do you have an identical twin sister?"

"No." Cold chills pounded down Janalou's spine, creating alarm in every cell. "Tell me more about what's on the news."

"The reporters say her name is Saree Naisbet and she's been missing since late May, about the time you and I met."

Shock roared through Janalou, ferocious as an angry lion. But she didn't utter a sound. Because she couldn't. She could barely breathe. All she could do was clutch the phone and hope Cherilyn continued.

"Apparently the police arrested her father and stepmother for murdering her and hiding her body. They've been held without bail for weeks and will appear in court tomorrow to be officially charged with the crime. I'm surprised neither of us saw the news before now."

Janalou's stomach dropped about a foot. But she didn't gasp. She was still too stunned to make a peep.

Papa and Belle had been arrested. Who had reported her missing? And why did they think she was dead?

Because she had disappeared, and hadn't left a note or any trail for them to follow?

While her brain churned, Cherilyn filled her in on more details.

"Apparently her old boyfriend, who was in Europe, called the morning after Saree came up missing. When her stepmother said she'd run away, the guy didn't believe her, so he called the police. They went to the house and found blood in several rooms, including Saree's bedroom. The dresser and bed had been pushed against the door and the police had to enter through the window they found open. They speculated her parents did that to make it look like she ran away. But they were apparently too hung over from drinking or not smart enough to get rid of the incriminating evidence. The crime lab checked the blood smeared on her bed and on the floor in several rooms with the records in Saree's doctor's office, and it matched."

Janalou thought she might faint. She didn't. She did drop the phone, though. Her nerveless hands had turned numb.

From far away, she heard Cherilyn's voice. "Janalou, are you there?"

She picked the phone back up, forcing her nerveless fingers to clutch it tight. "Yes. I'm here. And that girl isn't my twin. It's me."

"You?" Cherilyn gasped. "I was afraid you might say that."

"What channel are you watching?"

"CNN."

"I'm going to hang up now," Janalou said. "I have to think."

"Call me if you need any help."

"Thanks. I will."

She hung up, went to the conference room, and turned on the TV.

But the news Cherilyn had heard was over and probably wouldn't be repeated for thirty minutes or so.

Janalou sat at the big conference table, plopped her elbows on the edge, and held her head in her hands. She felt like crying. But she was too numb. She felt guilty. Very, very guilty. Her father and Belle had been arrested weeks ago and held without bail.

She had to go home. Back to South Carolina. But first she had to tell Kree. And his parents. She had to admit she had lied.

It was going to be one of the most difficult things she'd ever done. They'd never trust her again.

Her new life was over. She knew that as surely as she knew she didn't want to go back and face Papa or Belle. They would probably kill her if they ever got their hands on her again.

It's too soon, her brain cried. *I've barely begun my new life. I want more time.*

But she didn't have a choice. Guilt and decency demanded that she do whatever she could to get Franklin and Belle released as soon as possible.

Martina arrived at work before anyone else. Janalou couldn't look her in the eye.

"You okay?" Martina asked when Janalou avoided looking at her.

"No. Actually I'm not."

"If you're sick, you should go home. Want me to call cab?"

"No, thanks. I'll wait for Kree." Janalou didn't have it in her to tell Martina she wasn't sick. She was sick at heart. Her whole life was down the tube. *Would everyone hate her when they discovered she had lied? Pretended to be an orphan? Was this God's way of punishing her for basing her new life on lies?*

The instant Kree arrived, Janalou said, "I need to talk to you. In private."

He took her elbow and guided her down the hall to their shared office. "What's wrong?" he asked as he shut the door.

"I, a, that is," she cleared her throat and tried again. "My real name isn't Janalou. I changed it because I ran away from my papa and stepmother. They aren't dead as I led you to believe. My stepmother abused me and I've been afraid she might find me, and make me go back and then she'd beat me again."

Instead of getting angry and confirming her fear, his expression softened. "I hoped some day you would open up and tell me more about yourself."

"Do you understand what I just said?"

"I think so."

"I lied about being an orphan. I'm not. And Papa and my stepmother have been arrested for murdering me. Even though there's no body. Apparently they'all be charged formally tomorrow, in court." She was shaking so bad, her teeth rattled.

Kree wrapped his arms around her. "Slow down. Let's go over that again."

Janalou shook her head. "No. Please. I don't have time. I need to go."

"We have to take the time, Jana. I need to know where you plan to go."

"South Carolina. Spartanburg. I have to return and let everyone know I'm alive. Papa's in jail. And my disappearance put him there."

"When did you hear about this?"

She twisted out of his embrace, feeling unworthy of his touch. "Cherilyn called a little while ago, and said she heard the news on CNN. She recognized me from the photo, but she thought it might be my twin or something."

Kree took Janalou's arm again and led her to conference room. He closed the door, then turned on the TV.

A female reporter on CNN was rehashing the news. "I have this information from a reliable source," the petite black-haired woman said. "One of the three couples who ate dinner at the Naisbet home the night their daughter disappeared last May has agreed to testify that Franklin Naisbet reprimanded his daughter, Saree, after she kicked his friend under the table. The woman believes the man did something improper. His hands were beneath the table, and she's certain he groped young Saree. The husband isn't quite as sure, although he grudgingly admitted that Saree did look very upset. And in talking to some of the Naisbets' neighbors, it's common knowledge that Belle Naisbet shouted at her stepdaughter routinely."

Janalou buried her face in her hands. "Turn it off. Please turn it off," she sobbed.

Kree did. Pulling his handkerchief from his hip pocket, he gave it to her, then wrapped his arms around her again. "You must have lived through hell."

"I wanted it to stay behind me, not dragged out for the whole world to know," she cried. "It's sordid and ugly."

"You have nothing to be ashamed of, Janalou."

"That's not my real name."

"You changed it, so as far as I'm concerned, it is. You left the name Saree behind. We'll go back and help your parents, but you're not staying there. I won't let them near you. I promise. They'all never hurt you again."

Never had Kree felt more protective. He hadn't been there to help Bethany, but by the grace of God he would be with Janalou and he wouldn't let her down. She needed him. And it felt good to be needed. At last he knew why.

His parents arrived a few minutes later. Sensing Janalou was too upset to explain, he said, "You stay here. I'll go tell Mother and Dad."

He left her in the conference room, and explained everything to his parents in their office, finishing with, "I'm going to stand by her. She needs me."

"Of course she does," his father said.

His mother shook her head. She looked upset, but he didn't give her time to voice her thoughts. "Don't judge her, Mother. She had her reasons. She lived through hell."

His dad looked grave and concerned. "You'll fly back with her, won't you, son?"

"Of course. She can't go alone. Those people may deserve to get out of jail, but they're monsters. I don't intend to let them near her, ever again."

"Good."

"I'm proud of that decision," Helen said, wringing her hands. "I don't understand people who abuse their children."

"Neither do I," Kree agreed, relieved neither of his parents had judged Janalou harshly.

When he returned to the conference room, she raised her head. Tears still streamed down her cheeks. She wiped them with the handkerchief he had given her.

"I think I should talk to your parents before I leave," she said.

"You don't have to. I've already explained."

"For my own sake, I think I do."

He took her hand and she stood. Before they took a step, his parents walked into the conference room and closed the door behind them.

Janalou took a deep breath, and cleared her throat. "I can't excuse my lying. It was wrong and deceitful. My only defense is that my stepmother is an awful person when she drinks. I ran away because I was afraid she might kill me during one of her drunken attacks. But I never dreamed she would be accused of murdering me while I'm still alive."

"You don't have to say any more," Max said.

He picked up the remote, flipped on the TV and they watched the news together. When a photo of Janalou flashed, everyone including her, drew in sharp breaths.

"Looks exactly like you," Helen said.

"It's my graduation photo," Janalou said, trying to swallow the lump in her throat. "If it's all right, I'd like to leave now. The sooner I get back to South Carolina, the sooner Papa and my stepmother can be set free."

"You don't have to ask our permission to go," Max said. "You work for us, but we respect you and understand what you need to do."

"You'll let us know if there's anything we can do to help, won't you?" Helen asked, and Janalou wondered if she really meant that.

"Yes. And thank y'all." She felt so untrustworthy. "You've been kind and I hate knowing I repaid your kindness and friendship with lies and deceit."

"Stop feeling guilty," Kree said. "You're being too hard on yourself. We understand."

She looked up at him, standing beside her, holding her hand. "I guess I should go home and pack a bag."

"Could you call back east, and not have to return?" Helen asked.

Janalou shook her head. "I don't think that would work. Anyone could call and claim to be me. I'm sure the judge will want to see me in person, and make sure I'm really alive." She sucked in her bottom lip and tasted blood. She'd been so agitated she must have bitten her bottom lip. "I can't believe I didn't know about this until today. It must have been in the news before, weeks or months ago when they were arrested or something."

"We've all been busy this summer and haven't watched much TV," Helen said.

Janalou could hardly believe Helen was defending her, trying to make her feel better. "You're a wonderful woman, Helen. I've learned a lot by watching you this summer. If I ever have children, I hope I can be as understanding and supportive as you are."

Helen smiled. "I'm sure you'll be a good mother, Janalou. You're a dear girl, and you remind me of my best friend when I was growing up."

"I do?" she gasped.

Helen nodded. "Your eyes and lips, your whole face looks like hers and I suppose I held myself back at first because you remind me how much I've missed her throughout the years and wished we hadn't lost track of each other after I moved here."

Touched to tears, Janalou looked at Kree again. "I should call for plane tickets."

"I'll take care of that, and I'll drive you home to pack." He guided her toward the door.

She turned back to look at his parents, saw the worry in their eyes, and wished she could say something to ease their distress. But she couldn't think of a single word. All she could think about was returning to Spartanburg, and having to face Papa and Belle again.

"We wish you well, Janalou," Helen said.

"Yes," Max echoed and when she glanced back, she saw tears in two sets of eyes.

Twenty

After she finished packing, Janalou said, "I appreciate your offer to go with me, Kree, but y'all don't have to. I hate to drag you into my problems. I can do this by myself."

He folded his arms across his chest, his expression adamant. "We're supposed to be engaged. What would it look like if I let you go alone?"

Janalou shrugged. "Your family might hate me for lying and pretending to be an orphan."

"You saw my parents' reaction. They aren't judgmental. Neither are my sisters. They'all not only understand my going with you, they'all expect it." His tone brooked no argument, so she gave up. If his voice hadn't convinced her, the look in his eyes and the determined set of his jaw did.

"All right. Thanks. I really don't want to go there and face what I have to alone."

He smiled. "I know that."

She tried to smile too, but it was feeble at best. Her heart ached, and her soul felt very old and weary, like it had already lived several lifetimes.

This summer had been the happiest of her life. Had her happiness come to an end? Would she still be welcome here after everyone knew she had lied and deceived?

And would she be able to leave Spartanburg after Papa and Belle were set free? Would they find a way to keep her there and punish her for being accused of her murder?

Leaving South Carolina had taken a lot of courage.

Going back would take even more.

Janalou hadn't been this nervous since the night she'd left, back at the end of May.

As Kree drove to the airport, her hands shook. She clasped them together on her lap, and forced herself to think of something other than the ordeal ahead. Only then did she think about Duke, who had assured her more than once that he would help her if she ever needed it.

"I should call Duke. If I don't, he'll probably show up later to drive me home, or back to the apartment."

Kree extended his iPhone. "Call him. Do you know his number?"

She nodded. "By heart."

Duke answered on the first ring.

"Have you seen the news?" she asked.

"Yes. Are you all right, lass?"

"Yes. I'm on my way to the airport. You won't need to pick me up tonight."

"I understand."

"Thank you for everything you've done, Duke."

"You're welcome, lass."

After the call ended, she called Cherilyn and asked her to call Reina.

Fear clutched at her heart as they continued to the airport. Focusing on her new life helped. Had she only known Kree less than three months? It seemed so much longer. He, his family and friends acted as though she belonged there, and she had looked forward to spending the future in California. How she hoped she could return.

~ * ~

After they boarded the plane, tension held Janalou in a firm grip. Although grateful Kree had insisted on coming with her, she dreaded having him meet Papa and Belle. She didn't intend to introduce them, but he would see them in court, and know she had lived with one terrible person, Belle. Would he think what Belle was like had rubbed off on her?

More thoughts crowded in, and turmoil churned inside. How would Papa and Belle react when they saw her? Would they embarrass her in front of Kree? In front of the entire world? There were bound to be reporters at the trial. Did she have any hope of avoiding them?

During the drive to the airport, she had tried to warn Kree and tell him what Belle was like, but still she worried. Would he think less of her once he met her and Papa? If their places were reversed, she might think less of him. It shamed her to admit that, even to herself. Maybe she did have flawed characteristics like Belle. Maybe they just exhibited themselves in different ways.

Shame whipped at her, making her insides feel raw. She hadn't been ashamed of Papa until he married Belle. Then she'd been ashamed of them both. Now she was ashamed of herself, too.

Her stomach tied itself in knots.

She didn't eat lunch and couldn't concentrate on the in-flight movie. All she could do was worry. And fret.

~ * ~

Knowing Janalou was nervous and upset, Kree decided she might be better off if they talked. "I'd like you to tell me about the night you left home."

She licked her lips. "It's not a pretty story."

"I'd still like to hear it."

"My parents had a dinner party. Afterwards, my stepmother struck me, and I dropped a stack of china plates. She bloodied my nose, and I was afraid if I stayed, she might do worse."

"She's the one who gave you those black eyes?"

"Yes."

"Not your father?"

"No."

"Did he ever hit you?"

"No, but Papa never believed me when I told him about Belle's abuse either."

"How did you get away?"

"Belle was screaming at Papa, so I raced to my bedroom, threw things into a pillow sham, and crawled out through the window. I ran all the way to the bus station, where I had stored my backpack and money in a locker. I was so glad that night's bus was late. I was afraid Papa and Belle might find me if I had to wait until morning."

"Your life must have been a nightmare."

"It was after Papa married Belle. He changed, and drank too much. That's one of the reasons I was so impressed with you for not drinking."

"Tell me about your friends. Will any of them be worried about you?"

She shook her head. "Probably just Margie, but she's in Europe with her grandparents and cousins this summer. I planned to call her when she got back, at the end of August, and let her know I'm okay, and that I won't be going to college with her."

"Where had you planned to go?"

"I earned a scholarship to the University of South Carolina, but I'm not going to stay in the East. I hope someone else can use it."

"Have you contacted the university to let them know you won't be using the scholarship?"

"Not yet, I plan to."

~ * ~

By the time their plane landed in South Carolina, it was after seven in the evening. They collected their luggage, and Kree rented a car. Then he drove to downtown Spartanburg, found the Veteran's Highway, and pulled into the parking lot of the Marriott Hotel on the north end of town where he had made reservations.

After they checked in, he said, "Let's take a walk after we unpack, and get some exercise."

"That's a good idea."

He smiled, and patted her shoulder. "Call me when you're ready."

"Will do."

They met in the hall a short time later. He took her hand before they strolled outside, south, toward town.

When he saw a restaurant across the street, he said, "You didn't eat lunch. Let's go have dinner over there."

"Another good idea."

~ * ~

Knowing she needed nourishment to keep up her strength, Janalou forced herself to eat. It wouldn't be smart to collapse in court.

Back at the hotel, Kree said, "I don't want you to take this wrong, but you don't have to spend tonight alone."

She gazed up, afraid to believe what she saw in his eyes. Warmth. Caring. And love? "Thank you, but I think I need to be alone tonight."

"I understand."

How could he when she didn't understand herself?

After they returned to their respective rooms, Janalou's fear and trepidation mounted. She could hardly wait to get tomorrow over with. Would she still have a life in California? Would Kree want her to return? Or would he be so repulsed by Papa and Belle that he'd want to be freed from their pretend engagement?

Somehow Janalou made it through the night.

Morning finally dawned.

She showered, dressed and met Kree for breakfast. But she couldn't force more than two bites of toast down. She did manage to swallow most of her orange juice.

Not sure when the trial was scheduled to convene, they arrived at the courthouse early.

The instant she and Kree entered the building, Janalou saw her old boyfriend, Tony. He looked as shocked to see her as she was to see him.

Once he had made her pulse race just by being near. Although that feeling was gone, her heart raced for a reason she couldn't discern.

She chalked it up to nervousness. The thought of facing the judge and Papa and Belle in front of half the town and people she might not know, made her sick to her stomach. Reporters worried her, too.

Tony stood with four other people, but the strangers' backs were toward her so she focused on him. He looked more mature. His shoulders were broader, he stood taller, and he was handsomer than the last time she'd seen him. But he wasn't handsomer than Kree, and he didn't stir her the way Kree did.

"Hello Tony," she said, conjuring a smile, but how, she couldn't fathom.

"Hi." He still looked startled. Shocked. She couldn't decide which. "I—we came to watch the arraignment today, and I, we..." he gestured at the four people beside him. "We thought you were dead. I'm glad you're not, that you're alive and safe." He looked from her to the girl at his side, his expression still dazed. "I have some people I'd like you to meet."

Janalou followed his gaze and gasped as she stared into the eyes of a girl who looked exactly like her—the same age, the same height, the same hair color, the same eyes. It was like looking in the mirror. Only their clothes and hairstyles were different. Janalou wore a full blue skirt and pink blouse while the other girl wore a tailored beige suit and her black hair was long, but not as long as Janalou's, and it was contained by a neat clip behind her head while Janalou's hair was loose, and flared around her shoulders like a cape.

While they stared, a memory stirred, and the words slipped out before she could stop them. "Janalou loves Jeri Sue."

The girl's cheek dimpled when she smiled. "Jeri Sue loves Janalou."

"And Winnie the Pooh loves both of you," the strange young man finished.

Janalou swung her stunned gaze to him. His name slipped from her throat with amazing swiftness. "Paul?"

He nodded, then grabbed her close, squeezing her in a bear hug. "You remember me? Us?"

Startled by his fierce hug, yet strangely comforted by it, and too confused to think straight, Janalou shook her head. "I remember the words—the names, but I don't know who you are."

"I'm your brother," Paul said, drawing slightly away so he could gaze into her astonished eyes. "Jeri Sue is your sister, your twin sister, and these are your parents. Our parents. Reva and Taylor Madzen."

Janalou staggered backwards. And bumped into Kree. "Sorry," she mumbled, too shell-shocked to say anything else.

Madzen? Very close to Madsen, the name she had chosen for her new identity.

Was she hallucinating? Was she so afraid to face Papa and Belle that she'd made up something to fill her head?

While Kree steadied her, his warm hands on her cold arms, she searched the anxious faces of the woman and man watching her.

Finally she swallowed, and forced the words through her constricted throat. "You're my parents? But Franklin Naisbet is my papa. And Belle's my stepmother."

"No." The distinguished looking man and attractive woman both shook their heads, and Janalou realized she was holding her breath.

"We're your parents. We're sure of it. We've already gone through blood and DNA tests," the woman named Reva said, "to make sure."

"You remember the rhyme, and your brother's and sister's names," the man named Taylor said.

"But how did Franklin Nesbit come to act as my papa?" Janalou asked, too astounded to rationalize or even think beyond that one question.

"You were kidnapped," her mother, Reva, said.

Janalou's mind reeled. Possibilities and memories attacked her brain. All she could ask was, "When?"

"When you were three and a half years old."

She frowned. "Fifteen years ago?"

Tears glittered in the pretty woman's sad blue eyes as she shook her head. "More like seventeen."

"I just turned eighteen."

"You're almost twenty," Jeri Sue said. "Our birthday is at the end of this month."

Too bewildered to think straight, Janalou said, "My birthday was in June. I'm eighteen. I graduated from high school at the end of May."

"They cheated you out of two years of your life." Paul shook his head, his eyes filled with disgust.

"They did more than that," Taylor, the man who claimed to be her real father, said. "They cheated all of us out of being a family."

Janalou tried to stay calm. But she failed. Tears flooded her eyes and anguished words tumbled from her lips. "All this time I thought he—Franklin—was all the family I had, and when I ran away, I didn't even have him."

Paul grabbed her back into his arms, comforting her as only a big brother could comfort, as he must have comforted her when she was young and small. "You'll never know how much we've missed you."

"That's right," Jeri Sue said. "I cried myself to sleep night after night because you were gone, and I wanted you with me."

Janalou had forced the memories so far back in her mind she had forgotten them until now. Like a huge body of water bursting through a weak dam, they attacked, one memory stacking upon another. As a child she recalled saying over and over again, *"My name is Janalou. Janalou Madzen."*

But Papa—Franklin had squeezed her shoulders until they hurt, and repeated with firm emphasis again and again, *"No, your name is Saree. Janalou is someone you must have dreamed about."*

"I want Jeri Sue and Paul and Mommy and Daddy."

"I'm your daddy now, and you can't have Jeri Sue or Paul. They're gone. They're dead. You'll never see them again. We're you parents now. You belong to us."

"I want Winnie the Pooh. Winnie the Pooh loves me."

"Winnie the Pooh was part of your old life. Now you have a new one. You must get used to it or you'll break your new mama's heart. She loves you and she's waited a long, long time to get you."

The memory of crying in her new mother's arms made Janalou pull away from Paul. She tried to flash a smile before she hugged Jeri Sue. Then swiping at her tears, she turned to the woman she knew in her heart was her birth mother.

"I forgot until just now. Franklin brainwashed me and made me think you were all dead. But I missed you so. I cried and cried, and said my name was Janalou, but Franklin wouldn't let me call myself that. He forced me to say my name was Saree. He told me you were all nothing more than a memory, and I had to forget you. But I didn't, not entirely. I dreamed about you, lots of times, over and over again."

She hugged her mother, then turned to Taylor. "He lied to me." She said that as though she still couldn't believe it. But her brain knew the truth.

"Yes," her real father said, pulling her close, and giving her a fatherly hug. "You're our daughter, and we'll do whatever it takes to punish Franklin. And we'll do it together, as a family."

He released her and she flung her arms around her mother, and didn't know who trembled most as they embraced again. After she kissed her mother's soft smooth cheek and inhaled her faintly familiar perfume, she opened her arms to her father again.

Somehow her young mind had made a distinction between Franklin and Minnie and her real parents. "I never called them mommy or daddy. I called them mama and papa. I never knew why. Until today."

Holding her close, Taylor patted her back, his voice hoarse with emotion when he spoke. "Thank God you're alive, and we've finally found you."

Tears still slid unchecked down her cheeks when he released her. "How did you find me?"

Her father gave her arms a gentle squeeze. "Paul met Tony last spring in college, and invited him to visit us in London this summer."

"London?" Surprise whipped through her. "You—you live in London?"

Jeri Sue smiled. "Our father is an important man, sis. The president appointed him as Ambassador to the U.K."

Janalou felt her eyes widen and her brows rise. "You're an ambassador?"

Taylor smiled. "Yes, but let's get on with our story." He nodded at Tony, who continued the interrupted explanation.

"When I met Jeri Sue, I mentioned you because you look so much alike. After she told me her twin had been kidnapped years ago, I tried to set up a meeting with you. But by then you had left Spartanburg, and Frank and Belle claimed they didn't know where you'd gone. They said you left without explaining."

"I did. I made plans to disappear, and I ran away."

Tony hiked his brows. "I've always wondered why you never answered my letters or returned my phone calls or texts or emails."

Anguish gushed through Janalou. "I never got them. I used to wonder if Belle intercepted your letters and destroyed them."

"She must have, because I sent several. I sent emails too, and lots of text messages."

"I never received them, either. Belle confiscated my cell phone, took my computer away, and cancelled our internet connection. I used a computer at school and one at the library, but you must have changed your email address, and I didn't know how to let you know I'd changed mine to Yahoo."

"Why did she do those things?'

Janalou shrugged. "She's an awful person. That's why I ran away. I couldn't live with her or Franklin any longer. When she drank, she turned abusive."

"They're both paying for their abuse now by being behind bars," Paul said. "They've been held for weeks without bail."

"But now that I'm here, they'all be set free."

"Not for long," her father said, his voice tight. "When we heard about the murder accusation and the trial, we had to be here. Now we'll make sure they're punished for kidnapping."

"Yes," her mother said. "It hurt so much to discover where you were too late, but we decided we needed to see that justice prevailed."

Kree reached for Janalou's arm. He had been quiet the whole time, but she hadn't forgotten he was there. Placing her hand over his, she smiled up at him through her tears.

"I'd like you to meet a very special man." She smiled at her family, too. "This is Kree Winterton. He has helped me a lot this summer, and I owe him so much."

"You don't owe me anything," Kree said, his voice calm, but his expression looked as amazed as her own must be as he offered her the use of his snowy white handkerchief.

"Yes, I do." She had never been more aware of his aura, or his inner strength. She'd always been proud to be associated with him. Right then, she was doubly proud because he looked calm, and she felt soothed by his presence.

Jeri Sue laughed, reaching for her left hand and staring at the ring. "You're engaged."

While she stared at the diamond solitaire, Janalou considered explaining it was a fake engagement, but she decided to wait until she had a chance to talk with Kree in private. They were fooling his family. Maybe he wanted to pretend with hers, too. Maybe he might even want to make it real. She hadn't really dared to hope that before, but now she felt more worthy.

To her astonished amazement, Duke Guggles, dressed in a dark business suit, white shirt and striped green tie, tapped Taylor on the shoulder. "I've arranged for an empty room down the hall where you can have some privacy, Ambassador Madzen."

Janalou gasped. "Duke! What are you doing here?" The answer dawned before he could reply. He had been watching over her, protecting her. Now she knew why. "You knew who I am, didn't you?"

He nodded. "Yea, lass, I knew. We'll talk later. This time belongs to your family."

Still befuddled, she nodded and walked with them down the hall to an empty room.

The reunion was like nothing Janalou had ever experienced or expected to happen, and all the more wonderful because of that. They hugged her again and laughed, shook their heads and cried, then shared memories, asking and answering questions, and making her feel as though she truly was a beloved member of their family.

Finally her father said, "It's five minutes to ten. We should all compose ourselves before we enter the courtroom."

They did.

And found seats together on the front row. Janalou sat near the aisle with Kree on one side and her father on the other. She clung to

Kree's hand, her nervous stomach rumbling so loudly she wondered how many others could hear it.

The bailiff ordered everyone to stand while the judge entered. After he sat down, everyone else, except Janalou, sat as well. The judge looked out over the audience, his gaze on Janalou when she stepped into the aisle and said what she had rehearsed so many times in her mind, "Your Honor, may I approach the bench?"

The attorneys on both sides of the room turned to look at her. So did Franklin and Belle, seated with their attorney. Janalou heard Belle's hissed gasp. "It's her. She's back. We can be released."

"Silence," the judge ordered, his stern gaze on Belle before he turned his attention back to Janalou. "What is your reason for wanting to approach the bench, young lady?"

Her gaze never left his. "I came to stop this trial. I'm the person Franklin and Belle Naisbit have been accused of murdering, but as you can see, I'm not dead." She took a couple of steps, and paused, still watching him. "Although Franklin Nesbit may not be guilty of murder, I think he is guilty of kidnapping me when I was a child. If so, he deserves to be in prison, behind bars for a very long time."

Pandemonium erupted in the courtroom. People jumped up, talking, shouting, waving, pointing.

The judge pounded his gavel. "Quiet. I insist upon quiet or I'll clear the room."

When order was restored, Janalou's real father stood, and stepped to her side.

"Who are you?" the judge asked.

"My name is Taylor Madzen. I'm Ambassador to the Court of St. James in the United Kingdom." His strong voice rang with authority. He looked important and sounded impressive, and Janalou felt immensely proud when he added, "I am this young woman's real father, and I wish to press charges against both of the accused. Belle Naisbit worked in my office years ago under the name of Belle Sharp. I wouldn't be surprised to discover she was involved in the kidnapping, if not completely responsible. She tried to seduce me, but I spurned her attempts, and terminated her employment. Perhaps that's why she stole my daughter."

More pandemonium erupted. The judge ordered the courtroom cleared, except for the accused, the attorneys and Janalou's real family. Kree, too, of course, stayed. So did Tony.

The judge stood. "We'll discuss this in my chambers."

Everyone followed him there.

Franklin didn't waste time proclaiming who was behind the kidnapping. The instant the door closed, he blurted, "It wasn't me who kidnapped her. Belle mastered-minded the whole thing. My wife, Minnie, wanted a daughter, and Belle convinced me that the Madzens had two, plus a son, and they didn't need three kids. She convinced me I'd be doing them a favor, taking you off their hands."

He spoke to Janlou instead of the judge or her real parents. Janalou wished she could sympathize, but she couldn't find it in her heart to forgive Franklin. Maybe someday, but not yet. Not only had he gone along with the kidnapping, he had stolen something very precious from her. Her family. And they had suffered too, for years, wondering whether she was alive or dead.

To Janalou's relief, Belle kept her mouth shut, as though she knew that anything she said would only make things worse.

When all the explanations had finally been made, Franklin and Belle were charged with a new crime and remanded back into custody.

After they led Belle away, Janalou said, "May I please speak to Franklin Naisbet? I have a few questions I'd like to ask."

She looked from the judge after he nodded to Franklin standing by the door, his wrists in cuffs. "Why did you marry Belle?" she asked, not caring who heard. "She turned our lives into a nightmare."

Franklin looked ten years older than the last time Janalou had seen him. He raised his arms, tried to ram his cuffed hands through his thinning hair, and succeeded in making a few wiry wisps stand on end.

"I paid Belle a hefty sum after she kidnapped you. She convinced me it was necessary for the adoption papers. But years later, when she discovered Minnie was dead, she found us and demanded more money. I said I wouldn't pay her another cent. Then she changed her mind. Demanded that I marry her or she'd go to the authorities and tell them I'd kidnapped you. I didn't know what to do. I loved Minnie to distraction. I'd have done anything for her. I did. I stooped low enough to help her get a child because she always yearned for a daughter, and we couldn't have one of our own. She didn't know you were kidnapped. I never told her. I'm sure she would not have approved."

"What did you tell her about how you got me?"

"Nothing. Belle had documents that looked like legal adoption papers, and Minnie signed them, believing everything was above board."

"Yet all those years you knew I'd been stolen—kidnapped. Weren't you afraid you'd eventually get caught?"

"Sometimes," he admitted, and dropped his chin. "We moved to a different state, so I hoped it was unlikely, and after a while you stopped mentioning them so I hoped you'd forgotten you had another family."

"I didn't forget entirely. I dreamed about them often, and always wondered if I'd invented them."

"I can't tell you how sorry I am that I got involved with Belle, but I need to warn you about her." Franklin swallowed. His thin face looked haggard.

"She was afraid of you, Saree. That's why she kept you from going out, and why she didn't want you to have friends. She was afraid if you had too much freedom you might remember your family, and try to find them. Then we'd be in trouble for kidnapping you. I never wanted to hurt you. Never. Please believe me."

"I'll try," Janalou said, although she thought it might take a long time.

In the hallway, when they left the judge's chambers, Janalou saw Duke again. He winked, a grin covering his cherubic face. She stopped to talk to him. "Did you see this in my future?"

He nodded, his eyes twinkling. "Janalou Madszen, spelled with a z, not an s. Didn't I say ye'd chosen a foine name for yerself, lass?"

"Yes, you did. You knew all along, didn't you?"

"Yea, lass. I knew."

"Why didn't you say anything?"

"I intended to, but ye got sick and then engaged, so I decided to let things run their natural course without interference. May wasn't the right time. You had other things going on in your life then, and Franklin and Belle deserved to be punished. I thought it wouldn't hurt to let them stew in jail for a while. And your real parents were in Russia and traveling through Europe so I elected to wait. But for those who deserve good, fate oft has a way o' rewarding them, as it has now rewarded you, lass, and your real family."

"You're not going away, are you?" she asked as he began to turn.

"Not far, lass. I'll be around fer a time, so don't fret yer pretty head."

Twenty-one

Kree and the Madzen family left the court house together. He had been astonished by everything that had happened. Seeing Duke Guggles there was just one more surprise.

Who was he? Why had he been on the bus that night in May? Why had he warned him about the storm that night in the Truman Library? And why had he followed them here from California? He'd seen him on the same plane, but hadn't mentioned it to Janalou, just as he hadn't mentioned seeing Duke almost every time they went anywhere together. Had he been following her on purpose?

A huge crowd stood outside the courthouse. Most were young people, who began to chant, "Saree, Saree, hooray for Saree. Saree, Saree, hooray for Saree."

"Do you know all these people?" he asked.

She nodded, tears flooding her eyes again. "They were high school classmates."

"They weren't in court," Jeri Sue said. "I wonder how they got here so soon."

"The phones were probably ringing off their hooks, all over the valley," Paul said.

The tears glistening in Janalou's eyes spilled onto her cheeks as she nodded. Her gaze swept the crowd, and Kree wondered what she was thinking when a smile curved her lovely heart-shaped lips.

A group of protective guards closed around them. Kree glanced at the long stretch limo waiting at the curb. Several men shooed reporters away, clearing a path to the white Lincoln.

"Saree, Saree, hooray for Saree," the crowd continued to chant, pushing against reporters and protective agents in an attempt to get closer to Janalou.

Kree had his first inkling of what her life could be like when she raised her hand and waved.

Her father stopped. "Would you like to say some-thing?" he asked Janalou.

She nodded, and the ambassador raised his arm. A hush fell over the crowd. Even the reporters kept quiet.

Janalou smiled as she looked at her classmates. "I'd like to thank y'all for coming here. I never realized I had so many friends. Thanks for your support. Y'all may never know how much it means to me."

Kree swallowed a gulp. She reminded him of an elegant princess addressing her loyal subjects. Suddenly he realized he had to let her go. Set her free. Give her time to spend with her family, and get to know them. It might take years to recapture what they'd lost, if they were fortunate enough to recapture it, but he couldn't stand in her way.

He couldn't imagine what it would be like to have grown up away from his parents and sisters. For the first time in a very long time, he realized how fortunate he had been.

And for the first time ever, he stopped blaming his parents for Bethany's death. Maybe she'd had a reason to end her life. That thought came as a surprise.

So did the next one. *He loved Janalou, loved her as much or more than he had loved Bethany.*

When Janalou's family began to walk again, the crowd parted. Surrounded by protective agents, Janalou and her entourage proceeded down the sidewalk.

After everyone climbed inside the limo, the chauffeur drove them to Greenville.

Sequestered in the Madzens' private suite at the Westin Poinsett Hotel, they ate a catered lunch in privacy, and spent the afternoon and evening talking, conversing, trying to catch up on some of the years they hadn't shared.

Kree was a bit surprised when Taylor Madzen said, "I've arranged for you to have a room here tonight, Kree. Janalou will share her sister's room. As you might imagine, none of us wants to let her out of our sight."

"Yes, I can imagine." Kree smiled at the not-so-subtle hint that the ambassador didn't intend to let them share a room as so many young couples did these days. He considered saying they hadn't been sleeping together, but didn't.

His idea to turn the fake engagement into a real one had receded. He couldn't marry her. They had grown close and he'd wanted their engagement to be real. But love and romance had no place in their relationship. Friendship was all they could share. Maybe not even that. She belonged in London with her family and he belonged in California, half a world away.

In spite of that pep talk to himself, disappointment squatted on his shoulders like a heavy cloud. He wanted her permanently. But apparently, that wasn't meant to be.

This morning he had watched and listened, caught up in the drama being lived out. At first Janalou had lost her pallor, her face had gone ghostly white. But she had held up, and done what needed to be done. He was immensely proud of her. Although she had suffered in the past, she had endured and grown into a lovely young woman. *Once a princess, always a princess.* She possessed sterling qualities, and someday a lucky man would be fortunate to share her life.

Kree drew in a deep breath. She should be emotionally drained. He was. He smiled at her. "Could we talk for a few minutes?"

"Sure." She hooked her elbow around his and led him from the room where they had spent most of the day with her family. In another room in her parents' spacious suite, she let go of his arm before she spoke. "I imagine you want to talk about the engagement."

He shook his head. "Not tonight. Maybe tomorrow. Right now I just want to know how you are."

Her eyes glowed as he'd never seen them glow. "I'm fine. I doubt I could be better. How are you?"

"Drained."

Her smile turned sympathetic. "We've all been through a lot today. Have you called your parents?"

"Once, but we just had a brief conversation. I'll call again when I go to my room. They're probably wondering what's going on now."

"I'm sure they are." Janalou sat on one of the overstuffed chairs and waited for him to sit too. "I need to call Cherilyn. Will you call Reina? Or should I?"

"I'll call her. You'll probably be busy trying to catch up with your sister."

Janalou nodded and rose. "I need to go thank Tony for his part in reuniting me with my family. I'll see you in the morning, Kree. I hope you sleep well."

Tony? An emotion Kree could only describe as jealousy skidded through him. He told himself he had no right to be jealous. But the feeling persisted anyway.

After she left, he realized why. Tony had glared at him off and on all day, and the look in his eyes seemed to say, *'You can't have her. I knew her first.'*

Kree didn't want to give her up, especially not if it meant she might turn to Tony. The possessive feeling darting through him was as foreign as jealousy. He didn't like either emotion, but they couldn't be ignored.

Alone in his room, Kree rammed his hand through his hair. Again he admitted the truth. He loved her. But he couldn't tell her. That would make her feel obligated, and he wanted what was best for her, not for him.

He spent half the night convincing himself he couldn't let his emotions rule him. Regardless of what Tony had been to Janalou in the past, and regardless what he might be in the future, Kree needed to set her free. And if he didn't do it soon, he might blurt that he loved her, and find himself incapable of letting her go.

~ * ~

In Jeri Sue's bedroom, the twin sisters were both too excited to sleep. They talked and talked, and talked some more, knowing it was impossible to catch up on all the years they had missed sharing, but happy in the knowledge that they had a lifetime to share their thoughts and memories, their hopes and dreams.

Eventually, Jeri Sue said, "I remember the last Christmas we had together before you were stolen. We both got twin dolls and pretty new velvet dresses that matched our dolls' dresses. Yours was green and mine was red. We put on our new dresses, held our dolls and stood in front of the Christmas tree so Dad could take our picture. After you were gone, we had it framed and put on my dresser. I never played with my doll or yours. I kept them in their boxes and saved them so they would still be new if we ever found you. They're stored in the top of our closet at home."

"Where is home?"

Jeri Sue smiled. "I'm sorry. Everything is all new to you. We live in Philadelphia. It's a great city. You'll like it there."

"I'm sure I will." Janalou smiled too. "I missed you without even knowing you existed. It was lonely growing up as an only child."

"It was lonely being an only twin, too. You've been in my thoughts so much."

"Now we can share our lives for as long as we live."

Jeri Sue nodded. "Most of the summer we believed you were dead. Finding you aren't has made today the happiest day of my life."

Janalou hugged her again. "Mine, too."

"There's something else you might not know."

"What?"

"Your girlfriend, I think her name is Margie, also called Franklin and Belle, about the same time Tony called them. I think she was as responsible as he was for getting the police involved. She's in Europe, but her parents raised a real ruckus, and after the blood analysis, they insisted that Belle and Franklin be arrested for your murder. When you get a chance, you might want to thank Margie and her parents."

"I will. Thanks for telling me."

Jeri Sue smiled. "You're more than welcome, sis." She reached for her hand and squeezed. "I can't believe how much I love you." Tears filled her eyes. "I've wished for this day a hundred thousand times, but it's still difficult to believe we're finally together again. All these years I've felt like part of me was missing. Now I feel whole again."

She sniffed, and Janalou used Kree's handkerchief to dry her tears. "I feel the same way, Jeri Sue. I missed you without knowing exactly what I missed."

"Promise me we'll always stay in touch."

"We will." Fresh tears brimmed Janalou's eyes. "I'm so happy I can't control my tears."

Jeri Sue took Kree's handkerchief and wiped Janalou's tears. "I feel the same way."

~ * ~

In the morning, before breakfast, Kree found time to talk to Janalou alone again. "You belong with your family now. You have a lot of years to catch up on. You don't have to return to California."

She smiled, and reached out to touch his arm. "You're wrong. I must return. I have a job that I like very much, and I'm studying to pass the real estate exam. Besides, your family thinks we're engaged and I'd like to move in with you." She paused, patting his arm, acting more comfortable touching him now that he knew the truth.

"I put you off before because I didn't realize Janalou is my real name. I believed I was living a lie, and I couldn't live with you while that fought with my conscience." She paused, swallowed, then said, "Not long ago I had an attorney help me change my name legally. I also got a new social security number, and made the correction on my withholding form."

"I'm glad. Did you ever consider telling me?"

She nodded. "Many times."

"Why didn't you?"

"I kept losing my nerve. I was afraid you might hate me if you knew I had lied."

"I'll never hate you, Janalou."

She swallowed, and smiled. "You're right about belonging with my family right now. My parents want me—both of us, to return to London with them. Can you take time off and go with me?"

Not ready to give her up yet, he nodded. He needed to see her in her new surroundings, and make sure she got along well with her real family. He also wanted to see if Tony went with them, and if he acted possessive, although he tried to convince himself that was none of his business.

"Jeri Sue and I want to celebrate our birthday together in a couple of weeks," Janalou added, "and I want to see where Mom and Dad live. I've never been to England. Have you?"

"Yes, however, I'd like to see where they live too." *And how you'll be living once you realize that's where you belong,* he thought, grateful he'd been invited to go with her. "You're sure your parents won't mind if I tag along?"

"I'm sure." Her eyes twinkled with happiness. "You're more than welcome. They consider you part of the family, and I'd rather not tell them we're not really engaged. That can wait until we—until later, can't it?"

He couldn't believe how relieved those words made him feel. All he said was, "Sure. That works for me."

~ * ~

Although Janalou had already called Cherilyn twice, she called again after breakfast. "This is almost too incredible to be true," she repeated.

"Yes," Cherilyn agreed again. "I've been glued to the TV, watching all the news. You're famous. A celebrity."

Janalou laughed. "Not really, but I feel incredibly lucky. I can't tell you how happy I am."

"Are you coming back to California?"

"Yes. Of course. But I'm going to London first. And Kree's going with me."

"I hope you have a wonderful time, and a safe journey."

"Thanks. I'll call and keep you posted about what's going on."

"I'd appreciate that." Cherilyn laughed. "I have some news too. I'm going out with Brad a lot. Misty and Toby adore him, and his son, Jamie. And I think we might get serious."

"That's wonderful," Janalou said, truly happy for her, and wishing she felt the same way about her relationship with Kree.

"Even if I don't get serious with Brad, I'm thinking about buying a house, but I want to wait until you pass your exam so you can help me find one. I want to be your first sale."

"That's great," Janalou said, smiling.

"I've got the TV turned on," Cherilyn said, changing the subject, "and you're in the news again." She laughed. "Don't let it get you down."

Janalou laughed, too. "I won't."

~ * ~

Cherilyn was right. Overnight Janalou had skyrocketed from a nobody to a blooming celebrity. Everyone wanted to talk to her. Reporters, dozens of them. Talk show hosts. Even the paparazzi.

Her father and the protective agents he had hired helped her avoid them all.

While they were finishing lunch, the President of the United States called and personally congratulated Ambassador Madzen for finally locating his missing daughter and being reunited with her.

After their travel plans had been discussed in great detail, Janalou said, "I'd like to go see Margie's parents before we leave. Jeri Sue said they helped get Franklin and Belle arrested, and their home was like a safe harbor to me last year. I'd like to thank them in person."

"We understand, and we'll go with you," her father said.

"Yes," her mother agreed. "We don't want to lose you again."

"Not much chance of that." Janalou smiled, something she did constantly. "Now that I know who you are, I'll never lose contact again."

Kree and Tony accompanied them, along with Jeri Sue and Paul. For the moment they were like one big happy family.

"Margie's still in Europe," her mother said, after she invited Janalou and everyone inside her nicely appointed home.

"I know. Do you have a number where she can be reached?" Janalou asked.

Mrs. Blanchard nodded. "She has her cell phone, but it doesn't always work. This week they're in London, staying at the Hyde Park Hotel." She picked a scrap of paper up off the coffee table. "Here's the number. Feel free to use our phone. I'd like to turn the speaker on and listen to your conversation."

"Of course I don't mind," Janalou said. She owed Margie and her family big time. None of them had ever forsaken her, and she would always be grateful.

"Hi Margie, it's me," Janalou said, when her friend answered. "I'm with your parents and I'll be flying to London tomorrow. I'd like to see you. How long will you be there?"

"We'll stay here until you arrive," Margie gushed. "I'm so glad you're alive, but I almost can't believe it. The police found blood that matched yours all over the house. What happened?"

"To make a long story short, I cut my hands and feet. That's why they found blood. But why did you call? Is anything wrong?"

"No. Nothing. It's just that my two cousins are both boys, and I feel left out sometimes, so Grandma suggested that I call and invite you to travel with us. She and Grandpa agreed to pay all your expenses. Can you imagine my distress when I called and Belle said you'd run away? Her story sounded fishy, and I've never trusted her, so I called the police. I wasn't just worried. I was alarmed, afraid she might have hurt or killed you."

"Thanks, Margie. If you hadn't called when you did, there might not have been any blood for the police to find."

"You promised you'd let me know if or when you left," Margie reminded.

"I couldn't call. I didn't know where you were and I didn't have a phone."

"I gave you our itinerary."

"But I left in such a hurry I didn't take it with me. I had to get away. But I intended to call in a few weeks, when I knew you'd be home. Anyway, I can't thank you enough for calling the police. If you hadn't, Belle and Franklin might not have been arrested, and I wouldn't have returned to Spartanburg, and I wouldn't have met my real family. I have a twin sister, a wonderful older brother, and my parents are the greatest."

"I know. We saw the news on British TV. It's really big news over here since your father's the Ambassador to the U.K."

Janalou frowned, surprised, although she realized she shouldn't be.

"When will you be here—in England?"

"We're leaving tonight."

"Great. Call me after you arrive. This is our last place to visit and Grandma said we can stay until I see you."

"I'll call as soon as I can."

"That's wonderful." Margie cleared her throat. "I know this is asking a lot, but I'd really like you to join us for the rest of our trip. We're going to Scotland and Ireland when we leave London. Can you go with us?"

"I'd love to, you know that, but I can't now. I need to spend time with my family. And I also have obligations in California. A new job. Even a fiancé."

"You're engaged?" Margie gasped.

"Yes."

"I'll want to hear all about him. What's his name?"

"Kree Winterton."

"Is he there?"

"Yes."

"You can tell me all about him when we see each other in London."

"I'll do better than that. I'll bring him with me."

Margie laughed. "I'll look forward to meeting him."

"Prepare yourself to be impressed."

Margie laughed again. "I'll do that."

"I guess we should hang up now."

"Yeah, I suppose we should. Call as soon as you can."

Janalou laughed, too. "Count on it."

Twenty-two

To ensure their privacy, her father had reserved the entire top section of the DC-10 for the flight to Heathrow. Judging by their expressions, Kree and Tony were as impressed as Janalou when they boarded the plane and were ushered up the small circular flight of stairs, near the first-class section.

After their flight was airborne, everyone unfastened their seatbelts and stood, congregating in a circle, close together. The men took off their suit coats and ties, making themselves more comfortable. Janalou unfastened the clip holding her hair behind her head and let it fall loose. Then she sat down between Kree and Jeri Sue, across from her parents, Paul and Tony.

"I think you're going to be impressed with where we live," Jeri Sue said.

"I'm sure I will be," Janalou said, still basking under the warmth of her new-found family. "Are you and Paul there all the time?"

Jeri Sue shook her head. "We're both still in college in the U.S., but we spend as much time in London as we can during the summer and between semesters, or whenever we have a long holiday weekend or school break. This year will be wonderful because you'll be with us for Thanksgiving and the Christmas holidays, won't you?"

"I'd like to be." She flashed a smile at Kree, too keyed up to contain her happiness. Then, turning back to Jeri Sue, she asked, "What college do you attend?"

"Vassar. Paul's in law school at Cambridge."

Remembering her scholarship, Janalou realized she could use it now that she didn't have to worry about Belle and Franklin, but she preferred to continue along the path she had forged in California. As soon as she passed the real estate exam, she would help Cherilyn find a house and earn her first commission. The thought made her happy.

She glanced at her father. "Tell me what you do as an ambassador."

He smiled as Paul answered for him. "As personal representative of the President, Dad oversees the American Embassy, as well as the Consulates General in Edinburgh and Belfast, and he liaisons with an office in Cardiff, too."

"Being an ambassador includes a ton of political and social responsibilities," Jeri Sue added. "In addition to all the things he does at the embassy, he and mom visit and entertain dignitaries all over the world."

"To say I'm overwhelmed is putting it mildly," Janalou said. "Never could I have imagined my life might include all of you and so many marvelous privileges. I can't help feeling like I'm in a dream—a marvelous one—and that I might wake up and find myself deeply disappointed."

"This is no dream," her father said. "We're finally reunited, thank God."

Smiling at him, Janalou said, "You must be very busy."

"I am." He winked. "So is your mother. Everything she does makes me look good."

Janalou turned to Reva. "I feel as though I'm living in a wonderful fairy tale. If I had ever suspected Franklin wasn't my real papa, and tried to conjure a family, never in my wildest fantasy could I have guessed that I might belong to such a loving one, or that my father is such an important man."

Her mother reached out to embrace her again. "Without you, our lives were never complete. Now they are."

"Yes," Paul agreed. "After you were stolen, I blamed myself because I'm the oldest and I thought I should have protected you."

Her mother shook her head. "It wasn't your fault, Paul. For years your father and I blamed ourselves, too, but we weren't there and neither were you. None of us could have prepared for a kidnapping we didn't foresee or expect."

"How—when—was I kidnapped?" Janalou asked.

"You and Jeri Sue were invited to a birthday party. Your sister got sick, but we decided to let you go without her. I drove you to the party and your little friend's mother promised to drive you home. But apparently Belle showed up disguised as our regular sitter, and said I had asked her to come pick you up. The woman had no reason not to believe her, so she let you go without question. When she failed to bring you home, I called."

"And she fainted when she heard someone had picked you up more than an hour before," her father said.

Janalou searched her head for memories. "It happened so long ago, I can't remember the birthday party, or being picked up by anyone strange. All I remember is that I cried for my family and I was told I'd never see any of you again."

"Were they good to you?" her mother asked, her forehead wrinkled in concern.

"Yes." Janalou nodded. "All the time I was growing up. Even after Minnie died, Franklin and I got along. But when he married Belle, everything changed." She shivered, then added, "I hope you don't blame the woman who let me go."

"It was difficult not to blame her," Taylor said. "She should have been more careful. Her husband was also in politics, and she knew people who hold public office sometimes have enemies."

They continued to chat, each one taking turns adding their thoughts or asking questions. For Janalou it was priceless, a time to be cherished.

~ * ~

They were due to arrive at Heathrow late that night which would be morning in the U.K., but no one felt sleepy.

"I'm so excited about England," Janalou said after the flight attendant cleared their meal trays away. "I've dreamed about going there all my life."

"A lot of us have had the same dream," Jeri Sue said, grinning.

"I've dreamed about you, too," Janalou said.

"And I about you. I'm so glad we've been reunited. We still have a lot to catch up on."

"Yes," Janalou agreed. "Tell me about your home in London."

"Our home."

Janalou nodded. "Yes, our home."

Their parents seemed content to listen and both smiled as Paul said, "The ambassador's house is named Winfield House and it's spectacular. Set in Regent's Park, it stands behind fifteen-foot iron gates on land that was once part of a great forest."

"I love listening to you as much as I love being with you. Please tell me more."

"Mom's the history buff," Jeri Sue said. "She gives the house tours, so she can explain better than anyone else."

Smiling, Reva said, "Let's get something to drink. We have a long flight, and I'll be happy to fill you and Kree in, if you're interested."

"We are," he said, his expression full of admiration.

"What would you like to drink?"

"Something that doesn't have caffeine or alcohol," Janalou said.

Her father asked the flight attendant to bring drinks. She did, along with ice and long-stemmed glasses.

"We're ready," Kree said, sounding as eager to hear about the Ambassador's residence as Janalou was. He set his cranberry juice down, and put his arm around her shoulders. She snuggled close, dazzled by his nearness and the comfort he provided while she waited for her mother to begin.

Reva took a sip of her cranberry juice. "The history of the house goes back a long way. Half a century before the Norman Conquest, the land belonged to the Abbey of Barking. Over the years, King Henry the Eighth hunted there, Queen Elizabeth the First used it to entertain dignitaries, and King James the First offered the property as collateral to raise money to go to war. King Charles the Second had the whole area 'disparked' and toward the end of the seventeenth century, Lord Arlington was given one of the first private leases. In England, even today, many homes are built on land owned by the Crown and as the lease nears its end, the purchaslng of a home becomes less desirable."

When Reva paused, Jeri Sue smiled and interjected, "You'll absorb Winfield House's history, whether you intend to or not, Janalou. It has a way of creeping inside your soul, and becoming part of you."

"I hope so," she said. "I heard it was owned by Barbara Hutton, the unhappy Woolworth heiress, and she donated it to the government to be used as the ambassador's home."

"That's right. But there's a lot more to the story than that," Reva said.

"Please tell us everything," Kree invited, his hand caressing Janalou's shoulder, and making her insides quiver.

"At one time, the house was actually two buildings, connected by a single-storied hall referred to as the tent room which was spacious enough for receptions. By 1920, most of the villas were neglected and abandoned. The leases on offer were short and expensive. Lord Rothermere, a newspaper magnate, was the last owner when all that remained of the original interior was the entrance hall. In 1936, the house was partly destroyed by fire. That's when Barbara Hutton bought it. Three years earlier she had inherited forty million dollars from her grandfather."

"I can't imagine having that kind of money," Jeri Sue said, grinning.

"Me either," Janalou said. "Please continue, Mom."

Reva smiled. "The world-famous heiress was twenty-four, and married to Count Haugwitz-Reventlow. Concerned about threats from someone to kidnap their son Lance, they decided to give up their London house near Marble Arch and look for something bigger and more secure.

"Friends suggested that St. Dunstan's Villa might be an excellent site. Impressed by the peace and security of the grounds, Barbara bought it and got permission for the old white stucco Regency villa to be torn down and a red brick Georgian house to be built in its place."

Reva brushed her dark hair back, and smiled at Janalou. "Should I go on, or do you want to get some sleep?"

"I'm too keyed up to sleep. Tell us more, please.

Kree nodded. So did her father, Paul and Jeri Sue.

"Barbara engaged two decorators, and an expert on carpets and French furniture who had renovated the Woolworth town houses in New York, plus a woman who had consulted with them on furnishings for the previous Reventlow London house. Oak parquet floors were laid, eighteenth century French paneling installed and marble bathrooms fitted. Several thousand trees and hedges were planted, a ten-foot high steel fence erected and a modern security system installed to protect the property."

Janalou turned her head to take in her surroundings again. She still could hardly believe she was here on an airplane with her real family. She loved history and was impressed by her mother's knowledge.

"In 1937," Reva added, "Count and Countess Reventlow moved into Winfield House, which they named after her grandfather, Frank Winfield Woolworth. Barbara decorated the house with antique Louis Fifteenth furniture, Persian carpets, Chinese art objects and art. The house may have given her some happiness and security, but if so, it was short lived.

"In 1939, with World War Two about to erupt and her marriage to Count Reventlow ending, Barbara returned to the U.S."

"Did the house just sit empty?" Janalou asked.

Reva shook her head.

"The Royal Air Force barrage balloon unit commandeered it. They boarded the windows and balloons festooned the gardens where officers played football, which is soccer in England, and they jocularly called themselves "Barbara's Own.""

"Did they take care of the interior?" Kree asked.

Reva shook her head. "Actor Cary Grant, who married Miss Hutton in 1942, visited the house and afterwards he heard Edward

R. Murrow criticize her in a radio broadcast for abandoning her home. Mr. Grant called the journalist and asked him to go see for himself what was happening. On the next day's broadcast, Murrow apologized to Miss Hutton. Although their marriage didn't last, Cary Grant always felt she was never given proper credit for her generosity."

"Was the house ever bombed?" Janalou asked.

"Some near misses damaged the roof. The house was also used as an Air Crew Reception Center to screen prospective Royal Air Force pilots. I doubt anyone paid much attention to upkeep because moisture ruined the parquet floors. In 1944, a fly bomb exploded forty yards away, killing one cadet and injuring twenty others. Six weeks later, Winfield House ceased to host the RAF unit, although it was later used as an American Officers' Club."

"What happened after the war?" Kree asked.

"Barbara returned about a year after it ended, and found buckled floorboards, peeling walls, broken windows and dangling wires. She telephoned her New York lawyer and told him she wanted to give the house to the U.S. Government to be repaired and used as the official residence of the American Ambassador to the Court of St. James. Her generous patriotic offer was accepted in a personal letter from President Harry Truman."

"That was very generous," Janalou said, smiling.

Reva nodded, and there were smiles on everyone's faces as she explained, "For the token price of one American dollar, Winfield House passed into official American ownership."

"You've impressed me with your knowledge, Mom," Janalou said.

"Me too." Once again Kree caressed Janalou's shoulder. She wondered if he realized what he was doing, and found herself a little surprised when she saw Tony glaring at them.

"Mom impresses us, too," Paul said, winking. "She's a terrific hostess. You'll see that when we get to London. We're all very proud of her."

"I agree," their father said, his fond smile resting on his wife as he reached for her hand.

"If you hadn't run off at the beginning of summer," Tony said, his tone caustic, "You would already have seen Winfield House."

Janalou's backbone stiffened at the snide remark, and she couldn't help defending herself. "Belle blackened both of my eyes. I should have left sooner, but if I had, I wouldn't have met Kree." She smiled up at him, and he gave her shoulder a reassuring squeeze.

Her mother reached out to cup her cheek. "We're so glad you're with us now, Janalou. All of us love you."

Jeri Sue nodded agreement.

So did Paul.

Janalou's eyes teared up again. "I can hardly believe you're my family," she said for about the tenth time. Wiping fresh tears, she said, "This is so incredible. So wonderful. All my life I wanted siblings, but all I had was Minnie, the woman I thought was my mama, and Franklin. He was a decent papa until he married Belle." The memories of Minnie's death made her sad, and more tears slid down Janalou's cheeks.

Her father reached over and dried them with his handkerchief. "Don't fret about Franklin any more. He'll be punished through the court system. That's all behind you now. You need not be afraid, ever again."

She smiled through her drying tears. "I love you all so much, and a couple of days ago I didn't even know you were real. I thought you were just people I dreamed up to be my pretend family."

"We've always loved you," Paul said.

Reva smiled. "I hope you'll feel as at home in London as we do."

"I'm sure I will," Janalou said.

A little later, soothed by Kree's gentle arms, and stroking hands, she closed her eyes, her head resting on his shoulder.

She hadn't slept much the previous night. She'd been too keyed up, and she and Jeri Sue had talked most of the night. The night before that she'd been worried about going to court and seeing Franklin and Belle so she hadn't slept much either. But tonight, after two sleepless nights, despite the noisy airplane engine, Janalou slept soundly in the arms of the man she loved.

She awakened when someone raised the window shades and bright sunlight streamed into the aircraft.

"We're almost there," Kree whispered.

"Did you get any sleep?"

He nodded, and smiled a sleepy smile.

He still had his arm around her shoulders. The other had fallen onto her lap. She pulled a little away, very aware of him and their close physical contact. "I hope your arm didn't fall asleep, too."

He kissed her forehead, sending her heart into a tailspin. "I wouldn't have minded if it had."

~ * ~

At Heathrow, they walked through Customs as though they were royalty, surrounded by protective agents. Porters followed with their luggage, all marked with special tags.

Outside, two gray-unformed chauffeurs met them, waiting to drive the Ambassador and his family to London.

"Our U.K. drivers are Rolls Royce-certified," Paul explained while the chauffeurs stacked luggage in the trunks, or boots as the Brits called them.

"And the drivers are very proud of that distinction," Jeri Sue added. "Because that means after they retire, they can drive new Rolls Royce cars to their first destination."

Paul grinned. "They have to be good to maneuver on some of England's twisty, winding roads."

"I can hardly wait to see some of those," Janalou said, so excited she bounced on her heels.

"I'll take you and Kree for a long drive while you're here, if you're up for it," Paul offered.

"I'm sure we will be." She glanced up at Kree. "Won't we?"

He nodded, his smile warm.

But that exchange earned another unpleasant sneer from Tony, who jammed his hands in his pockets, anger in his dark eyes. This time the scowl included Paul, but she didn't understand why. He was Tony's friend.

She was grateful for Tony's part in reuniting her with her family, but she didn't know how to handle him. Although he had been her boyfriend, they hadn't communicated for two years and she no longer felt close. Besides, her heart belonged to Kree.

"Paul, you and Tony ride with your mother," her father said, smiling at Janalou. "You," he said to her, "and Jeri Sue and Kree will ride with me."

Janalou flashed him a grateful smile. Tony's scowls were getting old, and she was glad they'd be separated during the drive.

They piled into the limousines. Protective agents with short-cropped hair, dressed like Secret Service agents in dark suits, white shirts and conservative ties rode in both cars.

Her father's black limo led the small entourage from Heathrow. Eager to see as much as possible, Janalou laughed. "Instead of Entrance and Exit, the Brits use In and Out."

"Right," her father said.

"What other words are different from ours?" Janalou asked as Jeri Sue reached for her seatbelt.

"For one, the freeway is called a motorway," Jeri Sue said, "and you should fasten your seatbelts. Failure to do so could result in a hefty fine."

Delighted to be in England and with her family, Janalou enjoyed the sights along the motorway. Having Kree there with her made everything more exciting. She was glad he had agreed to accompany them. *But how long would he stay? And when he left, would their relationship end?*

Twenty-three

By the time they reached London, Janalou felt like a different person. Everything was new and strange to her.

During the hours she had spent with her real family, her emotional baggage had shifted up, down, up, down. Part of her low self- esteem had disappeared, yet she had trouble trying to decide who she really was.

She was still struggling with conflicting emotions when the chauffeur stopped by the gate at Winfield House.

"Welcome home, Ambassador," the guard greeted them after her father rolled his window down.

"This is my daughter, Janalou," he said, "and this young man is her fiancé, Kree Winterton."

"We heard the good news, sir. Pleased to meet you, Miss Madzen and Mr. Winterton."

"The pleasure is ours," Kree replied.

Thinking it unnecessary to speak, Janalou merely smiled.

As she stepped out of the limousine, Janalou gazed all around, hardly able to believe she was really in England. Even more difficult to accept was that she was with her real family.

Winfield House was all Reva had described and more. The reception hall ran almost the entire length of the house.

"The front entrance was added in 1954," Reva explained, "after it became the ambassador's residence."

Guiding them toward French doors that opened to the terrace and garden in back, Reva added, "Drawing rooms are on the right, family dining room, state dining room, kitchen and staff offices to the left."

"Staff offices?" Janalou asked, feeling more out of her depth with each step she took.

Jeri Sue grinned. "Yes. Mom and Dad both have secretaries. There are protective agents always hanging around too, plus we have an excellent cook and housekeepers who make sure everything stays sparkling clean."

"That's great," Janalou said, once again shaken by the enormity of the changes in her life.

She glanced at Kree and saw doubt in his eyes. Recalling their conversation when he'd said he didn't want to be related to a politician, her breath caught in the back of her throat. *Would her father's position make a difference in their relationship?*

While they toured the ground floor, she brushed that worry aside and tried to enjoy herself.

Jeri Sue reached for her hand afterwards. "Come, I'll show you my room upstairs. I hope you'll want to share it. That will give us more time together." She lowered her voice to the hushed tone of a conspirator. "We can talk at night, when everyone else is asleep."

Her dark eyes, so much like her Janalou's, sparkled.

"I'd love that," she said, smiling and loving her twin more with every word they shared.

"I'll take Kree up to his room," Paul said. "We can meet back down here after we unpack." He raised his hand to cover a yawn. "It's easier to fly west with the sun, than east against it. Does anybody want to take a nap?"

Janalou shook her head. So did Kree. "We slept on the plane, and I think we're both anxious to explore London," she said.

Paul grinned. "All right. But you're not going anywhere without me."

"Without us," Jeri Sue said, raising her finger and twirling it in a protective gesture.

After they unpacked, Janalou made a quick call to let Margie know they had arrived, and promised to call again later.

Back downstairs, her father said, "I've assigned a protective agent to you, Janalou. His name is Monty, and from now on, he'll go everywhere you go."

"I appreciate your concern, but with Belle and Franklin behind bars, I 'm safe now, aren't I?"

Built like a linebacker for a pro football team, Monty shook his head. "There's always a possibility that somebody might try to abduct you or your brother or sister to get something from your father, Miss Madzen."

Understanding dawned, and Janalou resigned herself to having Monty accompany her wherever she went.

"What can we see today?" she asked Jeri Sue.

"Paul and I thought you and Kree might enjoy the Tower of London. We've already seen it, but we'd enjoy going again with you."

"I'd like that. How about you, Kree?"

"Sounds interesting." His eyes met hers, and held them captive until Paul spoke again.

"Are you going with us?" he asked Tony.

Tony nodded, his gaze an angry glare.

After a quick lunch, they left, along with three agents. A chauffeur drove them in one of the black limos they had ridden in from the airport.

At the Tower, after they stood in line to purchase tickets, Janalou saw Duke behind them. Now that she was reunited with her family, she'd probably live in a semi-fish bowl atmosphere.

Turning to Monty, she said, "I'd like to talk to that man."

"Do you know him?"

"Yes. He protects me, kind of like you, but he's self-appointed."

"Go ahead." But Monty followed her.

Plunking her hands on her hips, she asked, "What are you doing here?"

"Yeah," Tony butted in. "Who are you, anyway?"

A tic in Duke's cheek evidenced his annoyance. Ignoring Tony, he straightened the green cap Janalou had given him in June before he spoke. "Watching over you, lass. Making sure no harm befalls you."

Duke glanced at Monty, then back at Janalou. "I shan't force my presence on ye, however, I shall be nearby in case ye need me."

She smiled her thanks, grateful for all he'd done.

Instead of wearing all green as he had in California, or a dark business suit as he had at the court house in Spartanburg, Duke wore gray trousers and a black shirt, and he looked as much like a tourist as anyone.

When they joined a tour group inside the grounds, Janalou thought it uncanny how Duke blended in with the background. He wasn't nearly as noticeable as the three big burly agents assigned to her, Jeri Sue and Paul. Their suits made them stand out like sore thumbs.

Knowing she wouldn't be allowed to go anywhere alone for a long time, if ever, Janalou chewed on her bottom lip. This was going to take some getting used to, and she hoped it didn't bother Kree too much.

Everyone enjoyed the tour, and the things they learned.

"I can hardly believe William the Conqueror had the foresight to erect eight foot thick walls at the base of the ancient tower," Janalou said as she gazed at the big blocks that had been used to build the fortress. The old gray stones looked weathered, but she had a difficult time believing they had stood there for almost a thousand years. *Talk about history!*

"King William must have been brilliant," Kree said in a low aside, moving again to deflect Tony who kept trying to stand closer to Janalou.

Back outside, their guide, a Yeomen Warder, who called himself a 'Beefeater,' pronounced 'Beef-a-teer,' pointed at a large gray square stone. "That's the spot where Ann Boleyn was beheaded."

A shiver went through Janalou as she conjured a beautiful queen kneeling down in front of the stone and regally facing her death with her hands tied behind her back.

But she smiled when the Beefeater Yeoman explained, "Roses are delivered every year on the same day by an unknown entity, and placed on the ground where the queen lost her life."

At the end of their tour, they lined up at the Jewel House to see the heavily guarded Crown Jewels.

"Have the jewels always been stored here?" Janalou asked, looking at the line stretching out in front and behind them.

"Since about the fourteenth century when Westminster Abbey was found to be unsafe," Paul answered.

Sometime later, their group finally entered the Jewel House.

Enclosed in a table-like glass display cage in the center of the room, each of the five crowns was distinct. All were exquisite. St. Edward's Crown, worn by each monarch when being crowned in Westminster Abbey, was the most ornate. All were heavily decorated with some of the world's most extraordinary diamonds and jewels.

They also saw the gold Ampulla and Anointing Spoon, the Armills or bracelets—ancient biblical symbols of regality, the new gold bracelets that were made for Queen Elizabeth the Second in 1952-53, along with the Sovereign's Sceptre with Cross which were used in the coronation ceremony.

Having never seen anything like them, Janalou marveled at their beauty. "They're gorgeous," she said.

"Right," Kree agreed.

As they left that small chamber, it started to rain.

Tony, who had brought an umbrella, opened it and elbowed his way between Janalou and Jeri Sue to keep them dry. That earned him a grateful look from the twins, and a scowl from Kree.

Just outside the tower grounds, Paul bought two black umbrellas from a souvenir stand and handed one to Kree.

"Thanks," he said. "I need to change some dollars into pounds."

"It's too late today," Tony said. "The banks are closed."

"We can do it tomorrow," Janalou said, perturbed by Tony's clipped tone.

~ * ~

At home, Janalou found a private corner, and called Margie again.

"I'm so anxious to see you, I can hardly wait," she said, her emotions almost getting the best of her.

"Me, too," Margie said, sounding just as excited. "How are you doing?"

"Okay, although I'm kind of overwhelmed."

"I'll bet. I heard Tony called the police the same day I did. Do you still like him, even though you haven't seen him for a couple of years?"

"Not like I used to." Janalou glanced over her shoulder to make sure he hadn't moved closer. "I told you I'm engaged."

"Yeah. How—when did you meet him?"

"On the bus. I had an appendicitis attack and he called an ambulance and went to the hospital with me. After my surgery, we traveled by car, just the two of us."

"Wow," Margie said. "Will I see him tomorrow?"

"Yes. He'll be with us. Have you decided where we should meet?"

"Yeah. Grandma made reservations for tea at the Ritz at 3:30pm."

"That's great. I'm really looking forward to our get-together."

"Same here."

~ * ~

The next afternoon, Janalou, Kree, Paul, Jeri Sue, and Tony headed for London in two cars. Three service agents once again went with them. Duke followed in a separate car, with his own driver.

"Does Tony have to go everywhere we go?" Kree whispered, drawing Jeri Sue's attention as well as Janalou's.

Glad they and their agents were in a car without Tony, who had ridden with Paul, Janalou nodded. "I don't know how to exclude him."

"Do you still having feelings for him?"

"No."

"Of course she doesn't," Jeri Sue piped in. "After all, she's engaged to you."

Janalou stared down at the diamond ring on her hand, still not sure what was going to happen.

The small party reached the Ritz Hotel for the first seating for afternoon tea.

Already there, waiting in the lobby with her grandmother, Margie rushed across the foyer and hugged Janalou hard.

"It's so good to see you."

"You too." Goose bumps shot up her back as Margie hugged her back. All summer she had wondered if she'd ever see Margie again.

After they broke apart, she introduced everyone, including the protective government agents. She would have introduced Duke, but he kept to himself and didn't get close enough.

~ * ~

As Tony had on the plane and again at Winfield House, he tried to work his way to sit beside Janalou. Kree made sure he was always on one side, but he couldn't protect her other side. And protect her is what he felt he should do.

To his relief, Jeri Sue said, "Tony, I'm sure Margie wants to sit next to Janalou and Kree. Why don't you sit between me and Paul?"

Tony complied, but his disgruntled expression showed his displeasure.

Kree held a chair out for Margie, then one for Janalou, his hostility toward Tony escalating, especially when he said, "Margie, you've grown up to be a beauty."

"Sure I have." Margie rolled her blue eyes with what Kree interpreted as mischief. "That's why I have so many guys banging on the door day and night begging me for dates."

Janalou laughed, her eyes sparkling with humor. "You'd probably have more if you gave them any encouragement."

"I will if I ever meet the right one." Peeking around Janalou, she said to Kree, "Tell me about yourself."

"What would you like to know?"

"Where you're from, to start with."

"Lodi, California."

Margie's smile faded but before she could speak, Tony said, "That's clear across the country. Surely you're not going to live there now that you've been reunited with your family, Janalou."

Not only did he sound condescending, he acted as though his opinion mattered more than anyone else's.

"We're engaged," Kree said, "so I think where we decide to live is our business, not yours."

"Engaged?" Margie's grandmother shrieked, almost falling off her chair. "You're engaged and no one told me?"

Janalou extended her left hand so Margie and her grandmother could both see the ring.

"Wow! That's some rock." Margie jumped up and hugged Janalou again. "Congratulations. I'm so happy for you."

"Thanks," Janalou said, her voice full of emotion that Kree couldn't interpret.

Tony cleared his throat, drawing attention again.

Kree fisted his hands under the table. If he and Janalou hadn't been engaged, he was sure Tony would try to move right in, and take up where they'd left off years ago. He was beginning to re-think his idea of breaking up with Janalou. Maybe she needed him to keep Tony at bay.

Kree breathed a silent thank-you to Jeri Sue when she said, "I'm sure you'll be very happy, wherever you live."

Janalou's warm smile looked like she appreciated her twin's comment. Still, Kree wondered if she harbored any interest in Tony even though she had denied it. The guy was intelligent, good looking, and he had decent manners. But Kree didn't like the way he kept trying to monopolize her attention. Or the conversation.

~ * ~

A waitress in a black uniform with a white lace-trimmed apron served crustless sandwiches made with white bread. Some had sliced cucumbers. Others had sliced eggs. Both had butter but nothing else on them. Everyone sipped orange juice, and because it seemed like a tradition, most of them also drank creamed tea, although Janalou would have preferred hers with lemon.

When scones, strawberry jam and thick, clotted cream were served, Janalou said, "Would you and your relatives like to visit Winfield House tomorrow, Margie? Dad won't be home, but Mom said she'd give you a tour, and you could stay for lunch."

Margie nodded, laughter spilling from her lips. "I hoped you'd invite us there. Grandpa will be awed and my cousins will be in shock."

"And I'll be delighted," her grandmother added.

"Tell me about your travels," Janalou said. "I'll bet you've had a ball."

"Yes, we have," Margie said, sobering. "But it would have been nicer if you'd been with me. Being the only girl with two boys has had some drawbacks."

"What have you most enjoyed?" Janalou asked.

Margie smiled again. "Everything we've seen and done has been great, but if I had to choose one thing here in England, it would be Stratford-Upon-Avon."

"Why?"

"Because the village is so quaint, the buildings hundreds of years old, and I heard loads of stories about June brides and other traditions."

"I plan to drive Janalou and Kree to Stratford day after tomorrow," Paul said.

Once again Tony glared. He was leaving in the morning, and the others had planned to stay home, relax, and have a quiet day until Janalou's mother cleared her calendar and encouraged her to invite Margie and her relatives for lunch.

When the sweet pastries arrived, Janalou watched the by-play between Kree and Tony. It was apparent they didn't like each other. Every time Kree frowned at her former boyfriend, her self-esteem soared.

If Kree didn't like the attention Tony gave her, maybe they had a chance for a future. Hope swelled inside, and made her smile. When she first met Kree, she didn't feel good enough for him, but now her background gave her back some of the confidence she'd once had. What could she do to convince Kree to turn the pretend engagement into a real one?

~ * ~

A reluctant Tony left the next day. "I need to go home and spend time with my family before I return to college," he explained for the fourth time.

Kree knew how many times Tony had repeated those words because he'd kept track. He disliked Tony and his glares, and was glad to see the last of him. Sure, he had been partially responsible for reuniting Janalou with her family, but he acted as though they should all get down on their knees and thank him time and again.

Yes, Kree was glad to have Tony go. When the door closed behind him, Kree heaved a sigh of relief. It would be nice to have some time alone with Janalou, her sister and brother without Tony butting into their conversations or trying to monopolize both girls' attention.

After a leisurely British breakfast of bangers, eggs and cold white toast, the foursome sat in the luxurious lounge, chatting and laughing.

"What's that?" Janalou asked, nodding at a small bright pink piece of furniture that resembled a velvet foot stool.

"Let me demonstrate." Jeri Sue took off her shoes and tucked her feet inside the soft velvet folds. "This is what it was used for in the olden days—to keep a lady's feet warm. Without central heating, houses were cold and drafty, and the only heat came from fireplaces."

After Jeri Sue pulled her feet from the small tufted foot stool, and put her shoes back on, Kree saw Janalou studying another oddity—a shiny, flat shield-like wooden circle that stood on a stand, level with her face while she sat.

"That was a shield for women's faces," Jeri Sue explained. "Years ago they wore heavy wax-based make-up and the heat from the fireplace would melt it, so that thing protected their faces and kept their make-up intact."

"This place is as good as a museum," Janalou said.

"We think so too," Paul agreed, grinning, "and we're so glad you're here now sharing it with us."

Janalou laughed. "Me, too."

~ * ~

Margie and her relatives arrived promptly at eleven-thirty.

They were as impressed with Winfield House as Kree had been. He tagged along while Reva gave the tour, and hoped he remembered half of what she said so he could tell his family, Jason, and Reina. They would likely be all ears when he went home.

When they were seated in the family dining room and salads had been served, Paul said, "I have a brain teaser. There's a five letter word in the English language that is also one letter of the alphabet. It's only one syllable. Does anyone know what it is?"

Kree's mind skimmed the alphabet twice before he knew the answer. He glanced at Janalou, wondering if she had come up with it. When she quirked an eyebrow at him, he knew she had. They had both heard the word more than once yesterday. Funny how they sometimes communicated without having to speak. Even more surprising was her sharp alert mind. He'd come from thinking she was as shy as a rabbit the first time he'd seen her to thinking she was one of the most brilliant people he had ever met.

He looked across the table at Margie and saw her wink at Janalou.

"I can't think of any letter that's a five letter word," one of Margie's teenaged cousins said.

"Think about being in England," Janalou suggested. "What do people do when they go to the bank, or while they wait for a bus?"

When Margie's cousin looked baffled, his grandfather said, "Should I tell you, Nate?"

He nodded.

"Q. They queue up."

"Right," Paul said, a twinkle in his eyes.

"I have one, too," Jeri Sue said. "What is greater than God, more evil than the devil, poor people have it, rich people don't want it, and if you eat it, you'll die?"

Once again Kree's brain skimmed over the possibilities. When he came up with the answer, he thought it was too simple to be right, and waited for someone else to speak first.

Margie's grandmother smiled. "I know because I've been getting emails for years."

"What?" Paul asked, and Kree realized the ambassador had trained his children to draw other people into the conversation instead of monopolizing it, as Tony had done.

He glanced at Janalou, and saw by the look in her eyes that she knew the answer.

"Tell us," Margie's other teenaged cousin, Sam, urged.

"Nothing," his grandmother said.

"Nothing?" Sam looked perplexed, then he laughed. "Well, it does fit all those questions."

"I have one." Janalou pulled a pen and notepad off the sideboard and wrote for a few seconds. Then she said, "If each letter of the alphabet is assigned a number, one through twenty-six, then 'a' would equal one and 'z' would equal twenty-six. The words 'hard work' would be written this way... and she showed them a sequence of numbers: $8+1+18+4+23+15+18+11$. "Those numbers equal ninety-eight percent. Knowledge is this sequence," she said. Once again she showed them some numbers: $11+14+15+23+12+5+4+7+5$. "They equal one hundred percent. Attitude, see here how it's written: $1+2+20+9+20+21+4+5$. "They also equal one hundred percent. Now look at Love of God. The formula is this." She pointed to the numbers on the page: $12+15+22+5+15+6+7+4$. "And that equals one hundred and one percent," she said. "From this we can conclude with mathematical certainty that while hard word and knowledge will get you close, and attitude will get you there, it's the love of God that will put you over the top."

She had not only impressed Margie's relatives, Janalou had succeeded in impressing her own family and Kree as well. Pride swelled inside him. How many other things would she say or do to surprise and amaze him?

"Would you like to hear some of our Southern jokes?" Janalou asked.

After Kree, Jeri Sue and Paul nodded, she said, "What is a country club's definition of a faithful husband?"

When everyone shook their heads, Margie laughed and answered. "His alimony checks arrive on time every month."

"What is a country club's definition of natural childbirth?" Janalou asked then.

Unable to answer, they all shook their heads again, and turned their eyes to Margie, who grinned as she answered, "No makeup whatsoever."

By the time the visitors left, Kree knew something about each one. Without Paul and his sisters, that wouldn't have happened. They had worked as a team, and Janalou fit right in, helping to draw out Margie's relatives, and make them feel at home, just as they had made Kree feel as though he belonged.

~ * ~

Dinner that night was smaller than usual, just Janalou's family and Kree. Without Tony vying for Janalou and Jeri Sue's attention, or monopolizing Paul, Kree enjoyed himself immensely.

"You have a fantastic cook," he said to the ambassador. "The food is delicious. I've probably gained weight." With a grin, he accepted a second helping of lamb and mint jelly.

"We're fortunate to have Norma. She's a terrific cook," Paul said, and everyone nodded agreement.

A big part of the dinner discussion revolved around the embassy. Although Kree had never been interested in politics, he found himself fascinated by the problems the ambassador faced each day. By the look on Janalou's face, he knew she was fascinated as well.

Kree accepted a second helping of trifle, a colorful mixture of fruit, Jell-o, and diced cubes of white cake, topped with heavy whipped cream. "I've never eaten trifle before. I could get used to it, real easy," he said.

"Me, too." Janalou also accepted another scoop. "We'll walk off the calories tomorrow when we go to Stratford," she said, smiling.

"Good idea." Kree licked his lips, and his insides clenched when Janalou licked hers too. He wanted to kiss her, hold her close, and never let her go. Could he tell her that and not ruin her life?

Twenty-four

They got up early and Paul drove them, with three agents in tow, to Stratford-Upon-Avon to tour Shakespeare's birth place.

"I understand it took four days to travel here from London when Shakespeare was alive," Paul said after they reached their destination.

"Life moved at a much slower pace back then," Jeri Sue added. "Sometimes I think it moves too fast now. Before long, Paul and I will have to return to the States for school."

"I should leave, too," Janalou said. "I'm so glad we have time together now."

"We're all happy about that," Paul said. "Why don't you stay with Mom and Dad?"

"I'm studying to pass the real estate exam, and I need to go back to work." She glanced at Kree to see his reaction, disappointed when she couldn't decipher his expression.

The first place they visited was the house where Shakespeare was reputed to have lived. Part of one wall was exposed to show the old-fashioned daub and wattle construction. Kree studied that, then turned his attention to the crude etchings on the glass window panes.

Looking at Janalou, he said, "Some of these things were etched here four or five hundred years ago. Kind of boggles your mind, doesn't it?"

"Yes. England is full of history, everywhere we look."

"Yeah," he agreed. "Makes you want to stay here a long time, doesn't it?"

She nodded. "There's so much to see."

He grinned. "And so little time."

His grin looked forced or sad. Janalou didn't know which. When he reached for her hand, she moved closer, so happy she thought her bubble might burst.

During the journey back to the ambassador's residence, Kree said, "I made a plane reservation for the day after tomorrow. I think you should stay, though."

"I will for a little while," Janalou agreed. "As I mentioned, I'd like to celebrate my real birthday with my twin, and the rest of my family. I wish you could stay, too."

"I can't."

"I know, and I understand."

~ * ~

Parting was difficult. Janalou managed without crying only because she knew she would see Kree again soon. "Give everyone a hug for me, will you?" she asked before he climbed in the limo that would take him to Heathrow.

He arched his brows. "Everyone?"

"Well, maybe not your fishing friends," she said, forcing a smile.

"Maybe you should show me how."

She wrapped her arms around his broad shoulders and hugged him.

"Are you going to kiss me?" he asked, his husky voice very close to her ear.

"Do you want me to?" she teased.

"Yes."

Happily she complied while her mother, Paul and Jeri Sue watched.

"He's a great guy," Jeri Sue said after he left.

"He's the man I love," Janalou said, her voice quivering with emotion.

Jeri Sue smiled. "Can't say I blame you. Hope I meet someone I can love someday."

"I'm sure you will," Janalou said, swiping at the moisture escaping from her eyes.

"You don't have time to cry," Jeri Sue said. "Come on, I've got something to show you."

"What is it?"

"If I tell you, it won't be a surprise."

Up in the room they shared, she pulled an album from a drawer. "I had this air-freighted from our home in Philadelphia. It arrived yesterday but I waited to share it, thinking it would help take your mind off Kree's leaving."

"What is it?"

"Our first photo album. I thought you might like to see us when we were little."

Janalou smiled away her tears. "I would. Thanks for saving it for today."

From the first moment she had discovered her family, she had felt close to them, but she grew even closer during the next days they shared. Delighted to have a sister, they spent hours after everyone else retired talking, sharing their innermost thoughts. To her surprise, Jeri Sue felt the way she did about so many things.

Paul was just as special. Having a big brother was wonderful. Janalou felt unusually close to him and didn't know why. Because they had come from the same womb?

They spent hours catching up on details of their lives. Having siblings made Janalou feel more confident, more secure, as though her identity had always lacked something. Now it was complete. Her stay in England was all she could have wished for and more. Each day was pure pleasure. Each night a treasure to savor.

During the last week in August, she celebrated her birthday with Jeri Sue, and with mixed emotions. On one hand, she felt spoiled for celebrating her birthday twice in two months. On the other hand, she felt cheated out of the two teenage years she had missed. Suddenly she was twenty, and part of her resented not getting to be eighteen for more than a couple of months, or ever having a chance to feel nineteen. She couldn't help blaming Belle and Franklin for stealing those years from her.

She pushed those thoughts from her mind with an impatient twinge. Franklin had stolen enough of her life. She shouldn't let him steal any more, not even a single minute. She shouldn't even think about him.

But sometimes she couldn't help wondering what he was going through, or how he was. He'd been her papa most of her life and she had loved him even after he'd married Belle and allowed her to rule their lives.

After dinner when she saw the gaily wrapped gifts, she shoved all unhappy thoughts farther aside. She was where she belonged. With her family. Her real family.

Her parents gave her a new cell phone and two credit cards, an American Express and a MasterCard. "After you return to California, we'd like you to keep in touch on a regular basis," her father said, nodding at the phone.

"Every day wouldn't be too often," her mother added.

"She's right. And if you need anything, don't hesitate to use one of those cards," her father said.

"I don't know how to thank you."

"Thanks are unnecessary. We were robbed of your childhood, but we want to share as much as possible now, and we consider it a pleasure to have the chance to help take care of you."

Janalou reached up to hug him. "The pleasure is all mine, Dad."

When she unwrapped Jeri Sue's gift, the doll dressed in green velvet from that long ago Christmas, the last before she had been kidnapped, tears puddled in her eyes. "How did you get this?"

"I called the man who takes care of our house in Philadelphia, and told him which closet it was stored in, and asked him to Fed Ex it, along with the album we looked at after Kree left."

Gazing at the doll, Janalou said, "She's so precious."

"Here's something else," Jeri Sue said.

When Janalou unwrapped that package, she found the photograph Jeri Sue had mentioned of the two of them when they were three, wearing the red and green dresses that matched their dolls. Tears clouded her eyes, and she could hardly see. "Thank you. This is so special. Are you sure you want to give it up?"

"I've had it for years," Jeri Sue said. "Now it's your turn. Besides," she winked again, "I had a copy made for myself."

Janalou laughed. "Thank you again."

"You're more than welcome, sis."

The doll brought back more memories, and she felt very sentimental as she unwrapped Paul's gift, a silver tea set he had seen her admiring at a gift shop in Stratford. "Thank you," she said, humbled by her family's generosity.

Norma, the American cook, brought in a cake.

"Make your wishes at the same time," her mother said, "before you blow out the candles."

Janalou closed her eyes and wished Kree would love her and want to share the future. More tears glossed her eyes as she recalled celebrating her eighteenth birthday with him and her new friends in California. She missed him terribly. But being with her family was marvelous. A dream come true. Still, she was getting anxious to return to Lodi.

~ * ~

"I've never been in love," Jeri Sue said later, after they changed to pajamas and climbed in bed. "Is love as wonderful as everyone says it is?"

Janalou nodded. "Every time I see Kree, I feel warm way down deep inside. Sometimes just being near him makes my insides tremble."

Jeri Sue grinned. "That makes me happy, but I think Tony has feelings for you, too."

Janalou shook her head. "Tony was part of my past, and I'm grateful for his part in reuniting us, but I love Kree. Being separated is difficult."

"I can imagine. He seems like a terrific guy."

"He is."

"How long will you stay here in London with us?"

"Until next week. I should return to work. I've been studying for the California real estate exam, and I need to get back and finish. My test is the week after Labor Day."

"When will you come back to England?"

"As soon as I can."

"Paul and I will be here for Thanksgiving. I hope you'll be here then, too."

Janalou smiled. "I wouldn't miss a chance to spend Thanksgiving with all of you."

"Maybe you could invite Kree. And his parents, too," Jeri Sue suggested. "There are plenty of bedrooms for them to stay here, if you think they'd like to. I'm sure Mom and Dad will agree."

"I'll talk it over with them. If they do agree, I'll ask the Wintertons."

"Since you're staying until next week, I could fly back with you," Jeri Sue said. "I need to get ready for school. The flight would give us more time together."

"That would be marvelous." Janalou toyed with a strand of her long hair. "I'm torn between leaving London and staying. And I'm just as torn about staying in California and returning to London."

"I'm sure Mom and Dad will miss you," Jeri Sue said. "Try to come back as often as you can."

"Don't worry, I will."

"Has it been difficult adjusting to us?" Jeri Sue asked then.

Janalou shook her head. "No, not difficult. Different. And wonderful, too. But I can't forget the other people I love either. They treated me like family when I thought I no longer had one."

Jeri Sue nodded. "I understand."

After they turned off the lights and she heard her twin's even breathing, Janalou's thoughts roamed. Thinking of the doll Jeri Sue had given her reminded her that she had nothing from her childhood in South Carolina. She'd left everything except her memories behind, but she wouldn't mind having something that had belonged to Minnie, the woman who had mothered her for so many years. Thinking that was impossible, she told herself she didn't have a permanent home yet, and no place to store or keep mementos anyway. But she planned to take the doll and photograph Jeri Sue had given her back to California.

~ * ~

During the flight back to the U.S., Monty and another agent sat behind Janalou and Jeri Sue in first class. She saw Duke beyond the curtain, in the first business class row. He was like a shadow, silent and often unseen, yet always there. For some strange reason, his presence made her feel safer than Monty's did, even though he worked for the government and was trained to protect her.

She and Jeri Sue parted tearfully in New York. "I miss you already," she said, then hiccupped.

"I feel the same way," Jeri Sue said, "but I have an idea."

"What is it?"

She pulled her phone from her pack. "I'll call and we can talk until one of us has to board our plane."

"Fantastic. Glad you thought of it." Talking did help, and Janalou silently blessed her parents for the new phone, even though she had the one Kree's parents had given her in June. Someday she would to return it, even if she and Kree didn't end their phony engagement.

Alone for the flight across the U.S, except for Monty and Duke sitting beside her, Janalou thought about seeing Kree again. He lived in her thoughts, a constant reminder that she loved him. She hoped when she saw him again that he would say he'd missed her, too. Maybe then they could discuss sharing the future for real.

Kree met her at the airport. Two seconds with him had her in a dither. Her pulse trembled, her knees shook, and she almost forgot to breathe when he wrapped his warm, strong arm around her. She was tempted to lean closer, melt against him, reach up and draw his lips down to hers. But she didn't have enough nerve.

She was shocked when he turned her to face him, and crushed her against his chest in the sweetest kiss she'd ever known.

"Welcome back," he murmured, still holding her close after the kiss ended.

"Thanks," she whispered. He'd stolen her breath, and she almost couldn't find her voice. "It's good to be back."

"We've all missed you."

"I've missed all of you, too."

Reina, Cherilyn, Misti, and Toby peeked around the corner.

"Hi," they chorused, waving like long lost friends.

Janalou smiled. Had they watched Kree kiss her? Had he done it to impress them? Did the kiss mean anything to him? *How could it mean nothing when it meant to so much to her?*

"Welcome home," Cherilyn said, her eyes sparkling with laughter.

"Thanks. After two long flights, I'm glad to be here."

Kree released her. "I told Mom and Dad we'd meet them for dinner, if you're not too tired."

"I'm not." In spite of the long day, Janalou agreed with her brother. Flying west and following the sun was less tiring than flying east against the sun. She decided to call Paul first thing in the morning and tell him she appreciated his wisdom. Even if she had been tired, she was too excited to sleep.

Monty and Duke followed them to the restaurant where they met Kree's parents.

While they ate, Janalou's enthusiasm overflowed. She told everyone about her family, Winfield House, and a lot of the things she had seen and done.

"What did you most enjoy when we went to Stratford-Upon-Avon?" Kree asked.

Janalou smiled. "Ann Hathaway's thatched roofed cottage. I liked the story about courting, and the explanation of where the term spooning came from."

"Why don't you share that with us?" Helen said, her smile bright.

"Okay. Young men used to sit beside their favorite young lady with her father on a bench across from them in the huge Inglenook fireplace, making sure the young man kept busy whittling a spoon for his future bride to keep his hands off her, while she stitched a shirt for him to wear on their wedding day."

"What did you think about the explanation for so many June weddings?" Kree asked.

Janalou laughed. "You mean because that's the one month of the year when everyone took a bath?"

He nodded with a grin. "Apparently it was an annual ritual."

"I'm glad I didn't live then. I'd hate not being able to bathe or shower every day," Janalou said.

"You saw and learned so much," Cherilyn said. "I'm impressed."

"Me too," Helen added. "It must have been difficult to leave your family."

"It was. But Jeri Sue had to return to college, so we flew back together, and Paul left a couple of days ago. He's in law school. I'm planning to fly back to London as often as possible." She paused, took a breath and smiled at Helen. "By the way, you and Max and Kree are invited to spend Thanksgiving with us. Mom assured me they have plenty of bedrooms, and we'd like you to stay with us at Winfield House."

For the first time since Janalou had met her, Helen looked flustered. She raised her hands to her chest, her fingers tapping the vicinity near her heart. "That would be wonderful, but we wouldn't want to intrude."

"You wouldn't. I've told them how wonderful you've all been since I moved here, and they're eager to meet you. On Thanksgiving morning, we'll go to St. Paul's Cathedral so Dad can speak to ex-patriots who live in the U. K. and are interested in hearing his message from the President."

"Gosh. Makes me wish we could be there with you," Sirena said.

"Maybe you can be, next year," Janalou dared to suggest.

~ * ~

After Kree drove her home, Janalou wasn't surprised when Monty said, "I've arranged to live in the apartment next to yours."

She nodded.

With Duke living across the grass, she never went anywhere without one or both men.

Duke continued to drive her to and from work. And whenever she had errands to run, he often drove her and Monty, too.

To her relief, Martina left her alone, and rarely made snide comments. Janalou maintained her distance, afraid to believe Martina didn't resent her.

Almost every day she talked to her parents and Jeri Sue. She talked to Paul often as well, mostly during weekends when he wasn't quite as busy studying or attending classes.

Each day when Janalou saw Kree's handsome face, her heart melted. His warm gaze and sensual smile went to bed with her at night, and woke up with her every morning.

Yes, no doubt about it. She was in love. She wanted to shout her love to the world. She yearned to tell him. But didn't. What if he didn't love her? Wouldn't that be terrible?

~ * ~

One night while Janalou was studying for the real estate exam, Jason called. "I took the real estate test a few months ago. Would you like somebody to help you study?"

"Yes. That would be great."

"Are you studying tonight?

"Yes."

"I'll be right over."

"Great."

For the next few nights, he showed up after supper and drilled her on questions that might be on the test. After he left one night, Cherilyn knocked on her door.

"Come in," Janlou invited, moving aside so Toby and Misti could enter, too.

"What's up?"

"I'm ready to look at houses. When can you show some to me?"

"Are you still seeing Brad?"

Cherilyn nodded. "He's wonderful, but he isn't my reason for wanting a house. The kids need a back yard. We all need a place we can really call home. We can start looking now, and if it's okay with the Wintertons, we'll close after you pass your exam. That way you'll earn the commission."

"I'd be delighted to show you some houses whenever you have time, and I'll mention your idea to Kree's family, to see if that's okay with them."

When she mentioned it the next day, Sirena said, "I have some houses to show today. Why don't go with me and observe?"

"I'd love to."

She did, and watched and listened and learned.

"This is for practice," Sirena said when they were in the third house with an elderly couple who had wandered off, along the hall to see the master bedroom again. "I'll let you write up the contract, if they find a house they want."

"That would be wonderful," Janalou said. "But will it be legal?"

Sirena grinned. "Yes. I'll be there to help."

Back at the office, Sirena walked Janalou through the sales process. After one phone call to the seller, the couple signed the contract, left a substantial down payment, and departed.

Sirena smiled. "A sale gives you a good feeling, doesn't it?"

Janalou nodded. When she earned her first commission, she intended to start paying Kree back. With that in mind, she called the hospital in Indiana and the surgeon's office, and found out how much she owed him. The amount was even more staggering than she had imagined.

When he came into the office they shared, she said, "Cherilyn wants to look at houses. Would you take us to see some in the next day or so?"

Kree shook his head. "I'm going fishing up north, by Fort Jones. Why don't you ask Sirena or Jocelyn to help you?"

Disappointed, she forced a smile. "Okay." He had time to go fishing with his friends but never seemed to have time for her.

On Saturday during the Labor Day weekend, Janalou took Cherilyn to see several houses. They had dropped Toby and Misti off at Reina's, and it felt odd not to have them around.

"I liked the second house we saw," Cherilyn said after they looked at six. "But I'm a bit confused after seeing so many. Could we go see that one again?"

"The open house is over. I'll call the owners." Janalou pulled out her cell phone. After identifying herself, she said, "My client would like to see your house again. Would it be all right if we came by sometime?"

"Of course," the owner said. "We were just going out. Feel free to use the lock key."

"I love this house," Cherilyn confirmed after they walked through every room again, and stood staring out at the back fenced yard. "It will be perfect for us."

"Are you sure you want to buy right now? What if things get serious between you and Brad?"

"Then we'll have two choices—whether to live in his house or mine." She bit her bottom lip, then said, "I don't know if we'll ever be serious about each other, and I don't want to wait any longer to have a house. Do you understand what I'm trying to say?"

Janalou nodded. "If you decide to get married, you don't want Brad to think it's just because you want to live in his house, right?"

Cherilyn nodded. "Having my own will prove I don't need what he can offer financially. That's what his first wife wanted so he's a bit gun shy now."

"If only life could be a little bit simpler," Janalou said, thinking about Kree and his lack of attention since her return.

Cherilyn laughed. "If only. Those two words pack a powerful meaning."

"Right."

Back at the office, they sat down and Janalou wrote up the offer-to-purchase contract. As Sirena had said, making a sale did feel good. It also gave her a sense of power, like she could control her own destiny.

She could hardly wait to tell Kree she could afford to start paying him back. She was just as anxious to tell him she loved him, but she didn't have enough nerve yet. He'd never mentioned the 'L' word.

Twenty-five

During the oral real estate exam, Janalou didn't have to answer all the questions before they told her she had passed.

Ecstatic, she rushed back to the office.

Kree, Jocelyn and their parents were out, but Sirena was there and Janalou dashed to her door. "I passed my exam."

"That's terrific." Sirena gave her an enthusiastic hug

Watching them, Martina didn't smile, but she did say, "Congratulations."

Not long after Janalou got home from work, her cell phone rang. She pulled it from her backpack and flipped it open.

"Hello."

"Hi," Jason said. "Did you pass your exam?"

"Yes, and I'd like to celebrate." Without really thinking about it, she said, "If I fix dinner, will you eat with me?"

"Yes. That would be great."

He arrived while she was setting the table. She had also invited Duke and Monty, and couldn't help wishing she were celebrating alone with Kree, but he acted remote and she didn't know what to say or do to break through his wall of silence.

The foursome sat down at her small table and ate the chicken dinner she had cooked. Afterwards Monty and Duke left. Jason helped her do the dishes, then they turned on the TV.

Shortly after he left, Kree called. "I'd like to come over, if it's all right."

Her heart brightened. "Of course it is."

"I'll be there in a few minutes."

~ * ~

Having deliberately held himself away from Janalou since their time together in England, Kree had reached a difficult decision. He loved her, and wanted what he thought was best for her, and that was making sure she returned to England to be with her parents.

He had given himself time to get used to the idea. Now he had to act. If he waited much longer, he wouldn't be able to follow through with his good intentions. He'd been looking for an excuse, and finally had one.

~ * ~

When Kree arrived, his hair was a mass of unruly curls, as though he'd run his hands through it in agitation.

Janalou smiled, hoping to cheer him. "I have good news. I passed my real estate exam."

"I know. I heard."

She studied him, trying to decide what to say next, and settled on asking, "What's wrong?"

He cleared his throat. "Jason was here tonight. Why?"

"I invited him to dinner because he called to congratulate me, and I wanted someone to celebrate with and you weren't around."

"Why didn't you celebrate with Cherilyn? I thought you did everything together."

"We do share a lot of things, but she had a date tonight."

"Did she?" His voice sounded bored, and as cool as the air-conditioning blowing down on top of them from the ceiling vent. "Martina told me in front of my parents and sisters that you've been seeing Jason behind my back, here in your apartment so you're all alone. Can you imagine how stupid that made me feel?" Kree didn't wait for an answer. "It's time to end our false engagement."

Janalou's heart fell half way to her knees. "He—Jason only came over to help me study."

When Kree didn't comment, she squeaked, "Is there anything I can say that might change your mind?"

"No." He stuck his hands in his pockets and paced back to the door. "Please resign and leave the company before I get back from my fishing trip."

"You're going fishing? I thought you just came back…"

"I'm going again. And under the current circumstances, I'm sure you'll agree that sharing the same office is out of the question. If you don't have enough nerve to resign immediately, I'll tell my family."

His voice sounded strained, and his unbending posture looked as uncomfortable as his awkward expression.

Janalou felt as though her heart might break. Maybe it already had. "Please don't do this," she begged. "I haven't been seeing Jason behind your back. Tonight's the only time we did more than study, and all we did was eat. Duke and Monty were both here, too. You must know Martina's jealous, and wants to break us up."

He shook his head, and reached for the doorknob.

"Can I ask some questions before you leave?"

"Only if you hurry."

"If this hadn't happened, is there any chance that you might have considered turning our engagement into a real one, and possibly getting married some day?"

"Yes." He turned the knob and opened the door. "But that was before I realized one man isn't enough for you."

"That isn't true."

"Isn't it? What about Tony? Martina said he's called every day since you returned."

She shook her head. "If he has, I haven't talked to him."

Kree stepped outside.

"Wait," she begged. "I think I'm in love with you."

He gave her a long look. "I think you were fooling yourself all along. You'll be over me in no time at all."

But she was certain she wouldn't. She'd never been more sure of anything.

Pride did its best to surface. She didn't want to be like a dopey old lady who fell off a wagon and didn't have enough gumption to get up and take care of herself.

Squaring her shoulders, she tried to act brave, tried to pretend Kree's words hadn't stung, and watched in silence as he yanked the door closed behind him.

Then she burst into tears. She wanted to call Cherilyn, but knew she was still out with Brad. Besides, it wouldn't be fair to dump on her.

She grabbed a box of tissues instead, plopped on the couch, and let the tears fall. She couldn't stop them. With a few swipes, she realized she was more miserable than she had thought possible, even more miserable than she'd been during that awful year living with Belle.

When the doorbell rang again, she swiped at her tears, and dashed across the room to grab the doorknob, hoping it might be Kree.

But it wasn't. It was Duke.

"I saw the lad go, and he looked mighty upset. What happened, lass?"

"Martina told him I'd been seeing his best friend behind his back, and he didn't believe me when I said it isn't true."

"Listen, lass," Duke said, his tone consoling, "some people are bridge people. They help others cross from one place in their lives to another. Look at the lad and his family as though they've been a bridge for you. They helped you get from your unhappy past to your future. Now it's time to cross another bridge. Go back to England. Spend time with your family. Live the life you were meant to live, the life you've been cheated out of living."

Her throat clogged, and she tried to think rationally, but all she could say was, "Kree wants me gone before he returns from his fishing trip this weekend."

"I'll make arrangements for you to return to England, if you'd like, lass."

"Thank you. I'm not sure when I'll be going yet. I have a lot to do first." She crossed her arms, and forced herself to calm down. Until tonight, Kree had been there when she needed him, so she owed him big time, and she would do as he asked, without making a fuss.

As she stood there facing Duke, her hope for a future with Kree died a painful death. She tried to look on the bright side, but couldn't find one.

After Duke left, the doorbell rang again. Hoping it might be Kree, she dashed across the room and opened the door. But it wasn't Kree. Jason had returned, and he looked as upset as Kree had been.

"Kree called and accused me of stealing you from him. Didn't you tell him all we've done is study to help you pass the exam?"

"Yes, but he didn't believe me. Martina made up stories, and he believes everything she said."

"He didn't believe me either. He said our friendship is over. Then he hung up on me. He's never done anything like that, ever." Jason stuck his hands in his pockets. "I wonder how he found out I came here tonight."

"Martina told him. She must have been spying on me."

Jason nodded. "That explains it. She's had her eyes on Kree forever."

"Well, there's nothing I can do about that."

"Your life's different now," Jason said. "You can't go anywhere without bodyguards, or without reporters hounding you for comments. Kree might be using us as an excuse to break up because he doesn't want any part of that kind of life."

"I think I've been pretty well protected from that sort of thing."

"Protected, yeah. A protective agent lives next door and another guy lives across the courtyard, and one or both of them follows you everywhere you go. We couldn't even eat without them tonight."

"I invited them to help me celebrate."

But she couldn't dispute that they were always around, always nearby. Having Monty and Duke close made her feel safe and secure.

She stared down at the floor, then back up at Jason, trying to sort her thoughts and form the right words. "I'm sorry about coming between you and Kree."

Jason shrugged. "He'll come around. If he doesn't, our friendship isn't worth saving." He opened the door. "If you want someone to fly to London with you, I'm available."

"Thanks. I appreciate that."

"I'll call tomorrow, to make sure you're okay."

She forced a smile. But when he left, she cried again.

When she finally had no tears left, she started to make plans. Part of her wanted to leave right then. But she had run away from South Carolina without telling anyone goodbye, and didn't want to do that again. Her new friends meant too much to be treated that way.

Picking up a notepad, she listed all the connections she had to sever, and the people she wanted to call. Before she finished, she was crying once more. *What if she never saw Kree again?* This felt like a divorce, and she'd always wonder if she might have salvaged it if she'd done something different. But what?

~ * ~

When Kree's phone rang, he didn't want to answer, but caller ID indicated Jason's name and number, so he picked it up. "What do you want?" he barked.

"If you choose to believe Martina instead of me and Janalou, you can go to hell."

Without waiting for a reply, Jason hung up. Kree called him back. Jason didn't answer his land line or his cell.

Kree felt like a jerk. Worse than that, he felt as though he had ripped out his own heart and stomped on it. He'd known when Martina told him Jason was spending time with Janalou that she might be lying, or that there had to be a reasonable explanation, but he'd seen red and used his anger to sever his relationship with Janalou.

Giving her up was something he felt he had to do. He had weighed his choices, and firmly believed he had no other choice.

She needed her freedom and time to spend with her parents and sister and brother. They had been separated too long already.

~ * ~

Every hour that moved Janalou closer to leaving California made the crack in her heart more painful to bear. Returning to England was her only option. But putting Kree and her new friends behind hurt because she loved them, and feared she might never see some of them ever again.

With a heavy heart weighing her down, she was a bit surprised at how easy it was to give up her apartment and end her obligations in Lodi.

Sirena agreed to follow up on the house sale to Cherilyn, which made Janalou's insides shrink. Nobody was indispensable, but not getting to close her first sale made her feel like a failure. She didn't intend to use that as an excuse to hang around, though.

On Monday morning, only one thing remained to be done. Close her bank accounts. Duke and Monty accompanied her to the bank on their way to the airport. Having earned enough to live on, she hadn't used much of the money she deposited when she first arrived, and had even saved some from paychecks.

Relieved that she had enough to pay Kree something, she had a cashier's check made for four thousand dollars, wrote a check to cash for what was left, and closed both accounts.

After she dropped Kree's check in the mail, they headed for the airport in a regular cab, not the shamrock-emblazoned one Duke usually drove.

Janalou still had one problem. The ring. She had removed the solitaire the night Kree broke their pretend engagement. If the diamond was real, sending it through the mail wouldn't be safe, and leaving it with his parents or sisters seemed tacky. Maybe she could ask Jason, who would be flying to England with her, to return the ring. She couldn't stop wishing Kree would be her companion instead.

She looked at Duke and asked, "Was your employer unhappy when you resigned as a taxi driver?"

Duke grinned. "Nay, lass. I always work for meself, so the hours are my own."

She thought that odd, but then most things about the eccentric Duke Guggles were strange. Maybe he really was an other-worldly being.

Jason met them at the airport, where they pre-boarded, found their seats in first-class, and settled down for the long flight over the North Pole.

~ * ~

Both of her parents were at Heathrow after she landed and cleared customs more than twelve hours later.

Janalou hugged each one while Monty and Duke, ever watchful, stood nearby with Jason. "You didn't have to meet me," she said, "although I'm glad you did."

"We may not next time," her mother said, smiling. "But today we couldn't resist." Reva's smile faded. "We're sorry about your breakup with Kree, but we're happy you've returned to spend more time with us."

"I'm happy about that, too." When Janalou's voice broke, her father pulled her close.

"We know this must be difficult for you, and we intend to keep you busy."

Tears clouded her eyes. "That's a good idea. I don't know who I am or where I belong anymore."

"You're our beloved daughter, and you belong right here with us." The conviction in Taylor's voice bolstered her tattered ego.

"With all my heart I hope that's true."

"We'll make it true," he said.

Janalou turned to Jason and introduced him.

Taylor shook Jason's hand. "Any friend of Janalou's is a friend of ours. How long can you stay with us, Jason?"

"A couple of days."

"It may take that long for your body to catch up to the time change," Taylor observed. "You're welcome to stay longer."

"I appreciate your offer, but I don't want to wear out my welcome."

"I'm sure you won't." Reva's smile was contagious, and Jason smiled too. "We usually try to convince visitors to stay a couple of weeks. One is usually too short."

Jason winked. "My mom says company is like fish and dirty laundry. After three days it starts to smell."

Reva and Taylor both laughed. Then she said, "Our home is big enough that I'm sure we wouldn't notice."

"Maybe I could come back another time. I just wanted to make sure Janalou arrived safely, without encountering any problems. I know she has a bodyguard, but I thought she might enjoy having a friend with her, too."

"I did. And thank you, Jason.

~ * ~

Accompanied by Monty the next day, Janalou and Jason visited Kew Gardens, ate dinner on The Strand, and went to the theater that night.

The day after that, driven by her mother's chauffeur, and again accompanied by Monty, they went to see Westminster Abbey and St. Paul's Cathedral.

"There's a bit of history about these two buildings you didn't hear from the guide," Monty said as they finished their tour at St. Paul's. "During the great fire in 1666, St. Paul's Cathedral perished, but Westminster Abbey, which represented St. Peter's Cathedral, survived. They used some of the treasures and money that belonged to Westminster to help pay for rebuilding St. Paul. Hence the saying "Robbing Peter to pay Paul."

Delighted by that tidbit, Janalou smiled. "Thanks for sharing, Monty."

"You're welcome."

From St. Paul's, the chauffeur drove them to the River Thames where they boarded a boat to Greenwich, a World Heritage Site.

They visited the Royal Observatory that housed the first accurate determination of Mean Time, and stood astride the Prime Meridian, with one foot in the eastern hemisphere and the other in the west.

They kept busy, and on Jason's last night, they ate at home with her parents, just the four of them. It was a cozy, comfortable evening, and after dinner Janalou led Jason to the lounge where they chatted about what they had seen and shared.

Finally she said, "I never had a chance to return Kree's ring. Would you take it back for me?"

"Maybe you should keep it." Jason looked very uncomfortable. "I doubt Kree wants it back."

Janalou shook her head. "It would always remind me of something that failed." She extended the small box where she had stored the ring. "Please. It doesn't belong to me anymore, and I'd feel guilty if I kept it."

"All right." He cleared his throat. "Do you have anything you want me to tell Kree?"

She shook her head. "I miss him, but I'd prefer you didn't mention that."

"I'll bet he misses you, too."

Instead of commenting, Janalou swiped at the tears gathering in the corners of her eyes. "You'll stay in touch, won't you, Jason?"

"Yes."

"Thanks. You've been a good friend. I hope you'll remain one."

He smiled. "Me, too."

~ * ~

After Jason departed, her mother asked, "Are you going to explain why you and Kree broke up.?"

Janalou considered saying it hadn't been a real engagement, but Kree hadn't told Jason, so she thought she should remain loyal to the pretense they had perpetrated.

"He thought I should come back here and spend time with you and Dad."

"Sounds like something a man who loves you might do. Is there any chance that you might reconcile?

"No. He doesn't love me as much as he loves someone else." She shook her head when she saw her mother's concern. "It isn't what it sounded like. She died a few years ago, but Kree said he'll never love anyone as much as he loves her."

Seated side by side on an antique settee, Reva reached for Janalou's hands, and gave them a gentle squeeze. "That's sad."

She nodded. "I agree."

"I guess that means he and his parents won't be coming for Thanksgiving."

"I'm sure Kree won't, but I'd still like his parents to visit us. They're wonderful people, and I think you and Dad would enjoy them."

"They're welcome here, if you're sure you want to see them again."

Janalou tried to smile. "I do, but Helen asked me to be sure their presence won't be difficult—for me or for you and Dad, before they make their final decision."

"Actually, I've been looking forward to meeting them," Reva said.

"Helen said the same thing about you."

Reva smiled. "When I was young, my best friend's name was Helen. We did everything together and shared all our secrets until she moved away."

"Where did you grow up?"

"In Reno. I was devastated when her family moved to California."

Goose bumps skidded up Janalou's spine. "Do you know what part of California she moved to?"

Reva nodded. "Lodi."

"Helen grew up in Reno, and she moved to Lodi when she was twelve."

Reva's eyes rounded with surprise. Or hope. "You don't suppose? No." Her mother shook her dark-haired head. "It couldn't be her. There must be hundreds of Helens in California."

"But probably not a lot in Lodi who grew up in Reno." She swallowed, suddenly remembering something else. "She, Helen, said I remind her of her best childhood friend. Maybe that was you, Mom." While she watched the mixture of emotions flitting through her mother's eyes, she added. "I miss Kree's family, Mom. They're special, and I'd like his parents here for Thanksgiving."

"Then by all means let's call and assure Helen we'd love to have her and her husband visit us."

Janalou winked again. "And you can ask Helen if she's your old girlfriend."

"Right."

After Janalou punched the number, Reva took the phone and pushed the speaker button so Janalou could hear the conversation.

"Oh, Reva," Helen said a few minutes later, her voice cracking with emotion. "I've always wondered about you, where you are, what happened to your life, and wished we'd kept in touch."

"Me too," Reva said, her eyes teary, and a quiver in her voice. "And when you and your husband come for Thanksgiving, we'll have a chance to renew our friendship."

"I'll look forward to that," Helen said, and then added, "You have a wonderful daughter."

"Thanks. We think so, too."

Janalou didn't say a word. She didn't want to interrupt the reunion between two childhood friends.

As she listened, she realized another bridge had been crossed. Perhaps her reason for going to California was to meet Kree's parents and reunite their mothers. And maybe that was part of the reason Duke hadn't interfered, and had waited for fate to run its natural course.

The crack in her heart began to heal, if only a tiny bit. What a small world, she thought. What a wonderful world. Too bad Kree didn't want to share any part of it with her.

Her mother beamed a bright smile when the call ended. "That was wonderful. I can hardly wait to see Helen again."

Janalou's heavy heart brightened with hope. "Just... Helen and Max are coming, right?."

Reva nodded.

"It's probably best if I don't see Kree again," Janalou said, trying to sound convincing, "but there's something I need to do."

"What is it?"

"Pay him back."

Reva's smile vanished. "As in get even for breaking up with you?"

Janalou shook her head. "No, nothing like that, Mom. He paid my medical expenses when I had surgery." She explained what had happened, including the two weeks they had traveled alone. "He took very good care of me. Without making it obvious, he always found a place for me to sit when we were in a museum so I didn't have to stand very long. For the most part, he kept us from doing more than one touristy thing a day so I didn't get overly tired. And he paid for everything we did, not just my medical expenses, but the car, gas, food, motel and hotel rooms. He even bought clothes for me."

"How much do you owe him?"

"I left him four thousand dollars, but I still owe him a lot."

"Don't worry, dear. We'll be happy to give you money to pay him back."

"Thank you, Mom. Thanks so much."

Reva wrapped her arms around her. "You're welcome, sweetheart, and you don't have to thank me. I'm glad we can help you."

"It will be such a relief not to feel obligated to Kree anymore."

~ * ~

Although her heart continued to ache, Janalou loved being in London, and sharing things each day with her parents. It was a time of renewal, a time of getting better acquainted, and although she missed Kree terribly, she cherished each moment with her mother and father. She knew this idyllic interlude couldn't last forever, but while it did, she tried to enjoy each day. If not for the heaviness in her soul, she would have loved every minute.

September and October clipped by at a fast pace.

November brought a deeper chill to the air, and fine misty rain Janalou hadn't experienced, along with much shorter daylight hours.

While her parents' work and full schedules kept them busy, Janalou explored London with an umbrella or brolly as the Brits called them, and her constant companion, Monty. Duke no longer accompanied or followed them. She wondered why he hadn't said 'goodbye,' and if she'd ever see him again. His absence created another ache inside her, and severed one more link to the happiest summer of her life.

She kept in touch with old and new friends online, and wrote a daily log of everything she did, proud of herself when she managed not to write about Kree or how much she missed him.

One morning at breakfast, her father said, "We're understaffed at the embassy and we'd appreciate your help, if you'd like to work there, Janalou."

She jumped off her chair and hugged him around the neck. "I'd love to work there, Dad, even if the only thing I can do is volunteer."

"We'll put you on the payroll. I'm leaving in fifteen minutes. Can you be ready by then?"

"Absolutely."

She dashed up the stairs, changed to a tailored dress with a matching jacket, transferred things to a purse and plunked the strap on her right shoulder, and was back in the dining room a few breathless minutes later.

Laughter sparkled in her parent's eyes. "It's marvelous to see your enthusiasm hasn't changed," her mother said. "Even when you were a little girl, you were always ready and eager for new adventures."

"It's nice to know you want to help me, too," her father added.

"And I'm glad you suggested it, Dad."

Twenty-six

Seated in his car outside Jason's apartment, Kree debated whether to go pound on Jason's door or leave. They had avoided each other since Janalou left, but Kree owed him an apology. Making up his mind to give Jason his due, he climbed out and locked his car.

"Hi," he said when Jason opened his apartment door.

Jason stepped aside. "Come in, Kree."

"Are you sure you want me to? You missed our last fishing trip."

"I thought seeing you might be awkward."

"We've been friends all our lives, Jase, and I don't want that to change."

"Me either," Jason said. "But I'm not happy about the way you ended things with Janalou."

"I'm not either," Kree grumbled as he walked inside.

Jason shut the door behind him. "I was about to call and order pizza. Want to stay and eat with me?"

"Sure." Kree sat while Jason ordered their favorite, a large combination with everything on it.

"You want to talk about Janalou?" he asked as soon as he hung up.

Kree nodded. "Are you staying in touch with her?"

"Yes."

"Are you planning to see her again?"

"Would it bother you if I did?"

Kree frowned, as jealousy whipped through him. "Do you have a thing for her?"

Jason shook his head. "I wouldn't do that to you, Kree. Besides, even if I were interested, she isn't. Before she left, every time your name came up, she got tears in her eyes."

That should have made him feel better. But it didn't. "I miss her."

"She misses you too, although she asked me not to mention that." Jason picked up a small box from his coffee table and extended it. "She asked me to return this."

Kree turned the box in his hands, studying it. "Is it the ring?"

"Yes."

Kree opened the box. The ring fell out, onto the floor. He picked it up off the carpet and stared, wondering if Janalou thought it was as fake as their engagement had been. But the diamond was real, as real as the misery he lived with, twenty-four/seven.

He looked up, stared at Jason. "You didn't answer my question. Are you planning to see her again?"

"I hope so, but I don't know when. I flew with her to England, but I only stayed two days."

"How's she doing?"

"Better now. She loves being with her parents and exploring England. She's working at the American Embassy, too."

"I thought she might be lazy after she got reunited with her wealthy family."

"Your family has money but that never made you or your sisters lazy, Kree."

"I know. I shouldn't have said that. Guess I'm looking for reasons to justify our breakup. She deserves more credit."

"Do you mean that?"

"Yeah. I didn't know I'd miss her so damn much. I feel as though I've lost an arm or a leg, or some other vital part of myself."

"Maybe you should call and talk to her. I'm sure she loves you."

Kree shook his head. "I'm tempted, but I can't. She might suggest coming back here, but if she returned and something bad happened, I'd feel responsible. Besides, I hate being chaperoned by a government agent."

"I kind of liked it," Jason said, grinning. "Made me feel important to have a protective guy around. By the way, did I mention that both those guys, the big bodyguard and the short cheerful taxi driver, ate with me and Janalou that night you got so upset and ended the engagement?"

"No." Janalou had said the same thing, but he'd acted like he didn't believe her. Relief and envy slid through him. Relief because she hadn't been alone that night with Jason as Martina had said. Envy because Jason had flown to England with her and still kept in touch.

He told himself to get over it. That didn't mean he did. "There's already been much moaning and groaning and gnashing of teeth on my part," he admitted with a rueful frown.

"Can't say you didn't deserve it." Jason said. "So what are you going to do about it?"

"I'm still trying to decide."

~ * ~

Later, at home by himself, Kree stretched out on the living room couch, stacked his hands behind his head and stared out the dark wall of windows, wishing Janalou could be there with him. Knowing she emailed Jason wasn't a big deal. Or was it?

He felt ostracized from fun. From life. From everything. Not a day passed that he didn't think about Janalou. He missed her laughter, her smiles, her intelligent wit, the sparkle in her beautiful exotic eyes, and the compliments she paid him.

Most of all he missed knowing they could have shared the future.

The extra desk in his office mocked him. He finally called and had it hauled away, wondering why he'd waited so long. *Had he unconsciously expected her to return?*

~ * ~

His mother walked into his office, interrupting his pitiful gloom. "Good morning, Kree."

He forced a smile. "Same to you, Mom."

"Are you all right?" she asked. "You look tired."

He resisted the urge to say he hadn't slept well since Janalou left. "I'm fine." He doubted he'd get any sympathy. Like Jason and Reina, his whole family thought he was nuts for letting Janalou go.

His mother set an envelope on his desk. "This came to our house in yesterday's mail, but it's addressed to you." She walked out before Kree could form a coherent thought.

The envelope had a foreign stamp—British. And familiar handwriting—Janalou's.

His insides clenched. He took a deep breath before he opened the envelope and pulled out a check and a sheet of embossed stationery, emblazoned with her mother's official title, Mrs. Reva Madzen, Wife of the U.S. Ambassador to the United Kingdom.

His eager eyes scanned the handwritten note.

Kree,

Enclosed is a check for the remainder of my medical expenses, including the ambulance, plus $2,000 for our trip across the country. If I've underpaid you, please let me know.

With sincere thanks, Janalou

He clenched his teeth, feeling as though he'd been punched in the gut. She had sent a $4,000 check before she left town. Now she'd written one for much more, drawn from a bank in Philadelphia with her signature. She was no longer the needy girl he'd met on the bus. And she hadn't underpaid him, she'd overpaid. Reduced his generosity to a trifle. Made it meaningless.

Guilt over the way he had terminated their engagement descended. All right. He suffered a mega complex. He owed her an apology. He shouldn't have listened to Martina. He should have given Janalou more credit.

Kree picked up the phone. But lost his nerve. She wouldn't want to talk to him. Too much time had passed. There was no bridge back to the past.

He tallied the memories they had shared. Each one made him smile. They also made him sadder.

Holding her close in the arch in St. Louis.

Cradling her in his arms all through the night during the storm in Independence.

Traveling through Kansas and stopping to take leisurely strolls every time one of them had the urge to exercise or stretch their legs.

Sharing passionate kisses in Colorado and Utah. Her responses had darn near driven him mad, just as they had when he kissed her on her birthday, and again on the Fourth of July and every time afterwards when he couldn't stop himself. Every single touch had left him wanting more.

At night when he had trouble sleeping, he wondered what life would be like if she hadn't left California. Would he have told her he loved her?

He reminded himself he still loved Bethany, and her memory would always get in the way of any happiness he might have found with Janalou. But that was becoming more difficult to believe. So what was he going to do?

Not a thing. Janalou was where she belonged—in England reunited with her family. And he belonged here with his. That was the most difficult to believe. They belonged together. Where no longer mattered.

~ * ~

"Do you have plans for Thanksgiving?" his mother asked when they were in the conference room with his father and sisters. They had just finished going over the October sales and discussing those still pending, along with old and new listings.

"No. Aren't you cooking dinner?" he asked.

She shook her head. "Your father and I were invited to England," she reminded. "So were you."

He couldn't believe he'd heard her right. "You plan to spend Thanksgiving with Janalou and her family?"

"Yes," his father said. "Turns out that her mother and yours were best friends when they were children."

Goose bumps rushed up his spine. "What?"

"We both grew up in Reno," his mother explained, her happy expression making him frown. "When Janalou put that information together, she arranged for us to talk on the phone. Reva and I had quite a reunion, and we're both beyond eager to see each other again."

"You can eat Thanksgiving dinner with us, Kree," Jocelyn said. "We're going to my in-laws, but I'm sure they'd be happy to feed you, too."

"You could join us, also," Sirena said. "We're eating with Brad's family, but they always have room for one more. With your appetite, you might enjoy two feasts."

Kree had an appetite, all right, but not for food. For Janalou. He didn't commit himself. His brain was busy toying with the idea of flying to England, and surprising Janalou. Asking, begging if necessary, for her forgiveness.

"Janalou was a catalyst," his mother said. "And we're grateful she entered our lives."

"A catalyst?" Kree echoed. "In what way?"

"She's the first girl you've shown a real interest in since Bethany died, and she gave us hope that you had found the right girl and were ready to settle down."

"My heart belongs to Bethany," he said, trying to convince himself that was still true.

"Not anymore," Sirena said, setting her coffee cup down with a loud thud. "We should have told you the truth long ago."

"We agreed not to," Jocelyn said, her quiet voice a stark contrast to Sirena's outburst.

"Yes, but we didn't do him any favor," Sirena insisted, talking about him as though he weren't there.

"Kree loved Bethany," Helen said, "and we wanted him to cherish his memories of her."

"She wasn't worthy of him, Mom. She was a liar, a cheat and a thief."

The vehemence in Jocelyn's voice startled Kree. Jocelyn was the quiet, subdued one in the family.

"That's pretty strong language," Max said

"I can't help it. We all know she cheated on Kree. She claimed she loved him, but she went out with other guys. I saw her with my own eyes. Not just once. Several times. And she didn't even try to act discreet. She flaunted his ring and was probably laughing behind his back."

"We agreed not to discuss this again."

"Maybe it's time we did," Sirena injected. "The medical examiner said she was pregnant, Dad. You can't dispute that fact, can you?"

Max shook his head, and Kree gaped at each member of his family as though they had betrayed him.

They'd known Bethany was pregnant when she died, and no one had told him?

They hadn't slept together and everyone knew that.

"She stole Mom's pearls, too," Jocelyn added, still excluding Kree from the conversation. "After they disappeared, Reina found them in Bethany's bedroom, hidden under her mattress. That's why she quit working for you. She was ashamed, and afraid Bethany might steal something else, especially after she got arrested for shoplifting."

"We agreed not to air Bethany's dirty laundry after she died," Helen said. "Let her rest in peace."

"Why should we?" Sirena pounded her fist on the table. "She didn't leave us in peace, and she's ruining Kree's life."

"It's his life," Max said. "If he wants it ruined, that's his choice."

"But he might never marry. And Janalou was the best thing that ever happened to him."

"Not in his opinion," his mother said.

"That isn't true." Kree finally found his tongue. "I love her."

"Then what are you going to do about it?"

"Tell her."

"When?"

"As soon as I work up the nerve to call or go see her."

"Don't wait too long," Jocelyn advised, her eyes filled with sisterly love and concern. "She might fall in love with someone else if you do."

An image of her with Tony flashed. Kree clenched his jaw until it hurt.

Back in his office, he clicked on line and made an airline reservation to Heathrow so he'd be there for Thanksgiving. But he didn't tell anyone. He wanted Janalou to be the first to know. He had to compose himself. Decide what to say. His speech and the way he presented it would likely be the most important one in his life.

Twenty-seven

There were days and nights when Janalou couldn't believe Kree had used such a lame excuse to break their pretend engagement. Part of her rejoiced that she hadn't slept with him. A different part wished she had. While another part wanted to cry, constantly.

Working at the embassy kept her busy and she almost lost track of time.

One dark, cold, night her father asked, "Have you thought about going to college? I enjoy having you at the embassy, but that won't last forever. I won't always be an ambassador, and your mother and I will go home. You may want to think about the future, and having a career."

"I appreciate your concern," Janalou said. "Actually, I was awarded a scholarship to the University of South Carolina. I called last month and asked if it's still available, and if I could use it in January. They said yes, so I think that's what I'll do after the holidays, if you and Mom approve."

"Of course we approve." Pride radiated in her father's dark eyes. "However, I didn't ask because we don't want you with us. We never gave up hoping we'd find you, and we put money aside for your education, as well as for Jeri Sue and Paul. You may attend any college you'd like."

"You could go here in England, to Oxford or perhaps Cambridge," her mother suggested with hope in her loving gaze. "That way we could see you often."

Janalou smiled, pleased their thoughts were in tune, happy she belonged to such a wonderful family. "I'd love to stay with you, but I've been here long enough to know you'll always be a part of my life, and I'd like to use my scholarship. Besides, Margie is in Columbia, attending the university with some of our other high school friends and I'd like to renew some friendships, especially after the overwhelming support they gave me that day we left the courthouse in Spartanburg."

"We understand," Reva said.

"Have you thought about the degree you'd like to pursue?" Taylor asked.

She nodded. "One in counseling. My life was good while Minnie was alive, but when Franklin changed, I didn't know anyone I could talk to except Margie, and she was as confused as I was by his behavior. I'd like to be able to help young people who might need help when or if their lives turn bad."

Taylor patted her shoulder. "That's an admirable goal. We're both very proud of you, Janalou."

"I'm proud of you as well. And I'm happy to be here. Thanks for never giving up the hope that you might someday find me."

"We owe your friend Tony a great deal for his help in bringing us back together," Reva said, a speculative look in her eyes.

Her heart knew if Tony had really cared about her, he would have made more effort to keep in touch. To make sure her parents knew she harbored no interest in him, she said, "Margie said it was her mom who called the police and insisted they go to the house. If she hadn't insisted when she did, they might not have found my blood, and no arrest would have been made." She paused before adding, "If Tony and Margie hadn't helped, I'm sure Duke Guggles would have made sure we were reunited."

"Duke's an interesting man," Taylor said, a thoughtful gleam in his gaze.

"Do you know anything about him?"

He nodded his black-haired head. "He's a special agent. So special nobody knows which branch of the government he works for. Some say he answers directly to the president. Whether he does or not, doesn't matter. He's good. Whenever he shows up, problems get solved."

"Is Duke Guggles his real name?"

Taylor shrugged. "I don't know. Most people call him Leprechaun'."

Weird sensations pulsed through Janalou as she recalled how easily he had drawn the truth from her. And Kree had confided that he'd been certain the scumbags who tried to steal her backpack on the bus had been stupefied when the driver returned their tickets and trash bags. *Had Duke been responsible?*

According to Kree, he had known about the storm in St. Louis and warned him not to drive in it. *What kind of man was Duke? And did he really answer only to the president?*

"I have some news to share," Taylor said then. "The district attorney in Spartanburg called today. Franklin and Belle have both been sentenced to prison for twenty-five years each."

Janalou knew she should feel relieved, but an uneasy chill shivered through her. They couldn't hurt her now. Still, she couldn't forget the venom in Belle's eyes while they sat in the judge's chambers in August. If Belle could find a way, would she try to harm her? Janalou told herself not to be paranoid, but worry remained.

~ * ~

The next day when she arrived home from the embassy, her mother said, "Franklin's attorney called today."

"Did say what he wanted?"

Reva shook her head. "Only that he'd like you to return his call."

Janalou was tempted to ignore it. But Franklin had been a good papa for a lot of years, so she called his attorney.

"Franklin would like to see you," his attorney said. "He'll pay your expenses, including room, meals and round-trip airfare if you'll visit him in prison."

"Is he ill?" Janalou asked.

"No. He just wants to see and talk to you."

"When?"

"At your convenience."

"I'll have to let you know." She fretted and stewed before she mentioned the conversation to her parents.

"Do you want to go?" her father asked.

"I have mixed feelings."

"Would it help if I went with you?" her mother asked.

"Could you? You're so busy, I didn't think you'd have time."

Reva smiled. "I'll make time. If you decide to go, I'd rather you didn't go alone."

"Thanks, Mom."

"You're welcome. We should leave as soon as possible so we can be back here before Thanksgiving."

Janalou nodded agreement.

"By the way," her mother added, "you received something in the mail from California today."

Janalou examine the envelope with apprehension. By the stamped date, she knew it had taken more than a week to arrive.

She opened it, and found another envelope, certain it didn't contain a letter. Double envelopes usually meant an invitation or an announcement. Who from? Cherilyn? Or Kree's family? Could someone be engaged? Planning to marry? The possibility of Kree with another woman sent more regret spiraling through her.

To her immense relief, she found an embossed invitation to Reina's wedding.

Surprised Reina had decided to get married, Janalou checked the time difference before she called. "I'm so happy for you, Reina. Congratulations."

"I be happy too." Reina said. "My man, he live south of San Diego, on Coronado Island. He own nice house, and I move there after we marry."

"I'd love to come to your wedding," Janalou said, wondering if her heart was strong enough to chance seeing Kree again.

"That wonderful news. I miss you and want to see you, Janalou. It has been too long."

"Yes," Janalou agreed. "It has."

After they hung up, determination bubbled inside Janalou. She was going back to California to Reina's wedding, and she would see Kree. When she did, she'd give him a piece of her mind, and tell him he was a coward and he didn't deserve her. Then she'd get on with her life. Go to college, further her education. She didn't need him. He wasn't the only fish in the sea.

Unfortunately, she couldn't make herself believe the lie.

With her emotions warring inside, she and her mother made quick arrangements to fly to the U.S.

~ * ~

At the prison, Reva and Monty waited outside the area where Janalou went to see Franklin.

"Thanks for coming," he said, leaning his head down to talk through the speaker at the bottom of his window. "I wouldn't have blamed you if you hadn't."

Janalou studied him quietly. He looked ten years older, as though he'd been on a permanent drinking binge, although she knew that was impossible behind bars. His face was wrinkled and haggard, his posture stooped like a beaten man, and his hair had streaks of gray.

"Are you all right?" she finally asked.

He pointed at a button on her side of the window and lowered his head to speak again. "You have to push that button or I can't hear you."

She did, and repeated her question.

He nodded. "I'm okay. I wanted to tell you I sold the house and I want you to have the profit. I know money won't make up for the way I treated you after I married Belle, but it will help alleviate some of my guilt. I'll be in here a long time, so I don't need it. Besides, I don't want Belle to get her fingers on one more penny that belongs to me. I've filed for a divorce, and I'm not giving her anything. My attorney already closed on the house sale and the money's been deposited in the bank, in your name. He can fill you in on the details."

Startled by his speech, the longest he'd uttered to her since he married Belle, Janalou said, "You don't owe me anything, Franklin."

"I think I do. I was your papa for a number of years, and not all of them were bad, were they?"

Janalou shook her head, unable to speak with her throat clogged.

"You can use the money to get an education, buy yourself a car, a new cell phone, a computer, new clothes. All the things Belle refused to let you have."

Too choked up to comment, tears filled Janalou's eyes.

"Don't cry, sweetheart. I don't want to remember you with tears in your eyes. You're with your real family now, and I want you to be happy. Please try. Minnie would want that, too."

"I'm sorry things turned out this way," Janalou managed to mumble.

"Me too." Franklin cleared his throat. "I don't mind paying for my crime. It ate away at me for years. That's why I started drinking." With a resigned shrug, he changed subjects. "I know a lot of time has passed, but if you want your clothes or anything that belonged to Minnie, you have a week to get them out of the house. After that everything will be sold or donated. The new owners plan to move in next month, before Christmas."

"I don't have a key to the house," she said.

"My attorney will make sure you get one."

Franklin glanced away, then back at her. "I need to say something about Belle before you leave. She's behind bars, but she has long arms that sometimes find a way of stretching out, beyond the law. She hates you and your father, so you need to be careful. Belle's a bitch, and if she can, she'll find a way to hurt you again. Don't ever forget that hell hath no fury like a woman spurned, and your father not only spurned Belle in private years ago, he spurned her and humiliated her again in public in August."

Cold chills scattered down Janalou's spine. She felt as though she'd been living in a dream world, and then rudely awakened. *Would Belle try to hurt her?*

Overwhelmed by a mixture of emotions, she cleared her throat. "I'll be careful."

"Good." Franklin glanced at the approaching guard. "I guess I have to go now."

"I'm glad I came," Janalou said, wondering if she would ever see him again.

"Me too." Franklin stood and her heart ached for him.

She wished she could give him a hug but with a thick glass separating them, it was impossible.

What did he have to look forward to? He'd be an old man by the time he finished serving his sentence.

And Belle would be an old lady, unless she somehow found a way to get released early.

Twenty-eight

Kree was used to being in control of his life, but things had changed after Janalou left. As Duke had alluded, their time together had been limited.

Kree hated not having her nearby.

Now Reina was getting married and moving away. Tomorrow. After talking with his family about Bethany, he had lost his connection to her. Truth be told, he'd lost it years ago. He'd just been unwilling to admit it.

Restless, he started to pace, out of sorts with himself and with the world. He should have flown to England right away instead of waiting until Thanksgiving. But he hadn't wanted to miss Reina's wedding.

With nothing pressing at the office, he had left work before noon. But being home gave him too much time to think. Janalou had left a chink in his armor. He loved her. And letting her go had been a stupid mistake. Even though he intended to see her again, his conscience nagged. He didn't deserve her. Or her love. She was too good, too decent for him.

Needing something to do, he opened his fridge, popped the tab on a can of soda, snagged a bag of potato chips and wandered back to his living room.

He wanted Janalou back. He'd missed a golden opportunity when she lived in California. Would she give him another chance? Had too much time passed? Was she involved with Tony again?

Kree's heart sank. *What if she didn't love him? What if she never had? What if she didn't want his love?*

Willing to take the risk because without her, life no longer held much meaning, he checked his watch. England was eight hours ahead of California, so it was evening there. Dinner probably ended an hour or so ago. He pictured Janalou with her parents sitting in the lounge, talking, enjoying herself, maybe with her dainty feet tucked inside that bright pink thing women used as a footstool. The vivid images made him more miserable.

Not knowing whether to call or wait until tomorrow and hope she showed up for Reina's wedding, Kree ran out of patience and picked up his phone.

Someone answered after the third ring.

"This is Kree Winterton. May I speak to Janalou Madzen, if she's there?"

"She isn't at home. Would you like to speak to her father?"

"Yes, please."

A few seconds later, the ambassador said, "Hello, Kree."

"Hello Mr. Madzen," he said even though he'd been encouraged to call him Taylor. "Can you tell me where Janalou is?"

"She and her mother flew to the States a few days ago."

"I know I have no right to ask where she is, but I love her, and I'd like to tell her."

"I'm glad to hear that, Kree," Taylor said. "Janalou went to visit Franklin in prison yesterday. They saw Jeri Sue and Paul today, and I understand Janalou intends to go to a wedding tomorrow night in California."

Kree's mood soared as elation poured hope through his veins. "Tomorrow?" he echoed to make sure his hearing wasn't impaired.

"Yes. I talked with them a few minutes ago. They have an early flight out of New York."

"Do you have a number where they can be reached?"

"Yes."

"Thanks," Kree said a few seconds later, after he wrote it down.

He hung up, his heart pounding, and called the hotel where Janalou and her mother were staying.

"Hello, Janalou," he said after he heard her wonderful lilting voice.

"Who is this?" she asked, sounding breathless and unsure.

"It's me, Kree."

"Kree-e-e?."

"Yip."

"Oh."

He smiled at her squeal of surprise. "Is that all you have to say after more than two very long months?"

"How did you get my number? Is something wrong? Are your parents and sisters okay? Or Reina? Has something happened to her?"

"Everyone here is fine. I called London and your father gave me this number. And yes, something is wrong. Very wrong. I miss you, and want to see you again."

"You do? Why?"

He cleared his throat, and took the plunge, "Because I love you."

Janalou didn't skip a beat. "As much as you love Bethany?"

"More. You won't have to compete with her memory. She wasn't what she appeared to be. My heart's empty. I need you to fill it up."

"When did you de—cide you love me?"

"A long time ago. Before you left. I was just too stubborn to admit it then. Besides, I thought you needed time with your family before you considered love, or me or marriage. Have you had enough time? Do you need more? Please don't say 'yes.'"

"Janalou's laughter filled his heart with joy. "Then what should I say? That I've missed you? That I love you? That I want to see you again, too?"

"All of those things."

"Consider them said."

"Thank you."

"Y'all are welcome."

She rarely said 'y'all' anymore, but her lovely Southern twang was music to his ears.

"I understand you're flying to California tomorrow."

"Yes. Reina invited me to her wedding. Will I see you there?"

"Yeah, but I don't want to wait that long. Could we see each other sooner? Would you come to my house? As soon as you get here?"

"Yes. I guess I could."

"I'll be home all day, waiting."

"I'll call to let you know what time we arrive, if that's all right."

"It's perfect."

~ * ~

Janalou said goodbye, hugging the phone to her chest after Kree hung up. "Kree loves me and wants to see me."

"It sounded as though you plan to see him tomorrow," her mother said, smiling.

"Yes. Isn't it wonderful?"

Reva nodded. "Love always is."

Barely able to believe Kree had called and said he loved her, Janalou floated on a cloud of wonder.

In bed she dreamed about him, happy dreams that ended with her in a white wedding gown and him in a white tuxedo floating toward each other above a carpeted aisle in a church.

~ * ~

As soon as they landed and deplaned in California, Janalou called Kree.

"We're at the airport. Mother and I will go check into the hotel. I'll take a cab to your house after we're settled. I should be there in a couple of hours."

"That's great," Kree said. "I'm anxious to see you."

Janalou's heart sang a happy tune. "The feeling's mutual, Kree."

"I know you want to see Kree as soon as possible," her mother said while they headed outside the terminal. "Why don't you go now? I'll check into the hotel, and you can join me later."

"Marvelous idea, Mom. Thanks." Janalou hugged her, and with Monty in tow, she hurried toward an empty taxi.

The cab ride seemed to go on forever. But when the driver stopped a block before they reached Kree's house, Janalou thought it might have been too short. Nervous about seeing him again, she said, "We're not quite there."

The driver pointed out the windwhield. "I stopped because I don't want to run over that girl out there."

Janalou looked out and saw Martina running down the middle of the street toward them waving her arms like a crazy person. Wondering if something bad had happened to Kree, Janalou's heart pounded as she opened the door, and jumped out.

Surprise whipped through her when Martina yelled, "Why are you here? Why did you come? You're not welcome. I don't want you here." She grabbed Janalou's arms and tried to turn her around, back toward the cab.

Janalou struggled to get free, but Martina had a determined grasp, and wouldn't let go. A startled grunt behind her snapped Janalou's attention around to Monty. His look of surprise before he crumbled, face down, on the ground, didn't look real. A knife stuck out of his back.

Shock registered half a second before someone jammed a sickly-sweet-smelling cloth over Janalou's mouth and nose. Martina's struggle ceased as another man shoved a cloth across her face, too. And then the world turned black.

~ * ~

Waiting for Janalou, Kree flipped from the loud music on his TV to a different station to watch college football. The game was in the final seconds when someone pounded on his front door.

Certain it couldn't be Janalou yet, he kept his eyes glued on the screen until he left the TV room. The game was tied, 21-21, with

Stanford on the thirty-two yard line, about to make a field goal attempt.

He opened the front door and forgot the game when Sirena and Jocelyn and their families rushed inside. "Have you heard the news?"

He shook his head. "What news?"

"Maybe you should sit down," his brother-in-law, Brad, said.

"Why? What's wrong? Did something happen to Mom and Dad?"

Everyone, including all four children, shook their heads. "No, Grandma and Grandpa are okay," said little Ben. "They're gonna meet us downtown."

"Why?"

"Janalou's in trouble. She's been duck-ted."

"Duck-ted?" Kree repeated, confused.

"Abducted. Kidnapped," Sirena clarified.

Kree's heart jumped up to his throat. "How could that happen? She doesn't go anywhere without a bodyguard, and Monty's good or he wouldn't have been assigned to her."

"It happened about a block from here, Kree. Didn't you hear any of the commotion or the sirens?"

"No."

"His walls are probably well insulated," Brad said in his defense.

"How did it happen?" Kree asked, his voice a hoarse croak.

"From what bystanders saw, one of the abductors stabbed her bodyguard in the back, and forced Janalou and another female into a van," Jocelyn said.

The hairs on the back of Kree's neck stood on end. "Janalou was coming here after she and her mother checked into their hotel. They must have changed their plans, and decided to come here first. But there would have been two bodyguards. What happened to the other one?"

Sirena shrugged. "Bystanders only saw one, and only one man was mentioned on the news.'

Kree backed up until his legs hit the couch. Then he sat down. Either that or fall. His knees had buckled and his whole body was shaking. *Monty had been stabbed and Janalou and another woman were alone and unprotected with hoodlums.*

"Does anyone know why she was abducted?"

Sirena shook her head. "Not yet." She took the remote from his nerveless hands, hurried to the TV room and clicked to CNN. The news was sparse, even on local channels, although a bystander had seen and recorded the entire abduction on his cell phone.

Kree watched with horrified fascination. The other girl was Martina, and she had been struggling with Janalou. Both were taken unawares by the two abductors.

"What was Martina doing with her?" Kree asked.

"She must have heard us talking after you called yesterday and told us Janalou was coming to see you today. We're sorry, Kree. We feel responsible."

Kree didn't know what to say. His shocked brain could barely think.

After several phone calls to London, he discovered the hotel where Janalou and her mother had made their reservations. He called Reva.

"I knew Janalou was anxious to see you so we separated at the airport," she explained with a quiver in her voice.

"Would it be all right if I came to see you, Mrs. Madzen?"

"Yes, please do."

"I'd like to bring my family, if that's all right."

"It is."

"We'll drive you to the hotel," Brad said after Kree hung up.

"Thanks." He didn't trust his own driving.

His parents met them in the hotel lobby. His sisters and their families agreed to wait downstairs and the threesome approached Reva's room together.

As soon they stepped inside, Janalou's mother rushed through the crowd. "Who are all these people?" Kree asked.

"Government agents and policemen." She used a tissue to dab at the tears in her eyes, beautiful expressive eyes that reminded him of Janalou. "Thanks for coming," she said after Kree introduced his parents. "I can't believe this happened. I should have stayed with Janalou. I shouldn't have let her go alone."

"She wasn't alone," Kree reminded. "Monty was with her."

"Has there been a ransom note, or anything?" his father asked.

Reva nodded, her gaze locked with Kree's. "They didn't waste any time. Belle has two brothers who want her released from prison." Reva twisted her hands in agitation. "They said when she's free, they'all let Janalou go. My husband is doing everything he can, but I'm sure the law won't allow Belle to be freed."

Kree had a gut feeling she was right. Even if by some miracle the authorities let Belle out of prison, they might never see Janalou again. He didn't say it out loud, though. Bad enough that he thought it. He suspected her mother feared the same thing.

~ * ~

Hours passed.

Kree hated every second. He glanced at his watch and frowned. "We're missing Reina's wedding."

"No," his mother said. "Reina put the ceremony off. She wants to wait until we find out what happened to Janalou."

Janalou's twin sister and brother arrived. "Dad's on his way," Paul explained after embracing his mother.

"It's happening all over again," Jeri Sue moaned. "It's not fair. I love her so much. Why can't bad people leave her alone?"

No one had any answers. Tears filled all the women's eyes, including those of his sisters, who had arranged for a sitter to take the children home and joined them, along with their husbands, in Reva's crowded hotel suite.

Kree decided he had to do something to find Janalou or he'd go crazy.

Just as he was about to make an excuse to leave, Duke Guggles walked through the hotel room door. His sharp gaze settled on Kree. "I'm going to rescue the lasses. Thought you might want to come along."

"I do."

Outside the hotel, Duke nodded at a squad car. After Kree and Duke climbed in the back, he spoke to the two officers seated in front. "Head north, on the freeway. Turn on the siren. Speed is essential."

"Will do, Leprechaun."

Leprechaun? Kree fastened his seatbelt, feeling caught up in a gory nightmare. Forcing himself to calm down, he asked, "Do you know where Janalou is?"

Duke gave a curt nod. "She's wearing the watch I gave her for her birthday, and it has a tracking device. Belle's brothers took her north, past Redding, near Fort Jones."

"That's where I go fishing," Kree said. "It has a good-sized river."

"I know that, lad, and I'm counting on your familiarity with the area, hoping it will come in handy."

Twenty-nine

As the police car sped north on the freeway with the siren blaring, Kree described the national forest area near Ft. Jones and some of the houses and cabins located along the river. Then he was quiet, amazed by all the devices Duke had at his disposal, and the speed and expertise with which he used them.

After the first hundred miles, the driver turned off the siren, and Kree asked, "Will the abductors' demand be met?"

Duke turned his green gaze to Kree. "As soon as the demand to set Belle free was made, prison officials placed her in solitary confinement under maximum security. Ambassador Madzen convinced them to let an undercover FBI agent in to learn how to mimic Belle's voice and actions. That agent will help me distract Belle's brothers while other agents rescue the lasses."

While Kree tried to figure out how they were going to accomplish such a task, Duke added, "People like Belle are only alive because it's illegal to kill them."

A buzzer sounded. Duke pushed the speaker on his phone. "Leprechaun here."

"This is Highway Patrol. We're staked out near the cabin where victims are being held. What's your ETA?"

"Ten minutes. Have all the FBI agents arrived?"

"Yes sir."

"Good. I'll call when we stop." Duke ended the call, a satisfied gleam in his eyes. "Belle's brothers are careless. It'll be easy to rescue the lasses right out from under their noses."

"We're there," Kree said, recognizing the national forest where he fished every year, and spotting a familiar cabin across the river.

"Pull off the road," Duke instructed the policeman who was driving, "and park behind those trees." For about the tenth time, Duke consulted a tiny screen on what Kree assumed must be a miniature palm computer. "The lasses are in a back bedroom by themselves."

When Kree saw a tiny image of Janalou sitting on a chair with her hands and feet bound, relief warred with fury. "How are you going to rescue her?" he asked.

"First thing is to cross the river."

"We missed the bridge. It's miles back."

"There's a footbridge, lad. On the other side, I'll meet up with FBI agents who will sneak around back. The woman disguised as Belle and I will distract her brothers while agents rescue the lasses. Once they're safe, the State Highway Patrol will close in and arrest the brothers."

Kree's heart had never beaten so fast. "I'm going with you."

"I expected no less." Duke nodded at a policeman. "Give him a bulletproof vest."

As soon as Kree fastened the vest, they started over the footbridge Kree could have sworn hadn't been there before, yet it didn't look new.

Worry that something might go wrong plagued him. Could Duke and the disguised female FBI agent keep both men away from Janalou and Martina so they could be rescued?

~ * ~

With her hands tied together and her feet bound to a chair, Janalou peeked out the small cabin window. It was dark, even though her watch indicated morning had come and gone. Clouds filled the entire sky, obliterating the sun, and gusts of wind buffeted the small cabin where she and Martina had been taken. The gloom outside increased her fear. She couldn't allow herself to think they might not get away. She had to be optimistic, for her sake as well as Martina's. In spite of the antagonism that had radiated from Martina until they finally made their peace last night, Janalou had been glad she wasn't alone with her captors.

Yesterday after she'd come to, the drive in the van had seemed to go on and on. She had no idea where they were, but it must be a long way from Lodi.

"I'm scared," Martina whispered.

"So am I," Janalou admitted.

"We're going to die, no?"

"No. We have to believe we'll be rescued or set free."

Instead of answering, Martina started to cry. Again.

"Crying won't help," Janalou said gently. "Calm down. We'll get out of this."

"Alive?"

"Yes, alive," she said with more conviction than she felt.

"Stop squawking like a wounded goose," one of their captors in the other room bellowed.

Martina quieted, and Janalou closed her eyes. Visions flashed before her eyes. One of Kree, wearing some kind of thick dark vest. Another of her mother's anguished face when she heard Janalou had been taken. Then one of her and Martina escaping through the window.

She couldn't imagine where the visions came from, but hope gleamed inside her as she stared at the window again. A small stream of sunlight broke through the clouds, and she had a sudden sense that Kree was nearby. "Kree's looking for us."

"How do you know?"

"I feel it, in my heart, and in my bones."

"You're crazy. Loco. I won't listen to you anymore." Martina tried to cover her ears with her hands, but with them tied together, she could only cover one ear.

Janalou heard a scratching at the window. When she saw two men dressed in camouflaged clothes, her heart jumped inside her chest cavity. *Were they special agents here to rescue them? Or were they just a different set of enemies?*

Then she saw Kree, with a finger pressed against his lips, indicating she needed to be quiet while he found a way to open the locked window.

Janalou nodded, then heard Duke's loud voice booming in the other room. She'd never heard a more welcome sound. She squelched a gasp when she heard a woman's voice in the other room, a voice that sounded exactly like Belle's. Her heart plummeted. What was Belle doing here?

Things happened so fast after that she couldn't remember the sequence. Within seconds, the men outside removed the window, frame and all, without making much noise, either. They climbed inside, untied her and Marina, then in seconds, had them both outside and racing through the woods, across the narrow footbridge she had envisioned moments before.

Janalou thought she must be hallucinating until she realized Kree held her hand all the way. His nearness soothed some of the fear gushing through her.

In the dense woods, she spotted police cars and bunches of uniformed officers.

"We're free. And safe," she gasped.

Relief and fear dueled in Kree's eyes before she tore her gaze away and climbed in a squad car.

"Don't leave me, ever again," he said, climbing in behind her and clasping her close.

"I won't," she promised.

"Sending you away was stupid. Will you forgive me?"

She smiled. "I already did, long ago.

The other door opened. Duke climbed in on her other side. "Where's Martina?" Janalou asked.

"With FBI agents. They'all take her home." Duke nodded at the policeman behind the wheel, and he shifted into reverse and backed up onto the dirt road.

"How's Monty? Janalou asked, rubbing her chafed wrists, and very happy to have Kree's strong arms still around her.

"He lost a lot of blood, but he'll be fine, lass."

"He's going to live. Thank God," she said.

On the paved road, they stopped where several other police cars had congregated. Janalou saw Belle's two brothers in handcuffs, and when Martina smiled and waved from one of the cars, Janalou smiled and waved back. During the long dark hours they had shared in captivity, they had managed to bury their antagonism and become tentative friends.

After the official business was concluded, Duke led Janalou and Kree to an unmarked car. "Get in. I'll be your chauffeur."

Seated on the backseat, Kree held Janalou close again, and they took turns asking and answering questions until Duke said, "I have a bit of information that hasn't been made public. When the FBI woman went in to see Belle in solitary confinement, she screamed and yelled herself into a stroke. Guards moved her to the prison hospital. She's on life support, but not expected to live. If she does, she'll be a vegetable, and unable to bother you ever again, lass."

"I hope that's true." Janalou hated to wish someone dead, but she couldn't imagine what miserable Belle had left to live for.

"Belle's brothers will spend a long time behind bars," Duke added.

"Where they belong," Kree said grimly.

Janalou nodded. She wanted to be alone with Kree, but knew she must be patient. She looked at Duke. "Are you really a leprechaun?"

"I'll let you decide that for yourself, lass."

He had lost most of his Irish accent. "Who are you?"

"An agent for the government. After the president assigned your father to the Court of St. James in the U.K., he asked me to look into your disappearance. Kidnappings often involve someone close to the family. I checked out everyone who worked for your father back then, everyone except Belle. By the time I tracked her to South Carolina and discovered she had married Franklin Naisbet, who had a daughter who fit your description, you were ready to graduate from high school. I suspected they had cheated you out of two years of your life, but I thought you were fine. While I was waiting for conclusive evidence to prove you are Janalou Madzen, I went to check on another young lass."

"Why were you on the bus that night? Was it a coincidence? Or did you know I'd be on it?"

"Pure coincidence. After I checked on Cherilyn and knew she was headed west, I decided to return to Spartanburg. Caught me by surprise when you boarded the bus, but I stayed on. It's that simple."

Everything he said sounded logical. But Janalou still thought he might be capable of magic. After all, he had shown up at crucial times, poised to help. And this time he had brought Kree. That in itself was a miracle.

"Why did you ride a bus back to Spartanburg instead of flying? Or driving?" she asked.

"I have an interest in Cherilyn."

"Is that why you remained on the bus when I went to the hospital, and let Kree stay behind with me?"

Duke nodded his white-haired head without taking his eyes off the road. "I knew I could see her safely to California and fly back to wherever you were. I was in Indiana before you left the hospital. I stayed in the same motel."

"Then you were in St. Louis and Independence?" Kree said.

"Yes," Duke nodded again, and although she couldn't see his face, she imagined a grin spreading across his cherubic face.

"You're very astute, Janalou Madzen. You, too, Kree Winterton. A pleasure to know ye both."

"I feel the same way about you, Duke," Janalou said. "Why do you have an interest in Cherilyn? What does she have to do with the government?"

"Nothing, lass. However, she's been treated poorly by people she loved and trusted."

Janalou suspected there was more to Cherilyn's story, but couldn't think of any other questions to ask Duke, so she turned her attention back to Kree. "I'm so glad you're here."

"Me too. And grateful Duke brought me with him."

"Guess that's my cue to leave." Duke pulled over to the side of the road. The squad cars behind stopped too, and Janalou suspected he intended to ride in one of them so she and Kree could be alone. At last.

"I've cleared your use of this car, lad," Duke said. "You'll make sure the lass gets back to her family safe and sound?"

"Yes, of course," Kree said. "Thanks for all your help. You're quite a man, Duke Guggles."

Duke opened the car door, and smiled after he got out. "One piece of advice, if ye don't mind, lad."

"Not at all. What is it?"

"Never stop believing in love, and you'll be happy forever."

Kree raised his hand and saluted Duke. "It's been a pleasure to know you, sir."

"Same feeling here, lad."

After he was gone, Janalou gazed at Kree, secure in the knowledge that at least one squad car would follow them back to Lodi. Not in any hurry, she asked, "Did you mean what you said on the phone?"

He arched an eyebrow. "That I love you?"

She nodded.

"Yes, I do love you, Janalou. With all my heart. I want you. The gouge you left inside me is as wide as the ocean, my regret for letting you go as deep as the Grand Canyon."

"What a beautiful thing to say," she said, smiling through her tears.

His expression somber, he cupped her cheek, sending more delightful thrills dancing through her. "Before I called you last night, I made plans to fly to England for Thanksgiving."

"You were going to surprise me?"

"Yeah. I decided not to let you know ahead of time because I didn't want you to refuse to see me."

"You'll always be welcome wherever I am."

"The same is true with me." The look in his eyes turned even more tender. "I want to marry you and spend the rest of my life with you. I'm not sure how we'll manage everything, but somehow we'll find a way for you to spend time with your family and live with me, if you'll marry me, that is. I'll move to London or back East or anywhere you want to settle."

"I'll do the same to be with you."

"Tell me you love me, too."

She smiled through her tears. "I do. Love you, too, that is."

"Then let's seal our re-engagement, our real engagement, with a kiss." Still seated on the backseat, he reached over the front seat and locked all the doors before he pulled her close.

Grateful for the dark-tinted windows, Janalou wrapped her arms around his neck.

The exquisite kiss made her pulse soar and healed the terrible crack in her heart.

"I don't think I'll ever be happier than I am right now," she said when the breath-stealing kiss ended.

"I hope you'll be happier when you're my wife."

She smiled at his hopeful expression. "I'm sure I will be."

And to her delight, and his, she was.

Of course, Kree was as well.

Meet *Peggy P. Parsons*

Stories have always lived inside Peggy's head and she often falls asleep and/or wakes up thinking about her characters. Her first full length novel was written while living in England after giving up her business career to join her husband who was seconded to the United Kingdom by his parent company. In the U.K. she served as both Treasurer and President of the American Women's Club of London. Upon her return to the U.S., she realized the 750 page manuscript should have been three separate novels, however, she was already working on her fourth story by then. Her love of writing keeps her near her computer, however, she stays active by taking classes in tap, jazz, clogging, and marching with the Jazzy Poms in parades, plus she teaches baton twirling, and performs on stage with the Rhythm Tappers of SCW, Az twice a year. She has served as Secretary and President of the Rhythm Tappers and is currently their Treasurer. She's also a member of RWA (Romance Writers of America) and belongs to two local chapters—Valley of the Sun and Desert Rose. Other favorite activities include spending time alone with her husband, plus their loved ones, traveling, and watching golf and football on TV.

Other Works From The Pen Of
Peggy P. Parsons

Glimpse Series

Glimpse Of Eternity — Transported back to the 1850's, Kacy meets the man she has loved and lost in other lives, but he refuses to believe the tales she spins.

Glimpse Of Forever — Hurtled back in time by an evil wizard, Jennifer finds her deceased husband, only to face losing him again.

Glimpse Of Never Ending Love — After traveling to the future, a stalker threatens Catharine, forcing her to turn to Tyler for help, but old fears make it difficult to trust him.

***

One Stolen Night — Pamela follows her dream of attending the University of Hawaii where she meets the legendary Robin, who steals more than her bruised heart.

Yours Till Niagara Falls — Kia fleets to her beloved Camp in the Adirondack's to mourn the loss of her family. When Jade shows up uninvited, she agrees to let him stay, even though she fears he might there for a sinister reason.

Paper Marriage — Rushed into a fake marriage, Analyn fights her love, unaware that Chandler's secret is the reason he claims he'll never love her.

Letter to Our Readers

Enjoy this book?

You can make a difference

As an independent publisher, Wings ePress, Inc. does not have the financial clout of the large New York Publishers. We can't afford large magazine spreads or subway posters to tell people about our quality books.

But, we do have something much more effective and powerful than ads. We have a large base of loyal readers.

Honest Reviews help bring the attention of new readers to our books.

If you enjoyed this book, we would appreciate it if you would spend a few minutes posting a review on the site where you purchased this book or on the Wings ePress, Inc. webpages at:
 https://wingsepress.com/

Thank you.